*Look for these exciting Western series from
bestselling authors*
WILLIAM W. JOHNSTONE
and **J. A. JOHNSTONE**

The Mountain Man

Preacher: The First Mountain Man

Luke Jensen, Bounty Hunter

Those Jensen Boys!

The Jensen Brand

MacCallister

Flintlock

Perley Gates

The Kerrigans: A Texas Dynasty

Sixkiller, U.S. Marshal

Texas John Slaughter

Will Tanner, U.S. Deputy Marshal

The Frontiersman

Savage Texas

The Trail West

The Chuckwagon Trail

Rattlesnake Wells, Wyoming

AVAILABLE FROM PINNACLE BOOKS

RATTLESNAKE WELLS, WYOMING

FRONTIER OF VIOLENCE

WILLIAM W. JOHNSTONE
with J. A. Johnstone

PINNACLE BOOKS
Kensington Publishing Corp.
www.kensingtonbooks.com

PINNACLE BOOKS are published by

Kensington Publishing Corp.
119 West 40th Street
New York, NY 10018

All Kensington titles, imprints, and distributed lines are available at special quantity discounts for bulk purchases for sales promotions, premiums, fund-raising, educational, or institutional use. Special book excerpts or customized printings can also be created to fit specific needs. For details, write or phone the office of the Kensington sales manager: Kensington Publishing Corp., 119 West 40th Street, New York, NY 10018, attn: Sales Department; phone 1-800-221-2647.

PINNACLE BOOKS, the Pinnacle logo, and the WWJ steer head logo are Reg. U.S. Pat. & TM Off.

ISBN-13: 978-0-7860-4484-9
ISBN-10: 0-7860-4484-5

First printing: May 2017

10 9 8 7 6 5 4 3 2

Printed in the United States of America

First electronic edition: July 2018

ISBN-13: 978-0-7860-4015-5
ISBN-10: 0-7860-4015-7

CHAPTER 1

Things had been relatively peaceful in Rattlesnake Wells, Wyoming. In recent days there were the usual quota of saloon brawls, a few incidents of drunks discharging firearms mainly to see folks scatter, and a domestic squabble or two. But nothing more serious than that.

Not to say, however, there wasn't still an undercurrent of excitement running through the town, due primarily to the announced opening of a spanking brand-new saloon in the New Town section on the north end of the city.

A saloon, especially in that part of town, wasn't particularly newsworthy in and of itself. The difference in this case was the much-ballyhooed opulence of the new business—as opposed to the quickly thrown-up tent saloons and gambling joints currently blighting the boom area as a result of the gold strike up in the Prophecy Mountains.

But, despite the general excitement, certain folks around town were neither happy nor impressed by what they were hearing—opulence be damned.

"It ain't that I mind facing tough competition," declared Mike Bullock, owner of the cleverly named Bullock's Saloon. "Hell, I've done that plenty of times before, in plenty of different places." He paused, his broad face bunching into a scowl. "But this Gafford character is starting to really get under my skin. I mean, a whole brand-new building, a fancy la-di-da name, an imported bar, even dance hall girls . . . you'd think that oughta be about enough, wouldn't you? But now this"—Bullock held up a poster emblazoned with large letters and colorful images and gave it a rattling shake—"*this* is pushing things too blasted far, says I!"

The paper Bullock was waving in the faces of Marshal Bob Hatfield and Maudie Sartain was an advertising flyer heralding the scheduled grand opening of the new saloon. The flyer featured all of the things Bullock had just mentioned in his agitated spiel, but with a bit more detail—like how the name of the new establishment would be the Crystal Diamond; how its main hall would feature an ornate cherrywood bar and a spectacular crystal chandelier both specially delivered all the way from San Francisco; and how the highlight of each evening's entertainment would be Miss Alora Dane and her Diamond Dollies performing dazzling song-and-dance routines.

But the real focal point of the flyer—the "this" that seemed to have Bullock on the brink of blowing his stack—was the event newly announced to kick off the Crystal Diamond's big opening. It was to be a shooting competition, open to all comers, offering as the first prize a matched set of gold-plated pistols with diamond-encrusted grips. Adding to the lure of the words, a picture of the pistols was prominently displayed.

"Gafford sure knows how to draw interest—you can't deny him that," said Maudie.

"I saw some of those flyers earlier. They're going up all over town," said the marshal. "I just hope that, in the process of drawing interest, those jeweled pistols don't also draw a heap of trouble. You combine a prize like that with a bunch of shooters and shootin' irons and a saloonful of who-hit-John, you got the makings for just about anything."

"There you go!" exclaimed Bullock, slapping the flyer down onto the table and pointing a thick finger at the marshal. "You'd be well within your rights to shut the whole shindig down, says I, as a public nuisance almost certain to start a riot."

Bob shook his head. "Come on, Mike. You can't be serious."

"You said yourself—"

"I said there'd be the *makings* of trouble. I didn't say it was a certainty or a guarantee, and therefore it's not something I can take legal action against. Comes right down to it, your place here—not to mention any one of the tent saloons or gambling joints along Gold Avenue—has got the same makings on just about any night of the week." Bob shrugged. "Minus the jeweled pistols and with smaller, more manageable crowds, that's all."

This discussion was taking place at a rear table in Bullock's Saloon, the oldest and most popular drinking establishment in Rattlesnake Wells. Except for a quartet of old-timers who sat quietly smoking and nursing their drinks as they played cards at a table toward the center of the room, the place was empty during this lull period in the middle of a weekday afternoon.

Mike Bullock was a balding, bullet-headed Irishman, only average in height but with a beer keg torso and thick, almost apelike arms ending in mallet-sized fists that had ended more than a few arguments and helped to quell many a brawl. Quick as his temper and fists were, however, he could also at times be bighearted and generous to a fault.

Maudie Sartain was his dependable right hand who helped with the day-to-day running of things— her duties ranging the gamut from tending bar when needed to ordering stock to serving as a sort of house mother to the hostesses Bullock employed to serve drinks and otherwise entertain male customers. A curvaceous, jet-haired beauty who made a habit of wearing dresses that proudly displayed ample cleavage, she'd long ago mastered the fine art of flirting without promising too much or allowing things to get out of hand. When some hombres got the wrong idea and tried to get too friendly with their hands because they were either too drunk or just plain too dumb, Maudie had also mastered the sharp-tongued reprimand or, if that wasn't enough, a sharp elbow where it would do the most good.

Tall, solid, square-shouldered Bob Hatfield— called "Sundown Bob" by some, due to the flaming red color of his hair—in addition to looking in on all local businesses from time to time in his role as town marshal, made particularly frequent stops at Bullock's.

It wasn't that the marshal was a heavy drinker or anything. He hardly imbibed at all, in fact, and especially not when on duty. He simply enjoyed the company of Mike and Maudie. Usually when he stopped in and lingered for any amount of time, he'd have a cup or two of Maudie's excellent coffee, as opposed to the dreadful brew he and his deputies made at the marshal's office, or sometimes some of the tea that she herself preferred.

Such was the case today, in fact, as he found himself sipping from a new blend that Maudie had insisted he try. It wasn't bad, but neither was it something he'd make a point of requesting the next time he came around. Yet, even at that, it was still better than what was waiting in the pot back at his office.

"Yeah, let Gafford go ahead and have his silly contest and draw his big, splashy crowd," grumbled Bullock, continuing his bitter lament. "Let's see how long all that lasts after the novelty has worn off. The ranchers and miners in these parts are hardworking men who want a fair measure to their drinks and a friendly atmosphere where they can bend an elbow, lay down a few cards in an honest game, and maybe pat a hostess on the bottom once in a while. They don't need all the hoopla of glittery chandeliers and high-kickin' dancing girls while they're being served watered-down drinks at jacked-up prices.

"What's more, when the Prophecies have coughed out their last gasp of gold dust—like always happens in booms like the one we're going through—then how long do you think August Gafford and his Crystal Claptrap will even be around? I was here before the first vein was tapped up in those mountains and I'll still be here when the last pickax is thrown down in frustration. Folks will remember that, and will keep it in mind. You'll see."

It was true enough that Rattlesnake Wells—so named for the nearby spring-fed wells that had originally caused pioneers traveling through this part of Wyoming on the Oregon Trail to branch off from their intended destination and instead settle right here, once they'd gotten rid of the numerous rattlesnake nests also to be found in the area—was undergoing a gold boom. In the space of less than four years, ever since the yellow ore had been found in the Prophecy Mountains just to the northwest, what had once been a quiet community serving surrounding cattle and horse ranches and a few farms, more than doubled in population and sprawl.

In addition to being a long-standing stop on the Rawlins-to-Casper stagecoach run, a railroad spur had also been added. The original layout of the town, running at a southwest-to-northeast angle and nowadays referred to as "Old Town," had stayed solid and largely unchanged. The growth sprawl, running off the northern point of Old Town and extending at an angle to the northwest, pointing toward the Prophecy Mountains, naturally enough came to be called "New Town." Its main drag was dubbed Gold Avenue, and lining it was every kind of hastily slapped-together structure one could imagine. Shacks and tents were predominant. Occupying these was a span of businesses that included shot-and-a-beer saloons, greasy spoon eateries, gambling dens, cut-rate equipment dealers, by-the-night sleeping cots, and whore cribs.

And the clientele for these businesses included every kind of easy profit seeker from swindlers and pickpockets to card sharps and pimps pushing their exclusive string of soiled doves.

It was hardly the kind of growth spurt that could be called uplifting for the original community. But along with the undesirables and the trash that poured in, so did a lot of money. And enough of that spilled over into Old Town to make the rest tolerable.

And now, for better or worse, right in the heart of the New Town sprawl, entrepreneur August Gafford would soon be opening his gaudy new saloon, the Crystal Diamond.

"Of course there are going to be customers who'll stay loyal to our saloon," said Maudie, her words aiming to soothe and reassure. "But you're also right in thinking that the novelty of Gafford's place will, in the beginning, most likely attract some of them to at least take a look and probably even throw back a drink or two."

"Any who do that, I don't care if they come back in here or not," declared Bullock, his scowl returning even fiercer than before. "In fact, I'd just as soon they didn't!"

"Now you're sounding grumpy and stubborn and, frankly, a little ridiculous," Maudie told him, demonstrating her standing with Bullock as being one of less than a handful of people who could get away with saying something like that to him. "What are you going to do—post a spy out front of the Crystal Diamond and mark off any of our regular customers who are seen going inside?"

"I'll know. I'll hear things."

"People have a natural inclination, not to mention a right, to be curious about something new and different. And that includes me." Maudie thrust out her chin defiantly. "I might want to take a look inside Gafford's place myself, once it opens. If I do, will you bar me from coming back in here?"

"Now who's being ridiculous?" Bullock growled in frustration. He looked plaintively over at Bob. "See what I have to put up with? Not only do I have that silk-tongued, fancy-pants Gafford trying to horn in on my business and steal my customers, now I've got treason threatened from within my ranks at the very highest level."

Bob couldn't keep one side of his mouth from curving up in a lazy grin. "Seems to me, Mike," he said, "that the biggest threat you're under right at the moment is the way you're gonna blow a gasket if you don't calm down. You said yourself how you've faced tough competition before and made it through. So you will again. Sure, the novelty of the Crystal Diamond is gonna cost you a few customers for a while. But, before long, things will level out and I bet you'll hardly notice the difference. My guess is that the ones who've got the biggest worry about being hurt by Gafford are the tent saloons and gambling dives currently pulling in business along Gold Avenue."

Bullock suddenly looked thoughtful and much of the tension seemed to ease out of him. "You really think so?"

"Stands to reason, don't it?" Bob said, aiming to add to the calmed-down reaction he'd already gotten. "If Gafford keeps his prices fair and can offer a glitzy setting complete with dancing girls and the rest, who with any sense would want to keep doing his drinking or gambling in a musty, mud-bottomed tent when he can walk a few doors up the street and do the same thing in so much better surroundings?"

"Sounds to me like those are some pretty good points," said Maudie.

Bullock heaved a big sigh. "Yeah, I guess they are . . . I guess, too, that I sometimes let myself get more riled up over things than I probably should."

"You think so?" Maudie responded, arching one finely penciled brow and putting an unmistakable dose of sarcasm in her tone.

"Okay, okay. I admitted it, didn't I? No need to rub it in." Bullock twisted his mouth ruefully. "But there's something about that Gafford skunk that just plain rubs me wrong, so don't be surprised if I let him get me worked up all over again before this is through."

Maudie smiled. "I'd only be surprised if you *didn't* get worked up over something on a regular basis. That would cause me to be seriously worried about you."

Bullock rolled his eyes and then cut his gaze to Bob. "See what I mean? She never lets up."

"And if I did," Maudie told him, "*you'd* be the one with something to worry about."

Speaking of something to perhaps worry about, right then was when three rough-edged hombres came crowding through the batwings, loudly stomping dust and caked mud as they boiled toward the bar like a pack of parched coyotes. And it didn't take long before one of them—the leader, judging by the way the other two held back and let him do most of the mouth-running—started in with some howling.

"Whooeee!" he cut loose. "I do declare this is one fine-lookin' establishment. I gotta admit, however, to bein' a mite perplexed. Is this really a saloon? Or is it a church? I know what the sign said outside and I know what it kinda *looks* like in here . . . but it's so dadgum peaceful and quiet, way more so than any other saloon I've ever been in, that I just can't be sure."

The one making the noise and drawing obliging snickers from his two companions was a tall, raw-boned specimen who might have been almost handsome before his nose got broken and reset so many times that it now looked like it had been put back together out of mismatched pieces. He had a narrow, V-shaped face with knife-edge cheekbones and small, yellowed teeth.

One of his pards was a dumpy Mexican with a round brown face, a drooping mustache, and greasy, curly hair spilling out from under the front of his sombrero and dangling down in the middle of his forehead. The other was a bland-looking individual, average in every detail except for a set of perfectly shaped and razored sideburns that looked as incongruous on his dirt-streaked, beard-stubbled face as a pair of ivory grips on a rusted pistol.

All three were clad in worn, dust-caked range garb that marked them as having likely been wranglers in the not-too-distant past. All wore guns holstered on their hips and Broken Nose, in particular, carried himself in a way that Bob immediately recognized as the mark of someone who fancied himself pretty handy with a shootin' iron. That, in turn, made all three of them worth keeping an eye on as the source for potential trouble.

Maudie sensed the same thing, as evidenced by her remark, "I got a feeling that here are three hombres we'd *wish* as customers for the Crystal Diamond." Even as she was saying this, however, she was rising up to go perform bartending duties for the trio.

In the meantime, as he leaned back against the bar, resting his elbows on the edge and hooking a boot heel over the brass rail along the base, Broken Nose focused on the near table where the four old-sters continued quietly playing cards. Addressing them, he said, "Hey, you bunch of grampaws. Any one of you happen to be a bartender or a priest? That might help me figure out this puzzlement I got."

Once again, his companions snickered and snorted at his great wit.

But one of the card players, Delbert Carey, a former soldier and railroad worker who still had more than a little bark on him, was neither impressed by Broken Nose's brand of humor nor intimidated by his loud mouth. Without looking around from the cards fanned out in his hand, he said indifferently, "What we are, you rather impertinent young pup, is of no consequence to you. And your so-called puzzle-ment, I assure you, is of equally little concern to us."

Broken Nose's reaction to this response was at first one of surprise, his eyebrows lifting high. But then, just as quickly, the brows came back down and knit-ted tightly above a glare aimed at Carey's back.

"Say now," he said. "You're a sassy old goat, ain't you?"

Carey ignored him.

Sideburns, also leaning against the bar, looked a little uncertain, like he didn't want to see this escalate into something more than it had to. "Too sassy for a priest, right?" he said. "So that's a good sign this probably is a saloon after all, wouldn't you say?"

"Either way," said Broken Nose, "I don't cotton worth a damn to bein' talked to like that."

Moving up on the back side of the bar and adopting a tolerant smile, Maudie said, "How about if I was to ask you gents what you'd like to have to drink? That more the way you'd like to be talked to?"

CHAPTER 2

The three newcomers turned their heads, each one openly and appreciably taking in the fetching sight behind the questions.

"How-dee!" exclaimed Broken Nose. "You not only are sayin' exactly the words we want to hear, darlin', but you are also lookin' mighty doggone fine while speakin' 'em."

"Thank you. I aim to please," Maudie replied. "So what can I pour you to add to your pleasure?"

"Red-eye. Some of the good stuff," said Broken Nose, slapping a palm down on the bartop. "You're lookin' at three fellas who have worked our tails near off back in Nebraska to put together a grubstake. And now we've come here of a mind to climb up into those Prophecy Mountains and not come back down again until we're packin' a fortune in yeller gold. But, before we do that, before we commence the diggin' and more hard work, we aim to have us a final round of hootin' and hollerin' down here on flat land."

"Well, you've come to the right place for that,"

Maudie said as she spread out three glasses and reached for a bottle of whiskey from which to fill them. "There's a good deal of hootin' and hollerin' gets done here most nights. Within reason, of course."

"Within reason," Broken Nose echoed, a lopsided grin spreading across his face. Then, raising his glass, he added, "You heard her, boys. Here's to keepin' our hootin' and hollerin' within reason."

In unison, three elbows bent and the shots of red-eye were tossed down. The emptied glasses had scarcely clapped back onto the bartop before Broken Nose was calling for more. "Do another round, darlin'. Just like that one."

"Be happy to, cowboy," Maudie told him with a smile. "But the way it works is, in order to keep my whiskey-pouring hand busy, my payment-taking hand needs to get in on some of the action, too."

Again the lopsided grin from Broken Nose. "What? We look like lowlifes who can't make good on our tab?"

"You could have a halo shining above your head," Maudie explained, "but the policy remains the same when it comes to drinking in here. You pay as you go."

"I'll cover that first round, Jax," said the Mexican as he dug into his pocket.

Broken Nose—Jax, as he'd now been identified—waved him off, saying, "No, I got it. Next one, too. On account of, once I get my money dug out, I'll also have me some further negotiatin' to do."

From his pants pocket, Jax produced a handful of coins and wadded bills. These he slapped onto the bartop. "There now, darlin'. Take what you need for two rounds of drinks. And then, after you've poured, tell me how much more you'll need out of that pile in order to arrange for me and you slippin' off somewhere private-like where we can make some music together."

Maudie hesitated in her pouring for just a fraction of a second. Then, after resuming the task and refilling the final glass, she set down the bottle of whiskey and said to Jax, "Unless I'm misunderstanding what you just suggested, I think you got a seriously wrong impression. We have gals on premises, some right pretty ones, who do the kind of 'slipping off' you seem interested in. They're still up in their rooms since they don't usually come down until more toward evening. But, if you don't want to wait, I can send word for a couple of them—ones I'm sure would meet your approval—to get ready and come on down now."

"Ain't none of that necessary," said Jax. "I've already seen what meets my approval. You. No need to do no more window-shoppin', not where I'm concerned."

"But that's where your wrong impression comes in," Maudie told him. "You see, I'm not one of the upstairs gals. I serve drinks, make friendly conversation with customers, and so forth, but that's as far as it goes."

Jax shook his head. "I ain't buyin' it. You work in a saloon, you parade around showin' yourself off that way"—he waved a hand indicating the manner in which Maudie's low-cut dress accentuated her fine bosom—"so the message is plain enough for me. You can be had—it's just a matter of agreein' on the right price."

"You're wrong, mister. To the point of being obnoxious and insulting. Much more of it," Maudie warned him, "will only get you an invitation to leave and not be welcome back."

Again seeming to want to mollify things, Sideburns spoke up, saying, "Why don't we just find somewhere else to spend our money and do our drinkin', Jax? This joint is pretty dead, anyway."

"No way," Jax was quick to respond. "Be a cold day in hell when I let some saloon floozy put the run on me and tell me not to come back!"

Up to that point, Bob and Bullock had been listening and looking on from where they still sat at the back table. Because of Maudie's proven capability for handling pushy customers all on her own, they hadn't seen any need to get involved in her exchanges with Broken Nose Jax. Until now. The threatening tone of Jax's last remark, however, made it a different matter. One that Bullock *did* decide to take a hand in.

As the stout saloon owner got to his feet and started toward the bar, Bob remained seated. Despite Jax's attitude raising the hackles on the back of the marshal's neck, the situation was hardly a legal matter warranting him sticking his nose in. In fact, he and his badge might only aggravate things more. Best just to leave Bullock and Maudie handle it, he told himself.

Marching up and coming to a halt beside Jax, Bullock got right to it. "You have some kind of problem with the way we run things around here, bub?" he wanted to know.

Jax turned his head and frowned down at the saloon owner. Bullock was three or four inches shorter than Jax, but he was broader through the shoulders by an equal amount, and the defiant thrust of his chin made it clear he wasn't the least bit intimidated by the taller man.

Nor did Jax show any sign of taking a step back from the demanding question put to him. "What's it to you, whether I do or not?" he asked in turn.

"My name's Bullock. Mike Bullock. If you paid any attention to the sign out front of this establishment on your way in, that oughta give you your answer."

"So you're the big he-goose around here. Is that it?"

"However you want to say it," Bullock answered. "What it boils down to is that a problem in my place is my business to take care of. So I'll repeat my question: Do you have a problem?"

"Damn right I do. A big one," said Jax. "I don't like havin' the ol' bait and switch game pulled on me."

"You'll have to spell it out plainer. I don't follow you."

"How much plainer does it have to be? You've got this little teaser behind the bar here"—Jax once again swept an arm to indicate Maudie—"paradin' around with her mams practically hangin' out, gettin' a fella all stoked up, and then, when I try to set a price for samplin' the whole package, she tells me it's no deal. Claims she ain't no 'upstairs girl.' What kind of shit is that?"

"It's called telling the truth. Maudie leveled with you. I heard her explain it clear as could be. We've got gals—hostesses, we prefer to call 'em—who are available for the kind of thing you're interested in.

But Maudie ain't one of them. She don't do that kind of work." Bullock's thick shoulders rose and fell in a shrug. "You're just gonna have to accept it."

"Like hell I will!" Jax's expression turned ugly and a bright flush of anger flooded his face. "I ain't ready to take that for an answer out of her nor you, either one. I say any woman who sashays around half-dressed in a joint like this is a saloon slut who deserves nothing more than to be treated like one. Now all I want to know is how much money I have to lay down to be the one to give her what her flauntin' ways are askin' for!"

"There ain't no price, you foul-mouthed, thick-headed fool," Bullock snarled. "And you'll be layin' down no more of your money in my place for anything. Down the drinks already poured for you and then hit the door. Get out of here and don't bother coming back."

"Supposin' I ain't ready to go?"

"You'll be leaving. Either by walking of your own accord, or being dragged out. The choice is yours."

The angry flush continued to color Jax's face as his mouth twisted into a sneer. "You'd like that, wouldn't you, you grizzled old scrapper? I can see by your flattened nose and the scar tissue around your eyes how you enjoy escortin' customers out the hard way. But if you think I'm gonna butt heads or bust knuckles with the likes of you, mister, you got another think comin' . . . What I will do, though, is bust a cap on your double-dealin' damn hide if you keep pushin' me!"

With those words, Jax reached down and drew his six-gun in a swift, unexpected move. It took only a split second before its muzzle was shoved square in Bullock's face and held steady mere inches from the tip of his nose.

"For God's sake!" Maudie exclaimed.

From where he sat, Bob saw Bullock's back go rigid and his hands ball into melon-sized fists. It was obvious the tough saloon owner was coiled tight, wanting badly to tear into Jax. But he didn't dare, not with a gun jammed practically up his nostrils. Not even Bullock's notorious quick temper was enough to make him that reckless.

As far as being reckless, Bob couldn't afford to be, either. Not for the sake of his friend. But, by the same token, neither could he just continue to sit and watch. The tableau had suddenly escalated into a life-threatening situation that the marshal not only had a right but an obligation to get involved in.

Slowly, measuredly, Bob stood up and edged toward those grouped in front of the bar. Out of the corner of his eye, Jax took note of his approach. The Mexican and Sideburns were positioned in such a way as to be more or less facing him. Their hands hovered close to the guns on their hips, but so far neither had drawn iron.

Ever the cautious one, Sideburns muttered, "You seein' this, Jax? We got a law dog in the mix."

"So what? That don't change the point of this, not a damn bit," Jax replied through clenched teeth.

"Might not be the best idea to keep wavin' a hogleg around, that's all I'm sayin'."

Never taking either his eyes or his gun off Bullock, Jax said, "I always had a hunch there might be a trace of yella runnin' up your spine, Reeves. Now's your chance to prove it one way or the other. Either stand your ground and back my play, or crawfish the hell out of here and never let me lay eyes on you again."

Continuing to move forward, his own hand clawed close above the .44 holstered at his side, Bob said, "Your man is giving you some smart advice, mister. You ought to be listening to him, not running him off."

"Ain't nobody runnin' nobody off, law dog," Sideburns was quick to say. Then, directing his voice back to Jax, he said with a scowl, "I'm backin' your play, Jax. I don't like it, but I'll back it."

Without bothering to acknowledge this and still without taking his focus off Bullock, Jax said to Bob, "If you want to talk smarts, badge-toter, you ain't exactly showin' many of your own. You're outgunned and outnumbered and I'm already primed to blow Mr. He-Goose's beak clean off if you crowd me too much. What the hell you lookin' to accomplish? You'd best back off and maybe, just maybe, this can work out with nobody gettin' serious hurt."

"Can't do that," Bob said flatly. "You're the one who needs to back off. Then maybe—just maybe— I won't have to blast you to hell and gone."

"You tell him, Marshal," Bullock growled. "Don't let this piece of trail trash buffalo you."

All of a sudden Jax's expression seemed to change. The double dose of Bob's counterthreat and Bullock's defiant bravado appeared to rattle him some, perhaps causing him to question the brashness of what he'd set in motion. Given this moment of hesitation on his part and the fact that Sideburns and the Mexican still had their own guns holstered, it could have been a good chance for Bob to make a decisive move—except for the problem of Maudie, whose position where she stood on the back side of the bar placed her directly behind Jax from the marshal's angle and thereby potentially in the line of fire. Bob wasn't ready to take such a risk.

But, at almost the same moment, Maudie realized for herself what a bad spot she was in. What was more, she also sensed the faint hesitation in Jax's aggression and recognized the opportunity it presented. Abruptly, she wrapped her hand around the whiskey bottle she'd used to pour the second round of drinks and thrust it out at arm's length, releasing it in a short toss that sent it across the width of the bar to thump against the shoulder of an unsuspecting Sideburns on the other side. The bottle didn't hit with much force but it was still enough to cause Sideburns to jerk away reflexively and bump against the Mexican beside him. As the bottle bounced off the jostled pair and fell crashing to the floor, Maudie dropped down low behind the bar.

The overall maneuver now gave Sundown Bob all the opening he needed.

If the speed of Jax's earlier draw had seemed impressive, it paled sadly compared to the lightning sweep of Bob's hand as it skinned his .44 and triggered it into action. Flame and lead spat from the barrel, the roar of the shot shattering the tense silence that had previously gripped the room. Jax's gun hand was swatted away as if by an invisible blow, and the weapon once gripped in it, torn from his grasp by Bob's bullet, went skimming down the length of the bar until it smashed into a pyramid of clean glasses stacked at the far end.

Jax's knees sagged and his free hand reached frantically to clutch stinging, empty, still-clawed fingers. An instant later, his knees had cause to sag even more and then buckle completely when Bullock immediately uncorked a sizzling right hook that sent him crumpling to the floor.

As Jax was going down, Bob swung his .44 in a short horizontal arc and centered it on the other two men as they finally, foolishly, decided to grab for their guns. "Don't even think it!" he warned them.

Predictably, Sideburns halted his attempt and jerked both hands, palms open, to shoulder height instead. But the Mexican insisted on following through. Or trying to. His hand closed on the grips of his gun but managed to do little more than loosen it in its holster before Bob's Colt roared again. The bullet it discharged this time smashed into the Mexican's shoulder, spinning him around and pitching him onto the edge of a nearby empty table. He hissed in pain and filled the air with Spanish curses, clawing the tabletop with his good hand, trying to hold himself upright, but failing and then collapsing to the floor.

CHAPTER 3

"You sure you don't want to throw those varmints behind bars, boss?" Chief Deputy Fred Ordway asked earnestly.

Bob's headshake was firm. "No. That'd make 'em even more bother than they're worth. Besides, we just got the jail cleaned out after the last two we had in there. These three claim to have a grubstake put together, so be sure they pay Doc Tibbs once he's done patching 'em up. After that, you and the Macy boys herd 'em on out of town. If they're still of a mind to go do some gold digging, give 'em an hour or so to buy supplies up in New Town. But that's all."

"What about giving 'em back their guns?"

"Not their handguns, no. They likely have rifles as part of their saddle gear. That'll be good enough for up in the mountains. Make sure they understand that if they come back to town for any reason in the future, they're to confine their dealings to Gold Avenue. And at the first sign of any more trouble out of them or if I see them down here again in Old

Town, I *will* toss 'em in the clink and throw away the key."

Deputy Fred nodded. "Got it, boss. I'll go on over to Doc Tibbs's office now and stick with the Macys until we're sure those skunks are on their way out of town."

After taking a final furtive glance at the voluptuous Maudie (and blushing faintly once he had), Fred turned and threaded his considerable bulk out through the crowd that had now gathered inside Bullock's.

Watching him go, Maudie said with a fond smile, "He reminds me of a totally dedicated puppy dog whenever he's around you."

"He's dedicated, true enough. Which I'm glad of and better off for," Bob said. "As far as the puppy part, he's proven more than once—to the surprise and misfortune of a few hombres who made the mistake of also seeing him that way—that he's got a bulldog side to him, too, when the need is there."

"Yes, I'm aware of that," Maudie replied. "I meant nothing disparaging by what I said. Fred has truly come into his own as a reliable lawman for our town, especially after all that trouble with the Sanders gang last spring. And the way he looks out for your two newer deputies, the Macy brothers, is equally impressive."

A half hour had passed since Bob had drawn his gun against Jax and his two companions. The sound of the shots blasting out of Bullock's in the still afternoon had quickly drawn attention. Not to mention a gathering of those hungry to hear all the gory details and thirsty to sample some of the fare from behind the saloon bar while they were being regaled. There was nothing like an outburst of trouble to draw a good crowd.

And none other than Mike Bullock himself, taking over duties behind the stick, was happy to provide these details, complete with colorful embellishments—and even happier to provide a steady flow of shots and beers to his listeners. Joining in this follow-up were Delbert Carey and the other card players whose game had been interrupted by the ruckus. They were now benefiting from said interruption via the drinks being bought them in exchange for also hearing their eyewitness accounts of the events that had occurred. Nor, as it turned out, were any of them shy about also laying things on a little thick.

Only Bob and Maudie were exhibiting any reluctance when it came to participating in the rehash. When his deputies showed up in response to the shooting, Bob had naturally related to them what had happened. After that, once his men took charge of the troublemakers, he didn't figure he owed a whole lot of explaining to anybody else. In fact, he probably would have taken his leave at that point if he hadn't seen how Maudie appeared a little shaken up in the aftermath of the trouble. So he steered her off to a table on the fringe of the pack and then stuck around to help her get settled down and to ward off her being bombarded by those wanting still another account of what had happened. A couple of the hostesses had come down from upstairs, and one of them had brought over a brandy for Maudie and a cold beer for Bob.

"If I wasn't already full up with deputies," Bob

said now, trying to lighten the mood a bit, "I might approach you about pinning on a badge. The way you tossed that whiskey bottle and distracted everybody so I had an opening to disarm Jax, you sure showed you've got enough grit for the job."

Maudie shook her head. "Don't tell me about grit. The only reason I did what I did was because I was scared—scared that either that piece of trash Jax was going to shoot Mike or that you were going to do something reckless enough to get your own self shot. Plus, I have to admit, I was worried about my own hide in case too much lead started flying around."

Bob shrugged. "Call it whatever you want. What you did was still brave and it for sure helped things turn out better than they otherwise might have."

"If you insist," said Maudie. Then, after taking a sip of her brandy, she added, "But I still don't recommend placing me on a list for future deputy candidates."

"Probably just as well," Bob responded with a wry smile. "In order for me to be able to pin a badge on you, you'd have to start wearing a shirt or some such. If you took to doing that on my account, I'd have half the men in town wanting to string me up."

Maudie's expression clouded. "After the crude way Jax came on to me—and he was hardly the first—maybe I *would* be better off dressing different, covering up more."

"Do what you think is best," Bob advised her. "But don't be in a hurry to let a piece of crud like Jax influence your decision."

Maudie finished her drink. "You're right. I'll be sure to keep that in mind." Then she smiled somewhat coyly. "Especially now that I've found out *you* take notice of the way I dress."

Bob felt his ears burn a little. Meeting her gaze, he said, "I've got eyes and a pulse, don't I? Fella'd have to be lacking both not to take notice of you, Maudie."

Her smile widened. "With you, I've too often been left wondering."

Before Bob could respond further, a ripple of increased excitement and a surge of louder voices ran through the crowd gathered in the middle of the room. It didn't sound like a sign of serious trouble but it nevertheless was something different, some new development. It piqued Bob's curiosity enough so that he stood up to peer over and through the bobbing heads that filled the room until he was able to spot what was taking place. Maudie stood up, too, but she was too short and the mass of bodies was too thick for her to make out anything.

"What is it? What's going on?" she asked.

"August Gafford and a gaggle of his followers just came in," Bob told her. He arched a brow. "This could turn out to be real interesting."

"It could be interesting or it could turn ugly," Maudie said with a concerned look on her face. "I'd better get over there behind the bar with Mike and try to keep him from saying or doing something rash. Wouldn't be a bad idea for you to work your way out into the crowd, either."

CHAPTER 4

"You've got a lot of brass showing up here," Bullock growled as soon as he saw Gafford shouldering his way up to a spot in front of the bar.

Gafford was a tall man of about fifty, impeccably dressed in a swallowtail coat and matching vest of powder blue. A modified, short-crowned top hat of the same color perched rakishly on a headful of wavy gray hair. His most memorable feature of all, however, was a set of big, bright teeth that he flashed at every opportunity.

He did so now, in response to Bullock's greeting, beaming a wide smile. "Yes, I suppose it does take a certain amount of brass to enter an establishment that regularly serves as a shooting gallery for the low-life ruffians it attracts as part of its clientele. But never let it be said that August Gafford is lacking in nerve or a spirit for adventure."

"In the first place," Bullock said in a strained voice, "my joint is as safe and free of riffraff—present company excepted—as any you'll find on the frontier. In most cases, I take personal responsibility for making sure of that. And, in the second place, that wasn't what I was talking about in the first place."

Gafford lifted his eyebrows. "Then what *were* you talking about? Could it be you were you referring to my mere presence here?"

"You hit the nail on the head, bub. That's exactly what I was referring to!"

By this point, all the other chatter in close proximity to the two men had died down and every ear and eye was focused on what would be said next.

"I find it rather surprising," Gafford remarked smugly, "that you would object to *anyone* inclined toward spending money instead of shooting up the place. Take some friendly advice, friend, and rake in all the income you can over the next few days. Because, in less than a week, after my establishment the Crystal Diamond opens up, I predict you'll be desperately watching a sad decline in paying customers of any stripe."

"That does it!" Bullock roared. "Out! Get the hell out of my place, you showboating windbag, before I come around this bar and fling you headfirst into the street!"

Gafford and those clustered closest around him surged backward at Bullock's outburst. But before it could escalate further, Maudie quickly moved up beside her boss and placed a restraining hand on his shoulder.

"Hey, take it easy, Mike," she said in a firm, soothing voice. "Haven't we had enough excitement in here for one day?"

"I got room for more," grumbled Bullock stubbornly.

"Then you ought to also have room for a little

friendly competition. If Mr. Gafford wants to come in here and spend some of his money—like he's been doing practically everywhere else in town—what's the harm in letting him throw some our way?" Here Maudie's voice rose a bit higher and louder and her eyes cut challengingly to Gafford himself. "In fact, if you let him stick around, I wouldn't be surprised if he was willing to really demonstrate his brass and that spirit he spoke of a minute ago by offering to buy a round of drinks for everybody."

This sent a new ripple through the crowd, one of anticipation. Attention was quickly locked on Gafford to see what his reaction would be. For a brief moment, the showy businessman appeared to be caught off guard. But then, with another teeth-flashing smile and a sweep of one hand in acknowledgment of Maudie, he said, "I've got to hand it to you, friend Bullock, your associate is every bit as fetching and shrewd as I have heard. But what the hell—go ahead and set up a round of drinks on me!"

What had been a ripple of anticipation now turned into a raucous swell of appreciation and shouted drink orders. Bullock found himself as trapped by Maudie's sly maneuver as Gafford was, having little choice but to start filling and shoving glassfuls of beer and whiskey across the bar and into grabbing hands. Maudie did the same, and the two hostesses swooped in to help as well, distributing drinks farther back into the crowd. At the same time, Gafford, struggling a bit to maintain a tolerant grin, produced a roll of bills from which he kept peeling off payouts.

By the time everybody in the room had been served at Gafford's expense (a few probably more

than once) and the frenzy was dying down, Bob
stepped up and leaned on the bar next to the big
spender.

"Well now," Gafford greeted him. "I may be the
man of the moment, albeit fleetingly, but *here* is truly
the man of the hour and the day by virtue of the way
you shot it out with those scoundrels earlier. I was
hoping I would run into you."

"I usually ain't very hard to find," Bob replied.

"No. Of course you aren't." Gafford gestured. "I
see you don't have a drink in your hand. Did you get
in on the round I just bought?"

"I passed, actually. But I'm good."

"Ah, of course. On duty and all that. Correct?"

"Something like that. Although it's a rule I've been
known to bend on occasion."

"As you have every right to do," Gafford proclaimed. "I hope you'll be partaking from time to
time at my new establishment when it opens. And,
needless to say, whenever you do, it will be gratis. It's
the least I can do—and the offer extends to your
deputies as well—considering your service to our
community."

"That ain't exactly a new concept on your part,"
Bullock said from his side of the bar. "The marshal
and his boys are treated that way by most businesses
in town."

"As they should be," said Gafford. "Nevertheless,
my invitation as far as the Crystal Diamond still
stands. Which leads me to another invitation I want
to be sure and extend—the one, as a matter of fact,
that brought me here seeking you out, Marshal."

"Oh? And what would that be?"

Gafford beamed another one of his toothy smiles. "I assume you've heard of the shooting match I am promoting as part of the grand opening of my Crystal Diamond?"

"Hard to miss hearing about it, what with all the flyers circulating around town and the talk they're generating."

"Talk is cheap. Takes money to buy whiskey," Bullock muttered to no one in particular.

"Not all talk is cheap," Gafford countered. "Ever since arriving in Rattlesnake Wells I've been hearing talk about its highly regarded marshal, how he is a quiet, unassuming family man except when hardcases show up to try and cause trouble. The incident here from just a little while ago, I think you'd agree, would be a good example of that. An example of the kind of incident that brings out the Sundown Bob persona, if you will, and the blazing gun skills that come with it."

Bullock shook his head. "Gafford, you can use more words and say less than anybody I ever heard or heard *of*. What the hell are you driving at?"

"And just for the record," advised the marshal, "I ain't exactly crazy about that 'Sundown Bob' moniker."

"Very well. I'll keep that in mind," said Gafford. "But the perception—and *proof*, you can hardly deny—of your gunmanship remains. *That* is the point I'm trying to get to. Simply put, if you aren't already planning on it, I am in hopes that I can encourage you to sign up for the upcoming shooting match."

"Hey now," said Bullock. "Much as it pains me to agree with any part of all this grand opening hoopla, that ain't a half-bad idea. You sure got the credentials,

Bob. Hell, the event is bound to take place—you might as well win it as anybody."

"*Had* you thought about entering?" Maudie said, joining in the discussion. With the details of the shooting having been told and retold and the round of free drinks now history, the crowd was starting to thin out again in a steady trickle.

Bob pushed his eyebrows up. "To tell the truth, no, I haven't given the contest much thought one way or another. After all, the flyers and the announcement only just came out this morning."

"So go ahead and start giving it some thought, then," urged Maudie. "You really should enter. You'd be certain to win."

"Odds-on favorite, that's for sure," agreed Bullock.

"And," said Gafford, "think how much excitement it would add to have Sundown Bah . . . er, I mean, the town marshal entered as one of the contestants."

A thoughtful expression tugged at Bob's face. "Now that you've all mentioned it, I gotta admit that the idea is sort of intriguing." His expression gave way to a somewhat sheepish grin. "But say I did win, what the heck would I do with a pair of fancy gold-and-diamond six-shooters? Wouldn't be like I could wear 'em on the job or anything."

"Why not?" said Gafford. "It only enhanced Wyatt Earp's reputation when he started packing the Buntline Special that was presented to him."

Bob's sheepish grin twisted wryly. "That's only because Earp's reputation was mostly just hogwash to begin with. Way I hear tell, other than that fracas at the O.K. Corral, he used a gun more for clubbing rowdies over the head than for doing any actual shooting. I suppose that long-barreled Buntline might have come in handy for something like that, but it sure as hell wasn't practical for much else. Certainly not for drawing quick and firing in a shoot-out."

Now it was Maudie's mouth that curved into a grin, a decidedly impish one. "If you resorted to that method around here, it could result in men lining up to purposely get clobbered over the head with a diamond-and-gold gun. They might see it as the closest they'd ever get to striking gold, in hopes some of the plating from the barrel scraped off on their scalp."

"If you're worried about packing around those fancy shooters, I got the perfect solution," said Bullock. He jabbed a thumb to indicate the large painting of a plumply voluptuous nude woman that hung on the wall behind the bar, centered amidst the display of liquor bottles. "Think how grand they'd look up there, bracketing Luscious Lucille. They'd look great and even add a classy touch."

"Now see here," Gafford was quick to sputter. "They'd add a touch of class this place could surely use, no doubt about that. But, if they're going to be put on public display anywhere, it rightfully ought to be my establishment. After all—"

"They can rightfully be displayed wherever the winner of the contest takes a mind to," Bullock said, cutting him off.

"Don't get started again, you two," Bob said, quelling any buildup of an argument. "Especially not since you're getting the cart way ahead of the horse. I haven't even signed up for the contest yet, let alone won it. Keep in mind there are plenty of good shooters besides me around these parts. And when news of this contest spreads, it's bound to draw the best of 'em."

"When *are* you going to start signing up shooters?" Maudie asked Gafford. "And when are you going to hold the contest?"

"Sign-ups, which will require a twenty-five-dollar entry fee, will begin first thing on the day after tomorrow," Gafford said. "A booth will be erected on the front steps of the Crystal Diamond and will be open for two days. The contest itself will be held on Friday, five days from now. At its conclusion, the doors of the Crystal Diamond will be opened for business."

"What about the big prize, the two jeweled guns?" Bob wanted to know. "Where are you keeping them and what steps are you taking to keep them safe? You haven't approached me or my deputies about anything regarding them."

"The guns will be here on tomorrow's train from Cheyenne," Gafford explained. "The same train will also be carrying Miss Alora Dane and her Diamond Dollies. All will arrive, I assure you, with a good deal of fanfare."

His tone growing annoyed, Bob said, "And when were you gonna advise me about any of this so me and my men could be on alert? You start parading around gold-and-diamond-encrusted guns, you don't recognize the chance for attracting the attention of some who might be inclined to make a grab for 'em without waiting to try their luck in a fair contest?"

"My apologies, Marshal, for not notifying you in a more timely manner," Gafford was quick to say. "I assure you, however, that I *do* recognize the risk of the guns attracting bad intentions from scoundrels looking to seize them. That is why I didn't announce anything about the prize guns earlier and why I have provided my own security to guard them until they are transferred to the possession of the contest winner. I certainly didn't mean to exclude you and your deputies from any involvement but, by the same token, neither did I want to burden you unduly on top of all your other responsibilities."

"Well, it sounds like you've taken *some* reasonable measures, at least," Bob allowed. "When you say you've got your own guard looking out for the guns, can you give me a name?"

"Simon Quirt. He's a former Pinkerton man who comes with high recommendations."

Bob nodded. "I've heard of him. A former Pinkerton and a few other things. But, from all reports, a competent man to have on your side."

"I'm glad you approve."

"I didn't say that. Not exactly. But you've already got him on the job so that's what we'll have to work with. I'll naturally want to meet with him after he gets in. Once those guns make it to town, they'll still fall under the general responsibility of me and my deputies, even with Quirt in place."

"I understand."

"Where will you be keeping them between when the train gets in and the day of the contest?"

"Abraham Starbuck has agreed to keep them in his bank's vault during the overnight hours and whenever they're not on display."

"Sounds like a good idea," Bob said.

"Mr. Starbuck has also agreed to be one of the judges in the shooting contest," Gafford went on. "I've also lined up Angus McTeague as a second."

"You're roping in some of the town's best men, I'll give you that," Bullock said grudgingly. "Nobody will question the outcome of the judging with the likes of Starbuck and McTeague making the calls."

"But I still need a third, a tiebreaker if necessary," Gafford pointed out. "At one point I was thinking I would ask the good marshal here. But now that the notion has arisen for him to enter the contest himself, that clearly falls by the way." The businessman paused to clear his throat before fixing his gaze directly on Bullock. "Another name frequently suggested to me, friend Bullock, was yours. Given how much disfavor you've exhibited toward me and my entire undertaking, I suppose it's a waste of breath to ask—but *would* you consider serving as a judge for the contest?"

Bullock blinked rapidly two or three times and looked sort of like a man who'd been asked to try on a pair of frilly bloomers. Then that look shifted into his familiar scowl. "You've got a hell of a lot of guts, Gafford. There's something else I've got to give you. And, for me, that usually goes a long way toward taking the measure of a man."

Now it was Gafford's turn to look disconcerted. "You saying you'll do it?"

"Go ahead, Mike," Maudie urged. "It's going to take place with or without you. Show *your* measure by being part of it and meeting the challenge of the competition head on."

Bullock's scowl held firm. "Never let it be said that I came up short when it was time to match guts with anybody . . . Bring it on, Gafford. You're damn right I'll be your third judge."

CHAPTER 5

When Bob went home for supper that night, he was immediately ambushed by his ten-year-old son, Bucky, who was armed with a ton of questions about the afternoon shoot-out at Bullock's.

"Me and some of the other fellas from school heard about it as soon as classes let out," explained the freckled, wide-eyed boy who shared his father's flaming red hair. "Naturally, we ran straight downtown to find out as much as we could. But you were still inside with a bunch of other people so I couldn't get no closer. I mean, seein's how I know better than to ever go in a saloon." He paused, his face forming a somewhat disgruntled frown as he cast a furtive glance over toward Consuela, Bob's housekeeper and cook. "Then Consuela showed up and made me leave. She said you'd probably be busy for quite a while and wouldn't have time to be bothered by a bunch of questions from us kids. She said it could wait until you got home."

"Plus," Consuela added sternly, "the proximity of a

saloon, even on the outside, is no place for a young boy to be hanging around."

Consuela Diaz was a pretty young woman of Mexican blood who also served as a surrogate mother to Bucky since the passing of Bob's wife, Priscilla, nearly three years earlier. Moreover, Consuela had been part of the family, in a manner of speaking, since before Bucky was born. Her father, Alberto, was the ranch foreman for Bob's dad back in Texas. And her older brother, Ramos, had been Bob's best friend throughout their teenage years and into early manhood.

When Ramos was savagely gunned down by a hired thug working for the greedy cattle baron trying to squeeze out everybody else—including Bob's father—within the territory he sought exclusive control over, Bob retaliated vengefully. This earned him the brand of an outlaw, dubbed "the Devil's River Kid" because of the wilderness area into which he fled to elude capture, and for a year and more he was also forced to avoid all but the most fleeting and secretive contact with his family, including his young wife and baby son.

It was during this period that Consuela, having blossomed seemingly overnight into a smoldering, dark-haired beauty from Ramos's gawky, irritating kid sister who'd had a crush on Bob since she was eleven, first began to assist in the care of Bucky. This was necessary due to the frail, failing health of Priscilla, whose condition was only worsened by the emotional strain of Bob's outlaw status.

Following a manhunt that chased Bob into the teeth of a fierce blizzard and left him believed to be dead, Consuela had accompanied Priscilla and Bucky to Chicago, where Priscilla originally hailed from and where they intended to start a new life away from the turmoil and painful memories rooted in Texas. It was there that Bob caught up with them, revealing himself not only to be very much alive but also freed now from the attention of those sworn to hunt down the Devil's River Kid.

Assuming the new surname of Hatfield over the Hammond that Bob had been born with, all four of them (Consuela included, in order to continue helping look after Priscilla and the toddler Bucky) had struck out to build a new life together. This eventually brought them to Wyoming, where Priscilla's poor health finally took its toll. Bob, Consuela, and Bucky had gritted their teeth and forged on until finally settling in Rattlesnake Wells, where Bob's decency, bravery, and skill with a gun had soon won him the job of town marshal. Together, they'd been building on that foundation ever since.

"As usual," Bob said now, in response to what had just been related to him over the kitchen table, "Consuela had it right. I'd like to think that I can always make time for you, Buck, but the truth of the matter is that certain things, like my job, will sometimes get in the way. You can understand how a shooting is a pretty serious matter, right?"

"Well sure, Pa," Bucky agreed as Consuela began filling their plates with generous servings of potatoes, peas, and pork chops. "I just wanted to make sure you were all right . . . And then I wanted to hear the details about how you blasted those three low-down hombres who were threatening to kill everybody in the joint!"

Bob grinned. He couldn't deny that he liked being hero-worshipped by his son. But at the same time, he recognized he had to be careful not to glorify the practice of settling problems with guns. There were plenty of others who'd be quick enough to fill a boy's head with those kinds of notions.

"That sounds like a pretty good story, pal," Bob said, digging a fork into his mashed potatoes. "But, as usual with those kind of things, I guess it didn't take long for it to be exaggerated. So let me tell you what really happened . . ."

Around bites of the delicious meal and in between questions from Bucky, Bob told the straight of how the incident had played out. He neither embellished nor altered anything, except for cleaning up the crudity of Jax's remarks to Maudie.

"So you see," he summed up, "there were three hombres involved, right enough, but only two of 'em actually tried to bring their guns into it. Plus, I had help from a gal throwing a whiskey bottle and from Mike Bullock throwing a walloping right cross."

"Wow, I'd've liked to've seen that!" Bucky exclaimed. "There are folks around town who say Mr. Bullock can throw a punch as hard as John L. Sullivan."

"I don't know about that," Bob said. "But he's gotten pretty good with his fists over the years from breaking up saloon brawls, that much is sure. I guarantee I wouldn't want to be on the receiving end of his punches."

"But you still saved the day," Bucky insisted. "Shooting the gun out of one skunk's hand after he already had it drawn and aimed, and then winging that second fella before he ever cleared leather. Sundown Bob galloped into action again!"

It was obvious that Bucky had been keeping up to date on his share of the dime novels that circulated among the boys in town, despite their parents' best efforts to confiscate the lurid tomes. Bob couldn't suppress another grin, even as he said, "You know I don't care for that name."

"I know, Pa. I wish you did like it better, though. I think it's pretty neat."

"Pretty neat for a character in a dime novel, maybe. But in real life folks just have regular names, and mine's Bob Hatfield. That's good enough for me."

"Okay, Pa." Bucky squirmed in his chair. "I've cleaned my plate," he said. "Could I be excused now?"

"Excused to go do what?" asked Bob.

"I promised Skinny Hutchins and some of the fellas that I'd let them know the real details on what happened at Bullock's after I got the chance to talk to you. There's almost an hour of daylight left—I thought I'd go do that. They're counting on hearing from me. Can't I go?"

"For dessert, I saved part of the pie from yesterday. And I have some cold buttermilk," said Consuela.

"Couldn't I have the pie later, after I get back?"

"Pretty risky, leaving me alone with pie and cold buttermilk. Don't know if I can promise there'll be any left when you get back," said Bob.

"Aw, you wouldn't do that, Pa. I trust you."

Bob looked at Consuela. "Boy must be powerful anxious to talk to his friends if he's willing to risk his pie like that. Okay, Buck, you can go ahead and make your report. But you be back before dark, hear?"

Bucky took off like a shot. When Consuela rose to go fetch his pie and buttermilk, Bob got up from the table, too. "Mind if I take that out on the porch, 'Suela? It's a pretty nice evening. We won't be getting many more before the chilly edge of winter starts slicing in."

"*Sí.* I will bring your dessert out."

Bob went out and sat down in the old wooden rocking chair he kept on the front porch. As part of his morning ritual in good weather, after he ate breakfast inside, Bob would bring a postmeal mug of coffee out here and sip it down slowly before heading out to assume his marshal duties. Coming out here of an evening was more intermittent, but he nevertheless enjoyed it whenever he did.

Bob's house sat at the top of a gradual slope overlooking the town. Directly below was what had come to be called the Point, the joining spot where New Town's Gold Avenue branched off to the northwest, toward the Prophecy Mountains where the gold strikes were, and Front Street, the main drag of Old Town, angled to the southwest. The old and the new; the quiet and settled contrasting with the boisterous and booming. Either way, it all fell under the responsibility of Bob and his deputies to keep the lid from blowing off.

At the moment, all looked peaceful and calm. Bob enjoyed such moments, savored them. But, on the other hand, he grudgingly admitted to himself that it would be mighty boring if there weren't other moments, like the one today with Jax and his cohorts, to spice things up a bit. As long as it didn't swing too far one way or the other, he told himself, he could be content.

Abruptly, Consuela was at his elbow, holding out a glass of buttermilk and a saucer on which sat a fork and a thick piece of apple pie. Bob took the fare, saying, "Thank you."

Consuela paused for a moment, examining the side of his head. "That bullet nick to your ear is healing nicely," she said. "There's going to be only a minor scar with very little meat missing."

"With no real scar to spark interest, it's gonna make a pretty lame story for me to tell in my old age," said Bob.

Consuela swept her skirt under the backs of her legs and sat down on the edge of the porch. "I'm sure you'll think of some ways to adequately embellish it between now and then," she said with a smile. Then, glancing upward, she abruptly switched subjects, noting, "It is a nice evening, isn't it?"

"For a fact," Bob agreed, sinking his fork into the pie. After he'd taken a bite, he said, "Aren't you having any of this?"

"Not right now. I'm too full. If Bucky leaves any, I'll have some before I go to bed."

"I'll see to it that he does leave you some."

"You needn't bother. He's a growing boy—let him eat."

"You spoil him sometimes."

"And you're too hard on him sometimes."

It wasn't a new disagreement between them. But, on this occasion, it didn't seem worth getting into any deeper.

Bob finished eating his pie. Consuela tipped her

head back and leaned against a porch post. The fine, graceful curve of her throat was outlined in a golden glow of the twilight while the rich blue-black of her long hair trailed down in deep shadow. Looking at her, Bob found his final bite of pie somewhat harder to swallow. He washed it down with a hurried gulp of buttermilk.

"I went down to Bullock's as soon as I heard about the trouble that had taken place. I got there ahead of Bucky and his school amigos," Consuela said, speaking quietly, in a matter-of-fact tone. "I looked through the window and saw you sitting and talking with the woman Maudie—the one who threw the whiskey bottle."

"That's right," said Bob. "She was kinda shook up by what happened. I was trying to calm her down."

"She's very beautiful, isn't she? And she dresses in a manner to assure that men take notice of her."

"Well, yeah," Bob said. He wasn't sure exactly what was going on, but he knew he wasn't particularly comfortable with it. "She's a bar maid in a saloon, 'Suela. Dressing the way she does sorta goes with the job. But you've met Maudie before, you know she's an okay gal . . . I mean, she's not, er, one of the upstairs girls or anything like that."

"Yes, I know. If she was that, I wouldn't be so troubled."

"Troubled by what?"

"By the way she was looking at you while you were 'calming her down.'"

"Aw, come on, 'Suela. You're reading more into it than there was, or is even close to being. Yeah,

Maudie is kinda, well, flirtatious, I guess you'd call it. But it don't mean anything."

"Don't be so sure," Consuela told him. "You foolish men are sometimes the last to see certain things."

She stood up to go back in the house. "It is never spoken between us, Bob, and I realize I may be stepping out of bounds to mention it even now. But you know how I feel about you, how I have felt since I was a mere girl. And I believe that, if you'll admit it, you have developed similar feelings for me. Yet I also recognize and respect that you are not done mourning your wife . . . So I wait. And will continue to wait . . . But not forever, and certainly not for another woman."

CHAPTER 6

Bob remained on the porch after Consuela had gone back inside. Dusk thickened into nearly full darkness. Bucky returned home just ahead of pushing it past his time limit.

"Your buddies satisfied with your report of the facts?" Bob asked.

Bucky nodded. "Oh yeah. They thought it was a great yarn, even if you only blazed it out with two gunnies instead of three. Skinny thinks you're the toughest lawman since Wild Bill Hickok. He says if you'd let people go ahead and call you 'Sundown Bob,' you could probably be almost as famous."

Bob chuckled. "I ain't looking to be famous, Buck. I just want to do my job and help keep our town a decent place to live."

"Well, I guess that's a pretty good thing, too," Bucky said somewhat reluctantly, clearly thinking it might be better for his pa to be more Wild Bill–like in his ambition and fame.

"I held back from eating all the pie, so you better

go have yourself some," Bob told him. "Then what about schoolwork?"

"I did most of it earlier. But I've still got a little left."

"Best take care of that after the pie, then. I'll be in after a bit."

"You're not taking a turn around the town tonight?"

"Not tonight, no. The Macy brothers are taking care of that. Everything's pretty quiet and I've had enough excitement for one day, thanks."

"Okay, Pa. See you inside then."

The screen door creaked and slapped shut and Bucky was gone.

Bob settled back in his chair and his thoughts returned to Consuela and the things she'd said. None of what she'd put into words was really new or startling, other than her unexpected jealousy over Maudie. It was true that Bob and Maudie had been carrying on a flirtatious relationship for some time. But, at least in his mind, that's all it was. He was certainly aware that Maudie was attractive and vivacious, and he supposed that played a part in why he enjoyed and looked forward to visiting with her whenever he stopped by Bullock's. And he supposed, too, that he enjoyed thinking she also found him attractive and interesting to talk to. Yet he'd simply never imagined the thing between them to be headed toward any kind of romance, serious or otherwise.

Where Consuela was concerned, however, it was a different matter. While he'd fought hard since the passing of Priscilla not to allow himself romantic feelings toward anyone, he nevertheless was aware that he'd grown very fond of Consuela. Hell, he loved her. Him, her, Bucky—they were a package, a family. He couldn't imagine them not being together . . . And yet he'd never expressed that to anyone—barely even to himself, and for sure not to Consuela.

"So I wait. And will continue to wait . . . But not forever."

Bob realized now that's precisely what he'd been counting on for all this time. That Consuela would be waiting for him when he was ready, was past grieving for Priscilla and the time felt right. To him. But how fair was that? To expect that of her, to make the assumption that a young, vibrant beauty like her would keep waiting without ever receiving a clear indication, not even a hint of how he truly felt.

"But not forever."

So now he'd been given a jarring reminder that there was a limit to how long he could take Consuela for granted. Still—no matter how much he knew he didn't want to lose her, didn't want her to *feel* like she was being taken for granted—he also knew he wasn't quite ready for the two of them to move on to something more than the way it was now.

The only answer, then, was to open up to her, not let her keep twisting in the wind. Confirm his deep feelings for her and then ask her to bear with him a little while longer until—

The sudden crack of gunfire shattered Bob's thoughts as well as the calm quiet of settling nightfall. He sprang from the rocker and stood for a moment on the edge of the porch, poised, feet planted wide as he scanned the town below and tried to gather into focus what was going on. Then he spun and ducked back into the house to grab his gun belt and holstered Colt from where he'd hung it on the back of a kitchen chair when sitting down to eat supper.

Bucky and Consuela, both wide-eyed, appeared in the kitchen doorway as he was buckling on his gun. "What's going on, Pa?" Bucky said.

"Don't know for sure. But there's some kind of trouble down in New Town, and I've got to go check it out." He paused, pinned them both with a hard glare. "You two stay here and keep inside until I get back. I mean it!"

It was the quick scan he'd made from his porch that told Bob the shooting was taking place in New Town. Along Front Street in Old Town, all the businesses except for Bullock's and the Shirley House Hotel were closed, their windows dark. There were lights glowing in the residential district on either side of Front Street, but all was quiet there. From the sound of the shots, it was clear that the trouble was emanating from somewhere along the sprawl of New Town's Gold Avenue, where the various tent businesses—the quick-buck gin joints, gambling dens, fleshpots, and the rest—were ablaze with lights and activity.

As Bob reached the Point and veered to begin angling up Gold Avenue, he drew his .44 and slowed the pace at which he'd been running. The shots were still popping and cracking from somewhere up ahead but, curiously, now that he was down here closer they sounded less distinct than they had from up on the slope. The noises blaring out of several of the tent businesses—banjo and piano music accompanied by drunken shouts and raucous laughter—were blurring the sounds of the gunshots and muting them from even being noticed by those inside the tents.

Bob edged over to a band of shadows on the left side of the street.

Just ahead was the massive shape of the newly constructed, three-story Crystal Diamond Saloon. Except for a pair of torches flickering atop tall poles out front, the building was unlit and cast in myriad shadows. Bob knew there also was supposed to be something else out front—a shotgun-armed guard, a man named Elmer Hyser whom Gafford had hired to watch the building because of Elmer's credentials as a former railroad detective.

As Bob drew nearer, he saw no sign of Elmer. And then, when he heard a fresh outburst of shots and the sounds of bullets cutting the air, some smacking hollowly against wood from inside the unoccupied, fresh-timber structure, he had a pretty good idea why. Either Elmer was involved in the shooting that was taking place—or he'd been removed from his post at the start of the trouble.

Skirting wide of the nearest pole torch in order to stay out of the oval of illumination it threw, Bob closed in on the about-to-be-opened new saloon. He paused for a moment in a dense, slanting shadow at the corner of the building. He listened intently as another lull fell in the shooting from inside. No sound reached his ears except the clamor from up the street. Something *did* reach his nose, though—a tangy, stinging chemical smell wafting out from the silence. It took him a moment to identify it as the odor of coal oil. A *lot* of coal oil.

What the hell?

Stepping up onto the wide, canopied front porch that ran across the front of the Crystal Diamond, Bob dropped into a half crouch and skimmed quickly past a broad window painted with designs and stylized lettering stating the establishment's name. He paused again at the edge of the front door. Pressing a shoulder to the frame, he leaned out cautiously and peered over the curved top of the nearest half of a set of batwing doors. The heavy, ornate inner doors that stood just inside the batwings—a feature that should have been closed and locked at this hour—were standing wide open. Faint light pouring through the gaping doors from the torches out front and through the windows on the north side of the big central room from the streetlamps strung along Gold Avenue made a few patches of murky visibility. But mostly the interior was shot with hard-edged shadows and impenetrable blackness. As Bob's eyes strained to try and penetrate this inky curtain, the stink of coal oil filled his nostrils more strongly than ever.

By now he had a pretty good idea of what was going on here. At least part of it.

Deciding to take advantage of the continuing lull in gunfire, he held his face just back from the edge of the doorframe and called out in a loud voice, "This is Marshal Bob Hatfield! Whatever this is about, I'm giving you the chance to end it before it gets too far out of hand! If you stop shooting, we can try to talk this out."

For an answer, three shots immediately poured out

of the darkness. One of the slugs whined just above the batwings and out into the street. The other two chewed into the doorframe only inches from Bob's nose, splattering slivers and chunks of wood as the marshal jerked back reflexively.

A voice crowed from inside. "That's how we do our talkin', Marshal! With lead! You want to have more of a conversation, step out farther in that doorway and have it with our bullets!"

Before he jerked back, Bob had caught a quick glimpse of the muzzle flashes as they spewed lead his way. They came from deep within the big room, at an elevated level. His mind raced, picturing the interior of the saloon as he remembered it from the times he'd visited during the construction. There was a stairway back there and a wide balcony running across the width of the room. So okay, the shooters who'd just opened up on him were up there on the balcony.

As Bob was reaching this conclusion, a different voice called from the shadows somewhere inside at ground-floor level. "We already tried that, Marshal. We got no farther talking to 'em than you did. They're drunk or crazy—or both—and flat-out won't listen."

Bob easily recognized the new voice as that of Peter Macy, one of his deputies. But, before he could respond, the shooter up in the balcony hollered down again, "That's right, we're drunk and crazy and we're by-God ornery enough to blast you law dog sonsabitches to bloody ribbons if you don't clear the way for us!" Another pair of shots rang out, this time aimed in the general direction of Peter's voice.

When things went quiet again, Bob called to his

deputy, "What the hell's going on, Peter? What's this all about?"

"We caught these skunks getting ready to set the place ablaze," came the answer. "There's two of 'em and they got coal oil splashed all over in there. Vern and me caught wind of it when we were walking by out on the street. That's what caused us to come investigate. Luckily, they left the torches they were gonna use—not lighted yet—down behind the stairs and we've got 'em trapped up above where they were spreading even more of the coal oil."

"You ain't got shit trapped, law dog! You'll see how trapped we are when we get ready to blast our way out of here!"

"Where's Vern?" Bob asked, ignoring the harsh words and inquiring about Peter's deputy brother.

"I'm back here, under the stairs, Marshal," Vern answered for himself. "I knew there was also a back stairs down from up there, so I came to cover it. Only it wasn't all the way finished being built yet, so I kicked out the lower support struts and collapsed the bottom half of it. If they think they can make the jump without breaking their fool necks and want to give it a try in order to come and reclaim their torches, though, I'll be glad to welcome 'em!"

"The only thing you'd better get ready to welcome, you back-sneakin' weasel, is a bellyful of lead when we *do* come down from here!"

Ignoring the balcony voice again, Bob said to no one in particular, "What about Elmer Hyser? What became of him?"

"He's gagged and hog-tied over there on the floor, not too far inside the door from where you're at.

They didn't bother killing him. They were gonna leave him like that, to roast alive when they got the fire going!"

"Ain't that much difference between a gun-totin' guard and a lousy badge-toter," one of the balcony shooters jeered. "Either one deserves whatever treatment they get!"

A surge of anger rushed through Bob. He gave in to it momentarily by triggering a pair of shots from his .44, aimed recklessly toward where he'd seen the muzzle flashes earlier. "The ones who deserve to burn are you two cold-blooded bastards!" he shouted through clenched teeth. "And that would be too good for you."

Taunting laughter rolled down in response. "You can cuss us all you want, Marshal, but you sure can't shoot worth a damn!"

Bob inhaled and exhaled a ragged breath. He cursed himself for the foolish display of temper, for uselessly wasting bullets instead of keeping a cool head . . . But then, from his angrily spat words, he got an idea.

"Vern," he called, "are those unlit torches back there within your reach?"

"Yeah, they're right here next to me," came Vern's voice out of the darkness.

Bob smiled devilishly. "Good. Have you got a match to light one of them?"

Vern didn't answer right away, like he either didn't understand the question or maybe he couldn't believe its implication. Before he could say anything, one of the would-be arsonists up on the balcony also caught on to what the marshal seemed to be implying.

"Wait a minute! What the hell are you doing talking about matches and lighting one of our torches? There's coal oil splashed all over down there. That weasel deputy starts fooling around with matches, this place and all its fresh-cut timber will go up like a tinderbox!"

"That was the general idea, wasn't it?" Bob called in a mocking tone. "Ain't that what you and your buddy came here to do?"

"But not with us in it, you damn fool!"

"Same basic plan, just with a little twist, that's all," Bob replied.

"You wouldn't dare!"

"Of course he wouldn't," said the second balcony voice. "He's just bluffin'. What kind of marshal would torch a building in his own town—especially a fancy, brand-new one like this?"

"The kind of marshal who don't have the patience to keep listening to a couple lowlifes like you break wind with your mouths," Bob answered. "The building don't mean all that much to me. It can always be rebuilt. But letting you two varmints get away with what you're trying to pull—that *does* matter to me. I flat won't allow it, and I'll do whatever it takes to stop you."

"I still say you're bluffin'!"

"Then all you have to do to find out is try me, big talker. You got three options: You can throw out your guns and come down those steps with your hands raised high. You can come down those steps with guns blazing and try to make a break for it . . . Or you can hold your ground and get carried out as chunks of charred meat shoveled into a wheelbarrow."

"I don't think that crazy bastard is kidding, Murphy! I think he means it," said one of the voices from the high darkness inside.

"Shut up, McQueen!" said the voice of the second arsonist. "I'm tellin' you, there's no way he'd purposely torch this building just to flush us out. That'd be plain insane."

Bob gave it a beat and then called, "How about it, Vern? You got that match ready?"

"Sure do," Vern called back.

Emitting a nasty chuckle, Bob said, "What do you say then, boys? Vern? Peter? Happens I *am* feeling a little insane—you with me?"

"Count me in," said Vern.

"Same here," called Peter. "All you got to do is say the word, Marshal."

"That settles it then . . . Strike the match, Vern!"

CHAPTER 7

"No! For God's sake, hold it!" wailed the voice of the one called McQueen.

"*You* hold it," said Murphy. "Don't even think about givin' in to 'em, McQueen."

"The hell I won't! I ain't gonna get turned into no hunk of charred meat—especially not for no lousy fifty bucks."

"You think they're gonna give you a fair shake if you walk down there? They'll either blast you to hell and gone as soon as they can see you clear, or haul you out front and string you up as a warnin' to others."

"Don't listen to him, McQueen," Bob called. "You're the one showing good sense—he's just trying to steer you more wrong than you already are."

"I know it! I should never have got talked into this in the first place," said McQueen. "I'm throwin' my gun down, Marshal. Then I'm comin'—"

"No, you're not," snarled Murphy. "You can crawl down on your belly if you want, you yellow dog. But you're leavin' me your gun and cartridges. I'll show you how a real man fights his way out of a tight spot."

"You do what you want, Murphy. But me, I'm playin' it just like the marshal said— Quit it! Let go, damn you . . ."

There was the brief sound of a struggle. Feet scraping on the floor, grunts of effort, and a garbled curse. Then there was the muffled roar of a gunshot and a muzzle flash partly obscured by a body jammed close. Then another, from a slightly increased distance this time, the muzzle flash much brighter. A moment later came the sound of cracking, breaking wood— a railing giving way—followed by the whoosh of something heavy falling through the air and splatting hard onto the floor below the balcony.

"There you go, you law dog sonsabitches!" crowed Murphy. "You got the yellow cur you wanted to join your pack . . . And now you're gonna get both barrels of *me*!"

Down the steps Murphy came in a rush. Invisible at first, like a raging phantom. Snarling and cursing, his feet clumping heavily, a pistol blazing in each hand. Until he descended into a band of weak light that poured in over the stairway from one of the north windows. Bob and his deputies were poised, ready. The instant the mad fool became a discernible shape—thick bodied, wild-eyed, and shaggy bearded—they all three opened fire.

A half-dozen slugs pounded into the shape, jolting and jerking it, spinning it crazily like a marionette with cut strings, until it pitched forward over the remaining steps and hit the floor with a sound eerily similar to the one made by McQueen's body just moments earlier.

The final barrage of shooting had at last drawn attention from some of the closer businesses up Gold Avenue. By the time Bob and his deputies got the bodies dragged out from inside the Crystal Diamond, quite a crowd had formed.

The bullet-riddled Murphy was as dead as a varmint could get.

Elmer Hyser, the security guard, was still alive. As he lay helplessly bound and gagged in the darkness, however, he'd suffered wounds from two wild shots, one to his thigh and another to his hip. The latter had resulted in broken bones that put him in severe pain and increased the difficulty in moving him.

McQueen was also somehow still alive and breathing . . . though hanging on by a mere thread.

With the doctor sent for and the crowd held at bay by Peter and Vern—giving particular admonishment to stay back from the Crystal Diamond, especially with torches or lanterns—Bob bent close over McQueen, comforting him as much as he could while at the same time attempting to get some information out of him.

With a red-rimmed froth of tiny bubbles forming at the corners of his mouth, McQueen gazed dully up at Bob and said, "I'm in a bad way . . . a-ain't I, Marshal?"

"It ain't good," said Bob, not wanting to lie to the poor devil. But then, immediately regretting that he hadn't offered at least some encouragement, he added, "We got a mighty good doctor in our town, though, and he's on his way. So just hang on."

"Two straight to the gut . . . R-reckon I know what that means."

"Try not to think about it," Bob urged him. "But tell me something . . . Why were you in there with Murphy in the first place? I heard you mention fifty dollars and getting talked into it—did somebody *hire* you and him to try and burn that building?"

McQueen continued to gaze up at Bob, but now it was as if he were looking *through* the marshal, seeing something somewhere beyond him. "Oh Lordy, Lordy . . . Ain't it shameful what a pitiful wretch will do for a handful of dirty coins?" There followed a quick, ragged gasp and then . . . nothing.

Long, lanky Doc Tibbs came hurrying up the street and moved directly to where Bob remained kneeling. "How bad is he?" he asked.

Without looking up, Bob said, "Depends how you look at it. He ain't in pain no more. He's dead." The marshal rose slowly to his feet and gestured. "But not Elmer over there. I don't think his wounds are life-threatening, but he's hurting plenty. He's the only one you can do anything for, Doc."

As Tibbs moved on to the wounded guard, Bob walked over and stood with the Macy brothers. "I wasn't able to get anything useful out of McQueen," he said. "But from what we overheard when they were still up on the balcony, I got the impression they were carrying out a job for hire. You fellas get the same feeling?"

"That could explain it. I can't think for another reason why they'd take it on themselves to try and burn down the place," said Peter.

"Anything else said, before I got here, that might support that notion?" asked Bob.

Vern shook his head. "Not really. Not a whole lot of talking got done. Except—like Murphy put it— with lead. I agree that them getting hired for the job makes sense, though. They got the look of a couple lowlifes who'd do about any kind of dirty work for money."

"Either of you seen them around before?" Bob asked.

"Not that I can say for sure," said Peter.

"Same here," Vern agreed.

Bob was in the same fix. Due to the gold strike, McQueen and Murphy were the kind of hard-luck nondescripts who came and went in a steady flow all up and down Gold Avenue. In any of New Town's smoky, crowded tent businesses on just about any night of the week, they would have blended invisibly in among others of their same ilk.

The marshal turned to the pack of gawkers who'd spilled out of some of those very same businesses and now were gathered close to catch a piece of out-of-the-ordinary excitement. "How about it, any of you?" he asked in a loud voice, his eyes scanning the anxious, hard-featured faces. "Anybody know either of these two men? Their names were Murphy and McQueen."

There was some general murmuring and grumbling. Then somebody called out, "Which one was which?"

"What the hell difference does it make?" responded Bob irritably. "I'm not looking for a verification of their names. I want to know how long they've been in town, where they've been staying, or who they've been hanging around with . . . Anybody?"

More murmuring, but nobody came forward with the kind of information Bob was looking for.

"Either they genuinely don't know, or they're afraid to admit any association with the skunks," said Peter.

Bob addressed the crowd again. "If I find out later on that somebody *does* know something but is holding out, it'll go hard on that person. But if you come forward in the next day or so—to me, or any of my deputies—what you have to say will be kept in confidence and there won't be any trouble. Spread the word on that."

Turning away from the Gold Avenue bunch, Bob saw a cluster of folks approaching from the direction of Front Street and Old Town. In the lead was Mike Bullock. Not far behind him came August Gafford and a short ways farther back was Fred Ordway, Bob's chief deputy. In between, Bob also spotted Titus O'Malley, the town undertaker.

"Jesus," Bob muttered, not quite under his breath. "We're gonna have half the state of Wyoming here before this is done."

Bullock marched up, puffing some from his hurried walk. "What in blazes is going on, Marshal?"

Bob's mouth spread in a sardonic smile. "Thankfully, blazes are exactly what's *not* going on, Mike."

"What's that supposed to mean?"

Bob jerked a chin toward McQueen and Murphy. "It means that if those two firebugs had gotten their way, this building we're all standing in front of would be one big bonfire right about now."

Gafford walked up just in time to hear the last part. "What! What are you saying—*my* building was going to be set on fire?"

"That's the way it was headed," Bob confirmed. "Lucky thing my deputies here were passing by on patrol and smelled the coal oil that had been poured all over inside to make sure there'd be no stopping it once it was touched off."

Gafford's eyes bugged. "Good God! I can't tell you how thankful—wait a minute. What about Hyser, my guard?"

"He's over there, being tended to by the doc. He caught a couple bullets but he's gonna be all right. He was headed on a lot worse course before that. They jumped him and hog-tied him, then forced their way in. They dragged Hyser inside, too, to get him out of sight. Way it looked, they were fixing to leave him there and let him burn alive as part of their dirty work."

"Good God!" Gafford exclaimed again.

"Who are—or were, I guess I should say—those two cold-blooded devils?" Bullock wanted to know.

"That's what we've been trying to find out," Bob said. "All we got so far is that their names were Murphy and McQueen. You recognize 'em, by any chance?"

"Never saw 'em before in my life . . . or theirs," Bullock answered.

"They're unknown to me as well," said Gafford. "So what did they have against me, then? Why would a couple of obvious bottom-scrapers be out to ruin me and my beautiful Crystal Diamond?"

Before responding, Bob glanced over to Fred, who

was kneeling next to the dead men and giving them a good looking over. Fred had as sharp a memory for faces as anybody Bob had ever known and regularly put that knack to good use by spending time in Gold Avenue dives on the lookout for known trouble-makers.

But on this occasion he had nothing to offer. Looking up to meet Bob's gaze, he could only shake his head. "Can't recall ever seing 'em around before, boss. Their names don't ring no bells, either."

"I repeat my question," Gafford said impatiently. "What could these two complete strangers have against me that would make them attempt something so appalling?"

"My guess—and making a guess is the best I can do right now—is that somebody hired 'em to do it," said Bob.

"But that still comes back to who—who wants to ruin me badly enough to hire a couple of arsonists?"

Bob cocked an eyebrow. "How about you take a stab at answering that? Who do you have in the way of enemies who might go that far to do you harm? You're a wealthy, successful man, the kind who cuts a pretty wide swath wherever he goes. In other words, you're the kind of fella who, generally speaking, has likely left a few ruffled feathers in his wake. Is that an inaccurate statement?"

"No, I suppose it's not," Gafford admitted grudgingly. "The resentment and jealousies of others commonly haunt a successful man. But to this level? I've never encountered anything to such a degree and can't think of anyone from my past who harbors that kind of rancor toward me."

"Maybe it's not all that far in your past," spoke up Bullock.

Both Bob and Gafford pinned him with looks that said they were waiting for him to elaborate further.

"We were talking about it in my place only this afternoon," Bullock reminded the marshal. "When I was fretting and moaning about competition from the Crystal Diamond, you were the one who pointed out that those a lot more threatened by Gafford's fancy new joint would be the other saloons and gambling dens right here on Gold Avenue." He made a sweep of his arm, indicating the tent businesses and shanties strung out to the north, just past the milling crowd on that side. "No offense to the hardworking, honest miners and other folks who trade there, too, but everybody knows that in among them are also scavengers and lowlifes who would do just about anything for a quick payoff."

"That's certainly an unsettling thought," Gafford said, scowling.

"I don't like it, either, but there it is," said Bullock. "By saying it, I'm admitting my own ill wishes and hard feelings at the same time. But while I dislike your showboating ways and may have expressed a desire more than once to belt you smack in the mouth, Gafford, I don't go in for this kind of dirty business. Not only that, I'll back you against anybody who does."

Gafford regarded him, his scowl gradually easing. "I believe you, Bullock. I'm well aware that we don't see eye to eye on most things, but I long ago took the measure of you as a man of his word and someone who would never stoop to something like this as a means of retaliation."

"That's good to hear, from both of you," Bob said. "And I tend to agree with Mike that most likely whoever did the hiring for this attempt to burn down the Crystal Diamond came out of New Town. But any retaliation for it, I expect to be left in the hands of me and my deputies. We'll continue to dig and ask around, try to get to the bottom.

"In the meantime, Gafford, you now have some added work to do to finish getting your place ready for the big opening. I'll have my men stand watch over it for the rest of the night. In the morning, you'd better hire yourself some more guards to replace Elmer and then a crew to scrub down all the coal oil that's been splashed to hell and gone. See me, if you want, for the names of some good, reliable men who'll give you an honest day's work."

Gafford nodded. "I'll do that, Marshal. Thanks for the offer."

Turning to his deputies, Bob said, "Okay, break 'em up. Clear everybody out, send 'em back where they belong. Let the doc and the undertaker finish their work. Shoo off the rest."

It didn't take long for his orders to be carried out.

Once they had the street mostly to themselves, Bob gathered his deputies in close. "You all heard what I told Gafford and Mike Bullock, right?" he said. "It's gonna be up to us to get to the bottom of this. I meant it when I said that I believe the culprit who hired McQueen and Murphy came out of one of the competing saloons along this strip. We're gonna have to keep pouring on the questions and maybe do a little leaning on certain individuals. Those two didn't just materialize out of thin air. Somebody had to have seen 'em before tonight, must have noticed 'em hanging around, talking to somebody . . . That's what we need to get to."

All three of the eager faces he was addressing nodded their understanding and agreement. "Okay. Peter and Vern, I want to commend you again on the good job you did here tonight spotting those two and stopping them before they got any further with their plans," Bob said. Before continuing, his mouth fell into a crooked grin. "As a reward for your good work, I'm gonna let you take the watch over this place for the rest of the night. Sorry about the sleep you'll miss, but you can divide it up in shifts however you want. Just make sure one of you is on the job and awake until morning."

"We'll work it out, Marshal," Peter assured him.

"I can spell them for part of the time, too, if you want," offered Fred.

"No, you take over bright and early in the morning," Bob said. "Stick with it until Gafford shows up with his cleanup crew. Then it's in his hands. For tonight, even though I realize you went off duty a while back, I do have some work for you before you go back on your own time.

"I want you to come with me and we'll make a pass through these Gold Avenue saloon tents and some of the gambling joints. Maybe we'll be lucky and catch somebody who's a little nervous and more apt to have a slip of the tongue while the pressure and excitement of what almost happened is still fresh in their minds. Be harder tomorrow after whoever was in on it has had a better chance to get their story straight and cover their behind. But that don't mean we'll let up—sooner or later somebody will crack."

"Sounds good, Marshal. I even have a couple most likely places in mind," said Fred.

Bob nodded. "I do, too. But we've got to be careful not to go in with our minds already made up, not until we shake something loose."

As Bob and Fred got ready to head up the street, Vern edged forward with an uncertain smile on his lips and said, "Speaking of a body not having his mind made up about something, can I ask you a question, Marshal?"

"Well, sure, Vern. What is it?"

"Back there a little while ago, when you asked me if I had a match and then called out for me to strike one on those two varmints up in the balcony . . . You *did* remember that I don't smoke or have any call to actually carry matches. Didn't you?"

Bob grinned. "What do you think, Vern?"

The young deputy's brow furrowed. "I guess I think, like I did then, that you were bluffing. That's why I went along with it and said I had one. But if I truly did, you wouldn't have really wanted me to light one of those torches. Right?"

Still grinning, Bob reached out and clapped a hand on Vern's shoulder. "Probably not. But, then again, my memory about another fella's habits and so on ain't necessarily as sharp as it used to be . . ."

CHAPTER 8

Their prowl through the Gold Avenue tent dives that same night had garnered Bob and Fred disappointing results. They got a number of furtive glances and a few nervous stammers, but not much more. Nothing they could act on.

In the morning, Bob rose with the sun, as was his habit. He ate his usual breakfast of boiled eggs and coffee, prepared by Consuela. The faint tension between them from last evening was nowhere in evidence. Bob was relieved at that, having plenty else on his mind to start the new day. Yet, at the same time, he knew the matter wasn't resolved.

Normally on school mornings, he waited before leaving the house in order to have a few words with Bucky once the boy had been rousted to get ready for classes. On this occasion, however, he waived that routine and asked Consuela to explain. He knew his son would be bubbling with more questions about the shoot-out at the Crystal Diamond, even though Bob had already covered the basics with him and Consuela upon returning home last night, and he simply didn't have time to get caught up in that again.

At the bottom of the slope below his house, Bob took a turn up Gold Avenue before going to his office down near the end of Front Street. He found Fred Ordway already on the job out front of the Crystal Diamond, having relieved the Macy brothers so they could go home and catch a few hours' sleep.

Fred, with his slightly stooped shoulders and well-padded stomach, could at times appear slow and shuffling, perhaps not overly bright. As more than a few hardcases had found out since he'd pinned on a badge under the mentorship of Bob, however, it could be a serious mistake to write him off so lightly. Fred and his plodding, methodical ways could be hound dog tenacious and bulldog tough.

Bob saw that kind of intensity and focus in his chief deputy's eyes this morning. Nobody had been more frustrated than Fred at last night's failure to turn up some kind of link to the two would-be arsonists, and Bob could tell he was chomping at the bit to get back to doing some more digging and questioning as soon as possible today.

"You must have landed on your mattress barely long enough to put a dent in it," Bob said, greeting him.

"You said to be here bright and early, boss, so that's what I am."

"You even take time for breakfast?" No matter what else, Fred seldom missed finding time to eat.

"As soon as Mr. Gafford shows up here," Fred explained, "I planned on making a stop at the Bluebird Café on my way down to the office."

"You be sure and do that." Bob rolled some kinks out of his shoulders and swept his gaze up the sprawl of Gold Avenue. This early in the morning there was scarcely a sign of activity. "I take it everything's been quiet here since last night?"

"Nothing but. I saw a few hungover miners heading out from the whore cribs farther down the line, but that's about it. Otherwise, you know that most people and businesses in New Town don't start stirring until closer to noon."

Bob grunted. "Too bad they try to make up for it by howling late into the night."

"I did have one visitor this morning, though." Fred stepped over to the front steps of the Crystal Diamond and picked up a burlap sack that he carried back and held out to the marshal. "Titus O'Malley stopped by a little bit ago and left this for you."

Bob took the sack, which had some heft to it and a faint jingling sound from within its bulky contents. "What is it?" he asked, unable to think what the town undertaker might be presenting him with.

"It's the personal belongings of those two varmints from last night, Murphy and McQueen. Mainly their guns and gun belts. But there's also a little something extra." Fred paused, waiting for Bob to pin him with a questioning look before continuing. "Titus said you needn't worry about him billing the town for the burial of those two. He said he already took his fee from the money they had in their pockets—close to fifty dollars each. His receipt for what he took and the balance of the money is in the bag there with the rest."

"Fifty dollars each," Bob echoed thoughtfully. "That's

a pretty healthy sum for a couple of hardscrabblers like those two appeared to be."

"Uh-huh. That's what I was thinking."

"Wouldn't be hard to conclude it amounts to evidence of sorts to back up our notion about them being hired for the arson job."

"Yeah. I was thinking that, too."

When Bob arrived at the log building near the end of Front Street that housed his office and the jail, he immediately poked up a fire in the top of the ancient stove and set a pot of coffee to brewing. The much-maligned stove gave off too much heat in the summer and not enough in the winter and was responsible for cooking the worst coffee in town—at least that's what Bob and his deputies laid the blame on for the vile mud that came out of most every pot they prepared. Bob didn't even bother hoping that the one this morning stood a chance of turning out any better.

While the coffee was coming to a bubble, Bob sat down at his desk and pulled from a drawer the accumulation of wanted posters and fugitive notices he had stored there. He was pretty sure there was nothing among them that tied to McQueen or Murphy. He had a good memory for names and neither of those tugged at his recollection. Neither did their faces, at least not in the conditions he'd studied after last night's encounter. But washed and shaven, their greasy hair cropped, and with a different name attached . . . it was a long shot, but just maybe he'd run across a match.

Bob was nearly finished going through the stack

without any success when the door opened and August Gafford came in. He was once again dressed nattily in a three-piece suit complete with cravat, making quite a contrast to the harried way he'd looked when Bob had seen him last, while he was still trying to come to grips with what had nearly been done to his new business.

"Good morning," he said in a booming voice. "And I mean that in a most sincere way, not the standard casual manner in which folks tend to use the term. When I think of the circumstances I *could* have woken to this morning, if not for you and your deputies, it is a very good morning indeed!"

"We already went through that last night," Bob replied. "Like I told you then, we just try to do our jobs the best we can."

"And I can attest that your best is mighty fine. Making me look forward all the more to living and doing business here in Rattlesnake Wells."

"Well, I hope it works out good for both of us," Bob said. "The time for your big opening is getting mighty short. I guess you'll know better after the Crystal Diamond has been running for a while, how it's going to work out for you business-wise."

Gafford nodded. "The ultimate test, that's for sure. But I already have faith everything will go fine in that regard. Some very key components to my saloon's success, as a matter of fact, will be arriving today on the train. Not only the prize guns for the shooting contest but also the performers who will give the Crystal Diamond one of its many distinctions. We discussed this yesterday. I just thought I'd stop by and remind you."

"I hadn't forgotten."

"I'm hoping, of course, that you'll be available to meet Miss Dane and her troupe with me. And I will be sure to explain to them how the quick attention and bravery of you and your men ensured that the Crystal Diamond is still standing for them to perform in."

"I'll be around," Bob said. "But you need to get a crew to work pronto on cleaning up all that spilled coal oil before an unintentional spark floats in from somewhere and does accidentally what those coyotes last night couldn't get done on purpose."

"Yes. Yes, of course," Gafford said anxiously. "I'm on my way there now. I just wanted to stop by and once again express my profound thanks."

"Consider it done. No need to keep saying it."

As he turned toward the door, Gafford said, "I already have some carpenters lined up to finish that back stairway and a few other touches. Your friend Bullock was kind enough to provide the names of some reliable men I intend to hire for the cleanup. As far as ongoing security for my establishment, as per your suggestion from last night, remember I have Simon Quirt, also arriving on the train, already in charge of the prize guns. Once he gets here, I thought I would turn the matter of broader security over to him as well. I'll make sure he discusses any arrangements with you."

"That'd be good. Like I said, I was wanting to talk to him anyway."

CHAPTER 9

By the time Fred got to the office, Bob had finished going through the stack of wanted posters without turning up anything useful.

Together, the two lawmen then spent most of the remainder of the morning trying to gain some background on McQueen and Murphy by other means. Bob's conversation with Gafford about cleaning up the coal oil gave him an idea to try and use the accelerant to possibly trace the pair. Returning to the Crystal Diamond, where a three-man cleanup crew was starting in with a strong mixture of scalding water and lye soap applied vigorously with stiff-bristled brooms, they found a partially emptied keg of the fuel and what appeared to be a newly purchased pail out behind the building. Up on the balcony, they found a second such pail.

From there they proceeded to Krepdorf's General Store in Old Town, the area's biggest retailer of such goods, hoping one of the clerks would remember a matching sale. Having no luck with this inquiry, they went back to New Town and began asking the same questions at the smaller, scattered businesses there that dealt in similar items.

On the fourth try, they found a fellow dealing hardware odds and ends out of a tent who admitted to selling the pails and a keg of coal oil that matched the brand of what Bob and Fred had found behind the Crystal Diamond. Trouble was, the sale had been to a single individual, a man who matched the descriptions of neither McQueen nor Murphy. And, since the hardware salesman had set up shop only a couple of weeks earlier, he didn't know the purchaser's name or anything about him other than he said he was clearing some farmland northeast of town and needed the oil to burn a pile of timber and brush that he'd cleared.

The physical description the hardware man provided—thirtyish, average height, dark hair and beard, dressed in standard working man's attire—was uselessly vague. But then, right at the very last, he did provide something useful by mentioning the horse he helped the alleged farmer load the keg onto. It was a tall palomino with a sizable notch missing from one ear—the result of a bullet, its rider claimed, that came too close while once fleeing outlaws on the trail.

"So the fella who actually purchased the coal oil might be the one who went on to hire Murphy and McQueen," Bob muttered as they walked away. "But the description we got for whoever it was—not even the part about wanting it to help clear farmland, which is an obvious lie—sure don't do us much good for narrowing it down any."

"Not the description of the buyer, no. But the

description of the horse he used to haul away his goods," Fred said, scowling thoughtfully, "now *that* is a different matter."

"How so?"

"Because I remember seeing that horse around before. Ain't that many palominos around to begin with, and especially not many with a bullet notch out of one ear. That's the part that stuck in my mind."

Bob reached up and absently touched his ear that had recently had its own close call with a bullet. "Just don't mistake me for no palomino," he muttered.

"That scratch of yours is nothing compared to the notch I'm picturing. This horse I'm talking about has a serious hunk of meat missing." Fred's scowl deepened. "Right at this minute, I can't recall exactly where or when I saw the blamed thing. But it wasn't too long ago, I'm sure of that. Just let me chew on it some—it'll come to me."

"Chew away," Bob told him. "We find that horse, we find the man who bought the coal oil. And that is one hombre I am mighty interested in talking to."

"I know, boss. It'll come to me."

On their way back to the marshal's office, Bob and Fred ran into the Macy brothers, who were headed that way also. "We've had some sleep and a late breakfast so we're reporting for duty," Peter announced. "We figured after the trouble last night and the train coming in today, you'd probably want us to be on hand as soon as possible."

"You figured right," Bob said. "As a matter of fact, the train is due in less than an hour and I figure it would be a good idea for all of us to be around for that. It's carrying the jeweled guns as well as the entertainers that are going to be a big part of what Gafford is counting on to make his saloon a success. If somebody is serious about knocking him out of business, they likely won't stop with that arson attempt last night. Strikes me that raising Cain with his show people might be something else that crosses their mind as a way to cause him grief."

"Makes sense," said Vern. "We got in their way the first time—no reason we can't do it again. Heck, we might even make a habit of it."

"Making a habit of getting in the way of troublemakers," Bob told him, "is kinda what lawmen are *supposed* to do."

CHAPTER 10

The train came hissing and shrieking into the station right on schedule, fifteen minutes past noon. There was less of a crowd gathered to meet it than Bob had expected—and less of one than August Gafford would have preferred, that was for certain. But Gafford, once again dressed in all his finery, played it to the hilt anyway. He was waiting on the station platform with huge bouquets of flowers for the ladies, and his booming voice was in fine form as it announced each member of the troupe.

There were five in all.

Miss Alora Dane led the way onto the platform to accept her flowers and a big hug from Gafford. She was a short woman pushing forty, by Bob's judgment, but wearing it very well with precisely applied makeup and lush, scarlet-painted lips framing a dazzling smile. Her hair was a carefully piled mass of blond, and her figure was spectacularly curved and boldly displayed by a form-hugging dress. Every red-blooded man who *wasn't* on hand for the arrival of the train that day and thereby not privy to this breathtaking vision would be mentally kicking himself for weeks to come.

The remaining two gals, the singers and dancers known as the Diamond Dollies, were definitely not hard on the eyes, either. One was a saucy redhead named Essie, the other a butter blonde named Becky, with smoldering brown eyes. Both were a half-dozen or so years younger than Alora, and Bob would later learn that their full names, respectively, were Estelle Pruitt and Rebecca Levitt. Although it wasn't mentioned during the public introductions, it turned out they were married to the musicians of the troupe— Oliver Pruitt, a plumpish, round-faced sort who played piano, and Lyle Levitt, a lanky banjo and trombone player whose broad smile revealed a set of prominently bucked teeth.

Once the entertainers were all presented and met with appreciative applause, Gafford signaled for one final thing to be brought out. A tall, lean, narrow-eyed black man clad in a charcoal gray frock coat and flat-crowned Stetson stepped forward holding a leather briefcase. As he moved fluidly across the platform, his eyes swept continually to all sides and the tails of his coat flared out slightly to reveal a pair of tied-down holsters encasing pearl-handled Colt .45s on each hip.

"That hombre's got the look of a gun wolf if ever I saw one," muttered Fred, standing beside Bob.

"Name's Simon Quirt," replied Bob. "And you're right—that matching set of holsters and hoglegs ain't just for show."

As they continued to watch, Quirt turned the briefcase flat and held it out to Gafford. Gafford unsnapped the clasps and opened the case. Then, taking it from Quirt, he tipped the open case slightly and held it up for all bunched around the platform to see. In hollowed-out pockets of maroon felt rested the brace of gold-plated and bejeweled dueling pistols, reflecting glints of sunlight as Gafford slowly turned them this way and that.

"Here they are, ladies and gentlemen," he proclaimed. "The much-heralded first prize in the shooting contest that will begin the grand opening of my new saloon, the Crystal Diamond. Up until now, Rattlesnake Wells has been in the midst of an exciting gold rush. But, in just a matter of days, I am going to add to that the dazzle of diamonds!

"See for yourself"—Gafford began dramatically sweeping one arm as he named off what it was he wanted to be seen—"first of all, these one-of-a-kind bejeweled pistols . . . Secondly, the glamorous Diamond Dollies, who will be performing exclusively at my establishment . . . And, last but by no means least, the most breathtaking jewel in all of the West, Miss Alora Dane!

"All of it right here in Rattlesnake Wells, for your distinct pleasure and enjoyment. Be sure not to miss a single event or a single moment of excitement!"

When the applause had died down and the crowd began to disperse, Gafford motioned Bob up onto the platform, where he made rather hurried introductions between the marshal and the entertainers. It didn't take long for Bob to spot that the bright smiles displayed for the public only minutes earlier were not nearly as wide or bright for him.

"The train that brought these weary souls into

Cheyenne was plagued with numerous delays and difficulties, making their layover before starting out for here very short and not terribly pleasant," Gafford explained. "Therefore, they are extremely exhausted and want little else but the restful comfort that awaits them in the rooms I have reserved at the Shirley House Hotel. For these reasons, Marshal, I trust you'll understand if we shorten the lengthier amount of time I planned on talking with you and your brave men . . . But only temporarily, I assure you. As soon as these good folks are adequately rested and refreshed, I will arrange that lengthier audience. I suggest dinner this evening in a private dining hall at the Shirley. Say seven o'clock? You and all of your deputies are urged to attend."

Bob had little choice but to concur. He'd had enough of an introduction to the troupe to suit himself, but didn't want to deprive his men of either the recognition they deserved or the chance for a fine meal at the Shirley. Whether or not Simon Quirt—the one member of Gafford's group Bob for sure wanted to talk with at greater length—would be part of the dinner, he didn't know. But he'd see to it they had their talk, one way or another.

"I trust, in turn," he said to Gafford, "that in addition to getting Miss Dane and the others comfortable in the hotel, you're also not going to waste much time getting those guns into the vault at the Starbuck Territorial Bank. It's right across the street from the Shirley."

"I assure you that will be taken care of posthaste," Gafford replied. Then he smiled. "In the meantime,

I further assure you that Mr. Quirt will continue to keep them very secure."

"I got 'em this far," said Quirt, leveling a flat gaze at Bob. "Until they're handed over to the shootin' contest winner, I fully intend to keep right on makin' sure nothing happens to 'em."

"That's real good to hear," replied Bob, meeting his gaze evenly.

A pair of wagons had pulled up alongside the platform during this exchange. One had rows of passenger seats bolted to the floor of its bed; the other had a common hauling bed already loaded with trunks, various-sized suitcases, and a handful of cased instruments. Gafford and Quirt found room to climb aboard the hauling rig. The entertainers were assisted into the seats of the other wagon and then both rolled away toward the Shirley House Hotel.

"Those wagons are carrying some mighty eye-pleasing gals," said Fred as his eyes followed them. "But why do I have a feeling they're also carrying trouble that we'll be dealing with before too much longer?"

"I don't know," Vern said, sighing wistfully. "But if it comes to that, all I can say is that I never saw trouble wrapped in such a fine-looking package as Miss Alora Dane."

Two men stood at the back corner of the train station. They'd been standing there, out on the fringe of the crowd, all during Gafford's introductions and bloviating. One of them had come in on the train; his suitcase rested on the ground beside him. The other had ridden up only a short time ahead of the train's arrival; his horse was ground-reined only a few yards away. The pair remained inconspicuously back out of the way after the crowd filtered away and the four lawmen had quit the platform and were making their way up Front Street.

The train passenger was tall, trim, dressed in a well-cut corduroy jacket and a black string tie worn at the throat of a boiled white shirt. A Colt .45 with a shiny black handle rode in a cross-draw holster on his left hip, and a wide-brimmed, cream-colored hat sat on a headful of gray-flecked hair. His facial features were clean-shaven and quite handsome, complete with penetrating blue eyes and a cleft chin.

The appearance of the second man, the horseman, contrasted considerably. His clothes were rumpled and dusty, his broad, hard-featured face unshaven. He had small, suspicious eyes set too close on either side of a blunt nose. The bottom half of his face was dominated by a wide, thick-lipped mouth that always seemed to have a cruel twist to it.

"I still say we should have hit the train out in the open country," said the unshaven man, whose name was Eugene Boyd. "We could have had those guns and the rest in our possession by now. After, that is"—here his mouth curved into a lewd smile—"we'd given those 'entertainment' gals a chance to do some *real* entertaining for us."

"You have a one-track mind, and the route more often than not goes through a sewer," said Clayton Delaney, the handsome man.

Boyd shrugged. "I don't pretend otherwise. Never have, never will. To my recollection, the kind of stuff I've done for you over the years ain't too often required a lily-pure outlook on things."

"I wish I could, but I can't deny that," sighed Delaney. "The difference between you and me is that I, on occasion, have had a twinge of remorse over some of the things we've done. I don't believe you ever have."

"When a thing is done, it's done," Boyd grunted. "Frettin' about it afterward only muddles a body's thinkin' about what's in front of 'im in the here and now. Frettin' and regrettin' don't gain you a damn thing except maybe causin' a misstep on account of havin' your mind clouded by what you can't go back and change anyway."

"You keep things nice and simple, I've got to give you that," said Delaney with a wry smile. "Which is exactly what I viewed hitting the train *not* to be. Yes, we could have gotten the guns and the rest quicker. But we also would have ended up with a posse or two— one of them likely manned by U.S. Marshals, since railroad interests would be involved—thundering on our trail."

"We've outrun posses before. Includin' ones with federal marshals in 'em."

"True. But it was never a hell of a lot of fun, was it? And it usually cost us some men in the bargain. *This* way"—he held up one of Gafford's flyers advertising the upcoming shooting contest—"we can accomplish the same end without all that grief. Hell, if I can win the contest, we'll gain what we want legally. How would that be for a change?"

Boyd scratched his bristly jaw and scrunched up

his face. "Don't know how it'd be. Ain't something I've tried very often."

"Well, look at it as a new experience, then."

"Uh-huh. Listen, I know you're a mighty good shot at plinkin' targets and such . . . But what if you *don't* win the contest?"

"Then we resort to a plan for *taking* those prize guns." Delaney scowled. "I mean to get my hands on them, one way or another. You know the reason why. But even if we do end up having to take them by force, it will still be easier relieving an individual of them rather than staging a train robbery. What's more, the only law we'd have to worry about—at least anywhere close—would be that bumpkin marshal and his deputies we just saw leave here. If any federal law decided to get involved, it'd be days before they could ever get up here to join in."

"Okay. I guess it holds together a mite better that way," Boyd allowed grudgingly. "The train opportunity is gone anyway. Like I said, I ain't one for frettin' and regrettin'. So I'll ride back and tell the boys how it is. How we'll just sit tight until we see which way that shootin' contest goes."

"On the day of the contest, I'll want you and one more man back in town," Delaney said. "If the contest doesn't go my way, then we won't want to waste any time in forming a fallback plan."

Boyd nodded. "Got it. The shootin' is on Friday, right?"

"That it is."

"Good enough. I'll see you then."

CHAPTER 11

Fifteen miles east and a bit north of Rattlesnake Wells, four men stood in an open area covered by brownish prairie grass reaching to the tops of their boots and dotted with numerous tree stumps. A little over a hundred yards away, in the direction they were facing, was a horse corral contained by weathered gray fencing. At their backs, in the distance, the ragged outline of the Shirley Mountains thrust up into the cloudless blue afternoon sky.

One of the men was considerably older than the other three. His name was Moses Shaw. He was of average height, bandy-legged, with thick, powerful forearms and solid shoulders in spite of his nearly sixty years. Stringy gray whiskers covered his chin and jawline and more streaks of gray were shot through his shoulder-length hair. He wore a patterned red bandanna around his forehead, no hat, and part of the hair falling over his left shoulder was gathered, braided, and tied with a leather thong marked by Indian designs.

The three younger men lined up beside him were

his sons—Wiley, Cyrus, and Harley. Wiley, the youngest, was tall and lanky, with a jutting chin and deep-sunken pale blue eyes. Cyrus, the middle one, was equally as tall, slim to the point of looking gawky and somewhat frail, with a prominent Adam's apple and a sizable gap between his two front teeth that caused him to whistle sometimes when he spoke. The oldest, Harley, was shorter, more like his father, stocky in build, with a broad, squarish face, squinty eyes, and limp, greasy hair spilling to his shirt collar.

Moses was holding a Henry repeating rifle, the stock resting in the crook of his left arm. His sons all held Winchesters in a similar manner. On the railing of the corral they were facing, four paper targets had been nailed. Each had a black bull's-eye dot, approximately an inch in diameter, painted on it.

"Well, there they be," Moses announced, tipping his head in the direction of the targets. "Equal distance, equal targets, weapons of choice. We each take three shots, measure the spread, see who comes out the tightest. Can't be no fairer than that."

"Pop," said Harley at the end of the row, "we really don't need to go through all this. Ain't much doubt who's gonna come out on top. You taught each of us boys about shootin' since we was knee high to a sway-backed hound dog. You saw to it we was all pretty good, but none of us ever came close to matchin' you."

"That may be true, Harley, and it's kind of you to give your old man his propers," Moses said. "But the truth is that you boys are all still young and full of vinegar. Me, not so much. I've slowed down considerable and I ain't so sure my eyesight ain't faded some.

Can't know for positive 'cause ain't none of us done any serious shootin' in a while. That's what I want to make sure of. I can't afford to pay for all of us enterin' that shootin' match in town so I want to be certain as I can that us Shaws are puttin' forth our best. And I ain't the kind of pa who lords it over his boys and don't give 'em a fair shot to stand on their own."

"Ain't nobody knows that better'n us, Pop," said Wiley.

"I'm proud to hear you recognize that." Moses paused and pulled his brows into a scowl. "But see here now. I'd better not catch any of you rascals holdin' back just to *let* me win, you hear? If I think that, I'll tan your dad-blamed hides. *That* I still got enough vinegar for."

The three sons cast their eyes momentarily downward.

Cyrus said, "Yeah, we know that, too, Pop."

Moses nodded. "All right, then. We'll shoot on down the line. Harley, you go first; I'll finish up."

And so it went. Inasmuch as it was a still, clear day and all four men were skilled marksmen, it didn't take long for the dull, flat cracks of a dozen shots to roll across the prairie.

When the shooting was done, the four Shaws walked up to the railing. The results were predictably close. Harley's pattern was well within the bull's-eye, holding right at a half-inch spread. Cyrus planted two rounds square in the center of the black dot but the third went wide, extending a whisker past the outer edge. Wiley's pattern was almost as tight as his older brother's but fanned out a sliver more than half an inch. It all became moot, however, when they got to

Moses's target. His three slugs were dead center and grouped so tight it looked practically like a single oversized hole.

"Real shame about that faded eyesight of yours, Pop," Harley said dryly. "Looks to me like you ain't lost a tick from the days when you was sharpshootin' for the Blue and got awarded all those medals in the war."

"Yeah, and what did it gain me?" Moses answered, his tone suddenly bitter. "I found out soon enough, when the war was done and they didn't need me no more, that a fella with a chestful of medals is just as poor and left out as a scrounger who stayed safe on the back lines."

Cyrus looked a little confused. "But ain't goin' after this here shootin' prize kinda the same thing?"

"Hell no, it ain't!" snapped Moses. "Take all those shootin' medals and ribbons from the war, put 'em in a sack, haul 'em to the bank, and what would you have? Nothing, that's what. Get you laughed out of the joint. But those prize shootin' irons, with all their gold and diamonds, now that's a different story. There you'd have value. You'd all of a sudden find yourself respected, a man of *stature*!"

Now it was Wiley who looked confused. "Didn't know we was ever interested in havin' stature, Pop."

"Maybe we are, maybe we ain't. Point is," Moses said stubbornly, "we'd have it if we wanted it. And it'd mean that a sharp aim and a steady trigger finger would by-God count for something, the way they ought to."

* * *

"Jeez, Swede, I sure hate doin' it. I really do."
Merle Conroy's mournful tone was matched only by
the expression he wore as he voiced this lament. He
was a beefy man in his midforties, thick through the
shoulders, thicker still and somewhat soft-looking
through the gut. A fringe of beard encircled the
lower half of a homely, bloated face boasting a pasty
complexion and red-rimmed eyes. On his head sat a
battered Stetson whose flat crown had once been
adorned with a band of silver conchos, though now
there were gaps where more of the decorative discs
were missing than in place.

"Do you hate it less than you'd hate havin' your
sorry ass thrown in Marshal Hatfield's jail? If you
don't, then I guarantee you'll damn well hate it less
than what I do to your incompetent hide if you end
up dragging me into this with you!"

Swede Simkins was narrow shouldered and lean,
less powerfully built than Conroy. But, at six-six in
height, he towered over the sallow-faced man by
more than half a foot. This, combined with a fierce
scowl, a commanding voice, and the surly attitude
that seemed second nature to him, clearly made him
the domineering half of the pair.

"Aw, come on, Swede," Conroy protested. "You
know better than that. I'd never rat on you or drag
you into any kind of trouble. I mean, you *are* part of
it—you're the one who sent me after that keg of coal
oil in the first place and had me take it to those other
two characters. But nobody will ever hear that out
of me."

"Hell, then I got nothing to worry about, do I?"
Swede sneered sarcastically. "At least those other two

jaspers had the decency to get themselves killed when they got caught. That leaves you as the only one who *can* drag me into it!"

"But I won't, I tell you. I ain't ever tripped you up before in all the years we been together, have I?"

"It only takes once," Swede hissed. "That's why you've got to get rid of that stupid damned horse of yours. You've got to do it before *he* trips up both of us."

Conroy hung his head, and his whole body seemed to sag.

The two men were standing in the partitioned-off storage area at the rear of a large tent supported by wooden beams. On the other side of the partition, the front three quarters of the tent comprised the Red-Eyed Goat Saloon, owned and operated by Swede. All around where they stood were crates of whiskey and barrels of beer. A collapsible army cot shoved against one wall marked Conroy's sleeping quarters. Out back of the tent, through the slit of a doorway hanging partially open, two staked horses were visible. One was a tall palomino, the other a sleek black blaze-face.

"If there ain't no other way, I guess I got to go through with it," Conroy said, his chin still down. Then, lifting his face, he managed a weak smile and added, "Ol' Sol sure has been a mighty good horse to me, though, Swede. That time the posse was on my tail, throwin' lead, and one of their shots blasted that chunk out of his ear? He never slowed a step. He just kept chargin' on, and pretty soon we were leaving 'em in our dust."

"I know. I've heard the tale a thousand times. And

I know how much Sol means to you," allowed Swede. "But it's that very damn notch in his ear that's got us on the brink of big trouble. If you hadn't used Sol to haul away that keg of coal oil, none of this would be necessary. But you did. And now Hatfield's fat deputy, after tracing the keg those other two morons left behind, is going all up and down Gold Avenue asking who belongs to a notch-eared palomino. How long do you think it'll be before that leads to you? And then, since everybody knows you work for me, guess where it's bound to lead next?"

"I get the picture, Swede." Conroy hung his head again. "I just wish there was another way, that's all."

"Well, there ain't! And the longer you put it off, the longer you're exposing our necks to the chopping block. So take that nag out into the rugged country somewhere. Take my horse along so's you got something to ride back. Put a bullet in ol' notch-head and get it over with. Then bury him."

Swede clapped a hand reassuringly onto Conroy's shoulder. "Use my Big Fifty Sharps, he won't feel a lick of pain. That's as humane as you can be. Afterward, when Hatfield or that fat deputy comes around—which they're bound to do—you say you sold that horse a week, ten days ago to some fella you can't remember the name of. That'll be the end of it. Not them or anybody else will be able to prove a damn thing otherwise."

Conroy neither moved nor said anything for a minute.

Swede took his hand away and, for the first time, his voice seemed to take on a trace of gentleness.

"You're gonna want to get a move on, Merle. Evening will be settling in soon."

Conroy gave a slow nod. "I think I'd rather do it in the dark. Then I won't be able to see so good in case ol' Sol looks back at me."

Swede sighed. His voice turned impatient, all trace of gentleness once again gone. "Whatever works best for you. As long as you get it done."

CHAPTER 12

"What's the sense in getting all spruced up at the end of the day?" Bob Hatfield wanted to know. "They've already seen me and met me once today. I made whatever impression I'm going to make. I don't see the point in going to all the trouble of trying to fiddle with it now."

"Well, you should," Consuela told him firmly. "You're the town marshal and you're attending a dinner with special guests in one of the Shirley House's private dining rooms. *That* calls for 'sprucing up' a little."

Bob looked plaintively over at Bucky, who was sitting at the kitchen table and grinning broadly. "I don't think you're gonna win, Pa," said the boy. "I've gone through this a lot, mostly on weekends when it's time for Sunday school. I always lose."

Evening had settled in and Bob had returned home, intending to relax a bit before heading down to the Shirley House for the get-together with Gafford and his entertainers. He thought he would do this while visiting with Bucky and Consuela as they were taking their own supper, maybe enjoy a big mug of Consuela's good coffee with them as they ate, and answer some more of the questions he knew Bucky still had bottled up about last night's shooting at the Crystal Diamond.

No sooner had he advised Consuela not to set a place for him and went on to explain why, however, than she began fretting and fussing about her ironing a shirt and laying out a change of duds and him getting washed up and shaved and so on.

"Scraping the whiskers from your chin and then putting on a clean shirt and your good suit coat," she insisted now, "is hardly the torture you make it seem. Plus it will be a good chance to wear that nice new string tie Bucky got you for your last birthday. After I iron your shirt, I will polish your dress boots and get them ready."

"Now, doggone it, 'Suela, you don't have to do that. Not for the likes of them," Bob said.

"I'm not doing it for them. I'm doing it for you, because you represent the town. You need to show everyone that you are better than to show up for a fine dinner in dusty boots."

Bob sighed and looked at Bucky again. "You're right. I ain't gonna win, am I?"

"Tried to tell you."

"She make you shave for Sunday school, too, does she?"

Bucky's eyes went wide. "No. But can I start, though?"

Bob laughed, reaching out to tousle his son's mop of hair. "Not quite yet. I'm afraid you might do too much damage trying to even *find* a whisker, maybe end up cutting your nose off instead . . . Come on, we can talk while I'm capitulating to the terms of this battle I've lost. I'll tell you some more about that shoot-out from last night. Then you can help me tie my tie."

A quarter hour before seven, Bob made his way down the slope from his house and angled onto Front Street, aiming for the Shirley House. As he approached, he saw his three deputies waiting for him on the boardwalk out front. As he stepped up next to them he got a better look in the illumination thrown by the lanterns hanging on the posts of the shingled awning. He could see that each of his fellow lawmen appeared freshly scrubbed, shaved, and all were decked out in clean shirts. The Macy brothers were tieless but Fred sported an oversized bow tie as well as a vest. The tie looked like it could have doubled as a ribbon on a woman's Easter bonnet.

The aroma of hair oil and bay rum hung heavy under the awning.

"Jeez, fellas," Bob remarked wryly, "careful not to stand too close together for any length of time, else the concentration of all those high-smelling fumes might set off a doggone explosion or something."

Yet, even as he said this, he was questioning his own laxity in wanting to prepare for this event. It had taken Consuela to prod him into sprucing up at all. But here were these three—none of whom had a steady woman of any kind in his life—who'd taken it upon themselves to clean up. Bob wondered if he was at risk of turning into some kind of slob in his advanced years. Well, not as long as Consuela was around. But if not for her . . .

"We've never been invited to dinner in no fancy place like the Shirley before," Peter explained. "We weren't sure what was appropriate."

"Don't worry. You look fine," Bob told him.

"Mrs. Nyby saw to it I fitted out proper," said Fred rather proudly. Mabel Nyby was the widowed landlady of the boardinghouse where he stayed.

"She did a right good job," Bob said. "But are you sure you didn't steal that tie off one of her bonnets?"

"Why, no," Fred answered earnestly. Then, frowning, looking suddenly uncertain, he said, "Why? Is there something wrong with it? I thought—"

"You thought right," Bob interjected, mouth stretching into a wide grin. "The tie looks great. I was just joshing you out of jealousy. Each of you looks just fine. Hell, we *all* look fine . . . So let's go on inside, give those dancing ladies a treat by showing 'em some of the best-looking Western hombres they're likely to lay their eyes on, and then eat a bunch of the Shirley's fancy cooking."

Which was exactly what they proceeded to do.

The evening went well, and even Bob, when all was said and done, had to admit to having a good time. Much of his enjoyment came from seeing his men so eagerly soaking up the experience. The food was excellent, the conversation was interesting and at times highly amusing when Gafford would spin an anecdotal tale from one of his many experiences, and the ladies were definitely exquisite to look upon.

It crossed Bob's mind more than once that he could be in for a very difficult time when it came to keeping the peace in Rattlesnake Wells over the next several days because it might take that long to wipe the dreamy looks off the faces of Fred, Peter, and Vern after their time spent in the presence of Alora Dane. How intimidated would potential trouble-makers be if they found themselves facing a bunch of lawmen walking around with glazed eyes and sappy grins?

Otherwise, the only drawback to the dinner as far as Bob was concerned was the absence of Simon Quirt. He still wanted some words with the former Pinkerton man. But then, thinking it through, he realized it was really no loss because the kind of discussion he figured to have with Quirt wouldn't have been a good fit for this evening's circumstances anyway.

When it was time to call it a night, Bob and his deputies departed together, as they'd arrived. Before leaving, each expressed his sincere gratitude for the invitation and the pleasant time that resulted.

Back out on the boardwalk in front of the Shirley House, Bob immediately sensed the letdown in his men. He understood, even though he didn't quite feel the same. The good news was that his earlier concern about them venturing out entranced and maybe walking into a post or something now didn't look like so much of a problem. He guessed their slumped shoulders and hangdog expressions were an improvement as far as going about their business, but it was still a pitiful thing to see in grown men. Pitiful enough to be annoying and to make Bob feel compelled to call them on it.

"For the love of Pete, fellas," he growled. "You three

have been shuffling your feet and looking cow-eyed to the point of practically slobbering a time or two tonight. And now you look like a bunch of sick pups. You act like you've never been in the presence of a pretty woman before."

"I ain't," said Vern. "Leastways none like Miss Alora."

"I hate to bust your bubble, kid, but under all that perfume and makeup she's near old enough to be your ma," Bob told him.

Vern blinked innocently. "So what? That don't make her no less beautiful."

"He's got you there, boss," Fred pointed out. "Besides, you're just joshing again, right? You don't think she's really that old, do you?"

"Okay, you caught me. I'll admit, your Mrs. Nyby has probably got her shaded by three or four years."

Fred cocked his head back. "Now I know you're joshing."

"Besides," spoke up Peter, "what difference does it make? She can be a hundred, but she's still beautiful."

"And that ain't to shortchange the other ladies, either," said Fred. "They're mighty pretty, too. But them being married and all, and with their husbands sitting right there . . . well, you all know what I mean. But when it comes to Miss Alora, there's no getting around how special she is."

Bob rolled his eyes. "You three are pathetic. I hope to hell after a good night's sleep at least one of you wakes up tomorrow morning with a clear head. Miss Dane is a mighty pretty woman, it's true. But in spite of the spell she seems to have cast on the lot of you, she ain't no doggone *goddess* or anything."

Vern opened his mouth to say something, but then changed his mind and bit off whatever the remark was going to be. Instead it came out, "Whatever you say, Marshal."

Bob scowled. "What I say is this: I suggest you all call it a night. If you happen to pass by a cold watering trough on your way home, stop and take a good long soak in it. Then, maybe, I'll have a chance of seeing some of that clearheadedness I'm hoping for in the morning. It would come in handy, since I figure tomorrow's gonna be another busy day."

"But what about tonight?" asked Peter. "Shouldn't a couple of us take a turn around town before—"

"I'll take care of that," Bob said, cutting him off. "You and the others just do like I told you. Work on getting your brains unscrambled."

CHAPTER 13

As he watched Fred and the Macy brothers drift off down the street, Bob loosened his tie and undid the top button of his shirt. Never a fan of ties for any purpose, he was particularly puzzled by the custom of knotting one on and then sitting down half-strangled to partake of a big meal. Unfortunately, it hadn't stopped him from stowing away more than his share of the delicious fare he'd just been served. Which made a late patrol around town not just an obligation, but also a good chance to walk off some of what he'd overconsumed.

Pulling out his watch and checking it, he saw that it was past nine; later than he'd thought.

Except for the Shirley House, the only other Old Town business still open at this hour was Bullock's Saloon, located diagonally across the street. Bob's first thought was to have a peek in there on his swing back, after working his way down Front Street checking locks and so forth on this side before turning back at the far end and returning on the other side. But then, on a whim, he decided to cross over and make Bullock's his starting point for patrolling this part of town.

One reason for this was that Bob fully expected Mike Bullock had heard by now about the dinner the marshal and his men had just attended. Given Bullock's testy feelings about Gafford and his high-handed ways, there was little doubt he'd have a disparaging remark or two. So Bob figured it would be better to go ahead and let him get whatever he had to say off his chest rather than let him stew about it all night and have even more of a head of steam built up by tomorrow.

The air was still and crisp as he crossed the street. A cold-looking slice of silver moon hung low overhead in a cloudless sky.

Keeping to habit, Bob paused just outside the entrance to Bullock's and gazed in over the tops of the batwings, giving the interior a good looking over before going in. There was only a modest crowd on hand tonight; two tables of card players and a half-dozen men lined up along the bar. Two scantily clad hostesses were milling about, one sticking close to the card tables and the other hanging nearer the bar.

As she did from time to time when other duties weren't required of her, Maudie was sitting in on one of the games. Her ample charms, though strictly untouchable, riveted the attention of most of the men in the room to the point of making the two hostesses all but invisible. Even Bob's gaze lingered for an extra beat or two as he scanned the room.

It might have lingered even a bit longer if it hadn't been drawn by another presence also seated at Maudie's table. Off to her right, two seats down, was

Simon Quirt. When Bob's eyes settled on him, he found the black man already looking back in that cool, calm way he had.

Bob pushed open the batwings and walked on in. When he leaned his tall frame against the bar and hooked a boot heel over the brass rail, Mike Bullock was right there on the other side, waiting for him.

"Well, well. It's heartening to see that—for the time being at least—our stalwart town marshal is willing to leave the trappings of higher society and still come to mingle for a time among us common folks."

Bob grinned. "Is that the best you got? I'm disappointed, if it is. I figured you'd be ready to unload some real ear-blisterers on me."

"Good. I hope you are disappointed," Bullock said sourly. "Then you'll have an idea how I felt when I heard you and your whole crew was over at the Shirley breaking bread with Gafford and his dancing girls. Did they flash their legs and put on a private show for you?"

"Nope. And thank God they didn't." Bob shook his head. "I already have three starry-eyed deputies looking like they got mule-kicked to the head and walked away with their brains scrambled."

Bullock grunted. "I can understand that. I got me a good look at that Alora Dane when their wagons came into town from the train station and I gotta tell you . . . If ever a fella could be knocked loopy from just the sight of a gal, she'd sure as fire be the one to do it."

Bob couldn't believe his ears. "Oh no. Not you, too," he groaned.

"What?" said Bullock, bristling indignantly. "Don't I have the right to take note of a pretty woman when I see one?"

"I wouldn't deny any man that right," Bob replied. He waved his hand in a flourish. "By all means, take note all you want. It just surprises me, that's all, that you'd look with favor on anybody—even a pretty package like Miss Dane—who's got anything to do with Gafford."

"Me and him sort of buried the hatchet. Don't you remember?" said Bullock. "First, at the prodding of you and Maudie, I agreed to be one of the judges in the shooting contest. And then, after those skunks showing out last night . . . well, it set me to around careless-like. really, I don't like the thought of how much business he might cost me with that fancy-ass setup he's getting ready to open. But, if it comes to that, if he bites into my trade too deep, then I got two choices—either I throw in the towel and give up the match, or I jazz up my place here and go right back at him, head to head. That's the way I've always done it before."

Bullock paused and frowned deeply. "That other fella, the one doing all the bellyaching and whining these past couple days, that wasn't me. Just like throwing in the towel wouldn't be. Never been my way in the past and I don't intend for it to be any-more going forward. Thinking back on it, I don't much care for that other hombre and don't want to meet him again."

"Good words to hear. To tell you the truth, I didn't care much for that other fella, either." Bob made

William W. Johnstone

another gesture with his hand. "What say we drink on it?"

Bullock's frown faltered. One furry eyebrow arched high. "You mean you're gonna have a drink with me?"

"Special occasion."

"It must be. I was wondering if you were ever gonna get around to plunking down some money for something, considering all the time you spend in here."

Now it was Bob's eyebrows that arched high. "I didn't say anything about buying, did I? I just said we should drink to a special occasion."

Both men had a good chuckle as Bullock said, "And so we shall," while filling two shot glasses with amber liquid. The drinks were emptied glasses clapped back onto the bar top.

That's when Simon Quirt walked silently up and leaned against the bar on Bob's left side.

CHAPTER 14

"If I'm not interrupting, Marshal," Quirt said in his easy drawl, "Gafford keeps remindin' me that you're wantin' to talk to me. Thought maybe now might be a good time."

Bob turned his head to look at him, then cut a glance momentarily over at the card game continuing without him. "Done with your game, I take it?"

"More like the game's done with me. At least for tonight. Cards just ain't fallin' my way."

Bob nodded. "Happens like that sometimes. Takes a smart man to know when it's time to step away for a spell."

"If I was real smart, I'd stay away for good. Over the years I fear I've pushed considerably more money into pots than I've pulled back out." Quirt shrugged. "But a man's got to fill his idle hours some way or other."

Bob looked around and his eyes fell on an empty table near the back of the room, the same one he'd been sitting at with Maudie and Bullock the other day before the trouble broke out with Jax Verdeen and his

companions. He turned back to Bullock and je
thumb, saying, "Mind if we use that back table for a
few minutes to do some chin-wagging, Mike?"

"Be my guest. It ain't like there's a big crowd fighting to lay claim to it. You gonna want anything to
drink?"

"Coffee, for me, if you've got any made up. Otherwise I'm okay," said Bob.

"Sounds good. Same here if you've got some," said
Quirt.

Bob led the way back to the table and they seated
themselves, each man hitching his chair so that he
was facing more or less toward the front door and
had his back angled toward a slice of the side wall.
They'd barely gotten situated before one of the hostesses came over and placed two steaming mugs of
coffee in front of them. Quirt spread some coins on
the table and told her to keep the change.

"You didn't have to do that, but thanks," said Bob.

"I believe in payin' my way." Quirt lifted his mug
and blew across the top, clearing the steam. The pool
of coffee in the cup was only slightly darker than his
skin. He had handsome, almost delicate facial features and was groomed to near perfection. A carefully
trimmed mustache flared back on either side and
connected with sideburns barbered just as precisely.

After taking a sip of his drink, he said to Bob,
"You're staring. That's not polite."

Bob flashed a somewhat sheepish grin. "Sorry. I
was just thinking what you said a minute ago—about
filling your idle hours."

"Oh?"

"As neat as you got your mustache and sideburns

trimmed, I reckon that must fill up a good deal of time right there."

Quirt looked puzzled, perhaps a little annoyed. "Is that what you wanted to talk to me about? My grooming habits?"

"No, not hardly." Bob took a drink of his coffee. "Although maybe I should. I got reminded just recently, as a matter of fact, how shoddy my own grooming habits are on the brink of becoming."

"That sounds like a problem you can probably get turned around all on your own, Marshal. If you don't mind, I'd like to move on to whatever it is you're wantin' to discuss with me."

"That's fair enough," Bob said. "Mainly, I'm interested in your intentions as far as how long you might be sticking around Rattlesnake Wells. Are you just here to get Gafford's prize pistols delivered, or will you be staying beyond that?"

"Would it be a problem if I said I was plannin' to stay for a spell?"

"Not necessarily. Not unless you make it one."

Quirt slowly took a cheroot from his shirt pocket and hung it from a corner of his mouth. Offering one to Bob got a headshake in response. So he snapped a match to flame with his thumbnail and lit up his own, puffing blue smoke.

"I never set out to make problems, Marshal," he said, shaking out the match and dropping it into an ashtray near the edge of the table. "Way I see it, I'm often called on to keep 'em from happenin'."

"That would fit with your history as a Pinkerton man. Preventing or solving trouble that the law sometimes can't—or won't—handle on their own."

"So you understand."

Bob nodded. "Up to a point. Couple things to add, though. First off, you're no longer with the Pinkertons. Secondly, I represent the law around here and I kinda like to think that me and my deputies do a pretty fair job of handling whatever troubles come our way."

"So I've heard."

"Also crosses my mind that you've made a name for yourself outside of your time with the Pinkerton agency."

Quirt smiled thinly. "Which term do you prefer? Gunfighter? Gunslinger? Hired gun? I've been called each of those things and don't really mind any of them. Fact is, I'm pretty good with these guns I carry and so I do make a living based on that. Like I'm doing now with this job of work for Gafford. But I've never broken the law with my guns or done anything to end up with my name or likeness on a wanted poster."

"Nope. You haven't, for a fact."

"So why are you so worried about the thought of me stickin' around your town for a while?"

"Never said I was worried. Just curious, that's all," Bob replied. "You ought to know as well or better than most what's likely to happen when a fella with your kind of reputation settles in one place for any length of time. Sooner or later, some beer-brave jackass or some punk on the prod, looking to make his own rep, will come around looking to challenge you."

Quirt nodded. "I've encountered that kind of thing, it's true. When I have, I've gone out of my way to try and walk wide of it. Sometimes I've been able to, sometimes not. When I couldn't, I always faced 'em straight up and made it a fair fight. You can't expect a man in my position not to defend himself."

"Of course not. All I'm asking is that—if you *are* planning on being around for a while, and such a situation arises—give me and my deputies a chance to help you walk around it."

"Sounds reasonable. But, just so you know, there've been times in the past where I couldn't count on the law, even if there was any around, to back me that way. Seen cases where the local badge-toters were the ones cheerin' loudest for the local proddie to put me in my place."

"I've heard tell of cases like that. Damn shame," said Bob. "But it ain't like that around here. We get our share of jackasses and troublemakers, especially with the flow in and out of New Town thanks to the gold boom—and sometimes me or my deputies have no choice but to plant some of the damn fools on Boot Hill ourselves. But I'd just as soon keep it where *we* are the ones making that call . . . whenever possible."

"Like I said, sounds reasonable. Should anything like that come up, I'll do my best to allow you and your men a piece of it . . . whenever possible."

Bob took a drink of his coffee. "Which brings us back around to the question of whether or not you intend to be staying in town for a while."

"To be perfectly honest, I ain't made up my mind yet. And that's not a dodge," Quirt said. "Originally, you see, Gafford hired me to get the prize guns here safe and guard 'em on through the contest. Soon as that was done, I more or less figured on takin' the next train out. But then this business about those polecats tryin' to burn down his place came up and now he's offered me a job to stay on longer and oversee keepin' the Crystal Diamond safe from any more attempts to do harm before it ever gets off the ground."

"Sounds like pretty good thinking on his part, if you ask me," said Bob. "Me and my deputies make regular patrols and try to keep a close eye on all the businesses in town. But we can't cover one particular place all the time."

"Gafford knows that. He's got the highest regard for you and your men. But he also knows, just like you said, that you can't be everywhere at once. That's why he wants me to keep steady watch over the Diamond."

"After the trouble last night, I'm surprised—even though you haven't agreed to anything long term yet—he doesn't have you stationed there now."

"Matter of fact, that's where I'm headed in just a little bit and where I'll be the remainder of the night. And you're right, I *would* already be there if I hadn't run into a fella I worked with in the past and recommended him to Gafford for taking on part of the duty."

"This fella got a name?"

"Yates. Cecil Yates."

Bob shook his head. "Can't say as I know him."

"No, you wouldn't. I know him from down in Arizona. He just got into town and was looking for work to finance a grubstake in order to go try his luck up in the gold fields. Starry-eyed fool, just like so many others. But he's a good man with a gun—not a fast draw necessarily, but steady-handed and sharp-eyed all the same. For the time being at least, his turning up was a break for me and a chance for him to start earning some money."

"Speaking of earning money, or earning my keep anyway," said Bob, "reckon I need to get about doing my job. I only meant to stop in here briefly at the start of taking a nighttime turn around the town. Still need to get that done."

"Didn't mean to keep you."

Bob drained his coffee. "You were just responding to what I'd been asking for. I appreciate that." He rose from his chair. "I'd appreciate it, too, if you let me know when you decide about whether you're staying on or not. Either way, for however long you're here, I hope you'll keep in mind what we discussed."

"I'll be sure and do that, Marshal."

Bob headed for the exit. He pinched his hat to Maudie on the way by, and gave a wave to Bullock, who was busy drawing a round of beers.

At the batwings he paused for a moment, standing off to one side and gazing out into the dimly lit street, letting his eyes adjust to the change in lighting from the well-illuminated interior of the saloon. Noting that the street seemed a little darker than usual, he guessed he'd find that a few of the lanterns posted at regular intervals along the way had burnt out. Old Ollie Sterbenz, who did handyman work around town and who took care of maintaining the lanterns and lighting them each evening, must be slipping, Bob thought. He'd have to remember to remind Ollie tomorrow to do an examination of all the street lamps and make sure their wicks and oil pots were in good order.

He was thinking this as he stepped out onto the boardwalk.

If the man positioned at the south corner of Bullock's building, in a deepened pool of shadow caused by a nearby street lamp—being one of the ones unlit—hadn't clumsily clunked his gun against something as he raised the weapon to fire, thoughts of wicks and oil pots likely would have been the last thing to ever cross Bob Hatfield's mind. As it was, however, that single metallic tick was enough of a warning—*just* enough—for Bob to react and save his hide.

He was able to hurl himself backward, back through the batwings, a fraction of a second before the gun went off. The thunderous, window-rattling roar of a double-barreled shotgun—both loads being triggered simultaneously—ripped apart the night, the twelve-gauge charges raking across the front of Bullock's and turning the batwings into shredded slivers of pulp hanging limp and ragged on their hinges.

CHAPTER 15

Bob scrambled back into the saloon so frantically that he nearly tangled his feet and fell. He struggled to remain upright even as the batwing doors were pulverized by the shotgun blast, buffeting him with a boiling cloud of dust and spinning wood shards.

Bob leaned into the cloud, sweeping the .44 from his hip as he shouted over his shoulder, "Everybody, get down and stay that way!"

Then, recognizing the shotgun roar had signaled the discharge of both barrels and calculating he had a few precious seconds before the shooter could eject and reload, Bob lunged forward and rushed out through what was left of the batwings. Cutting immediately and sharply to his left—the opposite direction from the double-barreled blast—the marshal made long, desperate strides for the north corner of the building while at the same time extending his right arm out behind him and blindly triggering three rounds. It was a matter of four urgent strides and less than two seconds, but it seemed more like two hours, and every inch of the way there was a puckering of nerves between his shoulder blades where he expected the next blast to slam into him.

He made the corner and pitched instantly to his left again, diving into the shadow-cut alley at that end of the building. This time he made no attempt to stay on his feet. He went into a roll and came up hugging the shadows pooled deep against the outer wall. Without conscious thought, his fingers automatically began replacing the spent cartridges in his Colt. But before his thumb could shove in the first fresh load, the shotgun went off again. The corner he had just rounded took the punishment from this discharge, more wood torn away, exploding into whirling slivers.

Bob's mind did some whirling, too, as he snapped shut the Colt's loading gate. He was momentarily torn between two courses of action he could take. He could once again take advantage of the seconds he had before the shotgunner was able to reload, and go tearing around the corner in a full-out charge with Colt blazing, hoping to score a hit before he was met by another blast from those twin barrels. Or he could play it safer and retreat back down the length of the alley he was in, circle around the rear of Bullock's, and try to come up behind the shooter.

The decision got made for him, sort of, when one half of his options—the one that involved charging across the front way—was suddenly removed as being even the slightest bit viable. This removal came in the form of a second gunman opening up from across the street, from another mass of thick blackness where a street lamp was not burning. The realization hit Bob belatedly that these unlit lamps had been snuffed out so his ambushers had some added cover of darkness.

The second shooter wasn't using a shotgun, but rather a repeating rifle. A Winchester, Bob judged from the sound of it. Whatever it was, it was pouring a hell of a lot of lead into his alley and making it plenty hot for him. Since the alley was fairly wide but offered nothing in the way of cover, he had little choice but to stick tight to the shadowy wall and keeping dropping back.

In fact, he decided, he'd better drop back all the way and be quick about it. If the rifleman across the way kept him pinned close at this end of the alley, it would give the shotgunner from the other side a chance to cross over and lean in with his gut-shredder. He wouldn't have to aim with any great accuracy—all he'd have to do was let loose and the spread, if it didn't kill Bob outright, would sure as hell cut him down.

But Bob was damned if he was going to fade back too easily. Targeting on the rifleman's muzzle flashes, he triggered three more quick return rounds with his Colt. It would've been nice to have heard a yelp of pain, indicating he'd scored a lucky hit, but none came. Still, it gave the ambusher across the way a reason to duck and hold his own fire for a minute as Bob's .44 slugs streaked in.

Trouble was, since he hadn't scored a hit, Bob knew his muzzle flashes gave the rifleman something to target on in return. With this in mind, he dropped low and shifted to the opposite side of the alley. The shadows weren't as dense there, but still murky enough to keep him from being clearly revealed. As he tensed for a return volley, the marshal began crabbing backward, where welcoming shadows grew deeper.

Surprisingly, the next shots to rip through the night came not from across the street but rather from the alley on the other side of Bullock's building. Only it wasn't another shotgun blast—it was the rapid-fire crack of a pistol. Bob slowed his retreat somewhat, puzzling at this. He had time to wonder for only a split second, though, before the shotgun *did* roar again.

Next came an unintelligible curse followed by a clearer shout of, "Cover me!" This was followed promptly by the rifle on the other side of the street opening up once more. Only this time it wasn't sending more lead in Bob's direction, it was aimed instead at the south side of the building.

What the hell!?

Taking full advantage of whatever was going on, Bob turned and ran the remaining distance to the far end of his alley. Rounding the corner, he saw a pale glow of light spilling out the back door of Bullock's. He pulled up short and raised his Colt. A moment later, a shadow moved within the spill of illumination and the stocky shape of Mike Bullock leaned cautiously out of the open doorway.

"Damn it, Mike, that's a good way to get your head blown off," Bob rasped in a harsh whisper as he stepped forward.

"I might say the same for you," Bullock replied as he edged out a little farther and revealed the sawed-off shotgun gripped in his meaty paws.

"I thought I told everybody to stay put."

"When somebody is blasting the hell out of

everything and threatening my saloon, I ain't likely to duck down and hide." Though muted somewhat by the mass of the building, a fresh burst of rifle fire from the street and responding pistol fire from the front of the south alley threatened to drown out his words.

"Who else is out here? Who's doing the shooting in the alley?" Bob demanded.

"That gunslinger-looking fella you was talking to earlier. He jumped up and boiled out the back just seconds after you pulled that crazy stunt of charging out the front."

"Damn! Don't anybody listen?" muttered Bob under his breath as he used the illumination from the doorway to finish reloading his gun. Then, brushing past Bullock, he added over his shoulder, "Just stay the hell in there and don't let anybody else come out. Will you try to do that? If we get too many people fumbling around in the darkness we'll only end up shooting each other!"

Bob edged around the corner of the building and into the south alley without waiting for an answer. As he picked his way forward, he could make out the shape of a man—identifiable by his wide-brimmed, flat-crowned Stetson—crouched behind a rain barrel near the mouth of the alley.

"Quirt! It's me, Hatfield, coming up behind you," he called ahead.

"Come on, then. But stay low," Quirt said without turning.

A handful of seconds later, Bob pressed up beside him. "There were two of 'em," he said. "You get either one?"

"No luck," Quirt answered with a shake of his head. "I had the shotgunner in my sights, but then I stepped on a loose rock and lost my damn balance just as I was gettin' ready to shoot. I hate to say it, but I missed him. He pinned me back with a wild-ass blast of his double-barrel long enough so's he could make it across the street with the shooter over there coverin' him."

"Are they still there? Can you tell?"

"They were a minute ago. Leastways, I know the rifleman was 'cause he was pourin' a lot of lead my way. But now they've gone quiet."

"Seeing that their ambush is spoiled, they might be ready to give it up," Bob said. "If they've got horses behind those buildings or anywhere close, they could make a getaway."

"So what've you got in mind?"

"There's one sure way to find out if they've high-tailed it or are still wanting to finish what they started—you cover me, I'm going to make a break for the other side."

Quirt nodded. "Yeah, that oughta do it. Then, after you make it over, you cover me."

"No need for you to risk your hide any more than you already have," Bob told him.

"The hell there ain't. I don't do half measure, Marshal. Besides, I missed a sure shot at that snake with the shotgun. I don't intend to let it go at that."

Bob could see it was pointless to argue. Number one, there wasn't time. Number two, it was evident he wasn't going to be able to talk Quirt out of it anyway. He hesitated a moment longer, scanning the opposite side of the street for sign of movement or any indication that the ambushers were still present. Seeing nothing, he sprang out of his crouch and into another long-striding sprint. He made it to the other side and pressed himself into the recessed doorway of a bootmaker's shop. He was breathing hard and the smell of new leather filled his nostrils.

No shots had been fired at him.

He motioned Quirt to come ahead and then leaned out of the doorway, Colt raised and ready in case the cease-fire didn't hold a second time. But it did. Quirt made it across and joined him in the doorway, his breathing only slightly quickened.

"Now what?"

"We spread out. I'll go this way, up alongside the hotel"—Bob gestured with his Colt—"you go a couple doors down and then cut back between the buildings there. There'll be trees and underbrush for a ways, then it opens up to grassy plains. Residences will be off to your right, but if these jaspers are making a run for it I doubt they'll go that way. They'll break for the open."

"Got it."

The two men separated and then plunged back between buildings as the marshal had indicated. Bob raced along the side of the Shirley House, where intermittent pools of light spilled from some of the windows. This helped him make his way but—as he was keenly aware—it also meant he was being revealed as a result. Skirting as far out to the edges of the light as he could, he continued on.

At the end of the Shirley House, the traces of light abruptly ended and a cluster of tall, leafy trees blotted out even what moon- and starlight there was. The sudden total blackness brought Bob to a halt. As he willed his eyes to adjust, he stood listening intently, trying to pick out any sound above his own breathing.

And then he heard a horse whinny, mixed with a man's muffled curse.

Bob lunged toward the sound, making his way through the trees more by feel than by sight. He bumped and scraped against the rough trunks but somehow remained steady on his feet. And then he was emerging from the tree line, and the sky overhead, no longer blocked by a canopy of leaves, bathed everything before him in a bluish silver light.

Twenty feet ahead, two men were struggling to get mounted on a pair of horses that apparently had been tied to a stand of scrub brush. To be more exact, only one man—fighting an injured leg—was struggling to haul himself up. His cohort, already mounted, was leaning over and tugging, trying to help get him hoisted.

Bob aimed his Colt in the air and fired a booming shot. "Halt! Freeze or die!" he shouted.

The pair failed to heed the warning. The mounted man jerked up straight in his saddle and swung a Winchester rifle into view. The other man stumbled and dropped to his knees, reaching up to claw desperately at the rifleman's stirrup. "Don't leave me, Reeves. Don't run out on me, damn you!" he wailed.

Reeves kicked the other clear of his stirrup and hollered back. "You worry about haulin' yourself up into that saddle!"

Half a second later the Winchester was spitting yellow-orange flame and sending bullets ripping through the air where the muzzle flash of Bob's warning shot had been seen. But by then Bob was three feet away and dropped down to one knee. He raised his Colt, took careful aim, and pumped two rounds into the man called Reeves. The rifleman flung his arms wide, throwing the Winchester clear, and tumbled backward off the rear of his horse.

The second man wallowed painfully on the ground, cursing, and tried to rise to his feet. Almost immediately he dropped back down, falling over onto one hip. From that position he flailed desperately. A long object thrust into view, moonlight glinting dully off its surface. The shotgun's twin barrels roared once more, splitting apart the night and belching flame and sparks. But the shooter's aim was reckless and low, doing nothing more than tearing a long gouge in the grass and disintegrating one of the scrub bushes.

With the shotgun blast still reverberating in the air, three rapid-fire pistol shots cut through. The shotgunner was knocked flat by the impact of the slugs and then hunched into a single lumpy rollover before becoming very still.

CHAPTER 16

Passing through hanging wisps of powder smoke, Bob and Quirt converged slowly, cautiously, on the fallen men. Only after they had nudged the prone shapes with the toes of their boots to make sure there were no signs of life did they holster their guns.

"Any idea who they are or what this was about?" asked Quirt.

"Pretty obvious they were out to gun me," said Bob. "As far as who they are, I heard this one called Reeves. That matches the name of one of three men I had a run-in with just the other day. You got a match? Let's have a closer look at the one you put down."

Quirt thumbed a lucifer to flame and held it over the former shotgunner.

"Yeah, that's Jax Verdeen," Bob confirmed. "See the way his wrist and two fingers are taped up? I shot a gun out of his hand during that fracas I mentioned. Must have wrenched his paw pretty good."

"Which explains why he was using a shotgun," mused Quirt. "Don't require the same dexterity it takes to work a handgun or rifle. With a scattergun, all you need to do is aim in the general direction and yank the triggers."

"Yeah. And he was able to do that good enough— damn near *too* good," Bob said bitterly.

Quirt blew out his match and said, "Which brings me to the question—meanin' no offense, mind you— why, if you had him under your gun once, you left him still walkin' around to come back for revenge?"

"No other word for it, I guess, but to call it a mistake on my part," Bob had to admit. "They said they were headed up to the gold fields, so I took a chance and let 'em go. Figured they'd work out any leftover anger or aggression with a pick and shovel. But I was wrong."

"Looks like I was wrong, too," said Quirt. He pointed down, adding, "That fresh wound on his leg shows that I didn't miss him completely back in the alley, after all. Still, in a manner of speakin', I guess we both had a turn at lettin' him get away."

"Thanks to that leg wound, though, he didn't get away clean. Not tonight. It slowed him down and kept him from being able to mount his horse before we caught up with 'em." Bob regarded the black gunman closely. "That makes me mighty beholden to you, Quirt, and those ain't words I say lightly."

Quirt looked somewhat uncomfortable under the intensity of Bob's gaze, seemingly unable to form a quick reply.

Before the moment turned too awkward, other voices called out from the street, where people were starting to mill in the wake of the now-silenced gunfire.

"Marshal Hatfield! Are you all right? Is everything okay?"

"Back here! Past the tree line," Bob called in response. "Bring some lanterns!"

In a matter of minutes, a cluster of men emerged from the trees. Three of them were holding lanterns high. In the lead were Fred Ordway and Mike Bullock. A little farther back Bob saw Peter and Vern Macy.

"We heard the shooting and came running as fast as we could, boss," said a breathless Fred. "What in blazes happened?"

"Couple of bushwhackers tried to gun me down," Bob answered. "If you take a closer look with one of those lanterns you'll see it's two of the skunks I tangled with yesterday in Bullock's Saloon—the ones I was foolish enough not to throw in the clink right then and there."

"By God, you're right," said Bullock, leaning over the dead shotgunner. "This is that Jax hombre, sure enough."

"The other is the one they called Reeves."

"There were three of 'em that day," said Fred. "What about the third, the Mexican?"

"If you remember, I smashed his shoulder pretty good with a .44 slug," said Bob. "I'm guessing he didn't feel spry enough to ride along for this try at revenge. If somebody was to backtrack the way these two came in, I expect the Mexican could be found waiting in an outlying camp somewhere up in the foothills."

"I'll take a shot at that come first light," offered

Vern Macy, who'd proven himself a good tracker on more than one occasion.

Bob nodded. "Take your brother with you. A wounded animal is the most dangerous kind."

Bullock abruptly stepped closer to Bob, raising his lantern. "Good Lord, man, look at your face," he exclaimed. "We need to get you to a doctor."

In the glow of the lantern, Bob's face appeared peppered with a dozen or more wood slivers from the exploding batwing doors. Several were superficial, but a number were large and imbedded deep. A mixture of blood and sweat was smeared across his forehead and running down the sides of his face.

Reaching up with one hand and tentatively probing with his fingers, the marshal realized the damage for the first time. "In all the excitement, I guess I never noticed," he said. Then, with a wry grin, he added, "Thanks for bringing it to my attention, Mike. Now it stings like hell."

"Go fetch Doc Tibbs," Fred said to somebody in the crowd.

Bob made a chopping motion with his hand. "No. No need to roust the doc for a few splinters."

"You were crazy in the first place, chargin' after that shotgun blast the way you did," drawled Quirt. "Now you ain't showin' no better sense."

Bob grinned wearily. "Bad habit of mine."

"Some of those are deep gashes. Bound to need a few stitches. You're a damn fool if you don't let the doctor look at 'em," insisted Bullock.

Bob suddenly felt too tired to argue. "Okay. I'll walk on down to his office, then. If he's gonna do some sewing, that's where he'll want to do it anyway."

Turning to his deputies, he added, "Somebody else we'll need to roust is the undertaker. Load these bodies on their horses and take 'em to him. After that, Fred, I gotta ask you to go back on duty, officially, and finish taking a turn through town. I'm afraid I didn't get very far. Hope you understand, by the time the doc gets done with me I think I'll be ready to call it a night."

"Sure thing, boss. You get patched up and go on home, don't worry about a thing."

"When we catch up with that Mexican, Marshal," said Peter, "what do you want us to do with him?"

"Haul him back here," Bob said through gritted teeth. "I want him to have a good look at how his two buddies made out and then we'll let him sit behind bars for a few days to think real hard on whether or not he wants to try his luck."

CHAPTER 17

Over breakfast the next morning, Consuela was still fretting and fussing about the damage to Bob's face and the close call he'd had at the hands of the ambushers. Both she and Bucky had been waiting anxiously when he got home the previous evening, so he'd already related to them the basics of what happened. As usual, he tried to downplay the danger aspect. But a couple of busybodies from town had gone on ahead and filled them in more graphically while Bob was being tended to by Doc Tibbs.

Bucky, though concerned for his father's well-being, was nevertheless enthralled by descriptions of the thunderous gunplay. And the resulting marks left on Bob's face, including a few stitches on his forehead to close up the bigger wounds, he saw as "battle scars" to be proudly displayed.

Bob felt pretty good when he left the house and headed down the slope toward town that morning. The stitches made it necessary to wear his hat pushed back a bit higher, but otherwise he had no particular discomfort from last night's activity.

At the marshal's office, he found Fred already present and a pot of coffee bubbling on the stove.

After exchanging good-mornings with his chief deputy, who usually came in a bit later, Bob said, "You're up and at 'em mighty early this morning."

"Figured it was a good idea. Wasn't sure how soon you'd get in or how you were gonna be feeling."

A corner of Bob's mouth lifted in a brief smile. "That's real thoughtful, Fred. But all I got were a few scratches to my face. Not that big a deal. Consuela has been fussing and trying to baby me all morning— I don't need any more, okay?"

"Okay, boss. Just trying to be helpful."

"I know. You always are." Bob went to the stove and poured himself some coffee. "You ready for a cup?" he asked Fred.

Fred made a dubious face. "Not yet, thanks. I haven't worked up enough courage yet. I expect it'll be as awful as always."

Bob crossed the room and sat down behind his desk, took a drink. "Yep. It is."

Fred hitched up a chair of his own. "Far as I know, Vern and Peter got off okay to try and track down that Mexican. They said they were gonna head out at first light."

"With any luck they should be back by noon," Bob said. "I hope so. Gafford is gonna start taking sign-ups for his shooting contest today and he plans on having those prize pistols on display while he's doing it. Sure to draw in some true marksmen, but also likely to draw the kind of riffraff who could cause trouble. We're all gonna need to keep a close eye on things to make sure none of it gets out of hand."

"You still thinking about entering?" Fred asked.

During dinner last night, Gafford had again brought up the prospect of the marshal participating in his contest.

"Yeah, I guess I am," Bob said with a resigned sigh. "Looks like I'm going to have to, the way Gafford keeps blabbing about it. Almost like a challenge I can't turn down."

"I'd be sorry to see you *not* try your luck. Heck, with you it ain't even really a matter of luck. You're flat-out one of the best shots around."

"Maybe. But there's plenty of other good marksmen around, too. For one, there's Vern. He's damn good with a rifle and I saw the way his eyes lit up last night when Gafford was talking about the contest."

"But I doubt he'd ever shoot against you," said Fred.

Bob frowned. "Why not? If he's got any reservations like that, I'll set him straight in a hurry. It's a contest open to everybody, may the best man win. And, as far as that goes, I've been so busy using a handgun lately that I haven't had much call to test my rifle skills. I'll have to fit in some target practice before the contest to make sure I'm not rusty as an old gate."

"I doubt you've lost your touch," said Fred. "But you're right about getting plenty of use out of your .44. And you dang sure haven't lost anything when it comes to that. If it was a pistol-shooting contest, nobody could touch you."

"Don't be so sure," Bob told him. "I saw Gafford's man Quirt in action last night—for which I've got to say I'm glad he was on hand. But my point is, just like

I told you at the train station, those .45s he packs ain't just for show. He knows how to use 'em plenty good."

"Well. Then it's lucky he's on our side, right?"

"Came in mighty handy last night," Bob allowed.

Fred shifted a little straighter in his chair. "Oh yeah. Something else about last night. While I was finishing up rounds, I did some more asking around about that notch-eared horse. I ran across an old prospector named Gibbs, who only comes into town once in a while, but he told me he thought he used to see a horse like that around the Red-Eyed Goat Saloon. And then I remembered—that's where I think I saw it, too. It used to be tied out back a lot of the time."

"Out back of the Red-Eyed Goat?"

"Uh-huh. There's a fella who sleeps back there, in the storeroom. Name's Merle Conroy. He's sort of a bouncer and handyman for Swede Simkins, who runs the place."

Bob nodded. "Sure, I know Conroy. Kind of a rough customer. The type who takes a little too much delight in pounding the hell out of the drunks he throws out of Swede's place. Not that Swede is much better."

"He's a foul-tempered cuss, that's for sure. Swede, I mean," said Fred. "When I went into the Goat last night to ask about Conroy or the horse, he got real belligerent and snotty. Said he wasn't Conroy's keeper, didn't know where he was, and for damn sure didn't know nothing about no stupid notch-eared horse. Then he went to bellyaching about me showing up wearing a badge and upsetting his customers, chasing away business."

"Not hard to see where the type of customers drawn to Swede's place could be a little skittish with a lawman in their midst," Bob said. "But I hope you didn't take no guff off him."

Fred waved a hand dismissively. "Nah. He's all mouth—unless him and Conroy are knocking around somebody too drunk to fight back. I stuck around and asked some more questions, just to irritate him. But nobody else in there was willing to tell me anything, either. So I left and went around back to do a little more poking around. I didn't see no horse, but the ground was trampled pretty good back there and I could definitely smell the leftover signs of a horse, if you know what I mean. I even poked my head into the storeroom and called Conroy's name. I didn't get no answer, so I didn't push it. But I got a hunch he might've been back there hiding."

"I got a hunch, too," said Bob. "And it tells me you're really onto something. Sounds to me like Swede was acting suspicious as hell. And, when you consider the Red-Eyed Goat is one of the most popular tent saloons on Gold Avenue, that makes it a prime candidate for losing business to the Crystal Diamond when it opens."

Fred's eyes widened. "Which makes Swede a prime candidate for *not wanting* the Crystal Diamond to open. And Conroy—who I believe the notch-eared palomino belongs to—works for Swede and does his dirty work . . . It all fits, don't it?"

"It sure as hell *could*," Bob responded. "We've just got to line the pieces up the right way and see if we can make 'em click into place. And, since we'll be spending time up on Gold Avenue today anyway, watching over the contest signing and the display of the prize guns, it'll give us a good chance to drop in on Swede again and see if we can't pin down the elusive Mr. Conroy."

Fred smiled. "I like the sound of that . . . a lot."

It was just short of noon when Peter and Vern Macy came riding back into town. They were leading a third horse, across whose back was tied the body of Chollo Raza, the round-faced Mexican who'd been with Jax and Reeves.

As they reined up in front of the jail building, Bob and Fred came out to greet them.

"We backtracked the way the other two came in and found him camped up in the foothills, just like you figured, Marshal," announced Vern.

"He acted cooperative at first," Peter added. "But then he made the fool move of going for a hideaway gun. Didn't leave us any choice but to kill him before he did one or both of us."

"Not much else you can do when they call the tune that way," said Bob. "Hate to say a man's life is no big loss, but him and his pards come as close as any. He made himself another customer for the undertaker. All that's left is to take him there."

Fred stepped forward. "I'll take care of that. You fellas have had a long morning in the saddle. Climb on down and stretch your legs, go inside and have a drink of cool water or maybe a cup of coffee."

"Much obliged, Fred," the Macy brothers said in almost perfect unison, something they had an eerie habit of frequently doing.

As Fred led the corpse-laden horse away, Bob called after him, "When you're done with that, Fred, go ahead and grab yourself some lunch. Then meet me over at the Crystal Diamond. I'll be hanging around out front where they're holding the contest signing."

"Will do, boss."

Turning to the Macys, Bob said, "How about you boys? Did you even take time for breakfast, let alone lunch?"

The brothers shook their heads. In unison. Then Peter added, "Though we did eat some biscuits and jerky on the ride out."

"Well, unless killing that Mexican upset your appetites—which it shouldn't, not for the likes of a varmint like him—then you need to get some vittles in you. So, after you've taken care of your horses, do like I told Fred and get yourself some lunch. Then come on down to the Crystal Diamond, too."

"You expecting trouble there, Marshal?" Vern asked.

"Could be. With those jeweled guns on display and a parade of gunmen being invited in, anything could happen. Plus we may have some related business nearby at the Red-Eyed Goat Saloon."

"Related? How?"

"Fred got a pretty good lead on the purchase of that coal oil that was used to douse the Crystal Diamond the other night. It's looking more and more like it traces to the Red-Eyed Goat."

"That ain't hard to believe. A pretty rough crowd hangs out there—you could find skunks capable of just about anything in that mix," said Peter.

Bob nodded. "I know. And we're aiming to smoke out a couple of 'em."

"We won't take long over lunch," said Vern. "We don't want to miss that."

"Speaking of not missing something, that reminds me," Bob said, locking his gaze on Vern. "You intend to enter that shooting contest, don't you?"

Vern looked caught off guard, maybe even a little startled. "Well, I . . . I hadn't made up my mind . . . I mean, I really haven't thought about it too much."

"Why not?"

"Well, I . . . That is, we . . . Peter and me, I mean, we got busy planning how we were gonna track that Mexican and all. There ain't been a whole lot of time."

"Gafford's only holding open the sign-up today and tomorrow," Bob reminded him. "And if he gets thirty entrants, which is the limit he set, he'll close it sooner than that. So if you've got a notion to enter, you'd better make up your mind."

"Yessir. I'll do that," Vern said.

Bob continued to eye him closely. "You wouldn't by chance have another notion, would you? A very silly one—like being reluctant to enter because you think it might make me sore to have you shoot against me?"

Vern had trouble meeting the marshal's gaze. "Well, I . . . ."

"You know what would really make me sore?" Bob cut in. And then, going ahead and answering his own question: "If, after all these months of working for me, you didn't know me any better than to think I might be small enough and petty enough to be bothered by something like that. *That* would chap my backside something fierce."

"You're right. Anybody who knows you oughta know better than that," said Peter, casting a stern look at his younger brother.

"That settles it, then. You're too good a shot not to enter that contest, Vern. You got enough money to cover the entry fee?"

Peter spoke up again. "I told him I'd chip in to help him cover it."

Scowling, Bob said, "It's still two weeks to payday. If it's gonna run you tight, I'll tell you what—I'll advance you the twenty-five bucks. In fact, I'll go ahead and cover it when I sign myself up. Then all you've got to do is put down your name and square with me when you do get paid." He paused and flashed a lopsided grin. "Of course, if you win that fancy gun, then my interest rate on the loan is apt to go up considerable."

Vern grinned, too. "Thanks, Marshal. If I'm lucky enough to win, you can bet I'll pay you back with interest."

CHAPTER 18

"Look at 'em down there. Swarmin' around that fancy-pants blowhard like bees buzzin' around honey." Swede Simkins's voice rasped bitterly. The bitterness in his tone was matched by the glint in his narrowed eyes as he glared down the street toward the crowd gathered before the Crystal Diamond Saloon. "What's so damned interesting about gettin' a peek at some jeweled pistols that are probably fake and can't even shoot anyway, and watchin' a handful of suckers sign up for a shootin' contest? Come around here on a Saturday night—or practically any other night, as far as that goes—and you can see your fill of shootin' for free."

"Might be gettin' a gander at those fancy guns that's drawin' 'em to begin with," said Merle Conroy. "But what's causin' most of those slack-jaws to stick around is the leg show bein' put on by those dance hall gals. That and the free beer Gafford's offerin' for as long as his keg holds out."

"Warm beer out of a keg sittin' in the noontime sun and some fat ankles bein' kicked up by three over-the-hill crotch teasers," grumbled Swede. "If that's what has got those idiots so het up, then there's more lunkheads around these parts than I ever figured. And it ain't like I reckoned brains as bein' in high supply hereabouts to begin with."

The two men were standing out front of the oversized tent that housed Swede's Red-Eyed Goat Saloon. Conroy was leaning against the signpost hung with a shingle bearing the name in sloppily painted letters. The heavy canvas flaps that served as a doorway to the establishment were open wide and pinned back, exposing an interior totally devoid of customers.

"Lucky for us it ain't brains what leads a body to drink," Conroy said. "It's a parched throat and a cravin' in the gut."

"Is it lucky for us that there ain't a blasted soul in here drinkin' at the height of the noon hour?" snapped Swede. "And where do you get off with that 'us' crap anyway? Are you the one with thousands of dollars stuck in a supply of liquor that all of a sudden ain't goin' down nobody's throats?"

"No. Not hardly. You've always run that part, the organizin' and the money, Swede," said Conroy. "But I been with you for such a long time that I just kinda think of what we got going as . . . well, *us*."

"Yeah, we've been together for a long time," Swede muttered. "Maybe long enough. Maybe too damn long."

"Aw, you don't really mean that."

"The hell I don't. You and that stupid horse and that stubborn fat deputy are really puttin' the screws to me. Bad enough I got this Gafford puke threatenin' to run me out of business, now I got to worry about the law comin' down on me."

"You'll outfox 'em, Swede. You always do."

Swede's jaw muscles visibly bunched and unbunched. "Even the slyest fox gets run down sooner or later. I ain't so worried about Gafford and his fancy show saloon. If I have to, I got tricks that slickster ain't never heard of to put the run on him. That lard-assed deputy is the one who troubles me more. I don't figure him showin' up last night was the end of it. He's bound to come around again."

"So what? He can't prove nothing. Not now that you made me . . . now that I got rid of ol' Sol." Conroy's expression took on the weight of sadness. "I'll stay out of his way as long as I can. And if he does corner me, we've got our story all made up, right? I sold Sol quite a while back to some farmer I don't remember the name of."

Swede scowled. "As long as you stick to that we should be okay. But if Deputy Fred ever gets around to bringin' the marshal with him, there's where the real pressure, the real test, will come. He's the one you got to watch out for, Merle. You can't let him trick you or make you fold."

"He won't, Swede. I know a few tricks of my own." Conroy's expression hardened. "Everybody's heard how he slipped out of that ambush last night. But that don't mean he can always be so lucky."

Swede's scowl turned into something resembling a smile but was really more akin to a wolf showing its fangs before the snarl escapes its throat. "That's the kind of talk I like to hear. The kind of thing that makes me feel better about knowing I can still count on you."

"You shouldn't ever doubt that, Swede," said Conroy. Then, sensing movement farther back up the street, he turned his head and looked that way. After a moment, a smile formed on his own lips. "Look yonder. Here comes something else that oughta help you feel better. Moses Shaw and his sons are ridin' into town. You know dang well that some serious drinkin' is gonna get done in the Goat tonight, now that they're here."

"Yeah," said Swede, looking not quite so elated. "Thing is, like usual when they show up, you just gotta hope they don't kill any of the other customers before they pass out."

CHAPTER 19

As he approached the Crystal Diamond, Bob was surprised to see how many people appeared to be gathered for the contest signing. He'd expected a fair number of gawkers coming by to look at the jeweled guns, mixed with a trickle of others interested in trying their luck as marksmen, but that was about it.

Drawing closer, he saw the crowd equaled or possibly exceeded that which had shown up at the railroad station yesterday. Spotting the keg of beer being freely distributed by Oliver Pruitt and hearing the plunk of Lyle Levitt's banjo accompanying the voices and tapping feet of Alora Dane and the Diamond Dollies, Bob began to understand what was attracting such a turnout.

A temporary platform of fresh timber had been constructed over the front steps of the Crystal Diamond. On one edge was propped the beer keg that Pruitt was manning. On the ground in front sat a small wooden table with the sign-up sheet and entry fee box for the contest placed upon it. At the other edge of the platform was the propped-open case holding the jeweled guns. And, in the center of the makeshift stage, the dazzling, smiling song-and-dance ladies were exhibiting a preview of their beauty and talent.

Bob walked up to the signing table. Angus Mc-Teague, who would be serving as one of the judges for the shooting, sat behind it on a wooden chair. Mc-Teague was a big, beefy man in his forties who still showed the rough edges from working his way up the hard way while at the same time showing some of the refinements, mainly in the way he dressed, from his recent successes. As one of the earliest and hardest-working men to go after the gold in the Prophecy Mountains, McTeague came out the wealthiest man in Rattlesnake Wells. He was now the head of the New Town miner's council and owner-operator of three current mines where others, but not McTeague, broke sweat. Yet he remained a down-to-earth sort, well liked around town, with a reputation for being strict but fair to his employees.

"Afternoon, Marshal," he greeted. "Been expecting you to show up."

Bob grinned. "If I'd known this sign-up was going to be such a big shindig, I would've come around sooner."

"Gafford seems to find a way to squeeze attention out of practically everything he does, at least as far as it relates to the opening of this saloon," said Mc-Teague. "I've been up in the mountains tending my mines for the past few days yet his name and talk of the Crystal Diamond was on practically every tongue, even up there."

"I can believe that."

McTeague arched a wiry brow. "Which is not to say, I might add, that your name and the escapades of you and your deputies over the past few days didn't go undiscussed, either. I got back into town late last night and practically the first thing to reach my ears was an account of the attempt on your life only a short time earlier. I see by your face that some of the details I heard weren't exaggerated. You've been a very busy fella."

"Yeah, I kinda noticed," remarked Bob. "Wouldn't break my heart to be unbusy for a spell."

"You think this shooting contest and Gafford's grand opening are going to lend themselves to that?"

"Don't you?"

McTeague's shoulders rose and fell in a fatalistic shrug. "Gonna be a lot of activity attracting a lot of people. Could be a breeding ground for some interesting things to happen. Especially"—he reached out and tapped a thick forefinger on the sign-up sheet—"considering some of the sterling individuals it has already drawn."

Bob leaned closer to take a look at where he was pointing. He was surprised to see a dozen names already on the list. The one where McTeague's finger was tapping wasn't so much surprising as disconcerting.

"Moses Shaw," he read aloud.

"Yep. Him and his whole sorry clan—all three sons," McTeague confirmed. "Not a damn bit less scruffy-looking or any more cordial than they ever are when they come to town."

"Sorta surprised they didn't all enter," said Bob. "Living out half-wild like they do on that pathetic excuse for a horse ranch, talk is they're all crack shots when it comes to hunting and providing for themselves."

"But Moses is the one—according to him at least—who was the decorated sharpshooter in the war," Mc Teague reminded him. "He gets a little liquor in him, there's no end to his laments about how he practically won the war by himself and then had his country turn a cold shoulder after the fightin' was done. His tale of woe never ends or never changes. And, like a lot of born losers, if he showed half as much ambition as he shows sorrow for himself, his lot in life could be way better."

"Yeah. The sad part is that his kind seldom changes," said Bob. "And he's got a ready-made audience to listen to all his woes in those three boys. Since that old Indian squaw who raised 'em took a notion to up and die, they don't have either the sense or ambition of their own to look up to nobody else."

"I've always kinda wondered what happened to Moses's first wife, the birth mother to those boys."

"Hate to think."

"Yeah, ain't that the truth."

Bob straightened up and turned his head to the left and then to the right, scanning faces in the surrounding crowd. "The Shaws didn't stick around after the old man signed up? Not even for some of that free beer?"

"Nope," said McTeague. "They bulled their way in close, shouldered everybody back while Moses signed and paid, then bulled their way back out. Moses told everybody in earshot that he didn't ride all the way into town for no stinkin' beer, he wanted some double-rectified busthead."

"Let me guess. Him and the boys headed straight for the Red-Eyed Goat."

"I didn't see for sure. But I expect so, yeah. That's where they usually hang out when they come to town. Moses and that ornery old Swede are about the only two that can stand each other. Two peas in a pod."

"Two crooks in a crack, is more like it," Bob muttered.

"How's that?"

"Aw, I probably shouldn't say," Bob grumbled, suddenly feeling surly for no particular reason. "But those two scoundrels have always rubbed me the wrong way. I know—leastways I got a hunch digging into me like a shovel—that neither one of 'em is on the up-and-up. But I'm blamed if I can ever catch 'em at anything so's I can prove it."

"You mean like Moses and his boys venturing south to hit the occasional stagecoach or rustle a few head of cattle here and there?"

"Those are the stories, yeah. They come to town—not all that often, thank God—and they're rowdy and rude and loud, and we've had to jail one or two of 'em overnight a couple times for being drunk and disorderly. But they've never broken any serious laws here in Rattlesnake Wells. I guess I ain't supposed to worry about what they do outside my jurisdiction. But I do. I don't like having 'em come around my town, not even once in a while, with the stink of law-breakin' on 'em."

McTeague smiled. "The law dog in you barks loud,

my friend. Which is, I'll quickly add, to the benefit of our town."

"Yeah. Well, Swede Simkins and his shithole of a saloon fill my nose with the same stink." Bob's jaw muscles clenched. "Reckon I'd be benefiting the town even more if I could find a way to get the goods on him."

"Maybe Gafford's success will fold his tent for you."

"You never know," said Bob, his expression suddenly relaxing. "Something might come up even before then."

McTeague gave him a questioning look. But before he could ask anything further, Bob leaned back over the sign-up sheet, saying, "Reckon I'd best go ahead and get my name down without wasting any more time."

After he'd written his own name, he made a small *x* on the space below it, explaining, "There'll be a young fella along in a little bit, one of my deputies, to finish filling that in. So his place is held. I'll go ahead and pay his entry now, along with mine."

"Good," said McTeague. "That takes us almost halfway to our thirty entrants already. Looks like it's gonna be a real good turnout."

As he pulled a handful of bills from his pocket and stuffed the proper amount into the deposit box, Bob scanned the rest of the names on the list. He knew most of them, but not all. "Appears to be a pretty good mix."

"Uh-huh. A real interesting one."

Bob's mouth pulled into a tight, straight line. "Long as it don't get *too* doggone interesting."

"Reckon that's in the hand of fate . . . along with you and your deputies."

"We'll hold up our end. Let's hope fate does the same."

"One way that might help you hold some sway over fate—at least as far as shooting results—is to make sure you've got yourself sharp and ready." McTeague pointed to a stack of papers on one end of the table. "Those are paper targets, duplicates of the ones that will be used in the contest. You're welcome to grab a handful if you want to take 'em and do some practicing."

"Not a bad idea," said Bob, helping himself to several of the papers.

CHAPTER 20

"Marshal! There you are! I've been on the lookout for you all morning!"

Apparently noticing Bob for the first time as the banjo playing and singing and dancing reached an intermission, August Gafford came hurrying over from the edge of the platform where he'd been hovering near the display of prize pistols. In his wake, the guns hardly went unattended. A stone-faced Simon Quirt and another somber, competent-looking gent whom Bob took to be the Cecil Yates Quirt had mentioned the previous evening, stood close on either side of the propped-open case.

"Good Lord, look at your face," exclaimed Gafford as he reached the marshal. "Quirt gave me a detailed account of the occurrences from last night and I see now he wasn't exaggerating one bit. We heard all the shooting from inside the hotel but I thought it best to stay put and make sure the ladies remained safe."

Bob nodded. "That was good thinking. And if it wasn't for an assist from your man Quirt, by the way, I might be carrying around some unwanted lead instead of just a few splinter cuts. I expect he's the type who may have downplayed that part a mite."

As he said this, Bob caught Quirt glancing his way, and so touched a finger to the brim of his hat, snapping it away in a kind of salute. Quirt acknowledged with a faint tip of his head but his expression showed nothing, and then his gaze returned to scanning the crowd.

"Yes. Yes, Quirt did mention that he got involved a bit in that terrible ambush attempt on your life," Gafford replied. "If he was of value to you, then I'm glad. That's wonderful. But what he talked about the most and was clearly impressed by—and this is from someone, I assure you, who is not easily impressed and even less likely to indicate such—was the way you rushed out to the street practically into the teeth of a shotgun blast!"

"It was *after* a shotgun blast, when I knew the shooter would need some reloading time," said Bob. "No need to make it out more than it was."

"That's our Sundown Bob for you," interjected McTeague wryly. "He don't allow no dressing-up of what he considers only doing his job. And, by the way he's glaring at me right now, I'm reminded that he also doesn't like being called 'Sundown Bob.'"

"Well, he's certainly earned the right to that courtesy, then," Gafford said. "But the bravery and vigor with which he and his men attack danger and threats to the community—that can hardly be overlooked."

Now Bob adopted his own wry tone as he said, "Keep right on talking, Mr. Gafford. You keep building me up like that, you're apt to convince me that me and my deputies are worth a lot more money. That'd mean a tax increase on the local businesses."

"Surely, Gafford," McTeague said, "you've learned by now how stories about daring gunplay and so forth get very exaggerated out here in the Wild West. Haven't you?"

Gafford held up his hands, palms out, in a gesture of surrender. "Thank you for reminding me, McTeague. As the good marshal suggested, let's not make more out of it than it was."

The three men shared a good laugh over the exchange.

Further discussion was held at bay by the approach of a tall, lanky man, fiftyish, with a weather-seamed face and wearing a buckskin shirt. "Excuse me, gents," he said in soft Virginia drawl, "but is this where one signs up for the shooting contest?"

Bob and Gafford stepped to one side and McTeague motioned the newcomer forward. "You bet it is, mister. Come right ahead and put down your name or make your mark. There is, I expect you know, a twenty-five-dollar entry fee."

The lanky man nodded as he moved the rest of the way forward. "Understood." In his left hand he casually held a Winchester '73 rifle. On his left hip, in a cross-draw holster hanging from a wide leather belt, rode a Schofield revolver. A bone-handled bowie was sheathed on the opposite hip. A well-worn war bag, buckskin fringed and designed with Indian beads, hung over his right shoulder, held there by a scarred, knuckly fist.

Leaning his rifle against the front edge of the table, the man swung down his war bag and from it withdrew a leather pouch tied with a thong. From this he extracted some neatly folded bills and held them out to McTeague. "Count it if you like."

McTeague shook his head. "Looks right to me. Go ahead and put it in the box. Then mark yourself down on the list."

As the lanky man put pencil to paper, Bob leaned in a little closer and watched him write *Ben Eames* in a neat, slightly cramped script.

Taking back the pencil that Eames held out to him, McTeague said, "Welcome to our little contest, Mr. Eames. Thank you for participating."

"Pleasure's mine. Just like it will be to take those fancy gold guns off your hands," Eames replied.

"Never hurts to be confident," said McTeague. "You look as though you've had that Winchester to your shoulder a time or two."

"You could say that," Eames allowed.

Gafford stepped forward and extended his hand. "Allow me to introduce myself, sir. I am August Gafford. I am the owner and soon-to-be operator—as soon as we have our grand opening, that is—of this fine establishment we are gathered in front of. I also conceived and organized the contest you've just entered and, as Mr. McTeague told you, we are grateful to all you participants who are coming forward to make it a smashing success."

Eames took the hand and gave Gafford's arm a vigorous pumping.

As the saloon owner retrieved his hand, wincing though trying not to show it, he said, "Perhaps you'd like to meet one of your competitors, who also happens to be the marshal of our fair city . . . Mr. Eames, Marshal Bob Hatfield."

Bob shook the lanky man's hand and it was quickly evident why Gafford had pulled his paw back the way he did. Eames clamped on with a firm, bone-crunching grip. Bob was always prepared for such tests, though, so he made sure to give as good as he got. The thing that caught him by surprise was how soft Eames's palm was, not nearly as rough and calloused as he would have expected.

"Passed near here a few years back when your town wasn't but a speck, just a handful of buildings," Eames said. "You've done a powerful lot of growing in the time since then."

"That's how a gold boom will change things. Some ways for the better, some ways not so much." Bob regarded him more closely. "If you don't mind my saying, I don't recall seeing you around before. You just passing through again?"

Eames smiled. "Am for a fact. Back when your town was just a speck, it was already too big for me. Size it is now, it for sure ain't my cup of tea. I mostly like keeping to myself, you see. I'm on my way down out of the Snowy Range, where I keep an old cabin and spend some time now and then in the warm months. On my way back to Kansas to hole up for the winter. When I heard about this contest and the prize of those guns, it occurred to me that if I could win 'em and then sell 'em off again, well"—Eames's mouth spread in a wide, sly grin—"I might could afford me a little tonier winter digs than what I originally had in mind."

"Sounds like a reasonable plan to shoot for," said Bob.

"The marshal here is one of the men you'll be shooting against," Gafford informed Eames. "You'll most likely find him among your toughest competition."

"That's all right. I'll do my best to see that he finds me the same. The shooting's on Friday, right? I'll be camping a ways out until then. You'll see me back in town on Friday."

McTeague pointed to the stack of papers on the end of the table. "We've got duplicate copies there of the targets that will be used in the contest. You're welcome to take some, if you like, for personal target practice."

Reaching for his Winchester, Eames said, "If I ain't got this baby sighted in by now, don't reckon a few pieces of paper are gonna gain me much." With that, the man in buckskin picked up the rifle, slung his war bag over his shoulder, turned, and threaded his way out through the crowd until he was gone from sight.

"Rather strange one, wouldn't you say?" remarked Gafford, watching him go.

"Strange enough, I reckon. But if he's the worst this shindig draws, I figure we'll be getting off lucky," Bob said.

Forty minutes later, Fred and the Macy brothers had shown up at the Crystal Diamond. They were in time to catch the last couple minutes of the final preview show scheduled to be put on by Alora Dane and her performing troupe for that day. To Bob's surprise and relief, his men watched the closing number, applauded heartily, gazed longingly as the ladies left the makeshift stage . . . and that was it. Despite the display of leggy high kicks meant to titillate and reveal considerably more in the way of feminine curves than had been present the previous evening at dinner, the deputies showed no sign of being thunderstruck like before.

Bob had no idea what to attribute this to. What was more, he decided not even to bring it up for fear of jarring the trio out of whatever had brought on this sterner behavior and causing them to revert back to the way they'd been acting last night.

Once the beer keg was empty and the preview shows were done, the crowd began to thin out. There was still some novelty left at getting a gander at the prize guns, but not that much. Two more entrants had signed up for the shooting contest by the time Vern filled in the blank left for his name, making a total of seventeen. For the first day of sign-ups, it was a turnout Gafford seemed very content with.

With reduced activity now in front of the Crystal Diamond and an early afternoon lull seeming to have settled over Old Town, Bob gathered his men around him and said, "I think this is as good a time as any to do some squeezing on the Red-Eyed Goat Saloon and see if we can't get some rats to pop out and reveal themselves. What do you say?"

"You know you're not gonna get any argument out of me, boss," said Fred.

"Just say the word," said Peter.

"All you got to do is tell us how you want to play it," added Vern.

"Fred is the one who sniffed this out to begin with. I figure it's only right for him to take the lead," Bob said. "The three of you march right in the front. I'll hold back. Fred, you start firing accusations and asking questions. Tell Swede you know about the notch-eared horse, that you know it belongs to Merle Conroy, and that everybody knows Conroy hops to Swede's bidding. Not to sound boastful, but I don't think Swede or whoever else is around will show you the same respect they would if I was there with you. I'm hoping they'll act a little nervy, maybe run their mouths a little carelessly. When I think the time is right, I'll show up."

"Sounds good to me," said Fred. "Let's go do some Goat herding."

CHAPTER 21

"What the hell's the big idea?" snarled Swede Simkins when he saw Fred walking toward where he was drawing a pitcher of beer behind the Red-Eyed Goat's bar, which amounted to a pair of thick planks nailed side by side and stretched over the tops of some upended wooden barrels.

With the breakup of the crowd down by the Crystal Diamond, a handful of customers had found their way into the tent saloon. Moses Shaw and his sons were seated at a large round table on one side of the room, and the other occupants were leaving a cautious space around them. Three men were bellied up to the bar; three more sat at a small table with one side jammed against a canvas wall. Cigarette and cigar smoke hung in the air in thick layers, and the low rumble of voices was coarse and sullen.

Swede continued his lament. "You figure to show up here every day and harass me in front of my paying customers? You got no reason and no right to do that. It ain't even legal, is it?"

Peter and Vern fanned out a few paces behind

Fred and came to a halt, standing still and quiet, feet planted wide.

Fred kept walking until his ample belly bumped against the edge of the plank bartop, sloshing some of the foam out of the pitcher.

"Who says I'm here to harass you, Swede? You got a guilty conscience or something?" Fred said in an easy drawl.

Swede scowled. "Why else would you be coming around?"

"Why, Swede. You're selling yourself short." Fred made a wide-sweeping gesture with one hand. "I mean, you got to face it, man. This is a warm, friendly place you got here. The atmosphere, the charm. Not to mention you and that bubbly personality of yours that makes a body feel right at home. Is it so hard to believe I'm coming back around just because I enjoy it so?"

"Yeah, it is hard to believe. You think I don't know when somebody's pulling my leg?"

Fred grunted out a short laugh and then turned momentarily to the Macy brothers. "You hear that, fellas? There's that keen wit and good-natured sense of humor I told you about."

"Yeah, I bet he's a real hoot when you get him going," said Peter.

"Anybody can see that," added Vern.

"Hey, Swede," called one of the three men from the table over against the wall. "You gonna bring that pitcher of beer over here before it goes all the way flat, or what?"

"Get up off your lazy, drunk ass and come get it if you're in such a big hurry," Swede hollered back.

"And don't forget to bring your money to pay for it, else you'll be making an extra trip."

"What the hell," grumbled the man. "What happened to your fetch-it boy, Merle? He brought us our last pitcher."

"Well, nobody's bringing you this one," Swede was quick to say. "Not unless I come and bust it over your complainin' head. I do that, it'll cost you double—for the beer and for the pitcher, too."

The saloon man seemed to think this was very amusing. He issued a growling laugh and raked his eyes across the men lined up at the bar, almost daring them *not* to laugh along with him. He got a few weak guffaws for his trouble.

Meanwhile, the drunk demanding the pitcher got to his feet and stumbled over to claim it. He tossed some coins on the plank, seized the pitcher in both hands, turned jerkily back toward his pals. The first lurching steps he took caused the beer to slosh violently and wet the front of his already greasily stained shirt.

"Careful you don't spill too much. You'll ruin the wax job on my floor," Swede called after him. Then he snorted out another garbled laugh, the joke being that a wax sheen on the hard-packed dirt floor of the Goat was about as likely as a pair of polished new boots on a coyote.

When he cut his gaze back to Fred, the smile fell from Swede's mouth and his eyes hardened. "All right, let's quit dancing around it, law dog. What are you looking for?"

"Same thing as the last time I was here, and the time before that," Fred responded flatly. "I want to know about that notch-eared palomino horse that used to be tied behind your place all the time. And I want to talk to your hired man, Merle Conroy, who I have reason to think the horse belongs to."

"You can see for yourself that Merle ain't here," Swede sneered. "Matter of fact, I ain't seen him since you was here last night. Far as I know, maybe the damn fool did something that's giving him cause to avoid the law. Though I wouldn't know anything about that, a-course. Just like I don't know nothing about that stupid horse you keep asking after."

"Conroy don't ride a palomino?"

"I don't know *what* kind of nag he rides. Or even if he has a horse at all. When he's in here working for me—which he's supposed to be doing right now, in case anybody'd like to know—he ain't exactly galloping around on a horse."

Fred frowned. "If you ain't seen Conroy in two nights yet he's supposed to be here at work now . . . that makes you kinda lax with your hired help, don't it?"

Swede spread his hands. "What can I say? I'm a pretty easygoing fella. Merle's been with me a long time. If he ain't showing up, he must have a good reason. Maybe he's sick." Swede's mouth spread in a lewd grin. "Or maybe one of the whore cribs up the line has got a new girl and he's fallen in love."

From behind Fred, Peter said, "Didn't this old drunk over here with the pitcher of beer say, just a minute ago, that Conroy brought him and his pals their first pitcher? How can that be if Conroy hasn't been around for so long?"

"Hey, hold on a minute," Swede protested. "How

many different questions do I gotta answer from
how many different badge-toters?"

"As long as there's a badge pinned to it," said Fred,
"you'll answer whatever's asked of you. If you're
smart, that is."

"Is that supposed to be a threat?" Swede's eyes
blazed. "I'm supposed to be intimidated by a fat slob
and a still-wet-behind-the-ears punk?"

"Like I said, only if you're smart. And if you know
what's good for you," Fred told him.

Swede licked his lips. "Can't you see that old drunk
don't know one day from another? Sure, maybe
Merle *did* serve him a pitcher of beer at some point.
But that could have been from the last time he was in
here. Or the time before that. In his alcohol-mushed
old brain it's all run together."

"How about I ask the old-timer for myself? See if
he's as brain-pickled as you claim," said Peter.

"Aw, whyn't you leave the poor old geezer alone?"
wailed Swede. "You can see he's drunk."

"Drunk don't mean addled permanent-like,"
argued Fred. "Go ahead, Peter, ask him if Conroy's
been in here lately."

"He ain't been, I tell you," Swede said anxiously.
"I ought to know what goes on in my own place,
oughtn't I?"

Before anybody could respond to that and before
Peter made it over to address the old drunk seated
at the side table, there was a commotion from behind
the canvas flap hanging down behind Swede, a curtain of sorts that separated the bar area from the
storage area at the rear of the tent. The meaty smack
of a fist striking flesh and bone rang out clearly.

An instant later, Merle Conroy hurtled backward out through a floor-to-ceiling slit in the canvas and crashed against the plank bar, nearly dislodging it from the barrel tops it rested across. The three men on the customer side of the bar jumped back, grabbing frantically to save the drinks poured before them. Swede grabbed just as frantically, managing just barely to keep the planks from tipping off and tumbling to the ground.

Immediately following the flailing Conroy came Marshal Bob Hatfield, stepping through the slit opening and reaching to grab Conroy before he had any chance to regain his balance. The marshal jerked him upright and shook him like a rag doll.

"What the hell's going on?" shouted Swede.

"We got a situation here that amounts to one of two things," Bob said through clenched teeth. Conroy hung loosely in his grasp, head lolling, fighting for consciousness from the blow everyone had heard, evidenced by a split lip with a trickle of blood running from it. "Since I just found this rat lurking behind that curtain," Bob continued, "I figure—since you claim not to know about him being anywhere close by, Swede—he must either have been looking to steal something . . . or, you're a low-down stinking liar and you knew he was back there all the time and the two of you were conniving to keep him out of sight in order to avoid talking to my deputies."

"How was I supposed to know he was back there?" Swede sputtered. "I ain't got eyes in the back of my head, do I?"

"No," Bob said, "and you don't have very many

brains inside that melon, either, if you think you can keep lying to the law."

"I don't know what you're talking about," Swede insisted.

Bob cut his eyes to Peter and gave a jerk of his chin. "Go ahead. Ask your questions of the old gent at that table. Find out if he saw Conroy in here just before we showed up."

The three men who'd been standing at the bar started to slink for the door. Bob stopped them short with a command of, "Hold it right there!"

Fred stepped in front of the trio to make sure they got the message. "How about you fellas?" he asked. "Can you do anything with those mealy mouths except suck down cheap whiskey? Did you know Conroy was in here and hiding behind that flap all the time I was asking about him?"

"You don't have to answer him, boys," Swede advised them. "He don't have no right to badger you that way and you got every right to have a few drinks in peace and quiet."

"How much peace and quiet anybody gets while they're in my town," Bob cut in, "is sorta up to me and my men. One of the places you got a good chance to get some, though, is behind bars in our jail. And one of the ways you got a good chance of ending up there is if I think you're withholding information in a legal investigation."

One of the three men hung his head and then rolled his eyes to look plaintively up at Bob. "Please, Marshal, we don't want to get caught in the middle of nothing. We just came in here to have a couple drinks and mind our own business. Honest, we wasn't really payin' much attention to—"

"*I* been payin' attention," interrupted a loud voice from across the room. "Me and my boys been lookin' on and listenin' the whole while . . . and not likin' worth a damn what we're seein' or hearin'."

CHAPTER 22

Bob turned his head and looked over at Moses Shaw.

"If you got something worthwhile to add to this," he said, "we'd be happy to hear what you've got to say. So we'll get to you in a minute. But first give us a chance to finish questioning these other men."

Moses shook his head. "No. That ain't the way it's gonna work. What I got to say I ain't gonna wait on. What's more, I ain't gonna be hoppin' to answer a bunch of your questions. What I'm gonna do is *tell* you a thing or two."

"Pop, maybe we oughta just stay out of this," said his middle son, Cyrus, a bit uneasily.

"You hush up," advised his older brother, Harley. "If Pop's got a piece to speak, best be lettin' him do it."

Moses stood up, glaring at Bob. "This ain't the first time me and my boys have come to town and run tangleways of you, Marshal. Seems like you and that fat deputy find a reason to plant yourselves in our way practically every time. And now there's even more of you, what with these two new pups I ain't ever saw before, puffin' out their chests with badges pinned on 'em. You're actin' more and more too big for your britches, and it's gettin' plumb tiresome, if you ask me."

"Nobody did," Bob reminded him calmly. "And if you button your lip pretty damn quick, there's a chance that maybe—just maybe—me and my big britches won't have to stomp all over you and your brood. My men and me are here about a matter that I don't think involves you, not unless you push it."

"That's exactly what I'm fixin' to do," growled Moses. "What you're up to involves me on account of it's interruptin' my drinkin' and carousin' . . . something me and my boys have been lookin' forward to for a good long spell."

"Then I suggest you go somewhere else to do it, and stay out of my way," Bob told him.

Moses's head wagged slowly back and forth. "Nope. We're settled here to get the ball rollin', and here's where we aim to stay until *we* say it's time to go. The only thing that leaves is for you and your star-packin' nancies to prance off. You can come back and bother Swede some other time, when we ain't around and you're not botherin' us in the bargain. Or try to root us out of the way now, if you think you got the stones for it."

Vern, who was standing closest to the Shaw table, turned to Bob with a bright flush of anger filling his face. "I don't stand by and take that kind of talk off nobody, Marshal. Either you give the word for it—or I'm wading in by myself!"

"And he won't be by himself for very long," said Peter.

Bob hesitated. This wasn't what they were here for. It was both unwise and unprofessional to be goaded by a pack of lowlifes like the Shaws. But Moses and his sons had been a thorn in Bob's side for a long time. His mind flashed to an old saying his father used to fall back on when he was too quick and too harsh to punish a rambunctious young Bob and then would have some regrets afterward. *"Well, I don't reckon it was a lick amiss,"* he'd say, trying to console himself.

Even if tangling with the Shaws wasn't really what they'd come here for, Bob decided, he didn't reckon it would be a lick amiss if that's what it came to.

"To hell with it," he said through clenched teeth. "Let's do some wading!"

Just that quick, the fight was on.

The Shaw brothers rose to their feet as one. They tipped over the table they'd been seated around, shoved it ahead of them, and came boiling around the ends.

Vern adroitly dodged to one side, causing the table to miss him. And then, cocking his fist as he rushed forward, he timed it perfectly so that the right cross he threw crashed solidly against the jaw of Wiley Shaw, landing the first punch of the fight. Wiley staggered back and might have lost his footing if he hadn't fallen into the grasp of his father, who held him up.

Fred wasn't quite able to move his bulk quickly enough to get out of the way of the skidding table. It banged against his knees and thighs. The contact made him teeter on the brink of being taken off balance for a couple seconds. But he held his ground and, in the end, gave a shove with his knee that sent the table skidding back several inches.

Trouble was, his skirmish with the table occupied Fred just long enough for Cyrus Shaw to lean in and bounce a bony fist off his chin followed by a left to his stomach. Even putting all his weight behind the punches, however, didn't provide much impact for the slight Cyrus—especially not against the substantial anchor presented by Fred. In response, the latter uncorked a whooshing backhand that landed with a meaty *splat!* Cyrus was spun around like a top, turning a full 360 degrees and sent staggering backward.

By that point, the stocky Harley had launched himself at Bob before the marshal was completely untangled from the still-groggy Conroy. The oldest Shaw son was an experienced brawler who knew how to put power into his punches so that they drilled in deep and were packed with hurt. Bob took a hard bang to the ribs and then an uppercut that damn near snapped his head off his shoulders before he was able to tie up Harley's arms and drag him into a clinch. Bob hung on tight, sucking for wind from the blow to the ribs and at the same time trying to quiet the bells the uppercut had set to ringing inside his head.

While Bob and Harley lurched back and forth, each struggling to gain advantage over the other, Peter ran from the farthest point opposite where the Shaws had been seated and made a running dive to land in the middle of the knot of bodies that had formed when Moses and Wiley had surged back to gang up on Vern. He succeeded in breaking apart the knot, each man splitting away, wobbly on their feet but nobody going down. And then, like pieces of a lodestone jumping back together, each party involved—four of them now—sprang inward again and began furiously raining blows on one another.

While that was going on, the three men who'd been standing at the bar made a successful bolt out the door. And the other trio, the ones sitting at the small table with the laboriously acquired pitcher of beer, dropped low and made their own exit by scrambling on hands and knees out under the bottom edge of the tent wall. The half-emptied pitcher of beer was left behind like an abandoned old friend.

Behind the precariously tilted plank bar, Swede was holding Conroy upright and trying to snap him out of the last of his grogginess. "Come on, man, get your damn head cleared," he urged. "This is your chance to make a break."

Conroy looked around blearily at the brawl spilling back and forth across the middle of the room. "Shouldn't we be helping them . . . the Shaws, I mean?" he mumbled.

Swede shook his head. A kind of sadness settled over his face and crept into his voice. "No. I fear the jig is up for us. I've been through this kind of thing before. The best we can hope for now is to stay out of jail—which is where those fool Shaws are surely headed. Otherwise, it's time to throw the key in the water bucket and kick the dirt from this town off our boot heels for good. At least we should be able to get away with enough to start over again somewhere else."

An even deeper sadness tugged at Conroy's face.

"Too bad there ain't one more thing we could be takin' with us."

"What's that?"

"Ol' Sol . . . I sure wish you'd've let me keep him, Swede."

In the meantime, the brawl was beginning to show some signs of running out of steam.

The Macy brothers were still trading blows with Moses and Wiley at a frantic pace. But sixty-year-old Moses was showing some definite fatigue, his shoulders slumping, his counterpunches coming slower and with less pop. A cut over Wiley's left eye was affecting his vision to the point where he was taking nearly two blows to every one he threw, and the latter were landing far less effectively than they had been earlier.

Ever since Fred's shattering backhand had rattled young Cyrus to his very core, the conflict between the two of them had amounted to something that resembled a game of keep-away more than an actual fight—with Cyrus ducking and dodging this way and that in order to keep out of the crushing grasp of the lumbering Fred.

The clinch Bob had locked in with Harley turned out to be something neither man wanted to release for fear of opening himself up to a punishing blow on the break. Finally, Harley made the mistake of momentarily exposing his face when he lifted his bullet head from the way he'd been keeping it tucked low and grinding against Bob's throat. Bob, taller by nearly five inches, took full advantage by slamming downward with his forehead and crashing it hard onto the bridge of Harley's nose. Harley yelped painfully. At the same time, Bob felt cartilage flatten and turn to pulp as hot blood gushed out the nostrils of the ruined nose and poured down over the marshal's cheeks.

Shoving Harley back a ragged step and a half, Bob immediately threw a roundhouse right followed an instant later by hard left. Blood flew from the bloody lump that used to be Harley's nose each time his head whipped to one side or the other. Stepping closer, Bob ended it with a swooping uppercut that started at knee level and streaked upward until his fist solidly clipped the point of Harley's chin. The oldest Shaw son flung his arms wide and fell straight back, rigid as a slab of timber, until his shoulders crashed heavily to the dirt floor.

Moments later, Moses was the next to go. Under a flurry of punches thrown by Vern, the old soldier sort of folded up. It started with a sagging of his knees and then the rest of him crumpled down, section by section, until he was a gasping heap with his fists hanging limply at his sides. His youngest son, Wiley, went down soon after, taking a vicious blind-side right cross from Peter that twisted him halfway around and then pitched him unconscious across his fallen father's legs.

That left Cyrus, the middle son. The escape artist who'd been nimbly avoiding Fred's grasp except for that one nerve-numbing blow. Distracted by seeing his father and brothers dropping all around him,

Cyrus's nimbleness faltered just long enough for Fred to finally clamp hold of the back of his shirt collar. The scrawny lad continued to squirm and twist, trying to pull away, but now that Fred had finally gained a hold he wasn't about to lose it.

Breathing hard, backhanding a trickle of blood from one corner of his mouth, Vern looked on with mild amusement. "You got a kind of slippery fish there, Fred?"

"You could say that," Fred replied, also breathing hard from his exertions trying to catch Cyrus. "Little turd is slicker than a greased pig at a rodeo."

"You want us to hold him for you so's you can clobber him one?" asked Peter.

Fred made a face. "Naw, much as I would like to land a good lick on the wiggly damn worm, that wouldn't hardly be fair. Besides, by the look of how his old man and brothers are laid out, he's gonna have his hands full tending to them."

"You damn right I'll tend to 'em," Cyrus snapped back defiantly. "And when I get 'em on their feet again, we'll take another run at you law dogs and we'll see who's left layin' the next time."

Bob stepped closer. "Son," he said wearily, "I don't have near the reluctance my kindhearted deputy does about smacking you in the jaw, I don't care how lopsided the odds are. You keep running your mouth, especially in that snotty tone, I will be very happy to show you."

Cyrus glared heatedly at the marshal for a moment, then clamped his mouth shut tight and said no more.

Bob nodded. "That's better. In case you haven't guessed, you and your clan are on the way to jail. We'll send the doctor around to your cell by and by. After that, you can think long and hard how smart it would be to get in any kind of hurry to tangle with me and my boys again."

CHAPTER 23

"So what were you hoping to accomplish? Find the few places left on your face that weren't already covered by scratches or scabs and see if you couldn't fill them in with fresh bruises? You've got one ear left, too, that you once again failed to get damaged."

Consuela asked these questions as she dabbed gently at Bob's face with an alcohol-soaked cloth. The marshal was seated on a wooden chair in his kitchen, Consuela hovering fussily over him as she applied the sharp-smelling cloth. On the other side of the table, also perched on a wooden chair, Bucky looked on with openmouthed fascination.

"Don't you think you're exaggerating just a mite?" Bob said in defense of himself and the recent events at the Red-Eyed Goat Saloon. "I only got hit once . . . in the face, that is."

"But how many punches did you land, Pa?" Bucky wanted to know. "Twenty or thirty at least, I bet. Right?"

Bob grinned with half his mouth—the half that didn't hurt quite so much. "Somewhere short of that many," he allowed. "But I got in some pretty good licks, all the same."

Consuela's expression grew even more troubled. "There can be nothing 'pretty good' about putting your hands—or fists—on the likes of human trash such as Moses Shaw and his sons. The two or three times I have had the displeasure of seeing them when they came to town was as close as I ever want to come. They have a stink about them and the look of pure evil. Just the touch of their eyes on a decent woman is enough to make her skin crawl. Behind the bars of your jail is a good start, but they belong locked away somewhere even deeper and more secure."

Bob almost wanted to laugh at Consuela's intensity. "How about the lowest pit in the bowels of Hell?" he suggested.

Her expression remained grim, not recognizing that he was teasing her a bit. "That might be a good start."

Bob sighed. "Well, my jail is the best I can do for now. Drunk and disorderly, interfering with an officer of the law in the performance of his duties . . . A night, or two at most, then I'll have to turn 'em loose. Putting them up any longer, feeding 'em and such, is more bother and expense than they're worth. And with the closing down of the Red-Eyed Goat—their favorite drinking hole when they hit town—maybe they'll have reason to come back around less frequently than before."

"Giving the wolf less sheep to prey upon does not change him from being a wolf," declared Consuela as she scrutinized Bob's face a final time to see if there was anything more she needed to do. "And what of the man who ran this Goat place? Him you did not put behind bars at all? I thought you were convinced he had something to do with the attempt to burn down the big new saloon that is about to open?"

Bob sighed again. He'd already gone through this with his deputies and was getting a little sick of explaining it. But, for Consuela, he was willing to exhibit some extra patience.

"The hardest thing for any lawman to accept," he said, "is when you're convinced, way down bone deep, that some no-good so-and-so is guilty of something . . . only you got no way to prove it. Not without contriving a piece or two of evidence, and if you start doing that then it puts you on the same side of the line as those you're up against."

The marshal shook his head. "That's where we were at with Swede Simkins, the hombre that ran the Red-Eyed Goat. Yeah, I feel certain he used his man Conroy as a go-between to hire those other two skunks to try and burn down the Crystal Diamond. But I don't have any proof. So, since Swede's ready to pull up stakes and leave town and no fire actually took place and the two directly responsible ended up dead, I'm willing to settle for that. It's the best we're likely to get. As long as Swede and Conroy steer clear of these parts and never show up in my town again, I can live with it."

"The last time you failed to put some *bastardos* behind bars, after the trouble at Bullock's just the other day," said Consuela, clearly unconvinced by Bob's rationale, "you almost were *not* able to live with it. They showed back up and came close to killing you."

"Thanks for reminding me," Bob replied dryly, his patience starting to wear thin, even with Consuela. "That's only about the twentieth time in the past hour somebody's brought that little piece of poor judgment to my attention."

Not liking to see even a minor disturbance flare up between his father and Consuela, Bucky abruptly spoke again. "You said you took off work early today because you had a surprise for us," he reminded Bob. "You're still gonna get around to that, ain't you, Pa?"

"You bet I am," Bob responded, grinning as his gaze shifted to the boy. "As a matter of fact, anybody who needs to do anything to get ready had better hop to it because in just a minute or two the first part of the surprise is due to come rolling up."

"Get ready for what? What is going to come 'rolling up'?" Consuela wanted to know.

Bob's grin widened. "Joe Peterson, from the town livery, is gonna be dropping off a buggy and team of horses for us. We're gonna take a ride out to Finn's Meadow. Before leaving town, we'll stop by the Bluebird Café and pick up the picnic lunch I arranged to be made up and waiting for us—ham sandwiches, pickles and potato salad, a big ol' jug of lemonade, and whatever else Teresa can think to throw in. Whatever she includes, you know it'll be tasty."

"We're going on a picnic? Oh boy!" exclaimed Bucky.

"Why not?" said Bob. "It's a nice day, we've got three or four hours of daylight left. We can spread a blanket, take on a good feed, and watch dusk settle in."

"I wish you would have given me some warning,"

said Consuela as she began untying her apron. Her lovely face looked thoughtful even as the corners of her mouth were being lifted by a pleased smile. "I could have prepared something here and made it unnecessary to—"

Bob cut her off, saying, "It wouldn't have been much of a surprise if I'd given you warning. This way all you have to do is choose a proper blanket and some eating utensils. Bring them, along with your appetite and your own willingness to relax and have a good time, and everything else is all set."

"Very well. I can do that," said Consuela, a wide, dazzling smile now on full display. "But this is so . . . so *unlike* you."

Bob scowled. "Which is exactly why, after we got done scuffling with those doggone Shaws earlier, I had me a thought on some things and decided a change was in order. Seems like for several days running it's been nothing but one no-account rascal after another looking to butt heads with me over some cockeyed reason. Cussing me, threatening my friends or my town, shooting at me . . . I figured it was time to take a little break from all that. I've got three good, competent deputies to handle things while I step away for a few hours. And who better to step away and spend some relaxing time with than my two most favorite people in the world?"

CHAPTER 24

"Hellooo! Hello, the picnic . . . Rider coming in!"

This announcement rang out from a fringe of trees running along the south edge of Finn's Meadow. It came in a strong baritone voice that easily reached the spot toward the center of the meadow where Bob, Consuela, and Bucky had spread their blanket in the shade of a towering oak.

As the three picnickers turned toward the voice, they saw a lone horseman emerge from the trees and approach them at an easy canter. The horse was a thick-chested roan gelding, its rider a trim, well-dressed man wearing a friendly smile, a black-handled Colt in a cross-draw holster on his left hip, and a wide-brimmed, cream-colored hat.

"Pardon me for interrupting," the smiling man said when he was close enough to rein up. "I heard some shooting a few minutes ago and thought it was worth coming to have a look. Once I had, I figured another good idea might be to let somebody know I was back there in those trees. You know, just to make sure no stray bullets got tossed my direction."

"I'm not in the habit of tossing around stray bullets," Bob told him. "I shoot in somebody's direction, I make sure I got good reason to do so."

"My pa's a town marshal and one of the straightest shooters around," Bucky added firmly. "In fact, what you heard was him practicing for a shooting contest that he's entered and is gonna win."

The stranger chuckled. "In that case, I wish I would have run into you a little earlier, son. Might have saved myself twenty-five dollars. You see, I've entered that same contest. But now, according to you, it doesn't sound like I have much of a chance."

"It's going to be a fair contest. Everybody will have their chance, mister," said Bob. "You just have to take into consideration that my son is a little biased."

"The way it should be. Wouldn't give you much for a boy who wasn't proud of his father."

Consuela stepped forward. "Would you like to take a break from the saddle for a few minutes, Mr. . . . ?"

The stranger inclined his head and pinched the brim of his hat. "The name's Delaney. Clayton Delaney. And I very much appreciate the offer, ma'am, but I don't wish to intrude any more than I already have."

"It wouldn't be that much of an intrusion," Consuela assured him. "We're mostly already done eating and, as you heard, have moved on to target practice."

"There's a leftover ham sandwich and plenty of lemonade still in that jug. You're welcome to light a spell," said Bob. "Maybe we can even burn a little powder together, get an idea what we're up against with one another."

"Ironically," said Delaney, "that's exactly what I rode out here for—to get in a little target practice. And a cup of that lemonade certainly sounds inviting."

Bob gestured. "Climb on down, then. Get out of the sun. Bucky will take your horse and put him with our team."

Once Delaney had dismounted, Bob went ahead and finished making introductions. When he'd finished, Delaney said, "I have to admit to recognizing you, Marshal. You were pointed out to me earlier today at the train station."

"You came in on today's train?" asked Consuela as she held out a cup of freshly poured lemonade.

"Yes, I did."

"Yes. Now I remember seeing you there as well," said Bob. "And later, when I put my name down for the contest, I remember seeing the name 'Clayton Delaney' already on one of the lines. But I had no way of connecting the two."

"Well, now you do." Delaney took a sip of his drink and declared it to be excellent.

"I wish I could take credit," replied Consuela. "But the marshal here made all the arrangements through the Bluebird Café back in town. This whole outing, as a matter of fact, was a surprise he sprang on Bucky and me—including his entry in the upcoming shooting contest."

"It appears to be a surprise that everyone is enjoying," Delaney assessed. "And if this lemonade is an example of what they serve at the Bluebird Café, then

I guess I know where I'll be taking most of my meals while I'm in town."

"The lemonade is just a start." Bob tipped his head to indicate the remaining contents of the picnic basket spread out on the blanket. "Like I said, there's a sandwich there you're also welcome to help yourself to. Was some pie once upon a time, but I fear that's long gone."

"I regret not having an appetite right at the moment. But, like I said, I definitely will be checking out the Bluebird in the near future. And, when I do, I'll make sure that I go there good and hungry."

"You won't be sorry," Bob told him. Then, trying to make the words sound casual and just a natural extension of their conversation, he said, "Figure to be staying long in Rattlesnake Wells, Mr. Delaney?"

Consuela gave Bob a look, signaling her disapproval that the lawman in him seemed ready to turn their conversation into an interrogation of the stranger.

If Delaney read it that way, however, he didn't seem to mind. "I rather doubt it, Marshal. Not that I find anything wrong with your town, mind you. But I'm seeking a somewhat larger community to settle in. I've recently spent time in both Omaha and Denver and found each of them to be a little *too* big and fast for my tastes. Cheyenne has a certain appeal, but I haven't made up my mind yet.

"The thing is, you see, I recently came into a bit of money via an inheritance. Nothing outlandish, I assure you, but nevertheless more than I've ever had at my disposal all at once before in my life. Enough so that I've made up my mind I want to invest it in something—some business undertaking—that will allow it to take hold, maybe grow a little, and provide me a comfortable income. Does that sound so crazy?"

"Not at all," said Bob. "Lot more sensible than the wild schemes too many fellas seem to chase after when they get their hands on some sudden money. What kind of business you thinking about getting into?"

Delaney emitted a short laugh. "That's about as undecided as where I'm aiming to settle. Thanks to an uncle who raised me from a little kid after my folks died in a tragic church fire, I gained some background in the hardware business. Uncle Nick had a small but well-established shop in Columbus, Ohio. He did some gunsmithing on the side that almost equaled what the hardware store brought in. He not only knew the workings and peculiarities of practically every kind of gun there was, he was the surest rifle shot I've ever seen. He taught me until I was mighty good myself. I could never hold a patch to him, but was still pretty decent."

"Is he the relative who left you the inheritance?" Consuela asked.

"Yeah, much to my surprise, he was."

"Why do you say to your surprise? Sounds like you and him had a kinda special relationship," Bob said.

Delaney's eyes took on a vague, faraway look. "We did . . . until a little disturbance called the Civil War came along. Uncle Nick was too old to go off to join the fighting. But I wasn't. Trouble was, we had drastically different ideas on which side I ought to go serve. Not even worth saying anymore which way we disagreed. But when I went against him, the last thing he said to me, as I was going out the door, was not to bother coming back because I was no longer any kin of his and there'd be nothing waiting for me if I ever showed up . . . So I never did."

"How tragic and sad," Consuela said in a soft voice.

Delaney looked at her with his faraway eyes, as if bewildered. Then, blinking several times, his expression cleared and his mouth broke into a wide, somewhat sheepish grin. "Holy cow, listen to me!" he exclaimed. "First I barge in on your picnic and then I depress everybody with my long, mopey tale of woe. What an ungrateful guest I turn out to be."

"You were only responding to questions put to you," Consuela said, sending another disapproving look in Bob's direction.

"Maybe so," said Delaney. "But you can't deny my response was awfully long-winded. The meat of it— what I should have gotten to a lot quicker in answer to the marshal's question—is that the kind of business I'm thinking about getting into is a modest hardware store or maybe a gun shop. Or maybe a combination of the two, like Uncle Nick had. After all, he *did* leave me the money, which means he must have forgiven me to some extent. So it kinda seems right that I pay him back by continuing the same line of business. Plus it's the only one I have any personal experience with."

"It sort of falls in line," Bob agreed.

"You could also say," Delaney added, "that even this shooting contest at the Crystal Diamond fits in with that line of reasoning. Almost like an omen or something. Down in Cheyenne is where I heard about the big shoot being planned up this way. Talk is that those prize guns are worth as much as two or three thousand dollars. That's a very tidy sum to add to what I've already got. So I win the contest on account of the shooting skills my uncle taught me, cash in the guns for as much as I can get out of 'em, and add that to my inheritance money, then find the right place to buy into and keep Uncle Nick's line of business continuing almost unbroken."

"It does almost sound like destiny," mused Consuela.

Bob's brow wrinkled skeptically. "Destiny . . . Omens . . . Hell, if it's so preordained, I may as well shoot myself in the foot right now and not even bother showing up for that contest on Friday."

Bucky, returning from taking care of Delaney's horse and catching just the tail end of Bob's remark, looked equal parts puzzled and concerned as he said, "Why in the world would you want to do something as crazy as that, Pa?"

Bob gave a dismissive wave of his hand. "Nothing to worry about, pal. It was just a figure of speech. Nobody's getting shot in the foot, least of all me."

"But you're still gonna do some more target shooting, though, ain't you? You and Mr. Delaney, like you said?"

As mentioned earlier, Bob had only just gotten around to telling Bucky and Consuela about his entry in the Crystal Diamond shooting contest on the ride out to the meadow. Consuela's reaction had been more or less neutral. Bucky, however, had been instantly enthused to the point of looking like he might blow up and bust if he had to wait all the way until Friday.

"If you're up for running some more targets and Mr. Delaney is still interested," Bob told his son, "I won't argue against giving my Yellowboy a bit more of a workout."

Delaney nodded. "Fine by me. Like I said, it's what I came out here to do anyway."

For the next forty-five minutes, Bob and Delaney took each other's measure with their rifles. In so doing, each man was pushed near to his limit, and together they put on an exhibition of marksmanship about as fine as anybody was likely to ever witness.

Bob shot with the '66 Yellowboy that was his personal favorite. Delaney used a Winchester '73. The latter, which Bob knew was the same model Vern Macy would be using in the contest and also the same as he'd seen carried by the confident, buckskin-clad Ben Eames at the signing earlier in the day, was fast becoming the most popular lever action rifle in the West. Bob expected he would be shooting against several '73s come Friday, so he welcomed the test of going up against this one in the hands of someone as skilled as Delaney.

Using targets supplied at the sign-up, duplicates of what was scheduled to be used in the official shoot, Bucky was kept busy running back and forth with the results of each round and then setting up fresh papers for the next. Each sheet was roughly double the size of a standard playing card, plain white background with a one-inch-diameter black circle in the center.

The targets were impaled at equal heights on the snapped-off branches of two saplings standing four feet apart off toward one edge of the meadow. The men fired three-shot rounds at each target on each tree before Bucky would bring in the results. Starting at about eighty yards back, the spread of the shot patterns for each rifleman kept repeating at no more than a whisker's difference. Bob's might be a tiny margin tighter on one round, but then Delaney would better him slightly on the next.

Gradually, they kept dropping back, increasing the distance from which were shooting. By the time they got to about a hundred and forty yards, the light had faded to a point where they were aiming as much by guess as by actual sighting. On the final round, Delaney outshot Bob cleanly. For the first time the difference in the spreads were significant—two of Bob's rounds, one on each target, just barely catching the black dot bull's-eye.

"That's it for me," the marshal announced. "We back up any farther, I won't be able to see the tree, let alone the target. You whipped me, Delaney."

"Naw, more like the darkness did both of us in," Delaney countered. "We go at it again in full, bright daylight, I'd hate to be anybody going up against us. You're one mighty fine marksman, Marshal. If I have to lose to somebody, I surely would find no dishonor in it being to you."

"Same goes for me," Bob told him. "Let's hope the bullets sail as true for us on Friday. If they do, I reckon we can at least expect to be in the thick of things."

"At the *very* least," Delaney amended.

CHAPTER 25

It was dark by the time they got back to town. Delaney, unfamiliar with the area, rode on ahead to take advantage of as much of the dusk as he could. Bob was in no hurry with the team and buggy.

The moon hadn't yet risen but there was plenty of silvery illumination from the early wash of stars. In fact, it made for a nice, soft-feeling mood. Bucky, on the seat between his father and Consuela, was having a hard time keeping from nodding off. He lost the battle frequently as they rolled along, his head and thick tangle of red hair tipping over onto Consuela's shoulder until a bump in the road stirred him into wakefulness again—though not for long.

More than once, when the boy's head was tipped in that manner, Bob glanced over at the picture made by the pair, together that way, and he would wonder what the hell was wrong with him for not accepting and openly embracing the obvious—that he was as much in love with Consuela as she was with him and all he had to do was say the word and the three of them could be officially bonded into the family they obviously already were.

He hadn't forgotten Consuela's words from just the other day: "*So I wait. And will continue to wait . . . But not forever.*"

If he wasn't careful, he warned himself, he would again be faced with the kind of empty ache he'd had to endure after the passing of Priscilla. That's how his forever would end up. The love of two beautiful, special women in a single lifetime was more than any one man had a right to expect. He'd better get his head straight before it all slipped away . . .

Bob dropped Consuela and Bucky off at the house before returning the buggy and team to Peterson's livery. When Bucky climbed down to go inside, Bob called after him to be sure and say his prayers before climbing into bed. Between yawns, the boy promised he would. In the doorway, Bucky stifled yet another yawn and looked back to say, "If the light had held, you could've beat Mr. Delaney at shooting. Couldn't you, Pa?"

Bob grinned. "I'd like to think so, pal. But he's mighty good."

"I guess," Bucky allowed grudgingly. Then, his mouth curving into a sly grin of his own, he added, "But nobody can outshoot Sundown Bob when he really sets his mind to it. Can they, Pa?"

"Reckon we'll find that out on Friday," Bob told him. "Now scoot on in to bed."

After the boy had disappeared, Bob reached up and lifted Consuela down from the buggy. Once her feet touched the ground, his hands stayed on her waist for some added seconds. When he took them away, she remained standing very close.

Gazing up at him, she said, "I had a very lovely time this afternoon, Bob. I hope you surprise us again in such a manner—and not wait so long next time."

"I'll make it a point not to," Bob promised. His expression souring a bit, he added, "I hope I didn't ruin it by getting into a shooting contest with that Delaney fella. I meant for it to be just the three of us. I had no way of knowing he'd be showing up, of course, but when he did I . . . Well, like I said, I meant for it to be just the three of us."

"That's all right," Consuela said, touching his arm. "We had a perfectly fine time both before and after he came around. To tell the truth, once the two of you started shooting I found it kind of exciting. And there's certainly no doubt that Bucky did. Now I'm looking forward to the contest on Friday more than I expected."

"You gonna be disappointed in me if I don't win?"

"Of course not. I may be disappointed *for* you, but never in you."

Bob's brow wrinkled. "How about Bucky? You reckon he might think less of me if I come up short?"

Consuela put her hands on her hips. "That's too ridiculous to even answer. The way that boy looks up to you, how can you think *anything* would diminish you in his eyes?" She paused, an impish twinkle forming in her luminous dark eyes. "Of course, if you *did* call upon your inner Sundown Bob to help give you a bit of an edge, I'm pretty sure he wouldn't mind that, either . . . Nor would I."

* * *

When Bob got to Peterson's livery, he was somewhat surprised to find Joe still there, at work in one
of the stalls on a nice-looking young stallion that had
pulled up lame. Bob had intended to take care of the
buggy team himself, stripping them down and releasing them into the corral. Joe told him not to bother,
that he'd take care of it as soon as he was done wrap-
ping the stallion's leg.

After sticking around to chew the fat for a few minutes, Bob headed up Front Street feeling loose and
relaxed, feeling good. The jail was in the next block,
however. Even though he had full confidence everything was in good hands and that stopping might
only unsettle his mood, the marshal couldn't bring
himself to just walk on by and continue straight home.

Vern Macy was sitting in a wooden chair in front
of the desk, cleaning his rifle, when Bob walked in.
"Hey, Marshal," he greeted. "Wasn't expecting to see
you any more tonight."

"Just dropped off the buggy and team we were
using. Thought I'd poke my head in for a minute,"
Bob explained.

"Well, everything is okay, the town's nice and quiet,
if that's what you're wondering," said Vern. "Leastways, as far as I know. Unless Fred and Peter come
back from patrol and report something different."
He paused, flashed a faint grin. "But I ain't heard no
shooting or explosions or anything."

"That's always a good sign," Bob said dryly. He
nodded toward the cell block at the rear of the

building, accessible through a heavy door that stood a few inches ajar. "How about our guests? They behaving?"

"More or less . . . Long as you don't count stinkin' to high heaven."

"You could close the door all the way," Bob suggested. "That'd block most of it out of the front area here."

"Yeah, but it would bottle it up all the worse back there. Sooner or later one of us would have to go back into the thick of it. Might be more than a human body could bear." Vern gave an exaggerated shudder before adding, "Besides, when Fred was training me and Peter he told us about a hundred times that when you got prisoners in the lockup you ought to leave that door open at least a crack so's you got a better chance of hearing 'em in case they're up to trying something sneaky."

"Can't argue that. Come to think of it," Bob said, "I think I was probably the one who drilled that into Fred when I was breaking him in."

"That would explain it, then. Fred holds pretty tight to most everything you say."

"The prisoners have any supper yet?"

"Corn bread and molasses. Some black coffee," Vern reported. "You said to keep it simple."

"That I did. Ain't like they're deserving of anything better."

"Hey! Is that the marshal I hear talkin'? Is that you out there, Hatfield?"

The raspy, unmistakable voice of Moses Shaw called out from the cell block. Bob made a sour face, cursing himself for not listening to his own better judgment when he'd had the chance to keep right on walking past the jail. He toyed momentarily with the thought of signaling Vern to deny his presence but rejected that as a display that would look too spineless to his deputy.

Sighing, Bob called back, "Yeah, I'm out here. What of it?"

"How long you figure on keepin' me and my boys penned up in this shithole, that's what of it. So I let the liquor take hold of me and my tongue a little too strong. Wasn't no serious harm done—just a good old-fashioned, knuckle-skinnin' scuffle is all. You can't keep us behind bars for very long just on account of that, can you?"

"Sorta depends on what all I decide to charge you with," Bob answered. "Skinning your knuckles on the heads of regular folks might not be such a big deal. But trading punches with law officers in the course of performing their duties, now that moves the bar up a few notches."

"You and your boys came out on top. Don't that count for nothing?"

"Not all that much"

"Aw, come on, man! I can't take bein' caged up like this. I'm already feelin' all itchy and squirmy and my throat is closin' up so's I can hardly breathe!"

"He ain't kiddin', Marshal," came the voice of one of the Shaw sons. "He's lookin' all wild-eyed and he's pantin' like an old dog pacin' on the end of a chain when he's caught the scent of a nearby bitch in heat."

"How about I have my deputy bring in a pan of cold water you can throw on him?" said Bob, at the same time giving Vern a wink. "But, then again, the splash of clean water on his mangy old hide might pitch him into an even worse fit."

"That ain't funny, you cocky damn badge-toter!" roared Moses. "Come say that to my face without a set of bars between us."

"There's another charge I can slap on with the rest—threatening and verbally abusing a law officer. You keep going, Moses," Bob told him, "you'll be spending the fall and a piece of winter in there."

"Since when did this quit bein' a free country? Can't a man even speak his mind anymore?"

Bob made no reply.

After a minute, his tone now lowered, almost a whine, Moses said, "Can't you at least step back here a minute so's we can talk face-to-face, Marshal? I'll keep a civil tongue, I promise."

Sighing again, Bob walked back, toed open the cell block door and stepped through. The mixed stink of sour body odor, liquor breath, cigarette smoke, and traces of urine and vomit washed over him. Light from a low-burning lantern affixed to the wall of the corridor running outside the block's two cells cast weak, shadow-cut illumination over the men in the cells. Moses and Wiley, his youngest, were in one cell; Cyrus and Harley in the other. All were bruised and haggard-looking, images better left in the dark.

"Make it quick, Moses," Bob said. "I'm ready to call it a night and head home."

"Yeah, I bet you are," said a leering Cyrus from the opposite cell. "I had me a hot little Spanish number waitin' back at the hacienda, like you do, I'd be in a damn quick hurry to head back home real often-like."

Bob spun and thrust out his forefinger like a saber.

"You watch your filthy mouth, you sniveling little bastard! I ever hear you say anything like that again, you'll come out of that cell walking on sticks."

Moses immediately joined in, saying, "Damn you and your gutter mind, boy! Didn't you hear me give my word this was gonna be a civil exchange?"

Cyrus scowled, looking torn between cowing under the lash of his father's tongue yet wanting to be defiant. "Jeez, I didn't mean nothin' by it, Pop. I was just sayin'—"

"You said too much!" Moses cut him off harshly. Then, gesturing to Harley, his oldest, he said, "Harley, you're right there by him. You be my admonishin' hand. Show your brother the consequence for his foul mind and for shamin' us all after I gave my word."

Harley's body poised but he looked pained, reluctant. His eyes went from Moses to Cyrus and back to Moses again.

"You heard me," Moses said in a gravelly voice. "Admonish him, I said. Do it!"

Harley tightened his right fist into a clublike ball and then, uncoiling suddenly, swung it in a vicious backhand blow to the side of Cyrus's head. The impact sounded like two slabs of meat slapping together, and the force sent the slender Cyrus pitching limp and loose-limbed onto a cell cot where he lay totally still except for the worm of blood crawling out one corner of his mouth.

"Jesus Christ! Stop that," blurted Bob. He wasn't able to halt the initial act, too late to fully comprehend what it was going to consist of until it explosively happened. But, despite his own outburst toward

Cyrus, he wasn't ready to stand by and watch further such punishment that might be directed by Moses and carried out by Harley.

Fixing a furious glare at Moses, he said, "That wasn't necessary! What the hell kind of father are you?"

Returning his own glare, Moses answered, "The kind of father who instills in his sons that a man's word is a sacred thing that must be honored—and any who fail to do so must be admonished severely and swiftly."

"A lesson taught the wrong way is no lesson at all," Bob insisted. "It can become a wedge that, if you drive it in deep enough and often enough, will force the exact opposite results."

"You let me worry about the lessons I teach my sons and how I go about enforcin' 'em," Moses said. "Ain't none of it any of your business."

"Maybe not—not as long I don't have to be a witness to it. Whatever you wanted to talk face-to-face about is done, Shaw. I got no time or interest in anything more you have to say."

As Bob turned to leave the cell block, Moses called after him, "You'd better let me out of here in time for that shootin' match on Friday, you hear? I put down my money and made my mark. I got every right to compete. If you keep me locked away it only means you know I'm good enough to beat everybody else. Freezin' me out will just prove one more time how everybody works at keepin' me down and preventin' me from gettin' the recognition I deserve for—"

Bob slammed the cell block door and turned the

old man's lamentations into a muffled, monotonous drone.

"You can crack that door again and listen to his bellyaching and smell the stink all you want—*after* I leave," Bob told Vern.

The young deputy shrugged. "Whatever you say." He'd finished cleaning his Winchester and had it leaning against the front edge of Bob's desk while he wiped gun oil from his hands with a soft cloth. The rifle was another '73 model.

Bob pointed. "That what you're gonna be shooting with on Friday?"

"What I figured," Vern said. "There a problem with that?"

"Not at all. From what I've seen you'll have a lot of company. Seems like most everybody is shooting a '73 except me and my Yellowboy."

"Not quite, though. Judging by the guns we rounded up after that fracas at the Red-Eyed Goat— well, what *used* to be the Goat—you won't be the only one not shooting a '73." Vern jabbed a thumb to indicate a collection of rifles leaning up against the gun rack on one wall. "Looks like Moses's weapon of choice is an old Henry repeater."

"Not a bad gun, either," Bob allowed.

"You gonna let him out in time for the contest?"

"Probably. Unless he acts up too much in the meantime."

"Be nice to get the stink out of here."

"Yeah, there's that. Also, after hearing so much about what a rip-roaring sharpshooter he was in the war, I'm curious to see what he's really got. An old

Henry or what have you, we both know it's more the man squeezing the trigger than the gun itself."

"For a fact."

Bob arched an eyebrow. "Speaking of which, I ran into a fella a little while ago out at Finn's Meadow. I was doing some target practicing after we'd had our picnic feed, he heard my shots and come over for a look-see. Turned out he's also entered in the contest. Name's Clayton Delaney . . . Ever hear of him?"

"Can't say as I have."

"Well, you're gonna. And I think he'll stick in your memory, same as he did mine." Bob twisted his mouth in a wry smile. "While we had some light left, me and him burned a little powder together. We stayed neck and neck until roughly about a hundred-forty yards. The light was getting pretty bad by then so we called it quits. I guess I could blame it on that—the poor light. Whatever the case, he plumb beat me on that last round. Didn't plant a single round outside the edges of the black circle."

"At a hundred-forty yards?"

"Give or take."

Vern emitted a low whistle. "Clayton Delaney, eh? Sounds like he'll be a pretty serious challenge."

"He'll be all of that . . . and then some."

CHAPTER 26

Back out on the street, Bob wasn't feeling quite as buoyant as he had upon first leaving Peterson's livery. He still felt pretty good, though. The time spent out away from everything and everybody—with just Bucky and Consuela, and then even after Delaney showed up—had been too enjoyable to be soured by the unpleasant encounter with the Shaws. He was damned if he'd let them have that much sway over him.

Not even the thought of possibly coming up short in the shooting contest bothered him that much—as long as it wasn't Moses Shaw who beat him. Normally possessing a very competitive nature, especially in his younger years, Bob was somewhat surprised by the ambivalence he felt toward the upcoming match. Naturally, he wanted to put in a good showing. But he'd grown secure enough in his own skin and in his sense of how others saw him, that if he failed to place first it would hardly be a crushing blow. In fact, to a certain degree, he might even feel a bit relieved at such an outcome. Should he win, he knew damn well there would be those with bitter, suspicious minds and poisonous tongues who'd claim the whole thing was rigged so that he—gun-blazing Sundown Bob, the local law—was a lock to come out on top right from the get-go. Bob didn't know why he let the potential mutterings of those kinds of people even cross his mind, let alone bother him, but they did all the same.

All he knew for certain was that, in the end, he'd do the best he could and things would turn out however it was meant to be.

"Hey, cowboy. No time to even say hi to an old friend?"

The voice, female, soft, and a bit smoky, came from a pool of shadows flooding the boardwalk near one end of Bullock's Saloon building. Turning his head, looking in that direction, Bob saw Maudie Sartain sitting there on a wooden bench under the narrow strip of shake-shingled awning that cast her in such murkiness. By contrast, only a few feet from where she sat, bands of golden light streamed from the front window and through the batwing doors of the saloon.

Bob walked over to her.

"You'd think a fella that attracts trouble the way you do," Maudie remarked dryly, "would stay a little more alert when he's out walking around. Especially when he's parading right down the middle of the street."

Bob grinned. "And you'd think a good-looking gal like you ought to keep herself planted in the light for her admirers to see, not faded back into the dark. So why *are* you out here all alone anyway?"

"Just catching a little fresh air, is all. We don't have a particularly large crowd tonight but there's a tableful of poker players who all happen to be cigar smokers and they're puffing hell out of their stogies, let me tell you. To make matters worse, one of them is Angus McTeague and he just got in a shipment of special cigars so he passed a couple out to everybody at the table. Nobody can stop carrying on about how great those special imports are. Maybe so, but all I know is that they stink to high heaven and I had to take a break from them."

"Tell you what," said Bob. "Without even taking a whiff of those stogies for myself, I invite you to go down to the jail and poke your head in the door—just for a second, that's all it'll take—and breathe in just a smidge of the odor from the guests we're putting up for the night. Then come back and return to your cloud of cigar smoke. I guarantee you'll find it sweet as a field of daisies by comparison."

"Gee, you make it sound so tempting. But I think I'll pass. At least, though, if you just came from there, maybe it explains why you came down the street in a daze like you were. You were half-stunned by that smell you're describing."

Bob planted one foot on the edge of the boardwalk. "Sounds like you got it all figured out. So I reckon I should be grateful for the diagnosis as well as for the fact you ain't an ambusher laying wait for me."

"There are different ways and reasons to ambush a man," said Maudie, gazing up, regarding him closely.

Bob shifted somewhat uncomfortably.

"Straighten up and lean back a little more into the light," Maudie abruptly instructed. When he'd complied, she said, "Good Lord, man. With a mug like that, you're the one who ought to be sticking to the shadows."

"Thanks a bunch," Bob responded, returning to his former position. "What did you expect after that shotgun blast last night rearranged your batwing doors—which I see Bullock has replaced quicker than my mug is gonna heal—so that instead of hanging on their hinges they were hanging off the sides of my face instead."

"I only caught a glimpse when that happened," Maudie reminded him. "Before I could get a closer look, you pulled that damn fool stunt of charging right back out into the blast. Ever since then, you've been making yourself mighty scarce around these parts."

"Been kinda busy."

"So I've heard. In addition to various other shoot-outs and shenanigans, as recently as this afternoon you decided to let Moses Shaw and his sons decorate your face a bit more with their fists. Now I can't verify all the reports I've heard but, judging from the peek you just gave me, I'd say the part about getting your face in the way of some fists was pretty accurate."

"Once again you seem to have it all figured out."

"And that would make your high-smelling jail guests the Shaws?"

"Another bull's-eye."

Maudie shifted over on the bench and patted the empty space beside her. With mock seriousness, she said, "You poor man. In your battered and stench-drugged state you'd better get off your feet. Come over here and sit down. You probably need some fresh air worse than I do."

This made Bob feel even more uncomfortable. A couple days ago he would have taken the seat and thought nothing about it. But now, in the wake of Consuela's recent remarks and the reflections that had been tumbling around in his head ever since, the marshal was a bit more hesitant. It didn't help that Maudie was once again wearing a dress that left her shoulders bare and revealed a generous amount of cleavage. Bob appreciated the view but at the same time he felt half-guilty for doing so.

Nevertheless, he settled onto the bench beside Maudie.

Regarding him closely, she said, "You seem so tense. What's wrong?"

"I thought we just covered that. A steady parade of varmints coming at you with bullets and bad intentions tends to put a fella on edge."

"You sure that's all there is to it?"

"Ain't that enough?"

Maudie frowned. "It's just that I've had this feeling you've been purposely avoiding me. And now—*after* you practically walked right on by without even noticing me—I can't help but sense you're ill at ease merely being next to me."

"Ninety percent of the men in this town would break a leg to be sitting where I am right now. Why would I feel any different?"

"That's what I'm trying to find out. Ever since I threw that bottle the other day and you shot those two men . . . then you and I had a moment when you went out of your way to talk with me and calm me down . . . It seems like something has changed between us."

Bob was feeling more and more uncomfortable, more pinned down. And increasingly annoyed. While Consuela's jealousy might be questionable, her expectations were at least somewhat understandable. After all she'd been through with Bob—their childhood years, his time as the Devil's River Kid, her care and devotion to both Bucky and Priscilla during periods when he couldn't be there, the healing and rebuilding phase they were still in the midst of—she had *earned* the right to certain expectations. But all Maudie had ever been was a flirtation, a friend. She'd never been led on to believe or expect anything more. And now for her to pressure Bob with . . .

Salvation from the awkward moment arrived in the forms of Fred Ordway and Peter Macy, coming down the street from the direction of New Town, returning from their evening patrol.

"That's a mighty leisurely pace you're stepping off there," Bob called out to them. "Things must be pretty quiet in town tonight."

The two deputies angled in his direction.

"Hey, boss," said Fred. "Almost didn't see you sitting there. You neither, Miss Maudie."

"Seems to be a lot of that going on," remarked Maudie.

"Be a shame to miss seeing *you*, Miss Maudie," Peter said with a smile. Then, realizing how that might sound, he dropped the smile and quickly added, "Uh, not that missing you would be a good thing, either, Marshal."

"Surprised to see you out and about, boss," said Fred. "I thought you'd be settled in at home by now, after your picnic."

"I just dropped our buggy and team off and was on my way home," Bob explained. "Made the mistake of poking my head inside the jail for a couple minutes to see how things were going there."

"You run into some kind of flare-up?"

"Not particularly. Just had to listen to some mouth-running from Moses Shaw."

Peter made a face. "Uh. And the smell, right?"

Maudie stood up. "I think I've heard enough about how bad the Shaws stink. So much, in fact, I'm beginning to imagine I can smell it wafting in the air clear from here. That being the case, I may as well go back inside and wrap myself in cigar smoke. Better the devil you know, right?"

"Hey, we don't want to interrupt the visit you and the marshal were having," said Fred. "You go ahead and sit back down. Me and Peter will mosey on our way."

"That's not necessary," said Maudie, moving toward the saloon's front door. "I need to get back inside anyway." She paused, looked back over her shoulder. "See you around, Marshal. Stop by for a cup of tea sometime."

CHAPTER 27

After Maudie disappeared through the batwings, Fred said, "Sorry if we barged in, boss."

"Nonsense," said Bob. "I called you over, didn't I?"

"Speaking of that—you asking about things being quiet in town, that is," spoke up Peter. "You'll be happy to hear that they sure are. Real quiet."

Fred nodded. "Reckon the Red-Eyed Goat being closed is part of the reason for that."

"Swede acted that fast, eh?"

"Not only closed down, but practically every trace of it has disappeared," said Peter. "Like it was never there."

"He pulled down the tent," Fred elaborated, "then folded it up and packed it, along with as much booze and barroom paraphernalia as he could fit, into a big old Conestoga wagon. That's where he's at now, stretched out on a bedroll underneath the wagon with a shotgun for company, guarding what possessions he's got left until he's ready to pull out at first light."

"What about the stuff he couldn't fit in the wagon?" Bob wanted to know.

"Sold it to other saloonkeepers and liquor dealers who were willing to pay cash and haul it off right away," said Peter. "Since everybody knew the tight he was in, you can bet he got raked over the coals pretty good on some of the payment he had to accept."

Fred's mount pulled into a hard, tight line. "Couldn't happen to a nicer fella. I'd've liked to seen him get raked over the coals even harder."

"I wouldn't have minded that, either, Fred," said Bob. "But it wasn't in the cards, not without any hard proof of what we suspect he tried to pull. I don't like it, you don't like it—but we're gonna have to get over it and move on."

Fred hung his head and scowled down at the ground. "I know, boss. I know. I'll knock off my grumbling."

"How about Merle Conroy? Any sign of him while Swede was packing up his stuff?"

"Not the slightest stir of dust," Fred answered. "And I was watching hard. Him, I would have given another hard shaking, no matter what. I don't know if I could have gotten anything to spill but, if nothing else, it would have been worth it just to hear him rattle."

Bob cut a glance over at Peter. "He been in this cheery a mood all evening?"

Peter rolled his eyes. "You wouldn't believe. My ribs plumb ache from trying to hold back all the laughter."

"Excuse me for thinking law and order is a serious

business and for letting slippery varmints like Swede and Conroy chap my hide," Fred huffed.

"Calm down," Bob said with an easy grin. "Keep right on taking the law serious, Fred. I wouldn't want you any other way. Just don't let it get you so worked up you blow a gasket or something."

At first, the tap on his hotel room door came so lightly that August Gafford mistook it for some obscure hallway noise that was of no direct concern to him. Only when it came a second, more insistent, time did he realize what it was.

Setting aside his snifter of brandy and rising from the overstuffed chair in which he'd been doing some light reading before retiring for the night, he snugged the belt of his dressing gown more tightly about his middle and shuffled to the door. Peering through the small, smudged peephole, he said, "Yes? Who's there?"

"It's Emerson. Let me in."

Gafford paused. Then, scowling fiercely, he undid the slide lock and chain and cautiously pulled the door toward him. He had it open only half a foot when the man on the other side impatiently shouldered it open wider and pushed in past Gafford.

"See here, damn it! You shouldn't be coming around here at this hour—nor any other," Gafford protested. "What's the meaning of this?"

"What do you think the meaning is?" said the man who'd just entered. He marched over to the decanter of brandy on the stand beside Gafford's reading chair, brushed off the glass stopper so that it dropped loudly onto the top of the stand, then hoisted the decanter high and took a long, gurgling swig of the amber liquid. After depleting the contents by nearly half, he lowered the container with a satisfied sigh. Turning back to face Gafford, the newcomer—despite identifying himself as "Emerson" from the other side of the door—now revealed himself to be the rather rustic, buckskin-clad individual who earlier in the day had put down his money and signed the entrants' list for the shooting contest as "Ben Eames."

"The meaning," he said, swirling the brandy casually in front of him, "is that I wanted what partners *always* want from one another—a meeting, a powwow, a chance to get updated and see how things are going."

"Things are going precisely according to plan." After closing the door behind him, Gafford's reply came in a somewhat strained voice. "As long as you don't foul it up by getting seen coming or going from here."

"Relax. I made sure nobody spotted me. And I'll do the same when I'm ready to leave."

Eames/Emerson started to raise the decanter for another drink.

"Good God, man," Gafford protested. "That's a top-shelf blend of liquor, not a batch of home-brewed busthead meant to be guzzled down merely for the sake of achieving a quick, cheap drunk."

The man in buckskin paused with the decanter only partly raised. He regarded Gafford under a sharply arched brow. "And there is exactly one of the things we need to talk about, partner. This *Ben Eames* role you arranged for me to assume, is getting old pretty damned quick. You think I don't know fine liquor? You forget that in my true identity of Benjamin 'Eagle Eye' Emerson, I spent many months as the toast of both coasts as well as the continent? I've been heralded by none other than Buffalo Bill himself as one of the finest sharpshooters extant, rivaled only by the likes of Annie Oakley and a small handful of others."

"Yes, yes. I'm well aware of all that. And it is exactly due to such renown that I suggested—and you readily agreed, I might add—that this job be taken under a heavy disguise. Your skill with a rifle, not to mention your training as an actor in those stage plays that Cody cast you in back East, made you the perfect choice." Gafford's voice lowered and his eyes bored harder into Eames as he added, "That, combined with the down-and-out condition you found yourself in after that incident in Boston, I thought presented a beneficial opportunity for both of us to—"

"Shut up!" Eames cut him off. "Must you mention that terrible Boston incident every time we talk? The girl *moved*, I tell you! She twitched at the last instant, just as my finger stroked the trigger, and there was no way to stop the bullet, nothing on earth I could do to prevent the horror . . ."

Eames's hand began to tremble, causing the brandy inside the decanter to slosh back and forth. Gafford walked over, took the decanter, placed a hand on the man's shoulder, and gently but firmly pushed him down onto the overstuffed chair.

"Take it easy," Gafford said consolingly. "I apologize for mentioning the matter. Every right-thinking person knows damn well it was a tragic accident. Those who cast blame and slammed doors in your face afterward, not allowing you any chance to redeem yourself, are pathetic and beneath contempt. What I'm offering you here may not be much, but it's fair compensation for some simple work. And, who knows, maybe afterward, if the Crystal Diamond takes off like I'm hoping and if you're interested, maybe I'll have something longer termed I can offer you."

Eames looked up at him. "Seriously? You think that's possible?"

"I wouldn't say so if I didn't mean it," Gafford assured him. "But first things first—you, in the guise of Ben Eames, have got to win that shooting contest the day after tomorrow. I've already explained to you where I stand money-wise, what makes it so crucial for me . . . I've got every dime to my name sunk in this undertaking and in those prize guns. If the Crystal Diamond *doesn't* take off like I'm gambling it will or if some sudden costly problem pops up, I'll be in a bad way. I've no more resources I can call on."

"Except the guns."

"Except the guns," Gafford echoed dully. "The guns *you* are going to secure in that contest and then covertly return to me for the balance of our agreed-upon fee. Once more in my possession, they will provide the security and collateral, if necessary, to help me weather any catastrophe that might reasonably rear its ugly head."

Eames passed the back of one hand across his mouth. "That makes me mighty important to you. Don't it?"

"I think I've made the answer to that abundantly clear."

Gafford took the decanter from Eames, righted a glass that had been standing overturned and unused on the serving tray, poured some of the brandy into it, and held it out to Eames. His voice shifting into a somewhat guarded tone as Eames took the glass, Gafford said, "I sense you're angling toward something. Most likely a renegotiation of some sort, unless I miss my guess. Is that what brought you here tonight?"

"You're a shrewd one, I'll give you that."

"Get to it, then. For all the good it's going to do you."

Eames took a drink. "You know it's funny how a man adjusts to certain conditions. There was a time, not too many years ago, during the period when I made my living hunting buffalo for the railroad, when sleeping on the ground out under the stars at night was so common to me that I thought nothing about it. That was when I developed my shooting skills, by the way. And as I long as I had food for my belly and a warm bedroll to wrap myself in at night, I was quite content."

Gafford sighed wearily, impatiently. "I really don't need a history lesson. I'm very familiar with your background."

"In that case," Eames went on, "you should have taken into consideration how far those days are behind me. How, in the interim, I grew accustomed to better accommodations. And how being alone at night out on the prairie—playing this rustic Ben Eames character you came up with—would give a man a lot of time, maybe too much, to think and reweigh his outlook on certain things."

"So spit it out, you greedy ingrate! There's no sense dragging on and on about it—how much more are you looking to get for holding up your end of the bargain?"

Eames bared his teeth in a cold smile. "How much more you got?"

"Nothing, you fool! Haven't you been listening? I've set aside money to cover my foreseeable expenses— including paying you the rest of what we agreed on for the job you agreed to do. But, after that, I'm flat until the saloon starts earning out. Even if I was willing to give in to your extortion, I've got nothing to meet it with."

"Talk around town, and even outlying, is that those guns might be worth as much as twenty-five thousand dollars. Maybe more. What if I was simply to keep 'em for myself after I win 'em? Ain't like I wouldn't have every right to do so. Came down to that, however much money you do or don't have wouldn't make a lick of difference to me."

Gafford snorted a derisive laugh. "The guns might command that much, but only through certain channels. Fumbling around as you'd be apt to do, trying to unload them in the wrong places, would yield only a fraction of that amount . . . and, very possibly, a slit throat and emptied pockets before it was done."

Eames sat up straighter in his chair. "Are you threatening me?"

"Only if you choose to call it that," Gafford answered calmly. "I prefer to call it an understanding that we need to reach once and for all. Especially you. For your own good. You see, part of the money I have earmarked to cover foreseeable expenses includes enough to insure payment to Mr. Simon Quirt. I don't believe the two of you have had the pleasure of being formally introduced. He was present at the signing ceremony today if you were paying attention—the dark-skinned gentleman with the icy eyes and the tie-down Colt revolvers hovering at all times near the prize guns? Mr. Quirt's job, in case you're slow at getting the picture, is to make sure that nothing un-planned happens to those guns. And what is planned or unplanned for them, as far as he is concerned, is determined strictly by me."

Eames drained his glass and this time the brandy appeared not to go down quite so smooth.

Gafford leaned over the lanky rifleman, and all of a sudden he seemed to be looming in a threatening manner. "Now, you listen, you washed-up, crawfishing piece of crud. We struck a deal and you're going to hold up your end. If you try to swerve me in any way or fail to win that contest or make another peep about holding out for a bigger cut of pay . . . I'll see you crushed like a prairie hen's nest under a herd of stampeding buffalo. If you insist, you may be able to make enough noise to cause me some embarrass-ment and trouble, but I promise it will be ridiculously minor compared to what you suffer in return."

Staring down at the hotel room's thinly carpeted floor, Eames's throat muscles gulped again, this time without anything for them to swallow. He said nothing.

Gafford straightened up. "Now get out of here. Make sure nobody spots your sorry ass leaving. I don't want to see you again until the contest. And I shouldn't have to tell you that if I have to come looking for you afterward—which is to say, if I have to send Simon Quirt looking for you— it will not be a pleasant experience when he catches up."

CHAPTER 28

Thursday in Rattlesnake Wells came and went largely without incident.

The closest thing to any kind of disturbance occurred when Moses Shaw and his sons were released from the lockup. They were their usual mouthy, belligerent selves but Moses held them in check just enough to keep them from earning another stay behind bars.

Outside the jail, Bob and his deputies had the Shaws' horses saddled and waiting, along with two extra mounts. "Me and Deputy Fred are gonna ride with you to the edge of town," the marshal explained. "There, your rifles—emptied of shells—will be returned to you. The cartridges are in one of the saddlebags—you'll have to dig around in order to find which one. You can reload once you're clear of town."

"You can damn betcha we'll be doin' that," promised Harley.

"But if I see you back *in* town sooner than an hour

before the shooting match tomorrow," added Bob, "we'll be relieving you of those shooters permanent-like."

"Now wait a blasted minute!" protested Wiley. "You can't do that. You can't freeze us out of town for no good reason."

"We've got a good reason. We don't want you mingling with decent folks who don't deserve truck with the likes of you," said Fred. "If that don't suit you, you're more than welcome to remain—back behind bars."

Wiley turned frantically to his father. "Can they do that, Pop? Is that any kind of legal?"

"They're the ones with the badges and all the sway . . . for right now," said Moses in a raspy voice. His cold eyes settled on Bob. "But one of these days, it won't be that way. After I win them gold guns, Marshal, and become a man of prominence in these parts—the kind the likes of you hop to the tune of and lick the boots of—then it'll be a different story."

"Don't count on it," Bob said flatly.

"What are we supposed to do between now and tomorrow mornin'?" wailed Harley. "Ride all the way back to the ranch just to grab a few hours' sleep and then ride all the way back again?"

"Ain't hardly our concern," said Fred. "Find a campsite somewhere and wait it out. That's all I can tell you."

"Better yet," spoke up Peter Macy, "find a water hole or a creek somewhere and soak some of the crud and stink off yourselves."

"I don't know that twenty-four hours would be enough to do much good, but at least I guess it might be a start," said Vern. Then his brows knitted. "But, for God's sake, don't even *think* about soaking those crusty hides of yours in any of the wells that provide our town's water."

Now Moses's eyes cut to him. "You and your brother got real disrespectful mouths, sonny. Like I told your boss: one of these days—and I predict it won't be long—you're due to be held to account for that kind of thing."

The second day of sign-ups for the shooting contest was much more subdued than the first. August Gafford was on hand, naturally, and the prize pistols were once again prominently displayed. There was no barrel of free beer, however, and although Alora Dane and the Diamond Dollies appeared for another show preview, this time it was a notably briefer performance than before.

The crowd drawn by all of this was considerably smaller the second time around. In the end, it was hard to say if the sparse turnout accounted for the diminished overall energy of the Crystal Diamond hoopla or if the reverse was true—the lesser energy accounted for the smaller crowd.

Nevertheless, the big events scheduled for the next day—the shooting contest and the grand opening of the saloon—were on the lips of most everybody in town, whether they came around the site or not. And seven more men stopped by to lay down their money and enter themselves in the shooting match. This made a total of twenty-four, a half dozen short of the limit but still a very challenging collection of marksmen. All in all, Gafford seemed plenty satisfied with the way things were shaping up.

As for Bob, this occasion that he had a hunch was possibly the calm before the storm allowed him to once again take a rare early quit at the close of the day. Actually, this was partly at the behest of Fred and Peter, who urged both Bob and Vern to knock off early, spend a relaxing evening, get a good night's sleep, and show up rested and ready for the contest in the morning.

Bob didn't know how Vern intended to fill this slack period, but the marshal had no trouble occupying his. For a time, he just sat in the chair on the front porch of his house, leisurely cleaning his rifle and carefully wiping down the cartridges he would be using.

For supper, Consuela put on a particularly fine spread of roast beef, potatoes, greens, and a sugar-glazed cake for desert. During the meal, she and Bucky revealed how they both had plans to be part of the festivities tomorrow. Consuela would be serving drinks and sandwiches at a food booth set up by Teresa and Mike Tuttle of the Bluebird Café. Since school had been canceled for the day, Bucky would be helping out by hauling dirty dishes back to the restaurant and fetching back trays of fresh sandwiches and slices of pie as needed.

Once supper was finished, the table cleared, and dishes done, they all three reseated themselves around the table and played dominoes for more than two hours.

When Bucky's bedtime rolled around, Bob escorted him up the steps to his room and the two of them got down on their knees, hands folded, elbows resting on the edge of the mattress. A God-fearing man, though his own church attendance was spotty at best, Bob tried to make sure Bucky regularly attended Sunday school as well as the main church service most of the time, and said his nighttime prayers on bended knee. Because his marshaling duties prevented him from being present for much of this, he was heavily reliant on Consuela, like so much else, to see it adhered to. It was all meant for the boy's spiritual well-being as well as maintaining a commitment to Priscilla, who'd been a very devout woman and who Bob knew would want their son to have a strong religious base.

"Now I lay me down to sleep, and pray the Lord my soul to keep," intoned Bucky softly, his eyes closed. "If I should die before I wake, I pray the Lord my soul to take . . . God bless my pa, Consuela, and my mother in Heaven. Also God, please bless all the sick and suffering in the world . . ."

When Bucky paused without tacking on an *Amen* to end the simple prayer, Bob opened his eyes and looked over.

Bucky's eyes remained closed but he sensed that his father was looking at him. "Pa," he said quietly, "do you think it would be okay if I was to add on a little something and ask God maybe to give you a bit of extra luck in the contest tomorrow?"

Bob grinned. "I don't think it would necessarily be a *bad* thing," he said. "But I expect God has got His hands plenty full with a whole bunch of other stuff way bigger and more important than guiding the aim of one particular man in a shooting contest. Don't you think it would be more reasonable to thank Him for the skill he's already given me—as well as the other fellas in the contest who are all likely pretty good, too—and then leave it up to us to take those skills and go the rest of the way on our own?"

Bucky didn't answer right away. He kept his eyes closed and his lips pressed tight together for a minute.

Then: "Yeah, I reckon that way is the best, Pa . . . Amen."

CHAPTER 29

The morning of the big day dawned sunless and gloomy. The sky was a flat sheet of metallic gray with a few wisps of darker, sooty-looking clouds curling around the edges. The air held a damp chill, and off to the northwest, somewhere above the mountains, a low belch of thunder could now and then be heard.

On the tongues of some—mostly those who preferred thumping the Good Book over pulling the cork on a good bottle—there was dour talk that all the hype and hoopla paid for by August Gafford to see his saloon get off to a bang-up start meant nothing if a heavenly dousing was on tap against it.

But so far not a drop had fallen, let alone a deluge, which left Gafford to loudly and confidently assure everybody that, at worst, if the rains came and postponed the shooting match, there would still be plenty to celebrate and enjoy when the Crystal Diamond officially opened its doors for business.

Bob arrived on the scene early, milling amidst others who seemed to be steadily gathering in spite of the threatening sky. Consuela, who'd gotten there even ahead of him, served him a cup of coffee from the Bluebird Café booth. She had on a blue-checked gingham dress and a frilly white apron this morning, as opposed to the brightly colored off-the-shoulder blouses and skirts she usually wore around the house. Her glossy black hair was parted in the middle and pulled back into a loose bun. But none of it really mattered, Bob thought to himself; you could dress her in a gunnysack and hide her comb for a week and her smoldering beauty would still show through. And in a crowd of people, it only stood out all the more by comparison.

"You're staring. What's the matter?" said Consuela, glancing down at herself and then reaching up to touch her hair. "Is there something wrong with the way I look?"

"If there is, I sure can't see it," Bob told her. "The only problem might come when Alora Dane and her Diamond Dollies show up. If they see a pretty gal like you out here serving sandwiches and pie, they might refuse to take the stage until you're removed from the premises—knowing they wouldn't be able to compete, no matter how much leg they show or how high they kick."

Consuela blushed. "What's gotten into you? A surprise picnic just the other day, a long evening spent at home last night with Bucky and me . . . and now compliments? I'm not saying I mind, I just don't know where it's all coming from so suddenly."

"Maybe I'm just smartening up in my old age."

"You're not that old, but I won't argue for fear of turning off whatever has triggered these changes."

Bob drank some of his coffee. "You know, I've

been doing some thinking about those prize guns. I mean, I thought about 'em before but not necessarily from the perspective of being the one who might win them."

"You should have thought about them in that way all along. You're an excellent shot and you have as good or better chance than anybody. Most people around town, in fact, see you as the favorite."

"Well, that's encouraging. But there are a lot of other good shooters on that list, too. You already know Vern and you saw another one the other day in that Delaney fella." Bob took another drink. "But what I was getting at is this: If I *did* happen to win, it could mean a lot to us. We could afford to fix up some of the chinks in that old house. Put in better windows, some nice curtains like you've talked about. Buy you a better stove and other foofaraws you've had to go without on a marshal's wages. Put a little aside for a rainy day, even some for Bucky to go to engineering school or some such when he's older. There's value in those guns way beyond just as show-off pieces, 'Suela. Value enough to even start thinking about—"

"Coming through! Important delivery coming through!" Bucky's announcement as he arrived carrying a tray stacked with sandwiches wrapped in waxed paper cut off his father in midsentence.

Consuela, who'd been hanging on Bob's every word, thrilled by every mention of "us" and "we" and wildly anticipating where he was headed next, had all she could do to hold back an outburst of frustration over the interruption. But she managed to control it somehow, saying merely, "Put the tray here" as she patted a spot on the booth's serving surface.

Bucky delivered his load, completely innocent of knowing he'd inserted himself into the middle of anything. "These are beef sandwiches," he told Consuela. "Mrs. Tuttle said she marked them with a *B* so you could tell. I have to go back now for some ham sandwiches and they'll be marked with an *H*."

"*B* and *H*," echoed Consuela. "That's simple enough."

"Mrs. Tuttle also said to tell you that in a little while, before it's time for the match to start, she'll be sending another lady to take over the serving here at the stand so you and me can go watch Pa shoot."

"That will be fine."

"Do you have any dirty dishes for me to take back for washing?"

"Hold out your tray. Here are some coffee cups you can return."

As Consuela piled on some cups, Bucky smiled up at Bob. "Won't be long now, eh, Pa? You're gonna win those fancy guns, I know you are."

"I'm gonna do my darnedest, pal," Bob told him.

"There you go," said Consuela rather hurriedly as she put the last of the dirty cups on Bucky's tray. "Be off with you, then. Careful not to break any. Try to bring back some clean ones along with the sandwiches. Tell Mrs. Tuttle that right now coffee is going the fastest."

"Will do."

As Bucky moved away, Consuela turned expectantly to Bob, hoping he would pick up with what he'd been about to say when he got cut off. But before he could say anything at all, another interruption showed up in the form of Deputy Fred hurrying through the throng.

"Better grab your Yellowboy, boss, and get on over to the firing line," he said. "They're wanting all contestants accounted for and ready so they can start off right on time, ahead of that rain that looks like it might be moving in."

"Isn't it awfully early? There's still plenty of time," Consuela protested.

"Yeah, but it's probably a good idea," Bob said. "By the time they get the order picked, the targets set, and everybody where they want 'em . . . sometimes it can be like herding cats."

"Just so you know, the Shaws showed up a few minutes ago," said Fred.

"That's too bad," Bob muttered.

"Looking rougher and ornerier than ever."

"They can look however they want to look. I can't help that. But at the first hint of trouble, we'll land on 'em with both feet."

"Don't let them distract you from the contest. They're not worth that," Consuela advised.

"Don't worry about that, Miss Consuela," Fred told her. "Me and Peter will keep a sharp eye on those Shaws so the marshal and Vern can concentrate all they need to on their shooting. I feel in my bones that one of 'em is gonna win."

"So do I," said Consuela. She reached out and took Bob's coffee cup with one hand. The other she brought forward and rested on his forearm for a lingering moment. Gazing up at him, she said, "I know better than any how the path of your life has not always been an easy one. You are a good man who deserves some good luck. My wishes are that today is that time. And the hopes and plans you spoke of . . . I . . ."

"I know," Bob said softly when she was unable to find the right words to finish. Then he grinned. "But hey, don't go painting that my luck has been all bad. I've got you and Bucky in my corner, don't I?"

CHAPTER 30

The contest started precisely at ten.

The range was marked out over a flat, open area directly behind the Crystal Diamond. Mike Bullock, Angus McTeague, and banker Abraham Starbuck were the somber-faced judges sitting on wooden folding chairs near the firing line. The prize guns, guarded by an even more somber-faced Simon Quirt, were displayed on a folding table that had been set up close by. A handful of nimble young boys who would serve as target runners were crouched in a pack on the sidelines, eagerly awaiting the call to bring in the first targets.

August Gafford, not surprisingly, did the announcing for the event. He started by introducing each of the contestants—to varying degrees of applause, the lowest response being only the meager hand-claps of the three Shaw sons for Moses Shaw—and then giving a quick review of the rules.

The initial round would be the twenty-four men shooting in six groupings of four, three shots each. The targets were initially set at eighty yards. Any round cutting outside the boundary, even marginally, of the one-inch-diameter center circle, meant immediate elimination. Rounds within the circle would be measured for distance of spread. The narrowest ones (ties were permissible) would advance; spreads measuring too wide would also mean elimination.

Bob shot in the third grouping of the first round. By the time he stepped to the firing line, three men had already been eliminated. The marshal grouped his shots at just a whisker over a quarter inch. Two other men in his group tied him, one was eliminated.

By the end of the first full round, seven of the starting twenty-four had been eliminated. The approaching thunder was growling more frequently and getting closer.

To hurry things along, the judges unanimously ruled to skip the ninety-yard increment and set the targets for the next round at one hundred yards.

Bob shot in the second grouping this time and once again advanced, keeping the spread of his rounds almost as tight as before. When the second round was completed, eight more men had been eliminated. The crowd of onlookers was increasing in size and buzzing louder with excitement. Bob blocked them out, concentrating on nothing but his rifle and the targets, taking cursory stock of the men left shooting against him.

Vern was also still in the thick of it, grinning sheepishly the couple of times he caught Bob looking his way.

Moses Shaw was still in it, too. No smiles, sheepish or otherwise, from him. Only an expression of grim concentration. The same expression, Bob thought, that he likely had worn as a Union sharpshooter picking off enemy soldiers. The long-standing question of whether or not those claims were true seemed to be answered once and for all here today. If the varmint *hadn't* shot in the war, like he said, he sure as hell was proving to possess the skill to have been capable of it. What was more, the scarred, battered old Henry repeater he was chewing up targets with looked like it might have been around for just about as long.

Nine men faced the targets at a hundred-ten yards. They were scheduled to shoot in three groupings of three.

Bob took the line first. He fired his rounds at a steady, unhurried rhythm, and the trigger stroke of each one felt good, solid. Like they'd gone right where he wanted them to. Still, at that distance, he knew his spread wasn't as tight as the previous times.

When the targets were brought in and examined, he learned he was correct. His spread was pushing close to half an inch. Fortunately, so were some others. When the measuring was done, four more shooters were eliminated. Five advanced—and Bob was one of them.

Five men now. Bob, Vern, Moses Shaw, Clayton Delaney, and Ben Eames, the buckskin-clad man looking to win himself some "tonier" winter digs.

A hundred-twenty yards to the targets. With the sky growing steadily darker, the clouds showing movement, the thunder getting louder. But no one in the crowd was departing, not even the women or the aged. If anything, more were still packing in. And none of the officials dared even *think* about stopping or postponing the balance of the contest.

The shooters took the firing line. As soon as he squeezed off his third round of this set, Bob knew he'd pulled it slightly. He cursed inwardly, certain he'd just scored an elimination. Once again, when the targets were brought in and examined, he proved to be correct. His third bullet had punched out near the edge of the circle, not breaking the boundary but nevertheless giving him an overall pattern spread of nearly three quarters of an inch.

"Tough break, Bob," said Mike Bullock, looking up from his judge's chair as he held out Bob's target.

Bob's mouth twisted wryly as he took the paper. "Guess I won't be able to let you hang those fancy guns over your bar for a spell after all, Mike."

"Sonofabitch!"

Looking around at the sudden exclamation, Bob saw Moses Shaw, standing before another of the judges, only a few feet down. He was crumpling up his paper target and throwing it to the ground. Bob turned and moved toward him. He sensed Vern fall in step beside him.

"Trouble?" Bob asked in a neutral voice.

Abraham Starbuck, the judge who'd apparently handed Shaw his target results, said, "Mr. Shaw didn't fare too well that last round and is unhappy with the evidence."

"You're damned right I ain't happy about it," Moses fumed. "This match should have been held off on account of these weather conditions." He whirled one hand in the air to help make his point. "The thunder, the wind pickin' up—it's too distractin' for a man to rightly concentrate, says I."

"You're entitled to your opinion, I suppose," said Starbuck. "But those conditions were being experienced by everyone else, too. There was nothing that focused them unfairly on just you."

Moses's sons were edging up to the front of the crowd only a short distance away. They looked sullen and ready for trouble, their eyes narrowed, their mouths curled into sneers. Each had a rifle in the crook of his arm. On either side close behind them, however, Fred and Peter stood poised and ready in case they tried to make trouble.

Bob saw fit to give them and their father a none-too-subtle reminder. "I warned you what would happen if you came back to town and started anything, Moses," he said. "I allowed you to return for the sake of trying your luck in the contest. Well, you put in a damn good showing but you came up short. Just like me and a lot of other fellas. I don't like it much, either, but that's the way it is. The only thing that leaves is to accept it like a man, not bellyache and whine about it like a spoiled brat."

"Yeah, I'll accept it," Moses snarled. "I'll accept that once again the Shaws get the shitty end of the shovel, just like always. Don't know why I ever let my hopes get built up that there was any chance for it to turn out different."

"Never mind that high-talkin' marshal and this whole stinkin' town, Pop," said Harley. "To hell with all of 'em. Us Shaws don't need no fancy-ass set of guns to make us amount to something."

"That's right, Pop," chimed in Cyrus. "They can take their stupid prize guns and stick 'em—"

"That's enough!" barked the marshal. "You were given a fair chance, you came up short, and now all you're doing is delaying the contest for everybody else who wants to see it finish up. So, since you've proven once again that you can't act civilized around civilized folks, take your lousy attitudes and dirty mouths and get out of here."

Moses stood his ground, glaring hard at Bob for a long, tense moment. Then he tipped his head in a barely perceptible nod. "Okay for now, Hatfield. Okay . . . for now."

A long, low growl of thunder rumbled across the sky as Moses spun on his heel and bulled off into the crowd, his sons leading the way, roughly shouldering a path through whoever got in their way.

Bob gestured to Fred and Peter. "You know the routine. Follow 'em to the edge of town, make sure they don't do anything rash. Get on back here as quick as you can."

A sudden, cold gust of wind whipped across the firing range and into the crowd, lifting hats and bonnets and causing ladies to bend forward quickly in order to keep their skirts from billowing up.

"We'd better hurry up and get on with this," hollered Angus McTeague, clutching a handful of fluttering paper targets to his chest. "This storm ain't gonna hold off much longer."

"By all means," agreed August Gafford. "The targets are now set at one hundred–forty yards. Who are our remaining shooters?"

"That means you. Better step up there, kid," Bob said to Vern.

Vern shook his head. Then, with a lopsided grin, he held up his last target and said, "Afraid not. I didn't get a chance to show you before ol' man Shaw cut loose, but that last distance did me in, too." The target he was holding out showed how one of his latest set of rounds had sliced a hair past the outer boundary of the center circle.

So it was down to only two remaining shooters. Clayton Delaney and Ben Eames.

The men stepped up to the firing line. Each looked very intent. Increasing gusts of wind buffeted them.

"Whenever you're ready, gentlemen," said Gafford, the expression on his face having turned oddly anxious.

The men put their rifles to their shoulders and fired quickly, confidently. Six shots cracked amidst another rumble of thunder. And then, like an exclamation point marking the conclusion, a pitchfork of lightning sizzled down across the western sky.

The target chasers came racing back with the targets. The three judges took the pieces of paper and leaned together, murmuring, heads bobbing.

After a brief examination, Abe Starbuck lifted his head and announced in a loud voice, "We have a winner—Mr. Clayton Delaney!"

CHAPTER 31

In the next handful of minutes, several things happened very rapidly.

No sooner had banker Starbuck sang out with the announcement of a winner than another lightning-thunder combination ripped across the sky. In the illumination from the lightning flash, wind-whipped, silver-gray sheets of rain could be seen dancing across the open plains to the west, headed straight for New Town and the throng of people gathered all up and down the edge of the shooting range.

Clambering up onto a chair to make himself more visible and to help his voice carry above the buzz of the crowd and the increasing din of the approaching storm, August Gafford shouted, "Everybody! Inside immediately! The Crystal Diamond is now open for business and we will hold the prize presentation in there!"

The rear, side, and front doors of the big saloon were instantly propped open and people—men, women, teetotalers, heavy drinkers, and everything in between—began frantically swarming for shelter.

As the first of the hard, cold rain sluiced down over the side of his face, soaking and bending down his hat brim, forcing him to wince and turn his head, Bob raked his eyes in a quick sweep to determine where he could be the most help. At the same time he naturally also sought to find the faces of Bucky and Consuela somewhere in the swarm. He knew they had been watching him shoot—he'd caught a glimpse of them standing together in the early going. But, once knowing they were there and accounted for, as the contest had proceeded and his concentration became more and more tightly focused on continuing to advance, he'd lost exact sight of them. Then, even as he was facing his disappointment at failing to make the cut, there'd been the flare-up from Moses Shaw to deal with. And now the blasted storm had cut loose.

It wasn't like Bob didn't think Consuela and Bucky couldn't withstand a little wind and rain, but he knew he'd feel a lot more at ease if he could *see* that they were gaining shelter okay. Nevertheless, he hung back, aiding others immediately around him, the elderly and the frail, making sure they didn't get too badly roughed up in the crunch to get out of the storm.

The side door was the closest point of entry for Bob and those in his immediate vicinity. To his right, he could see the judges, Gafford, and some of the other shooters making their way for the rear entrance. Vern was in among them, as well as Simon Quirt and Delaney, the contest winner. A corner of Bob's mouth quirked up as he noted that Delaney had a grip on the case holding the prize guns—they might not have been *officially* presented to him yet but he was stamping his claim on them all the same. And who could blame him? He'd damn well earned the right.

Another rumble of thunder rolled through the rain. At least that's what Bob took it for at first. But there was something vaguely wrong about it. Yes, it was a rumbling sound, but it seemed closer, lower. Not quite . . .

And then shouts of alarm were raised and women began shrieking. This was quickly joined by the unmistakable bark of gunfire.

Bob wheeled about, turning this way and that, eyes scanning the scene. His left fist tightened on his Yellowboy and his right hand hovered over the Colt on his hip. Then he saw them—two men on horseback, spurring their mounts hard, straight into the thick of the crowd off to his right, overtaking the knot of people where Bob had seen Vern and the others only a moment ago. The riders had their bodies hung low over the far sides of their horses, Indian style, alternately swinging their rifles like clubs or extending forward to shoot under the animals' necks. Through the mass of people, Bob couldn't manage a clear return shot. But even in the slashing rain he got a good enough glimpse of the attackers to determine beyond doubt that they were Harley and Cyrus Shaw!

From somewhere up ahead, more shots rang out and a fresh wave of women's shrieks cut the air. This ruckus seemed to be coming from *inside* the Crystal Diamond! Bob froze for a fraction of a second, bewildered, unsure as to the purpose of this violent outbreak and how to counter it without putting innocent citizens at even greater risk. As he wrestled with this moment of indecision, a third horseman came plowing *out* the side door of the saloon. Those in his way were either knocked aside like stalks of corn or trampled viciously under the chewing hooves of the horse.

A second rider emerged directly on the tail of the first. The propped-open door was torn from its hinges, crackling and shattering, sending shards of ragged timber flying like shrapnel, piercing and damaging some of the people who only moments ago had been clawing to squeeze through that very doorway.

Now many of the folks Bob had been assisting and herding ahead of him, trying to get them to shelter, were suddenly turning around and surging back against him in a desperate wave to escape the ruthless horsemen. The discomfort of some rain and wind were of small consequence compared to the threat of a bullet or falling under a horse's hooves. The marshal was jarred and battered by the human stampede, twisted this way and that, so he was barely able to keep his bearings let alone draw a bead on any of the attackers. Although he had yet to get a good look at the pair who'd emerged from the side door, he had no doubt they'd turn out to be Moses and Wiley Shaw.

Even as he cursed the identity of these cold-blooded marauders, Bob suddenly found himself face-to-face with one of them. Staggered, barely able to maintain his footing and balance after being repeatedly pummeled by the tide rushing back against him, he looked up and saw Moses Shaw, mounted on his horse, looming high above him. Moses's eyes were wide and wild, his teeth were bared in a maniacal grin, and he was backlit by a sizzling pitchfork of lightning that cast him in contrasting bars of shadow and brilliance that made him look like a spawn straight out of hell.

Moses raised his rain-glistening Henry repeater and aimed it at Bob.

Bob's right hand clawed for his Colt. But, for once, Sundown Bob's famed fast draw had no chance of turning the tables—his holster was empty, the Colt jostled loose at some point by the panicked horde fleeing back against him. As an alternative, he tried to swing the Yellowboy into play but even as he did so he knew he had no chance of succeeding.

"I told you it wouldn't be very long before you were held to account, Hatfield," snarled Moses.

A red tongue of flame leapt from the Henry's muzzle. In the same instant, a tremendous blast of thunder rattled the sky and caused the ground under Bob's feet to tremble. His awareness of this was very brief, however, as a streak of fiery hot pain snapped his head back on his shoulders and he had a fleeting sensation of starting to fall before he lost all sensation of anything.

CHAPTER 32

"Hang on a minute . . . I think he might be coming around."

The voice sounded murky, as if coming from far away. Yet somehow Bob knew it was actually quite close. The odd tone, he decided, was the result of being filtered through the dull ringing that filled his head. A dull ringing accompanied by a sharp, pulsing pain.

Gradually, he became aware of other sounds around him. Other voices, several of them, chattering excitedly; footsteps moving about hurriedly; groans of pain.

And then he remembered Moses Shaw's rifle firing at him from near point-blank range. This caused him to wonder if he were dead and if the voices he could hear were other souls clambering to get into the hereafter. But if this were the Pearly Gates of Heaven, there ought not be so much anguish, should there? Did that mean . . . ?

"Bob. Can you hear me?"

This time he recognized the voice. It was Mike Bullock's.

He tried to open his eyes but the lids felt like they weighed a ton each and refused to cooperate. Plus he somehow knew that opening his eyes to the light was going to send the pain in his head spiking even higher.

"Pa. You're going to be all right, you hear? You've *got* to be."

Bucky's voice. Quaking, intense, willing with all his might for the words he was saying to be true.

When he tried a second time, Bob got his eyes opened. The pain spiked just like he'd known it would. But it was worth it to see his son's face looming over him. A face streaked by tear tracks and obviously wracked by recent anxiety but now suddenly flooding with hope.

"Hey, pal," Bob managed to say in a raspy voice. He lifted one hand to stroke the side of Bucky's face. "Sorry if I let you down by coming up short in that doggone shooting match."

"That don't matter," Bucky was quick to respond, squeezing the words out between a half laugh and a half sob. "As long as you're okay, that don't matter at all!"

The pulsing pain subsided somewhat and Bob raised his head to try and get a better look at his surroundings. He was lying on his back on the floor of a high-ceilinged room—the main barroom of the Crystal Diamond Saloon, he recognized after a moment. He was still wet from the rain and outside, through the ringing in his ears, he became aware of the storm still ongoing, though somewhat abated.

Someone had placed a folded coat under his head. On all sides he could see other people laid out much like he was. Some were moving their limbs or heads, some were motionless. A few exhibited streaks of blood on their clothing. And Bob could make out at least two very still forms with an article of clothing spread smoothly over their faces.

Bob returned his focus to Bucky and the other faces hovering close about him—Mike Bullock, Maudie Sartain, and Angus McTeague.

"I know it was Moses Shaw and his boys," he said. "But . . . but what happened?"

"They came back for those damned prize guns that Moses felt cheated out of," said Bullock somberly. "They gave the slip to your two deputies, Fred and Peter, and came thundering back in on horseback. Clubbing and trampling, they rode straight into the mob of people just as everybody was scrambling to get inside out of the rain. In all the confusion, what with the storm busting loose and those maniacs riding roughshod over everything and everybody, a lot of people got injured, a few even killed."

Bob tried to push up on his elbows but a piercing pain lancing through his skull triggered a wave of dizziness that caused him to fall back almost immediately.

"Take it easy," Angus McTeague was quick to caution. "You didn't exactly make it unscathed yourself."

Bob reached up, probing tenderly. He felt a lumpy bandage perched atop his head, covering the direct source of his knifing pain. "I thought I was a goner," he said as the dizziness subsided. "Why wasn't I?"

"Just a freaky stroke of luck, was the only way the doctor could explain it," said Maudie. "The way your head was tilted, looking up at Shaw . . . the angle of his bullet . . . maybe he hurried his shot or jerked at the last second from a thunderclap. Anyway, the bullet cut a groove in your scalp and then, well, *bounced* without penetrating through to the brain and without even much bleeding."

"Jesus," Bob muttered. "I've been called stubborn and hardheaded more than a few times in my life but . . ." His words trailed off, his expression bunching into a scowl. "Did they get the guns?"

"Afraid so. They ripped the case right out of the hand of that Delaney fella, liked to tore his arm off."

"Where's everybody else?" Bob wanted to know. "Where is Fred and . . . where's Consuela?"

"Fred and Peter got wounded when the Shaws gave them the slip," said Bullock. "Nothing too serious, but they each took a bullet. Fred got it in the leg, Peter in the shoulder. Vern is over yonder, helping to—"

"What about Consuela? Where's Consuela?"

These questions were met by a tense, momentary silence. Until Bucky was the one to break it by saying, "They took her, Pa."

Bob's hand closed around his son's wrist. "What do you mean? Who took her?"

"The Shaws," Bullock answered. "They rode out of here with two hostages—Consuela and Alora Dane. They threatened to kill 'em if any posse came chasing too close."

Bob surged to a sitting position and then to his feet, moving so fast that those around him were startled into taking a backward step. All except Bucky. As soon as he was standing, another wave of dizziness hit Bob, and he lurched unsteadily. Bucky grabbed his arm to steady him and Bullock and McTeague moved back in to also assist.

Bob found himself suddenly fighting to catch his breath. "When was this?" he puffed. "How long was I out?"

"About half an hour."

"Where's Fred? Is somebody getting together a posse?"

Bullock frowned. "Didn't you hear what I said? Moses Shaw swore they'd kill those women at the first sign of—"

"And what did he say they'd do to them otherwise?"

Bullock had trouble meeting Bob's fierce glare. "He said that once they were sure of being in the clear, they'd let Consuela and Miss Dane go at some point where they could safely make it back to—"

"And everybody was willing to take his word on that?" Bob's voice was raised to nearly a shout by now. "Look around you. Do you think a piece of vermin who could do something like this can be trusted to keep his word? I can guarantee you he has every intention of killing those women, no matter what. The only question is what him and his twisted sons will do to them before—" Bob stopped short, not wanting to finish his thoughts with Bucky right there, gazing up at him. An expression of increasing alarm and dismay gripped the boy's face.

The marshal swayed unsteadily once again just as Doc Tibbs turned from his other patients and came hurrying over. "You need to lie back down immediately," Tibbs insisted. "You've suffered a serious head trauma and we must wait until—"

Bob cut him off. "Seems to me, Doc, that too damn much waiting has taken place already. So save your breath if you're gonna try and talk me into doing more of it."

"You push yourself too fast and too hard with an injury like that, there's a strong chance that all you'll do is finish what Moses Shaw attempted to begin with."

"If that's what's written, then that's the way it'll have to go," Bob replied. "But waiting here—split skull or not—and leaving those two women to the mercy of the Shaw clan . . . that I won't do. That I *can't* do."

Vern suddenly materialized at the doctor's side, a relieved smile on his face. "Marshal! Boy, is it good to see you up on your feet."

"The doc here don't agree with you. But that's another story," Bob told him. "Where are Fred and your brother?"

Vern pointed. "Over this way. Come on, I'll show you."

Bob took a step, lurched again. Vern and Tibbs were quick to assist him.

"Damn it!" Bob cursed his unsteadiness. "Just give me a minute—I'll get squared away with this."

They threaded their way through other citizens milling about, many in a state of semi-shock, some laid out on the floor due to injuries, like Bob had been. And here and there were the totally still bodies with their faces covered. Outside, the rain continued to hiss down, and infrequently there came a muted stutter of thunder.

"What's the extent of the damage?" Bob asked.

"Five dead," Doc Tibbs reported grimly. "About half a dozen injured seriously, at least that many more hurt to lesser degrees."

They reached a point near the saloon's front door where Fred and Peter sat on the floor with their backs to the wall. Fred's left pant leg was slit wide open and a bloodstained bandage was wrapped around his meaty thigh. Peter's left arm was in a sling that also bore some blood streaking.

"Thank God you're okay, boss," Fred exclaimed as he saw Bob approaching. But the elated expression on his face lasted only a moment before it collapsed into a look of regret bordering on shame. Hanging his head, he added, "No thanks to us and the sorry way we handled those Shaw skunks, letting 'em get the drop on us the way they did."

"We let 'em get their horses and then followed right behind, all the way to the edge of town," said Peter Macy, wearing his own forlorn expression. "They were mumbling and grumbling the whole way, mostly the old man complaining about how he got a raw deal in the contest. We couldn't hear every word they said, though, and somewhere along the way they must have passed some signals back and forth."

"Then, just when we were ready to turn back and leave 'em go on their way," said Fred, taking over the narrative again, "they wheeled on us with guns blazing. Cut us down and then tried to trample us. Warming up, I guess you could say, for when they got here." His voice caught on the last few words and he barely got them out.

"What's done is done," said Bob, feeling sympathy for his deputies but at the same time knowing there was no time for wasted emotion—neither to lay blame nor to offer consolation. "The thing now is to take what's left and try to make the best of it."

Fred and Peter lifted their faces. "Whatever you want from us, you know you got."

Bob turned to the doctor. "How bad are they? Are you finished patching them up? Will they be able to reasonably get around, function in a limited way?"

Tibbs scowled. "I've still got to dig the bullet out of Fred. I left it for the time being because I had more serious wounds to tend to. But it missed the bone and I'm pretty sure it didn't do any serious muscle damage. So, yes, after I get the slug out I suppose he'd be able to get around with a crutch. That's not to say there won't be a good deal of discomfort, however."

"Hang the discomfort. I can handle that," Fred said.

"As for Peter," Tibbs went on, "he got off a little better. His shoulder wound was an in-and-out. So there's no lead in him and, once again, no bone damage as far as I could see initially. But there's meat and muscle tear awfully close to the joint, which means a good deal of swelling and stiffness for a spell. But, with a sling, he, too, should be able to get around reasonably well."

Bob nodded. "Good. I need to put together a posse as soon as possible and—"

"Wait a minute!" the doctor protested. "I said these men could function reasonably well, but surely you can't take that to mean they're ready to ride out in a posse. As far as that goes, you're in no shape for such an undertaking yourself."

"If you'd let me finish," the marshal barked back irritably, "I never had any intention of putting these deputies in a posse. What I was trying to find out was if they could manage well enough to look after the town while me and my other deputy head up some men to ride after the Shaws. And as far as what I'm in shape for—until I keel over and can't haul my sorry ass back up again, I'll make the decisions on that!"

CHAPTER 33

On the back side of the Crystal Diamond Saloon, pressed close to the side of the building so that a section of roof overhang protected them from the rain, three men were huddled in conversation.

"You heard the marshal in there, making noises about forming up a posse," Clayton Delaney was saying, his words coming rapidly, anxiously. "I want you, Eugene, to be part of it. Say or do whatever you have to. Lie about your background, claim to have worn a badge and ridden with other posses in the past, if that's what it takes. Just make sure you get included in."

Eugene Boyd's broad face stretched with a sly smile. "Hell, I *have* ridden with plenty of posses in the past. I was always the one out ahead of 'em, that's all."

"This is serious, damn it," snapped Delaney. "I've got to get those guns back. The information they possess, the power that having such information will give to me, is crucial beyond imagination. Far more than the mere value of the guns themselves. I tried doing it what I thought was the smart way, and what did it get me? I even had them right in my hands. And then, once again, just like that"—he snapped the fingers of his left hand—"they were gone."

"You did a helluva fine job of shootin' in that contest, that's for sure," Boyd admitted. "I thought everything was a done deal."

"That just goes to show," Delaney fumed, "that lurking around the corner at every turn of your life, there's some no-good sonofabitch waiting to snatch away your hard-won gains. Remember that."

"No problem there. We learned that lesson a long time ago by always bein' the ones to do the snatchin'," Boyd reminded him. "That's why I tried to tell you we should've used our gang to snatch them guns off the train the other day out in open country."

"Speakin' of our gang," said the third man, a small-ish individual with a hangdog expression wrapped around an oversized nose that was the only thing giving him any real distinction, "are we gonna bring them into this now that the cow has kicked over the milkin' bucket?"

"You damn betcha we are. Ain't we, Clayton?"

"Naturally."

The third man, whose name was Chuck Peabody, raised a rain-damp hand and scratched at the whiskers on the side of his face. "That mean you're gonna come back with me then, Clayton? I mean, if Eugene rides out with that posse, you'll have to come and take charge of the gang, right?"

"Not necessarily. At least, not right away." Delaney raised and lowered his sling-wrapped right arm. "I played this up pretty good, letting on that it had been badly wrenched when that hellion on horseback yanked the gun case away from me. It does hurt, but not all that bad. The point is, it gives me a good excuse for not riding out with the posse. But it also means I can't suddenly ride off for some other undisclosed reason, either. It would be sure to look suspicious."

"Yeah, I guess it would," allowed Peabody.

"But hanging around here—for a little while, at least—isn't necessarily a bad thing. Since I'm not only one of the injured parties," Delaney explained, "but also have legal claim to the stolen guns, they're bound to keep me advised of all the latest developments. Who knows? It just might be that the local bumpkin of a marshal can somehow manage to retrieve those guns. In that case, they'll be returned to me and everything will still have the chance to work out smooth for us."

"Okay. Reckon that would be a welcome thing." Peabody frowned. "But where does that leave the gang, as far as the rest of the men knowin' what's up and what they're supposed to be doin' in the meantime?"

"That falls to you. You'll be taking instructions back on my behalf."

"Me?" Peabody suddenly looked very uncertain. "I dunno. What's the chances of Iron Tom or Largo or some of the others payin' any attention to what I got to say?"

"Because you'll be the direct link to me. In other words, you'll be doing the speaking, but I'll be doing the talking. They'd damn well better pay attention," said Delaney.

"And if there's any balkin'," added Boyd, "you can

remind 'em that it's just a matter of time before I'll be comin' back around again, and I'll settle the hash of anybody who gives you a hard time."

Peabody licked his lips, trying to put on a braver front than he was actually feeling. "Okay. If you fellas say so. What's the message I'm carryin' back to the others?"

Inside his well-appointed office at the Crystal Diamond, August Gafford was pacing furiously back and forth. The long cigar he was alternately clamping in his mouth or waving around to emphasize a point had filled the air with a slowly swirling cloud of blue smoke.

"Listen to 'em out there," Gafford said, jabbing his cigar toward the richly paneled door that led out to the main barroom of the saloon. "Three quarters of the town jammed into my joint on opening day and I ain't making a damn dime off any of 'em. We're in a crisis, so the only charitable thing for a civic-minded business leader like me to do is dole out free drinks to help soothe frayed nerves and calm poor terrorized souls." Gafford paused to wave both arms wildly, the one with the cigar in its fist making whirling patterns of smoke. "What about *my* frayed nerves? In addition to all the money being poured down undeserving gullets in the name of trauma, my goddamn golden guns have been stolen—*twice!*—right out from under my nose."

Sunk back in a heavily cushioned chair situated at an angle before the room's massive desk, Ben Eames cranked his head around with a scowl. "If that last part was yet another remark concerning my failure to win the shooting contest, I'm getting a little sick of hearing about it."

"I'm pretty sick over the whole business, too."

"Look, I never claimed to be the best shot in the whole world," Eames said. "No matter how good you are at something, there's always gonna be somebody better. Who could have figured that 'somebody' would pop up out here in the middle of no-stinking-where, Wyoming?"

"Yet he did. Of all the rotten damn luck!"

"In the end, it didn't really make a lot of difference," pointed out Eames. "Even if I *would* have won the guns, they'd have gotten snatched away from me just like happened to the other fella. There's where your anger truly needs to be aimed—toward that scurvy old Shaw rapscallion and his sons. They're the ones who tore hell out of everything and everybody and stole the guns in the process."

Gafford waved his arms again. "Don't you think I know that? Don't you think I have a special hatred built up for those unwashed dogs? The thought of them even *touching* my precious guns—let alone actually possessing them for any length of time—makes me physically sick to my stomach."

"What about 'em touching and possessing those women hostages they took?" Eames said with a distasteful expression clouding his face.

Gafford stopped pacing and leaned on the end of his desk. "You want the cold, hard truth? Here it is: If I had to choose one over the other, it would be my guns, hands down. If Alora Dane were here, all she'd represent would be another *expense*—on top of the loss I'm currently suffering due to the tragedy that's taken place. Exactly the kind of unexpected problem I told you I don't have the funds to cover. Not without those guns. That ought to make it plain enough why, as far as I'm concerned, they take precedence over anything or anybody."

Eames emitted a low whistle. "You're right. That's plenty clear and also a pretty damned cold outlook."

"Don't think I'm proud to admit it," Gafford said, setting his jaw firmly. "But, from my standpoint, it's only practical."

"But what happens if Hatfield's posse catches up with those thievin' varmints and retrieves the guns?" Eames asked. "With Delaney still on hand to claim 'em, that doesn't solve the problem of *you* not having them."

Gafford's jaw remained firmly set, the muscles at the hinge bunching visibly. "True enough. With Delaney still on hand, as you said . . . still alive, in other words."

Some of the color left Eames's face. "What are you saying?"

"Oh, come on, man, don't act so dense," said Gafford, straightening up abruptly. "I'm saying exactly what it sounds like—if something were to happen to Delaney before those guns were returned, then the claim to them would fall to the next man in line from the shooting contest. That would be you. And that, subsequently, would put me right back where I need to be. How much plainer do I have to make it?"

Eames passed the back of one hand across his mouth. "If something were to happen to Delaney . . . like him getting killed, you mean?"

"That's the blunt way of putting it."

"By me?"

"You're the one I'm discussing it with, aren't you? Why do you think I snuck you in here for this talk? You owe me for failing to win that contest in the first place."

"But I'm no killer!" Eames insisted.

"You're not? There's the grave of a young woman in Boston that many see as a testament proving otherwise."

Eames thrust to his feet. "Damn you! I told you to quit bringing that up!"

"Then quit backing me into a corner with your foolish demands and your shooting incompetence and now your gutless refusal to commit a simple act that would square everything."

"Murder is hardly a simple act. Not for me—no matter what you say or others may believe." Now Eames began to pace. "What about that other fellow you've already got on your payroll? That Simon Quirt you threatened me with before. If he's such a dangerous gunslinger, then murder ought to be right up his alley. Why not have him kill Delaney?"

"For myriad reasons," Gafford countered. "Number one, it would leave you—with your own hands unbloodied yet fully aware of too many details—in the position of having leverage over me. Number two, the money I am paying Mr. Quirt was based strictly on guarding the guns. So even if he *would* agree to take care of Delaney for me, I'm sure it would involve a significant additional fee. And you've heard repeatedly where I stand in that regard."

"If Quirt was responsible for guarding the guns,

then why aren't you holding him to account for failure, the same as you are me?"

"Because, technically, Quirt's job was done as soon as Delaney took the gun case out of his hands. So it still comes back to you not winning that contest, as we went to great lengths and considerable expense to arrange. Had you done so and everything else still happened exactly as it did, then all we'd be looking at would be the retrieval of the guns. Something I have faith that our fiercely determined marshal will accomplish." Gafford shook his head sternly. "But because of your failure, Delaney still stands in the way. Therefore it is your responsibility to do whatever's necessary to remove him as an obstacle."

CHAPTER 34

In the bedroom of his house, Bob was seated on the edge of the mattress, packing items into an old buckskin war bag that had been placed on a chair pulled up alongside the bed. Bucky was assisting by bringing him spare clothing and such from a nearby chest of drawers.

Although it showed many miles of use, the war bag was still plenty sturdy and reliable. Usually stored deep within Bob's closet, except for occasions such as the pursuit he was now planning, the bag and its contents dated back to his outlaw period as the Devil's River Kid. Chief among the ever-present items inside were a backup Schofield revolver Bob faithfully kept cleaned and oiled, extra boxes of ammo for the Schofield as well as additional .44 cartridges for the Colt sidearm and Yellowboy rifle he currently carried, a compass, and a pair of high-quality binoculars.

In times past, whenever a situation called for the war bag to once again be put to use, it usually had been Consuela—the only other person who knew the full story behind it—who'd drag it out of the closet and do the necessary added packing to have it ready for Bob. Her absence today wore heavy on Bob's mind, and for reasons far beyond not having her here to help make necessary preparations.

As he watched his father solemnly arranging things within the fringed bag, Bucky's youthful expression carried its own burden of concerns. "You're gonna be able to get Consuela back, ain't you, Pa?" he asked, badly needing to hear the reassurance.

"I sure aim to, pal. I'll do everything in my power."

"If anybody can do it, you can. That's what everybody says."

"That's heartening to hear. Faith ain't a bad thing. Let's hope I can measure up."

"You can. I know you can. But I keep thinking about what you told Mr. Bullock and the others back in the saloon. About how the Shaws might kill her no matter what. Either that or . . ."

"Stop it!" Bob said sharply. "Don't let your thoughts go there. Not ever. If you have faith in me like you say you do, then hold fast to that."

"I will. I promise." Bucky set his mouth firmly. "How about the other kind of faith? In God, I mean. Should I pray?"

"It sure can't hurt."

Bob closed his war bag and pulled it closed, cinching the leather thongs tight. He stood up. His head was still pounding dully but he hadn't experienced any dizziness for some time. He turned to Bucky, placed his hands on the boy's shoulders, and pulled him close. "Like we talked about, you'll be staying with Mike and Teresa Tuttle at the Bluebird Café while I'm away. They'll take good care of you, and I expect you to be on your best behavior. Understood?"

"I will be, Pa."

"Mrs. Tuttle is a good, devout woman. She'll help you with the praying if you need it."

"I think I can handle that part okay, Pa."

Bob lifted the war bag and slung it over his shoulder. "Come along, then. I'm to meet the men who are riding out with me down at the jail. I'll drop you off at the Bluebird on the way by."

Downstairs, as they went out onto the front porch, Bucky paused and looked back at the empty doorway.

"What's the matter? Forget something?" Bob asked.

Bucky shook his head. "No. It's just that it feels so strange for us to be leaving the house and not have Consuela standing there to see us off."

Bob felt it, too. There was a huskiness in his voice as he said, "She'll be back soon, boy . . . She'll be back."

As the day slid into early afternoon, the rain had diminished into little more than a mistlike drizzle.

After leaving Bucky with the Tuttles, Bob walked the rest of the way up Front Street to where a knot of men were huddled in the mist, waiting for him. Half a dozen of them were mounted. A seventh horse was saddled and ready for him to climb aboard. Among the others present, though not on horseback, he saw such familiar faces as Mike Bullock, Angus McTeague, and August Gafford. Fred and Peter were there, too, standing back closer to the front of the jail, looking on in grim silence.

Bob put foot to stirrup and swung up into the

saddle. Vern, who'd been holding the horse until he showed up, now turned the reins over to him. Then he handed over something else, saying, "Figured this might come in handy as well."

What he held out was Bob's .44.

"Somebody turned it in after finding it on the muddy ground back outside the Crystal Diamond," Vern explained. "I gave it a good cleaning, loaded it with fresh shells. It's got a full wheel."

"Obliged," said Bob. He took the gun, hefted its familiar weight and feel, then slipped it into the holster on his hip. "There. That's better." Grinning wryly, he added, "See? All that staggering I was doing a little while ago wasn't dizziness at all. I was just out of balance."

"I doubt the doctor would agree. Nor would he see any damned humor to it," said Mike Bullock, stepping forward. "For the last time, Bob, I'm begging you to reconsider. Especially your participation in it. Damn it, man, a bullet skimmed your head. You can't possibly be in any condition to—"

"We've already wasted too much time hashing that over. I'll not waste any more. I appreciate your concern, Mike—all of you—but my mind's made up. We're heading out."

"Godspeed to you then, if you insist."

"I do. If your intentions are good, as I know they are, then save them for the deputies I'm leaving behind. I expect the town will be pretty tame for a while, but I'm still asking a lot of two wounded men. And if any loudmouth takes a notion to try and throw any blame their way on account of what happened with the Shaws . . . well, hearing about it on my return would make me *very* unhappy."

"We'll see to it there's none of that," McTeague assured him. "Not that they can't handle it themselves. Take an arm *and* a leg away from each of them and they're still two of the finest men in town. Anybody with half a brain can tell you as much."

"I know that," said Bob. "I just don't want them to forget it."

Touching a finger to his hat in a kind of salute to the two men in question, Bob then wheeled his horse about and led his group off toward the north.

Some distance removed from the buildings of town, Bob signaled a halt. As the men reined up around him, he turned to face them and gave them closer scrutiny than he had back at the jail. He'd left it to Vern to pick those who'd ride with them, his only instructions being to choose hardened men who could shoot and withstand several hours in a saddle over rugged country. From the look of what he saw before him now, his deputy had done well.

Bob recognized most of the faces. Earl Wells and Heck Hembrow, two tough young riders for the Bar-K outfit; George O'Farrow, a bull of a man who did part-time work for Krepdorf's General Store and also loaded and unloaded freight at the train station; and Pecos Ryan, a soft-spoken newcomer to town who'd been a participant in the shooting contest and had given a good accounting of his skills. The fifth man was unfamiliar but had the look of a drifter who knew how to handle himself.

"Wanted to have this palaver out here where there weren't so many ears around," Bob said now, by way of explanation. "First, I want to say thanks to you men for being willing to sign on for this. The pay is next to nothing and what lies ahead ain't gonna be no picnic—you can tell that already by the weather conditions. And the hombres we're going after, just in case you had your eyes and ears closed back there earlier this morning, are some seriously dangerous characters. I just wanted to talk to you one more time to make sure you know what you're getting into."

The men returned his look. Nobody said anything.

"Earl and Heck," the marshal said to the Bar-K riders, "you boys have ridden with us before and I'm happy to have you. But you're not risking your jobs at the ranch for this, are you?"

"Mr. Kramer will likely be pissed at first, when we ain't there in the mornin'," replied Heck. "But when he finds out it was for a good cause, especially with those kidnapped women and all, he'll understand."

"Same for me," spoke up Big George O'Farrow. "My bosses will see this as something more important than the mule work I do. And, if they don't, then nuts to 'em. I was lookin' for a job when I hired on to them. I can always find another."

"With your reputation for working hard, George, there ain't a doubt in my mind," Bob told him.

The marshal swung his gaze to Pecos Ryan. "Can't say I know you very well, mister, but I know you can shoot powerful good. For what's at hand, that'll be a welcome thing."

Ryan grinned crookedly. "I may shoot well—but not good enough to win the contest. Therefore, I am out twenty-five dollars with no immediate job prospects." He shrugged. "So your posse wages are small, but at least they'll buy me some more bullets and maybe a plate of beans when we get back."

"I'll see to it they do. For sure," Bob promised.

"And that leaves me," said the remaining man. "My name's Eugene Boyd, Marshal. I've been a lot of places—some you'd know, some you wouldn't. None of 'em looked as good for stayin' as they did for leavin' behind. But in some of those places I packed a star, and the habit of wanting to see no-good skunks get their deserves sort of stuck with me. So, even though I arrived in your fair city only yesterday, I consider it a duty and an honor to ride on this undertaking with you to bring in those who did what they done earlier today."

"Well," said Bob, cocking one eyebrow, "if you can ride and shoot as good as you can talk, then it sounds like you'll be a good fella to have along."

"I'll hold up my end. You won't have to worry about that," Boyd said.

Before anybody could say anything more, the group's attention was drawn by the approach of a new rider galloping out from town. As he drew closer, Bob recognized him as Simon Quirt.

Reaching the posse, Quirt drew up alongside Bob and wasted no time announcing his intentions. "Afternoon, gents. Nobody invited me to the party, so I decided to invite myself." His eyes cut directly to Bob. "You know my reputation, you've seen me work. Any objections?"

Bob considered a minute before giving a nod toward Vern and saying, "I left the selection of the other men up to my deputy. It's only right to let him have his say on you."

Under Quirt's shifted gaze, Vern said, "My only question is why didn't you step forward earlier when I was asking for volunteers?"

"Hadn't made up my mind yet," Quirt answered. "Seemed to be some question at first whether or not the marshal here was up to being a part of it. No offense, Deputy, but I don't ride behind just anybody. With Hatfield in, though, I'm willing to saddle up."

"Sounds like you've got a pretty healthy independent streak," Vern said.

"You could say so. But that don't change the worth of my gun any. Plus, just a few minutes ago, I got word that an old friend of mine, a man named Cecil Yates—you remember him, Marshal, the fella I brought in to help guard the Crystal Diamond after the arson attempt?—well, he died from wounds he got when these fellas you're going after went on their tear. I figure I owe it to Cecil to hunt down the wolves who shot him, one way or other. I can either do it as part of your posse . . . or on my own."

"He's right about the worth of his gun," Bob said. "He proved that when he threw in with me against those two ambushers the other night. He'd be good to have on our side when we catch up with the Shaws. And I'd say he's given a pretty good reason for wanting in."

Vern made an accepting gesture with one hand. "If he suits you, he plumb tickles me. Welcome aboard, Mr. . . . Quirt, is it?"

"That's right. Simon Quirt." The gunman pinched his hat to the other posse members. "Pleased to be ridin' with you, gents." Turning back to Bob, he added,

"Sorry if I missed hearing it on account of arriving a little late, but what's our course of action?"

"I was just getting to that," Bob answered. Raising his voice slightly to address all of the men, he went on, "I expect most of you are probably wondering how we're going to track the Shaws in this rain. Well, the short answer is: We're not. Not at this point anyway. We're gonna bank on me thinking I know where they're headed and us riding hell-for-leather to catch up with 'em there, before they take off again and strike out in a more unpredictable direction."

"What do you know, Marshal? Where is it you think they're headed?" asked Vern.

"Their ranch," Bob said.

There was a muttering within the ranks. Then Heck Hembrow said, "Their own place? Lightin' straight for there would be kinda dumb, wouldn't it, Marshal?"

"Maybe so dumb it's smart," countered Bob. "Stop and think . . . I don't figure they came to town *planning* on raising hell and stealing those guns the way they ended up doing. It was strictly a spur-of-the-moment thing, a violent reaction born of Moses losing the match and feeling he'd gotten another raw deal, same as he's been moaning and fretting about for years. So now they're suddenly on the run with no thought given to what they're caught up in. That means no plan for what to do next, no supplies, no nothing—except the hostages they grabbed, who they're counting on to buy 'em some time and provide bargaining power if needed."

"I'd say having those women gives 'em a whole lot of bargaining power," said George O'Farrow.

"True. But dragging hostages along can also have some drawbacks," Bob pointed out. "Especially here at the beginning, they'll slow things down and they're bound to cause a certain amount of distraction within an undisciplined pack like the Shaws. All the more reason for us to move fast and sure in this early stage."

"But they've already got a two-hour head start on us," said Earl Wells.

"I'm well aware of that. But in those couple of hours, like I just got done explaining, I figure they've been slowed considerable by indecision and by the women they grabbed. Plus, if they're dropping somebody back now and then to check their back trail for pursuit, there's a little more time lost. In other words, they're not eating up ground near as fast as we can once we set spurs hard to our chase."

"Meaning you think we can catch up with them not too long after they make it to their ranch," said Quirt.

"That's what I think, yeah," said Bob.

"How far to their ranch?"

"About fifteen miles."

"Meaning it'll be coming on dark by the time they get there."

"Even if they believe there's nobody in close pursuit, you don't figure they're bold enough to hole up the night there, do you, Marshal?" said Vern.

Bob shook his head. "No. Especially not if this storm passes and they've got even a partially clear sky to travel under. The Shaws know this territory plenty good enough to move out under moon- and starlight."

"So," said Pecos Ryan, "even if you're right about them being headed for their ranch, our chance to catch them there will last only as long as it takes them to stock up on supplies and fresh horses."

"That's about the size of it," Bob conceded.

"Then hadn't we better get a move on?"

Bob scowled. "Of course. But we can't just go charging after 'em like a herd of thirsty beeves aimed toward water. If we close the gap fast enough but reckless enough for them to spot us, we're right back to putting the hostages at risk. That's why we need to work out the final details of our approach."

"Something tells me you've already got an idea in mind," said Vern.

"Matter of fact, I do. You've never had call to visit the Shaw place, Vern. But Earl, Heck—you fellas know where it is, right?" Once he'd gotten affirmative nods from the two Bar-K riders, Bob went on. "Straight northeast from here. Way I remember, the house and main corrals sit in a kind of shallow bowl. To the north and south are heavily wooded slopes. Unless they've done a lot of timber clearing in the last year or so, which I don't think they've got the ambition for, the trees to the south reach in especially close to the house. If we were to split into two groups and ride out wide on our approach to the ranch, each group closing in down one of those wooded slopes, then I'm thinking we'd have a pretty good chance of boxing in our quarry before they ever knew we were anywhere around."

"Sounds reasonable," said Big George.

"Vern, I'll take Quirt, make the swing to the south, and come in down the slope on that side. You take the rest of the men and come in on the other side."

"I do good in the dark. I can get in close without 'em ever knowing I was there," said Quirt.

"That's what I'm counting on. Like I said, the trees on that south slope reach in real close. I'm hoping just a couple men, moving slow and cautious, might be able to get far enough to grab the hostages—or at least be primed to do so—before the balloon goes up on the rest of it."

"And who cuts the balloon loose?"

"It'll be on my signal," Bob said. "The only thing is, I'm not sure what it's gonna be or how I'll give it. Let's just hope it will be clear enough when the moment is on us."

Quirt laced his fingers and stretched his arms forward, palms out, flexing until his knuckles popped. "Good. I like a plan that's not too binding, loose enough for some breathing room. When do we ride?"

CHAPTER 35

Consuela Diaz sat on the ground with her wrists bound behind her. She was cold, wet, frightened, and angry. One end of a rope, much thicker and coarser than the leather thongs securing her wrists, was looped around her neck; the other end was tied to the trunk of a cottonwood tree. There was only a small amount of slack in the rope. If Consuela tried to relax or lean too far away from the tree, the loop around her neck would tighten, choking her.

Beside Consuela, bound and tied in the same manner, sat Alora Dane. It was easy to see that the entertainer was equally cold, wet, and miserable. Her piled-up blond hair was partly fallen loose, her lipstick and mascara were smeared, and one strap of her brightly spangled dress was broken, leaving her ample bosom barely contained.

Yet, somehow, she still managed to look aloof and beautiful. How frightened she might be was hard to say. But that she was angry there was no doubt. She was plainly demonstrating this via the stream of words pouring from her mouth. The curious thing was, these angry outbursts weren't necessarily aimed at her captors but rather at one August Gafford.

"That silk-tongued sonofabitch," she was muttering, using an extensive vocabulary of words not too many people Consuela knew would consider ladylike. "If I live through this and ever get my hands on that no-good bag of phony promises, what I do to him will make what Indians used to do to their captives look like little more than a scolding from the pulpit!"

Consuela was afraid to ask for specifics.

"I can't pretend to know very much about your relationship with Mr. Gafford," she said. "But surely you can't hold him responsible for the acts of these desperate men we're now in the hands of?"

"The hell I can't!" Alora snapped. Then her tone dropped to a deep pitch meant to mock a male voice. *"Come West with me, my dear. Your fame will expand nationwide, you will be afforded every luxury imaginable, and I personally will see to your total safety."* Pausing to revert back to her normal voice, she added, "Well, excuse me all to hell if it seems like I'm being picky, but I hardly consider our present conditions to be the lap of luxury and I damned sure don't feel very safe in the company of our new escorts."

It was then that Consuela realized the woman was actually quite terrified and was using her anger toward Gafford as a means to try and counter that. "As long as we're still alive, there is hope," she said soothingly. "There are good people back in Rattlesnake Wells who will come after us and save us from these desperadoes."

"How can you be so sure?" Alora said. "You heard what the old man, the leader, told them as we rode away—if he spotted a posse on our trail, he'd kill us. Do you think for a second he would hesitate to do that?"

"Perhaps," Consuela replied. "Not out of compassion because, no, I don't believe that he and his vile sons aren't capable of such evil. But if they *did* kill us, that would eliminate us as a means to hold off a posse and would only spur the townspeople all the harder to catch up and seek justice."

"To hell with justice. If these scurvy dogs kill me, I want bloody revenge!" said Alora. "They're already owed that for the carnage they caused back there and who knows how many other things they've done to deserve it before now."

Consuela's expression saddened deeply and her gaze drifted somewhere far away. "With the town marshal among those left dead back there, without him to lead and control the pursuit I'm confident is coming . . . yes, bloody vengeance may very well be what results. Were he still alive, it would not sink to simply that. And, too, if he were still alive, our chances of being safely rescued would also be much better."

"Are you trying to build up my hopes, or tear them down?" Alora wanted to know. "And what makes you such a big fan of this marshal?"

"I knew him quite well," Consuela said with a quiet intensity.

Seeing the emotion on the girl's face, Alora softened her own tone somewhat. "Look, I'm sorry for your loss. I'm sorry for a lot of what happened back there, including, selfishly, the fix we're in . . . Maybe your marshal isn't really dead, maybe he was only wounded."

Consuela gave a slow shake of her head. "I'm afraid that's not possible. I saw him take a bullet to the head. I was only a short distance away."

In truth, she had been fighting her way through the panicked horde, headed *toward* Bob when she saw Moses Shaw fire at the marshal from near point-blank range. The scream she emitted at the sight was what drew Moses's attention to her. A moment later, he wheeled his horse, reached down to grab her by her long glossy hair, and dragged her up onto the saddle next to him. The last Consuela saw of Bob, he was lying flat and still on the ground with the crowd racing obliviously by, sometimes stepping on him.

She closed her eyes tightly now at the memory, as if doing so could also close the image from her mind. In those first minutes, as Moses galloped away with her, she remembered thinking that she didn't care if she died, too—in fact, *wishing* she were dead. But those feelings hadn't lasted long. She'd been through too much, had developed a core of inner toughness too strong, for her to give up that easily.

If nothing else, there was still Bucky, Bob's son. Consuela had lost sight of him in the chaos, but she knew he had to be back there somewhere now. She refused to believe the Fates would be cruel enough to have let any harm also come to him. Yet that meant he was a young boy who'd lost his mother in the past, now his father, and—temporarily—his surrogate mother. Despite her personal pain and heartbreak, Consuela swore she would not allow that to stand.

Whatever it took, she meant to find a way to survive and make it back to Bucky . . .

"What do you suppose they're talkin' about?"

"How the hell am I supposed to know what they're talkin' about?"

"Be interesting to know, that's all." Cyrus Shaw smiled slyly. "I know what I'd *like* for 'em to be talkin' about. Leastways one of 'em, don't make no difference which. Meanin' I'd like to be supplyin' something they'd surely be payin' attention to."

"Yeah, and then you know what would come next," said his younger brother, Wiley. "Pop would catch you at it and then he'd be the one doin' the talkin' and he'd be gettin' his points across with his fists and the toe of his boot. You ought to've learned that by now."

"Yeah, I've had lessons from him often enough," Cyrus said, running a hand over his ribs in remembrance of a particularly thorough teaching session. "I heard the words and got the message, but that don't mean it was enough to stop me from feelin' the things I figure I got every right to feel."

"That makes you an awful stubborn learner, Cyrus."

"Maybe stubborn. Maybe just not so doggone willing to bow down to the old man, the way you and Harley are so blamed willin' to do all the time."

"I wouldn't make a habit of sayin' stuff like that too often in front of Harley," Wiley advised. "And lettin' him hear you say it even once would probably be too often."

Cyrus scowled. "You leave me to worry about what I say or don't say in front of Harley. Speakin' of which, where in blazes is he anyway? He's been gone long enough by now to check our back trail all the way back to Rattlesnake Wells."

The two brothers were squatted in medium-high grass about twenty feet from the hostages, a distance sternly ordered by their father. Nearby, three horses stood tied to some scrub brush, resting and grazing disinterestedly on the wet grass. Except for other splotches of brush and the tree the women were tied to, the terrain where this halt had been called was wide open and mostly flat.

Moses Shaw stood apart from his sons and the hostages, another forty or fifty feet up a gradual slope reaching to the southwest. He stood motionless, hands planted on his hips, gazing toward the top of the slope. He seemed oblivious to the leftover droplets of rain running off the brim of his hat and down the back of his neck. His craggy features showed no more reaction than if they'd belonged to the stone face of a statue.

"The old man's gettin' impatient for Harley to show back up, too," said Wiley.

Cyrus looked curious. "How can you tell? He's been standin' like that, not movin' a muscle, ever since he walked out there a little bit ago."

"I don't know how, but I can tell," Wiley said stubbornly. "I hope to hell Harley does get back pretty soon. Otherwise the old man will get irascible and take it out on all of us."

"How the hell do you know a word like *irascible*?"

Wiley sighed wearily. "Because I pick up a book

and read it every now and then. You ought to try it sometime."

"Fat chance. What does it mean, anyway—that word *irascible?*"

"Means peevish, foul tempered. Easily provoked to anger."

Cyrus snorted a short laugh. "Well, hell, that ain't no hard conclusion at all. The old man is foul tempered and pissed off about something practically all the time."

"Yeah, but there are times it can get worse. And that's even less of a picnic than normal."

At that moment, Moses shifted his stance, turned, and started walking back toward Wiley and Cyrus.

"Good," said Wiley, straightening up from his squatting position. "He must have spotted Harley comin'."

Cyrus rose up, too, as Moses reached them.

"Harley's comin' yonder," said the old man. "He don't seem to be pushin' his horse unduly, so I'm guessin' he didn't see no sign of a posse on our tail."

Cyrus nodded. "Just like you figured. Right, Pop? I mean, what with us havin' a couple of their women as hostages and you tellin' 'em what we'd do iffen they came after us, you really put a kink in their tail."

"That's what I was aimin' for," Moses allowed. "But with townsfolk, you never can tell. Me puttin' a slug in the pumpkin of their marshal, I think, was the real deal-sealer. Havin' him go down was like takin' out the war chief of a pack of howlin' Injuns . . . leaves 'em all discombobulated for a while, not hardly knowin' which way to turn."

"In that case," said Wiley, grinning, "you put a kind of a jinx on 'em, Pop—you took out their head man *and* you grabbed a couple of their women for hostages."

Frowning, Moses said, "Speakin' of the women . . . They been behavin'?"

Cyrus lifted his brows. "Ain't really like they've had much choice. Not the way we've got 'em hog-tied. They been jabberin' some between themselves, but that's all."

"That's women for you," grunted Moses. "You can hang 'em over a pot of boiling oil and they'll jabber right up to the point where you drop 'em in. Only exception I ever saw was that ol' Injun squaw I took on after your ma passed givin' birth to Wiley. Ol' Majeilah. She was the quietest, most non-talkingest female ever there was. Had her nigh on to nineteen years and I don't think she spoke more'n a word a year in all that time."

"She maybe didn't speak in words," said Cyrus, "but she was all the time mumblin'. Putterin' around the house and mumblin' in some Injun lingo that didn't make a lick of sense."

"Don't speak ill of her," cautioned Moses. "She took on the lookin' after of me and you three hell-raisin' young boys . . . I'd say that earned her the right to go around doin' some mumblin' if she had a mind to."

Harley came riding down the long slope and reined up before his father and brothers.

"I rode a long way back, clear to the top of another high slope," he reported as he swung down from the saddle. "Not a thing in sight for as far as I could see in any direction. You plumb scared 'em off, Pop. They're hidin' back there in their shithole of a town, afraid to even stick a toe in our direction."

"Well, that's good. But that don't mean they'll stay put forever," said Moses. "Sooner or later they're bound to light out after us. We just got to be smart and make good use of the time we got so that, when they *do* set their sorry asses in motion, we'll have such a lead on 'em they won't have a chance of ever catchin' up."

"But we're still gonna go on to our ranch and stock up on supplies, ain't we?" said Cyrus.

"A-course. Supplies and spare horses for the long haul. But that don't mean we're gonna tarry there for very long." Moses gestured to Harley's horse. "Tie him over there with the others and let him catch a little bit of a breather before we move on. When we do, because he won't have rested as much as the other animals, let Cyrus take a turn on him. He's lightest. Then you take Cyrus's rested mount, me and Wiley will each take one of the women with us. We won't stop again until we make the ranch."

"What about those women?" asked Harley. "How long are we gonna lug them around?"

"Until I say otherwise," said Moses firmly. "Until I'm satisfied we've got all the use out of 'em we can get."

"I ain't sure what you mean," said Cyrus, knowing it wasn't a smart thing to bring up but unable to help himself. "But there's ways that I, for one, would like to get some use out of 'em that ain't got nothing to do with holdin' off no stinkin' posse."

Moses looked at his middle son, his lips curling as

if in disgust. "That mouth and mind of yours never rise very far out of the gutter, do they?"

"Aw, come on, Pop," Cyrus protested. "It's a natural inclination. You know there's times when me and Harley go visit the whore cribs back in New Town. What do you think we do there? This is the same thing, only these gals are a helluva lot better—"

"Knock it off, Cyrus!" Harley interrupted. "This ain't the time for talk of business like that. We got a lot more important things to take care of first."

Moses just continued to glare.

"All right," Cyrus said sullenly, wanting to be more defiant only unable to meet the fire in his father's eyes. "But I aim to see there's gonna by-God *be* a time for that kind of business!"

CHAPTER 36

"You can leave now. You've served your purpose," Clayton Delaney bluntly told the woman lying on the hotel room bed next to him.

The woman, a redhead barely clinging to her middle twenties and clinging even more tenuously to some still-decent looks that were wearing out fast, put a hand on Delaney's bare shoulder and said, "Why be in such a hurry, honey? There's always—"

"No, there's not," Delaney cut her off. "You've been paid. It's over. Now beat it."

Huffing indignantly, the woman slipped from the bed and began getting dressed. Delaney lay on his back, motionless, not paying any attention, just staring up at the ceiling. When the woman had her clothes and shoes on, she glanced over her shoulder as if wanting to say something more, but then decided against it. She left the room, letting the hard-slammed door make a statement for her.

After she was gone, Delaney continued to lie there. He'd hoped spending some time with a woman would calm him down, unknot the ball of frustration and anger that was clenched so tight in his gut. But it hadn't, not to any significant degree. In fact, the irony of it, being reminded how an interlude with another prostitute at another time and place was at the root of everything now tightened inside him, only left Delaney feeling more frustrated and restless.

He shoved back the thin sheet tossed partially across him, sat up, and swung his feet to the floor. Savaged his face with the palms of his hands, ran his fingers back through his hair. For a minute, he worked his right arm, the one that had gotten wrenched when the gun case was yanked from his grasp. After he'd stretched it some and rolled the shoulder around a bit, he lowered both arms and brought his elbows to rest on the tops of his knees.

So close. So damn close yet again.

He'd had the case containing the guns right in his hands, he kept thinking, only to have them yanked away in a matter of minutes. If he'd had the briefest spot of privacy within that same span of time, he could have gotten his hands on the note. Then, after that, as far as the lousy guns were concerned, he wouldn't have cared so much if they got stolen again. Hell, he wouldn't have cared hardly at all.

The wealth of the gold plating and jewel inlays on the outside . . . that was nothing compared to the value of the note secreted in the hollow handle of one of the weapons. The note that only Delaney and a precious handful of others even knew existed. What the delicately scripted words on that slip of paper meant to these individuals varied wildly and yet at the same time it all boiled down to the same thing: Power. Either maintaining it or trying to achieve it. For the time being, Delaney was in the latter category. But not for much longer, he vowed to himself. He'd tasted possession of those guns and that note twice now. It was just a matter of time before he sank his teeth in permanently.

It had all started more than a year ago back in Springfield, Illinois. It was there that the wife of a powerful U.S. senator had committed suicide. Before planting a bullet in her poor tormented brain, she had left a note detailing the cause for her distress. Her esteemed husband, it seemed, had, in a moment of desperation, murdered a young prostitute who was becoming too demanding and threatening to expose their numerous dalliances. Haunted by the deed, even after it was covered up sufficiently to protect his good name and standing, the senator had confessed to his wife what he had done. She, it turned out, was not strong enough to deal with either the betrayal or the thought of living with a murderer. Hence her departure from the world and the whole sordid matter and a note left behind to clear her conscience for the hereafter.

As luck would have it, her body was first discovered by a male secretary to the senator, a gambling addict who had some skeletons rattling loudly in his own closet. Recognizing the blackmail potential in the note but lacking the guts to use it in such a way himself, the secretary nevertheless pocketed the slip of paper and made no mention of it upon sounding the alarm over the wife's tragic demise. The powerful men protecting the senator went quickly to work and painted the suicide as the act of a frail, disturbed unfortunate who had long suffered from bouts of depression.

At the first opportunity, the secretary placed the pilfered note in the hands of Delaney, who at the time held the marker on the man's five-figure gambling debt. Delaney had been angling for some time to use this debt as leverage over the secretary in hopes of parlaying that into something he could use as influence over the senator. In one stroke, the suicide note served to satisfy the secretary's debt and simultaneously provide Delaney greater sway over the senator than he'd ever dared hope. Negotiations were quickly begun to force the senator to spearhead a controversial land deal that, once rammed through Congress, would eventually reap hundreds of thousands of dollars for Delaney and set him up for life.

Things were well under way and showing every sign of working out exactly the way Delaney was demanding when something so mundane as to be almost laughable happened. A common burglary occurred at Delaney's apartment building and his personal safe was cracked—the safe where he kept, among other valuables, the cased set of gold-plated, jewel-encrusted dueling pistols he'd recently collected in payment for yet another gambling debt. On a whim, after discovering that one of the guns had a secret hollow space in its handle, Delaney had tucked the suicide note inside. Whoever cleaned out the safe took the guns, as part of their haul, strictly for the gold and diamonds in evidence on the outside—without ever realizing the greater worth contained in the handle.

With Delaney no longer having leverage over the

senator, the land deal stalled. Desperate to gain control again, Delaney formed a ruthless team of hardcases and began chasing down leads to find out who was behind the burglary of his apartment. It took months of dispensing payoff money as well as several dislocated arms and broken jaws before they finally cornered the right thief. Once they did, the little weasel revealed before he died that he'd lost the guns in a card game to a man named August Gafford. Irony of ironies—right back to gambling once again at the core of it all.

After several more weeks, Gafford's whereabouts were finally pinned down. And with that came revelations of Rattlesnake Wells, the upcoming grand opening of the Crystal Diamond Saloon, and the much sought after bejeweled guns being advertised as the top prize in a shooting contest.

As he sat on the edge of the hotel bed reflecting on this, reflecting on all that had brought him here to this speck of a boomtown in the middle of the Wyoming wilderness rather than being surrounded by the comfort and opulence he so badly craved, Delaney could only heave an exasperated sigh. So close and yet so far. He'd actually held the guns in his hands once again, actually gained rightful claim to them . . . only to have them once again be taken suddenly, unexpectedly, away by another low-life piece of vermin who didn't even possess the brains to know what it was he truly had.

The only ones who fully understood what the guns stood for—besides the senator and his confidants— were Delaney's two gang chieftains, Eugene Boyd and Iron Tom Nielson. And even they didn't totally comprehend the power of the hidden note and what could be accomplished with it.

The clock was ticking on the land deal possibly being shelved for good if the senator wasn't ready to throw his full weight behind shoving it through. And, somehow, the crafty old bastard had sensed that Delaney's grip on the lever to control him had in some way slipped.

Delaney desperately needed to regain that grip and regain it firmly. He needed those damn guns back!

In a cluster of scraggly trees out back of the Shirley House Hotel, Ben Eames stood fidgeting nervously. He'd been doing this for the better part of an hour. A patch of grass under his feet had been mashed flat, and the wet ground underneath, even though the rain had let up some time ago and the late afternoon sky was now starting to clear, showed through in several places as muddy gouges from the heels of his boots.

From time to time, Eames slipped from his coat pocket a bottle of whiskey that he nipped sparingly from. He'd never mastered holding his liquor very well, in spite of all the time he'd spent trying to lose himself in various bottles of the stuff over the years.

"False courage," he muttered to himself. Holding the depleted bottle before him, as if studying it for the first time, he added, "But, then again, how much courage does it take to shoot a man in cold blood?" After regarding the bottle a moment longer, he uncorked it once again, saying, "Clearly more than I have without some assistance." And then took another swig.

Returning the bottle to his pocket, it made a dull clinking noise through the fabric as it brushed against the revolver shoved in the waistband of Eames's pants. The sound and the weight of the gun pressed against the side of his stomach reminded Eames of his skill with firearms of every type. Long guns, handguns, it didn't really matter. He'd long ago discovered that he could hit whatever he aimed at with whatever they put in his hands. It was just that he'd never aimed at another person before. Not intentionally. Certainly not the girl in Boston. It should have meant something that no formal charges had ever been brought against him over the incident, but that did nothing to stop the false claims and accusations that haunted him and followed wherever he went afterward, driving him nearly to the bottom.

But now that's what Gafford was demanding he do. Kill someone for real. Make right a perceived wrong . . . or be exposed once more and held up to public ridicule and blame all over again. The ringer who'd been brought in to swerve the contest but hadn't been good enough to pull it off.

Yeah. Ol' Eagle Eye Emerson. The last time he botched a shooting assignment, a girl died. Remember? Sure, and it turned out the poor thing was with child. Remember that part? Emerson's child, no doubt, that he was trying to avoid laying claim to along with his rebuff of the young mother— after he'd seduced her and no doubt had his way with her countless times . . . The cad . . . The murderer . . . The double *murderer!*

Eames could still hear those voices ringing in his head, in his mind's eye still see the printed words as they appeared in the newspaper accounts and editorials. The venom. The hate. He never wanted to experience that again. He couldn't stand it. They all believed he was a killer, anyway. So if that's what it took—to actually become a killer—in order to block out those voices, to not have to go through that all over again, then that's what he'd do. To hell with them.

Gradually forming this resolve as he brought his hand to rest on the handle of the gun at his waist, Eames glared balefully at the back side of the Shirley House Hotel. In there, second floor, room number eight. That's where he'd find Clayton Delaney. His target.

Gafford had provided him this information, along with a skeleton key he'd appropriated somehow with assurances it would open the door to number eight.

The plan was pretty basic. Eames, dressed now in garb totally different from the buckskins he'd previously been seen in, would go up to the room. If Delaney wasn't there and the door was locked, he'd use the skeleton key to let himself in. Then he'd wait until the target showed up, shoot him as soon as he stepped through the door, make his escape out the back. If Delaney was present when he knocked, he'd start shooting when the door opened, flee out the back when the deed was done. Either way, it would be quick, brutal, simple.

Eames licked his lips, surprised he felt so parched after the frequent hits he'd taken from the bottle. He considered taking another. But no, he'd had enough. There'd be plenty of time for that afterward. Or maybe if he had to wait inside the room for any length of time. But, for now, he didn't want to dull his senses any more than they already were . . . Not that one needed to be particularly sharp to stick a gun in somebody's face and start pulling the trigger.

Still, it was time to quit lollygagging and get on with it. Do your business or get off the pot, as the saying went.

Things were very quiet on this end of town. Even though the chaos around the Crystal Diamond had died down considerably, it remained the focal point of the majority of the citizenry. That was good; it meant they would be that much slower to react from up there to what Eames was fixing to do down here in Old Town.

Shifting the gun in his waistband, making sure it rode there good and secure, Eames stepped out of the scrubby tree line and started for the hotel. He was focused now, intent on going in and getting this over with.

Had he lingered just a few moments longer, he might have heard the sounds of the two horsemen reining up their mounts only a few yards in back of where he'd been standing . . .

CHAPTER 37

Clayton Delaney rose from the bed. After pulling on his trousers and boots, he went over to the washstand and poured some tepid water from the pitcher into the basin. He scooped several handfuls to his face, wetted and combed his hair, dried himself. Then he returned to the bed and finished getting dressed—gun belt, shirt, string tie, corduroy jacket. His arm and shoulder felt reasonably loose, without much pain, but he slipped the sling back on anyway. For appearance's sake.

He figured he would wander out and see if there was anything new in the wind. He realized, of course, that it was far too soon to expect a report back from the posse. But he also realized that he was feeling too restless to stay cooped up in this damn room, pretending to be nursing his hurt arm. Maybe he'd have a couple drinks, possibly a bite to eat. Maybe that would settle him down some.

But all the while he knew the only thing that would

really settle him down was getting his damn guns back.

Delaney was just reaching for his hat when the knock sounded on the door. He turned quickly, automatically stepping to one side, out of the direct line of the doorway. He started to reach for the Colt riding in a cross-draw holster on his left hip, but the restraint of the sling hampered the movement of his right arm and hand. So he rested his left hand instead on the grips of the Colt. He was fairly adept at shooting left-handed if he had to. But, other than the fact he wasn't expecting any visitors—unless it was the whore, coming back to try and earn more money—there was no particular reason to anticipate the knock meant trouble. Still, a man couldn't be too careful.

"Who is it?" he called.

A voice from out in the hallway replied, "Message for you, Mr. Delaney."

Delaney frowned. "A message from who?"

"I don't really know, sir. It's folded and sealed, with your name on the outside. The fella at the front desk asked me to bring it up."

The response sounded innocent enough to largely assuage the kind of suspicions and cautions that were second nature to Delaney. Plus, in his restless state he wanted so bad for *something* to happen that it also made him quicker to let down his guard.

So he stepped to the door, undid the lock, pulled it open.

In the brief moment Delaney had to study the man who stood there in the hallway, he thought he looked vaguely familiar. He might have gotten past the vagueness in another couple seconds if the man hadn't produced something else to concentrate on instead—the .44 Colt revolver he suddenly raised and aimed straight at Delaney's heart.

Whether there was a slight final pause on Eames's part for the task his heart wasn't really in, or Delaney's reflexes were just that good—by the time the .44 discharged its first round, the man meant to receive the slug was a blur of motion, hurling himself out of the doorway and off to one side in a frantic dive and roll. The bullet whistled across the room and smashed against the far wall.

As he sprang away, Delaney shoved against the door with his left hand, trying to slam it shut on the man with the revolver. If nothing else, it was meant to block the shooter's view for a second or two while Delaney scrambled to find some cover and make it back to his feet. He was also trying to unholster his own gun, but hampered by the sling and attempting to do it with his left hand while at the same time rolling across the floor wasn't working out very well.

Eames, in the meantime, undeterred by missing his first shot, fired again almost immediately. This round blew a large chunk out of the cheap door that Delaney tried to slam on him, causing it to swing back wide again until it slapped rattlingly against the wall. Eames entered the room, charging through a haze of powder smoke, and swung his gun to draw a bead once more on the man he'd come to kill.

He fired a third time at the frantically crawling, digging Delaney. The bullet tore a long gash across one bunched cheek of Delaney's butt and whapped loudly against the baseboard of the wall just beyond. Delaney yelped as he reached up, his sling finally tearing away, and tugged on the heavy wooden stand that held the washbasin and pitcher. He tipped the stand over and down—basin, water pitcher, and various grooming paraphernalia scattering in every direction—just in time to absorb Eames's fourth round. The bullet chewed deep into the wood but didn't manage to penetrate far enough to do any more damage to Delaney.

Finally, Delaney got his gun yanked free. Hunkered down behind the toppled washstand, without looking or really aiming—other than knowing he had the muzzle pointed in the right general direction—he raised his left hand and triggered off two rounds of return fire. The bullets whizzed wide of their target, but not by much.

Dropping into a wary crouch, Eames fired again. But all he got for his effort was to see one of Delaney's boot heels get blown away and fly against the wall, where it bounced off and came clattering back down.

Now Delaney had his Colt in his right hand. Having kept track of his would-be assassin's shots—five in total—he knew the man could have, at most, only one round left. Unless he had a second gun. Either way, Delaney was willing to try a bold move. Pinned down the way he was, he really had little choice. So he pushed up suddenly, to where he could see over the fallen washstand, and extended his arm to fire. Eames was right there, only a couple steps inside the doorway, framed by the light of the hallway behind him. He, too, had his arm extended, ready to shoot.

Both men fired simultaneously. Delaney got off two shots, but the second was adversely affected by Eames's slug tearing into the washstand directly in front of Delaney's face and kicking splinters up into his vision. So Delaney's second shot went harmlessly wide. But the one prior to that struck Eames high on his right side, breaking two ribs and tearing through a good deal of meat and muscle.

Eames spun around, crying out in pain, and staggered toward the hallway. He tried a desperation shot over his shoulder, but the hammer only clicked on an empty cylinder. Then another. Emitting a wail of pain and frustration, Eames lunged the rest of the way out into the hall. There, he turned unsteadily and broke toward the rear stairs in a lopsided, half-staggering run.

Delaney held off wasting another bullet. Wanting to follow through on the near-miraculous turn of events that had left him not only still alive but with a chance to actually gain the advantage in this conflict, Delaney scrambled desperately to crawl out from behind the toppled washstand and get back to his feet. Once he'd achieved this, he rushed across the room, stumbling awkwardly due to the one shot-off boot heel, and plunged out into the hallway. "Assassin! Stop that man!" he shouted at the top of his lungs. "He just tried to kill me! Assassin!"

Out in the hallway, he was in time to see his assailant starting down the stairs at the far end. Delaney snapped off a shot, but too hurriedly. The bullet tore wallpaper and blasted loose a shower of plaster dust from the slanted ceiling of the stairwell just above the fleeing man's head.

Seconds later, loud voices rose from farther down in the stairwell. Shouts. Curses. Delaney checked his fire once again, for fear of hitting an innocent hotel guest with a ricochet. But then, a muffled shot rang out from within the stairwell. Followed quickly by another and after that the sound of tumbling bodies.

Delaney ran in uneven steps to the end of the hallway and peered cautiously down. Below, on the first-floor landing in front of the rear exit door, three men lay in a tangle. One of them, the man who'd tried to kill him, lay very still and limp. The other two were kicking and shoving frantically to try and get out from under his dead weight. Both were wielding handguns. As they succeeded in rolling Eames away and clambering to their feet, they lifted their faces to gaze up at Delaney, and he was surprised to find he recognized them.

"Iron Tom! Largo! What the hell are you doing here?" he demanded.

Iron Tom Nielson flicked a glance down at Eames, then lifted his face again. "Helping to save your ass, by the look of it," he said. "Don't you think you should sound a little more grateful?"

CHAPTER 38

The bottom edge of the sun was touching the rim of the western horizon as the Shaws rode within sight of their ranch. The sky had finished clearing more than an hour earlier though the air remained cool and the thicker stands of grass still gave off silvery puffs of retained moisture as the horses' hooves plowed through them.

At the mouth of the wide, bowl-like area where the buildings were clustered, Moses brought his horse to a halt and leaned back in the saddle, eyes moving in a slow sweep of the scene. The main cabin, itself badly weathered and leaning and in need of repair, sat in the middle of a horse barn and a couple other shacks in even worse condition. Several tree stumps, left over from clearing the area and providing lumber but never pulled from the ground, dotted the floor of the bowl.

Consuela was plastered to the old man's back, bound there with her arms pulled forward so that they partially encircled his torso, and then her wrists tied with leather thongs to prevent her from pulling away. When Moses leaned back, his bony shoulders and the sour stink of him forced her to pull back as far as she could and turn her head in disgust.

"What's the matter, Pop?" asked Harley, reining up beside his father.

"Nothing in particular," Moses answered. "Just takin' the caution of lookin' things over good before we ride on in."

"You don't think it's possible for anybody from the town to have got here ahead of us, do you?"

"No. Hell no. But that don't mean some other polecat—a nester or some such—might not be still lurkin' around."

"I don't see no sign of anything, though, do you, Pop?" spoke up Wiley, who had Alora Dane lashed behind him in the same manner as Consuela was to Moses. "The horses are in the corral. Everything looks about the same as we left it."

"That's right," agreed Cyrus. "Same ol' shithole it's always been."

"To your ungrateful eyes and mouth, maybe," said Moses. "But that shithole, as you call it, has been home and shelter to the lot of us for a good many years. All through most of the growin' up of you boys. When your ma and me first settled here, it looked a lot better. Had what she called *'the promise of a fine home for us to raise a family and a place where we can grow old together.'* I remember her sayin' those very words. But then she got sick and died on us, and after that . . . well, it was just a place to stay, I reckon. A shelter from the storm, as they say."

"Don't look so down, Pop," Wiley said. "If it's long worn out from the hope of what it was in the beginning, that just means it'll be easier to leave behind. Right? And when we settle someplace new, where you and those gold guns will get the prominence and respect you deserve, then that will be a new and better beginning."

"Oh, la-di-da and bloomin' flowers," groaned Cyrus. "I wish I had me a fiddle to put a tune to all that mush."

"Shut up, Cyrus," barked Harley. Then, addressing Moses: "We ought to go ahead and ride on in, don't you think, Pop? We can get a fire goin', finish dryin' out, rustle up some hot vittles for our bellies before we pack up and get ready to ride out again. How's that sound?"

"Yeah, son. That sounds fine," Moses said, his gaze drifting to a spot on the hillside behind the house where two tilting wooden crosses poked up out of some weeds and poorly tended patches of grass. The graves of Moses's wife and the Indian squaw who came later. "But I don't want to tarry any longer than we have to."

After pushing their horses hard for several miles, Bob Hatfield had finally signaled a slowdown and he and Simon Quirt were letting the animals walk for a ways to rest and catch their breaths a bit.

It was the first chance the men had to talk at any length since Quirt had shown up and invited himself in as a member of the posse.

"How's that head of yours?" Quirt asked as they plodded along.

Bob said, "Well, I can tell for sure it must still be

resting on my shoulders okay. Elsewise it wouldn't hurt so dang much."

Quirt gave a shake of his own head. "I gotta tell you, that's the damnedest thing I ever heard of. A bullet bouncing off a skull like that."

"Uh-huh. It'll give me quite a tale to tell my grand-kids."

Quirt cocked a brow. "What's that name they call you—the one you don't like? Sundown Bob, is it?"

"That'd be the one."

"Well, there you go. Here's your chance to get folks to ditch that once and for all and provide 'em something different to call you. Something more to your liking."

Bob looked more than a little dubious. "Like what?"

"Hell, I don't know. How about something like 'Boulder-head Bob'?"

"Oh yeah. That's way better," Bob said dryly.

Quirt frowned. "You're mighty hard to please, you know that? Come on, you gotta admit—Boulder-head Bob, that's got kind of a ring to it."

"What I'll admit," Bob said, "is the first sumbitch I hear call me that, I'll throw in the clink. Then I'll come looking for you because I'll know you planted the idea in his head."

Quirt's frown turned into a grin. "I don't usually take well to threats. But, coming from you, I reckon I'd better choose a different tack. I mean, anybody who can bounce bullets off his noggin ain't some-body you want to mess with."

Bob just grinned, too.

They rode a ways farther in silence. Until Quirt spoke up again.

"This crew we're going after. The Shaws. You ever had any tangle with 'em in the past? Before the brawl I heard about the other night in the Red-Eyed Goat, that is."

"Some skirmishes here and there when they came to town," Bob told him. "Other barroom brawls, drunk and disorderly conduct that got some of 'em jail time on a few occasions. A couple instances of roughing up gals in the New Town whore cribs."

"I heard talk about 'em being suspected of some stagecoach robberies and probably a touch of rustling around the territory."

Bob nodded. "I've heard that kind of talk, too. And I don't necessarily doubt it. Trouble is, none of it ever took place within my jurisdiction and nobody ever had any hard evidence they could bring forward. A couple different U.S. Marshals came through and did some poking around, but they couldn't turn up anything they could act on, either."

"So, in other words, they're crafty and slippery polecats in addition to being plenty damned dangerous." Quirt set his jaw hard. "And, based on the way they tore so ruthlessly through a crowd of mostly innocents this morning, it wouldn't be amiss to add in downright evil."

"Can't see any argument against that," Bob allowed. "Old man Moses is the brains behind the bunch. If you want to call it that. In any case, he's leathery tough and bitter and seems to harbor a kind of hatred deep inside for all of mankind. Harley, the oldest son, is the toughest; quick tempered and violent on his own, and fanned all the more so when egged on by the old man. Wiley, the youngest, might be the only one with even a shred of decency in him. But he's been following the lead of the others for so long I expect it's too late to ever dig out that shred and have a chance for it to amount to anything. Then there's Cyrus, the middle son. He's twisted and snake mean in a deeper, darker way than any of the rest. Maybe the most dangerous one of them all."

Quirt looked over, regarding Bob closely. Then he said, "And he's the one who roughed up the whores, ain't he?"

"Yeah, he is," said Bob. "How'd you know?"

Quirt gave an indifferent shrug. "It's a pattern that fits the type, fits the way you described him. I ran into it more than once when I was with the Pinkertons."

Bob's mouth pulled into a tighter line and his jaw muscles bunched visibly.

Quietly, Quirt said, "It's the thought of him being close to those women hostages—especially the Spanish gal you have personal feelings for—that's driving you more than anything, ain't it?"

Bob shot a hard sidelong glance. "Best walk careful with your words, mister."

"Just laying it on the line for what it is, that's all," Quirt replied. "Not saying there's anything wrong with it or that you'd be doing any different if she *wasn't* part of it. Leastways not so far. But I just want to make sure you're facing up to the fact of your feelings, and how they may play into this. You got seven other men—including me—riding into it with you. *What* you decide and *why* you decide it could make a difference on how many of us ride out. That's all I want to get straight."

Bob exhaled raggedly. "How do you know about Consuela?" he wanted to know.

"Heard talk around town."

"Seems to me you have a habit of hearing a helluva lot of talk."

Quirt shrugged again. "Reckon I must be a good listener. For what it's worth, the talk about you and Consuela is very respectful. Except, that is, for those who think you're a blame fool for not getting around to making her your wife."

"Everybody's entitled to their opinion," Bob said through clenched teeth.

Quirt's expression turned solemn. "I saw it for myself this morning when your boy first told you the Shaws had ridden off with hostages and one of them was Consuela. You went from laying flat on the floor suffering a cracked skull to jumping to your feet and sounding the charge to go after 'em."

"That's still the way I feel."

"I know. You think I can't see that? My point is, there's only one thing that will make a man act that brave or that dumb—his feelings for a woman. So when this is over and we get her back, along with the other woman and the guns, I hope to hell you ain't gonna backslide into holding off any longer on finally telling her you love her."

Bob didn't say anything right away. Then: "I think I've come to recognize how I've done too much of that. Holding off, I mean . . . We get her back, I fully intend to correct it."

CHAPTER 39

"That's the only way it makes sense," Deputy Fred was saying. "If Eames had succeeded in blasting Mr. Delaney and then got away unseen or unrecognized, he must have figured that would leave him next in line for those prize guns when the marshal's posse returns with them."

"I guess," Peter Macy agreed somewhat reluctantly. "If we rule out robbery or a disagreement between the two—"

"I have explained to you time and again," cut in Clayton Delaney, "there was neither. The brunt of my money, except for the small amount I'm carrying with me for traveling expenses, is in a bank in Omaha. With very strict instructions on how to distribute it in the event of my demise. Walking up and blasting me, as you put it, wouldn't have gained Eames or anybody else any chance of getting it. And as far as even a hint of a disagreement between Eames and me, there was no such thing. We spoke maybe half a dozen words to one another during the shooting contest. Immediately following that, as we all know, bloody hell broke loose. I never laid eyes on Eames again until he showed up here and proceeded to open fire on me."

This discussion was taking place in the wreckage of Delaney's hotel room. Delaney himself sat on the edge of the bed, shifted rather awkwardly onto one hip due to the bullet burn down across the opposite-side cheek of his rump. Fred sat in the room's only chair, his crutch resting across his lap. Vern, one arm in a sling, stood next to him. Against the wall beside the sagging, bullet-ripped door leaned Iron Tom and Largo, who'd been introduced by Delaney as *"business associates of mine, just in from Cheyenne."*

"How you managed to survive all this, Mr. Delaney," Fred said, his gaze sweeping the room, "is nothing short of amazing. And then to have your two business pals show up when they did, just in time to stop Eames from making good his getaway . . . Your luck may have taken a bad turn when those prize guns got stole from you, but it sure swung back to the good side with the way you came out of Eames gunning for you."

"I guess that might be one way of looking at it," Delaney said sourly. "But sitting here with my guns still missing and a bullet-blistered ass and a bunch of scrapes and bruises from trying to dodge still more bullets, I can't say that *lucky* is exactly the way I feel. Still, I guess you're right that it could have turned out a lot worse."

At that moment, Frank Draeger, the owner and proprietor of the Shirley House, stuck his head through the open doorway. "Excuse me, gents. I just wanted to let you know, Mr. Delaney, that a new room—number eleven, just down the hall on the opposite side—is all freshly cleaned and ready for you, whenever you want to take your personal stuff down. I can send somebody to help with that if you want."

"No, my friends and I can manage," Delaney told him.

Draeger turned to the deputies. "O'Malley, the undertaker, is down on the back landing, ready to take the body away. He wanted me to ask you if it was okay to go ahead. And then, my wife, Freda, wants to know if it's okay to start cleaning up the blood."

Fred and Peter exchanged glances.

"Don't see why not, either one," said Fred. He pushed to his feet. "We'll come on down with you. I think we're done here and Mr. Delaney likely wants to get resettled in his new room. Any word on the doctor yet?"

Draeger shook his head. "Just that he's somewhere west of town delivering a baby. Soon as he gets back we'll see to it he's sent over to examine Mr. Delaney's, er, wound."

A handful of minutes later, Delaney and his cohorts had relocated to room eleven. With the door closed and locked and everybody else finally gone, it was their first chance to have any kind of private talk.

"Not to sound like I'm lacking in gratitude for the way you showed up and helped finish off that bastard who tried to kill me," Delaney started off, from where he'd again taken a seat on the bed in his awkward leaned-over manner, "but why the hell aren't you waiting outside of town like I sent word with Peabody for you to do?"

"Got a couple reasons for that," said Iron Tom Nielson. He was a large, lantern-jawed man with a shaven head fitted snugly inside a tobacco-brown derby hat. From one corner of his mouth protruded a half-chewed, unlit cigar. The "iron" tag had been with him since his time as a blacksmith's apprentice when hours spent each day wielding a set of forger's tongs gave him a grip "as strong as an iron vise" many would say later, after he strangled to death two men who made the mistake of picking a fight with him in a saloon. Because one of the victims was the son of a prominent local businessman who demanded revenge in spite of it being a clear case of self-defense, Iron Tom had fled ahead of a trial that was certain to see him sentenced to prison or hanging. Once branded a killer and a fugitive, that was the life he turned to. For the past half-dozen years he'd been part of Delaney's gang and had worked his way to the status of co-lieutenant along with Eugene Boyd.

"For starters," Iron Tom continued, "we're badly in need of supplies. Yeah, Peabody rode out and told us what had happened about the contest and the guns, how they got stolen away. And he said how you wanted for us to move in closer to town and be ready for action at a minute's notice. That was all well and good, but it didn't do nothing to replenish our grub, coffee, flour—none of that stuff."

"We been camped out there, waiting, staying out of sight, for nearly a week, man," Largo added. "We didn't stock up for that long a stretch. And then, when Peabody told us how everything was gonna be on hold for still longer, while you waited for a posse to chase down your guns, we decided we had to come in and tell you and then take back some supplies."

Largo was a half-breed Comanche, medium height, wiry and tough as old leather. His skin was deep copper, his eyes black and intense, and he had a thin-lipped mouth that turned down at the corners in a permanent frown. He had hair as black as a crow's wing, worn loose, so that it fell to his shoulders from under a battered, sand-colored cavalry hat.

At their words, Delaney looked properly remorseful. "I'm sorry, men. I guess I should have realized it if I'd stopped to think—but I had no idea your rations were so low. By all means, stock up and take back what you need. Do you have money?"

"We got enough," Iron Tom told him.

Delaney looked from one to the other. "You said the matter of supplies was 'for starters' . . . What else brought you in?"

"Restlessness," Largo was quick to reply.

"What's that supposed to mean?" Delaney asked.

"Among the men," answered Iron Tom. "Hell, I'll admit it—in me, too. And I think I can say for Largo as well. Damn it, Clayton, we're men of action. We came all this way to back you up on your play for those guns you want to get your hands on so bad. Then, at the last minute, when you made the decision to go for 'em in a different way—rather than holding up the train or whatever, like we figured we were coming along for—we naturally went along with your change in plans. After all, you're the boss.

"But now everything has been dragged out and we've been stuck out there in that open, empty country just twiddlin' our thumbs. It's starting to wear mighty thin. That damned storm gushing through this morning and catching us short of any decent shelter didn't help any, either."

"You think I don't feel the same way?" Delaney responded. "You think I don't feel the same restlessness? Every day that goes by that those damned guns and what they contain aren't in my possession is a day closer to losing a power- and moneymaking opportunity bigger than most men can even imagine."

"Speaking of moneymaking opportunities," Largo said, "another thing that ain't helping is knowing that those gold fields over in the Prophecy Mountains are so close by." He paused and his thin mouth curved briefly upward in one of his rare smiles. "You know how addle brained a lot of you white devils get when the smell of gold is in the air. Some of our men have got the scent and it's only adding to their itchiness."

"Bunch of damned fools!" Delaney spat. "Willing to go dig in the dirt for a wild risk at wealth when . . ." He let his words trail off and balled the fists hanging at his sides. He stood rigid for a long minute and then exhaled a ragged gust of air.

"You know what?" he said abruptly, rhetorically. His mouth twisted into a bitter smile. "Right at this moment, with everything that's happened the way it has, I wish to hell we *would* have gone the holdup route and taken those cursed guns at the first opportunity. I wish I'd never had this wrongheaded notion of trying to claim them the 'smart' way, the way that would leave us riding away clean, with no law on our tail." He chuckled with the same bitterness that had been in his smile. "Well, I got at least part of my wish. We got no law on our tail. But we also got no damn guns!"

Iron Tom frowned. "And as far as no law on our tail, I ain't even so sure that's exactly the case. Which is to say, they may not to be on our tail but that don't mean their law dog noses ain't twitching a bit where we're concerned."

"What's that supposed to mean? Say it plain," said Largo.

"What I mean is, it didn't seem to me that the one deputy, the young one who was asking questions back there in the other room, was altogether satisfied about Eames looking to kill Clayton only for the purpose of being next in line to claim those guns."

Largo looked puzzled. "But that *was* what he was up to. Wasn't it?"

"It's the only reason I can figure," said Delaney. "But Iron Tom's right—I got the same feeling about the young deputy being suspicious, not quite ready to buy that explanation. That's another trouble with hanging around a place too long when things are going wrong. Whether you're part of it or not, you can get caught in a wave of suspicion and then there's no telling what might turn up next."

Delaney smacked his right fist into his left palm. "Damn! More than ever I'm wishing we would have gone after those guns on the train. I'd pull the rest of our gang in and switch to our old ways right this minute if we had any clue where to find the damn things. The Shaws rode the hell off and the posse rode after them, but with the way it was pouring rain there'd be no way of picking up either of their tracks to even know where to start."

"Not so fast," said Iron Tom. "We might have a better idea about that then you think."

"How so?"

"From where we were camped—the farther camp, the one where we got damned near drowned before Peabody showed up to tell us to move in closer—we spotted some riders tearing hell-for-leather toward the northeast, just as the rain was letting up. We saw them, but they didn't see us where we were hunkered in. Anyway, we didn't hardly believe our eyes, not until Peabody came along and told us it was so, but Boyd was riding right there in the thick of 'em."

"So that was the marshal's posse I convinced Boyd to join," Delaney said, a tone of elevated excitement edging into his voice.

"Had to've been," Iron Tom allowed. "So, if you're serious about riding after those guns instead of continuing to sit here and wait for somebody to bring 'em to you, I say we got us a place to pick up the trail. We can take you back to where we saw the posse and start from there. Like I said, the rain was letting up by then, so their tracks from that point shouldn't be completely washed away like when it was pouring down. What's more, we've got Largo here—he can track a puff of smoke through a dust storm."

"Damn straight," said Largo.

Delaney stood up. "I don't need to hear any more. Let's do it. We'll track the posse and let them lead us to the Shaws and the guns. Then nobody—and I mean nobody—will stand in the way of us taking and this time by-damn keeping them!"

"No offense, but are you sure you're up to riding with us?" said Iron Tom. He gestured toward Delaney's rear end. "I mean, with your, er, wound it's gonna be mighty rough sitting a saddle."

"Don't worry about me," said Delaney. He grabbed a pillow off the bed. "With this and a bottle of whiskey to dull the pain, I can sit a saddle for as long as any of the rest of you. For what those guns mean to me—to all of us—I could gut out crawling through fire, Tom."

It only took only a moment of gazing deep into Delaney's eyes before Iron Tom snapped a firm nod. "I don't doubt you for a second."

"Good. Then let's go."

CHAPTER 40

The sun was all but set, filling the Shaw cabin with long shadows interrupted by pools of flickering illumination thrown by a pair of wall-hung lanterns and a single lumpy candle propped in the middle of the kitchen table. Moses Shaw sat at the head of the table, the case containing the prize guns lying open before him. His thick-fingered hands rested on the table, touching nothing. His eyes moved slowly, admiringly, over the contents of the case.

Standing to either side of Moses's chair, Cyrus and Wiley looked on. Both appeared interested, though not quite as mesmerized as their father. Especially not Cyrus, whose gaze frequently drifted to where their two captives were tied to the iron shutter bar hooks, one at each of the cabin's two front windows. Once again their wrists were bound and sections of coarse rope were looped around their throats and tied to the hooks, allowing minimal movement. Alora Dane's hair had completely fallen into a loose blond swirl by now and the front of her spangled dress clung even more precariously to keep at least one of her breasts from spilling free.

Consuela was more thoroughly covered by the gingham dress and apron that she'd worn to serve in the Bluebird Café food booth, but the skirt of the dress had suffered a long tear, leaving one of her long, shapely legs fully exposed by the way she was currently positioned in her restraints. When Cyrus's eyes lingered on the swell of Alora's breasts or Consuela's sleek, smooth-skinned leg, only then did his expression come close to the look his father got on his face from gazing at his guns.

Breaking the silence to inquire after his older brother, who had once again dropped back to check their back trail, Wiley said, "Shouldn't Harley be ridin' in pretty soon, Pop?"

Reluctantly tearing his gaze away from his guns, Moses looked around and said, "Don't worry, he'll be showin' up before long. Harley ain't nothing if not thorough. In the meantime, you two had better hop to packin' up supplies and whatnot for our trip outta here. If nothing is even started when he gets here, he'll be plumb angrified and I can't say as I'd blame him."

"Just exactly how long you figurin' for us to be away, Pop?" asked Wiley.

"Come on, for pity's sake. Ain't you figured that much out yet?" sneered Cyrus. "We ain't comin' back to this shithole nor anywheres near it. Not ever. After what we done in that town this morning, the only thing left for us around here is a hangin' rope."

Wiley looked a little startled. "Is that right, Pop?"

"I thought you understood. I thought that much

was clear," said Moses. "Yeah, your brother's right. We're puttin' distance between us and here and ain't ever comin' back."

"Where will we go?"

"Up Deadwood way, I'm thinkin'. Maybe a ways beyond, which direction I ain't fully decided yet."

"What will we do when we get . . . wherever?"

"We'll get by. Just like always. We'll stick together and get by." Then, brushing his hand gently along the side of the gun case, Moses added, "Only this time, no matter where it is, we'll have us something that will gain us a prominence and importance that's too long overdue."

Cyrus and Wiley went to their respective beds, each shoved back against a section of side wall, and began silently stuffing their clothing and personal effects into coarse grain sacks.

Moses remained seated at the table and swept his eyes slowly around the inside of the cluttered, filthy cabin that for too long hadn't seen any proper care. "The old place ain't much, I reckon. Like has already been said. Ought not have any remorse at all about leavin'. Yet, even still, it's been our home for a good many years . . . But everything and everybody passes. Turns to dust and then—maybe, maybe not—builds back up again. No doubt that's what'll happen here. It'll all turn to dust shortly after we're gone. Whether anybody ever sees fit to build it back up again, only the Almighty knows."

The old man's eyes came to rest on the two women. He'd seemed hardly to take any direct notice of them during all the hours they were being dragged along.

When he did so now, examining them very intently, the reaction both women felt was curious and troubling. They'd each been uncomfortably aware of the looks from Cyrus and even, to a more subtle degree, from Harley. The raw lust. But this look from the old man was something more, something deeper. And yet, suddenly, startlingly, there was lust there as well.

Turning away from his bed, holding the limp grain sack whose small lump of contents indicated the meager extent of his personal belongings, Wiley gestured toward the closed door that led to the cabin's only other room, Moses's bedroom, and said, "Want me to start baggin' up some of your stuff for you, Pop?"

Moses scowled, withdrawing his gaze from the two women. Gruffly, he said, "You know the rules about the privacy of my room. I'll take care of what needs to be done in there myself."

"Just tryin' to help, that's all."

Moses's scowl lessened. "I know. And for that I'm grateful. But here now, something else occurs to me we could *all* be grateful for. After what Harley said back there on the trail, I got me the cravin' for a hot, woman-cooked meal before we head out on our journey. Got a long, cold night ahead of us and no reason to expect much easier for who knows how long beyond that. A full belly to start out would be a welcome thing."

Cyrus looked around, frowning. "You sure we oughta take time for that?"

"I said so, didn't I?" snapped Moses. "One look makes it easy enough to tell that the painted-up floozy ain't gonna be no shakes as a cook. But I'm thinkin' the brown-skinned one, with the apron and all, is a different story. We got us a chunk of cured ham in the pantry, along with some taters and canned greens. I got me a notion she could do right fine with those fixin's." He returned his focus to Consuela. "How about it, señorita? Am I right? You *can* cook, can't you?"

Consuela met his eyes with a fierce glare. "*Sí*. I am an excellent cook—for humans. For animals, I don't bother."

Moses barked out a quick laugh. "Ha! A feisty one. A firebrand. That oughta add some spice to the meal."

"You ain't gonna let her talk to you like that, are you?" said Cyrus. "You want me to belt her one for sassin' that way?"

Moses's mouth spread in a tolerant smile. "In her fix, she's entitled to a little sass. Sign of spunk. Wouldn't give you a plugged nickel for a woman without *some* spunk." The smile went away. "Long as she don't overdo it. In that case we'd have to teach her *and* the floozy—just to make sure—where the line is that ain't to be crossed."

"For God's sake, do as he wants. Don't make it any worse for us than it already is," Alora urged Consuela.

Consuela considered the entertainer with a mixture of disappointment and pity. Then she returned her gaze to Moses. "Very well. Provide me something to work with, I will make you the best meal I can."

"That's better," Moses chuckled. "You heard the señorita, Wiley. Stoke up a fire in that cook stove and bring out those fixin's I mentioned. Plus some coffee for brewin' and anything else you can think of."

"Harley's comin' down the draw, Pop," Cyrus announced from where he was looking out the front door. "He's ridin' easy, don't appear to be in no particular hurry. The coast must still be clear."

"A-course it is," said Moses, chuckling again. "We put the fear of hellfire in those town nancies. I wouldn't be surprised if they not only ain't started out after us yet, but they're probably pee-dribblin' in their boots while still stayin' hunkered behind locked doors and drawn window sashes."

Wiley looked puzzled. "But you said before we couldn't count on 'em not comin' after us."

"In time, yeah. Just not quick-like. There's a difference." Moses jerked his arm in an impatient gesture. "Now, instead of standin' there arguin' and askin' questions, get a move on and start doin' what I told you!"

CHAPTER 41

"There," said Simon Quirt, pointing.

In the distance, against the sky's last pale streaks before evening gave way to full night, a curl of smoke was visible.

Bob nodded. "Uh-huh. That'd be about right. That'll be the Shaw ranch."

"And the smoke, indicating somebody is there, must mean your hunch was right—that's where they fled to."

"Appears so."

"Let's hope your deputy and the others are in a position to see the same thing and draw the same conclusion."

"I'm betting they are. I got a heap of confidence in Vern."

"From what little I saw of him, I have to agree."

"The quicker we close in the rest of the way, the quicker we can find out for sure about all of it." Bob paused for a minute, setting his jaw. "And the sooner we know for certain we've caught up with the Shaws, the better chance we've got of saving those women from any worse treatment than they may already have suffered."

Quirt gave him a sidelong look. "Hate to put it too blunt, but you figure those women are even still alive?"

"If that was softened so's not to be too blunt," Bob said, "I'd hate for you to blurt something right out. But to answer your question, yeah, I figure they're still alive. They've got too much worth as negotiating tools. Not to use against just us, but possibly in other ways farther down the trail. The thought of those women being killed don't trouble me as much as . . . well, other things."

"Okay, I get your meaning. You don't have to paint the picture no clearer than that."

"I hope to hell not. I don't want to think about it any more than I have to, let alone talk about it. Come on, let's close in on that smoke."

In order to prepare the meal for her captors, Consuela's wrists had been unbound. The loop of rope around her throat was left in place, its opposite end untied from the shutter bar hook and knotted instead around a leg of the heavy iron cookstove. This allowed her limited mobility—from the stove to the table—but no opportunity to try and make a sudden run for it.

All the while she was fixing the food, Consuela's mind was constantly churning. Observing, considering—looking for the slightest opening, anything that might give her the tiniest advantage, something unexpected she might be able to use as a weapon.

But at the same time, she knew with a sinking, gut-level practicality that current circumstances made any chance of escaping from these four vicious, heavily armed men all but impossible. What was more, even if she somehow managed to pull off that miracle for herself, there was the matter of Alora Dane, the other captive. Was Consuela willing to abandon her to her own fate, leave her to fend for herself?

On the one hand, Consuela knew that would be a difficult choice to make. On the other, what sense would there be in compromising the success of her own escape—*if* any opportunity presented itself—for the sake of trying to save them both? That would only double the odds against either of them getting free.

Above all, there was the thought of Bucky. Making it back to him, being there for him—that was Consuela's ultimate goal. Whatever it took to achieve that, she kept reminding herself—no matter the amount of suffering or humiliation, no matter how many difficult choices she might have to make—she must endure for the sake of Bucky. She must.

"Now that darkness is settling in," said Clayton Delaney, "are you sure you can still read the trail?"

His question was addressed to Largo, who was mounted beside him on a blaze-faced black gelding. Delaney sat a thick-chested pinto, the stolen hotel room pillow cushioning the seat of its saddle against Delaney's throbbing bottom. Milling about them, all having reined to a halt as signaled by Delaney, were

Iron Tom Nielson, Peabody, and four other riders, each one hard-eyed, bewhiskered, grim mouthed, and fairly bristling with firearms and other weapons.

In answer to Delaney's question, Largo's normally impassive expression appeared mildly affronted. "The sky has now cleared. There will be plenty of moon- and starlight." He paused, emphasizing the latter point with an upward sweep of his arm. "The trail, to me, is very clear. I can follow it easily."

Delaney nodded. "Good. That's what I wanted to hear. Any idea how far ahead of us they are?"

"Three, maybe four hours. At the point they passed here"—now Largo pointed to the ground—"they were moving fairly fast. With the darkness, they will slow. If we keep on steady, we will gain on them."

"Damn right I mean to keep on steady," Delaney said. "And damn right we'll be catching up with them."

"The only thing, then," spoke up Iron Tom, "is to hope that this posse is on the right trail that'll lead 'em to the Shaw gang."

"I refuse to contemplate otherwise," said Delaney. He shifted his position on the pillow, wincing slightly. "You heard what Largo said, these posse boys are riding hard after something. I got faith they're on the right scent. We stick with 'em, they'll take us where we want to go."

"You reckon they'll stop to make a night camp?" asked Peabody.

"I don't know. What I do know is that we don't stop until or unless they do." Delaney pulled his whiskey bottle, his pain duller, from his saddlebag and threw down a swig. Lowering the bottle, he added, "So keep your canteens in reach and some jerky to gnaw on as we ride, men. That's the best I can promise for right now. But when we succeed in running down what's out there ahead of us, then soon after that I can damn well promise high living for all who stick with me!"

"We hear you, Clayton," said Iron Tom, speaking for the others. "We came this far, we aim to stick. So let's get on with it."

Back in Rattlesnake Wells, August Gafford sat alone in his office at the Crystal Diamond Saloon. He felt sick to his stomach, sick to the point of thinking he might actually throw up.

Everything was going so wrong.

Hell, so much had already *gone* wrong. What else was left?

Through the office door he could hear the sounds coming from the saloon's main room. The murmur of a handful of voices, the clink of glasses now and then. The halfhearted banjo plunkings of Lyle Levitt, who'd shown up mainly to escape the boredom of staying holed up in his hotel room.

So very, very different from what the grand opening of the Crystal Diamond was *supposed* to be. The big kickoff that Gafford had been counting on, the fantastic gala he had put so much planning, effort, and money into . . . all a stupendously flat fizzle. No dance hall review, no swarm of high-spending customers, no nothing.

Alora Dane, the special attraction he had brought

in from clear back East . . . gone; kidnapped by the ruffians who'd put a blight over the whole day.

The much-ballyhooed prize guns, Gafford's ace in the hole . . . gone; taken by the same pack of vermin.

Ben Eames, also known as "Eagle Eye" Emerson, his insurance policy to make certain the guns stayed in his possession . . . a failure in the shooting competition, a failure once again in removing the obstacle that might still allow the guns to fall to Gafford, and then the ultimate failure in getting his worthless hide killed instead.

Not that Gafford gave a damn about Eames being dead. His ineptness deserved nothing better. But the alleged sharpshooter's demise removed all but the remotest chance for Gafford to get his hands on those cursed guns at a time when it was clear he was going to need their value more than ever. Short of outright thievery should the weapons ever come within his reach again, Gafford was in the direst straits imaginable. The dreadful opening of the Crystal Diamond—not to mention the days ahead that seemed destined to also fall short of expectations—guaranteed Gafford's immediate plunge into deep debt. And his borrowing power, with no collateral except for the failing saloon itself, was completely exhausted.

Furthermore, he had a nagging concern about the town deputies who were investigating the killing of Eames. Gafford couldn't shake the feeling that the lawmen had far-reaching suspicions. Did those suspicions include him? Despite the precautions he and Eames had taken never to be seen together or linked in any way, had they overlooked something? Was there something out there that those bumbling deputies might stumble over that would mean even more bad news?

Gafford's stomach rolled over and spasmed momentarily. He thought for sure he was going to throw up this time. But he didn't. After the feeling passed, he leaned back in his chair, beads of sweat popped out on his forehead and his breath coming more rapidly.

God, what had he done to deserve this? How could so much hard work and careful planning go so terribly wrong?

He reached for the decanter of brandy on his desk, removed the glass stopper, and peered down into the pool of amber liquid as if the answers were floating somewhere in there. Then, not bothering with a glass, he tipped up the whole decanter and drank thirstily.

CHAPTER 42

Moses Shaw felt almost as if he were bewitched. It had been years since a woman stirred any feelings in him. Hardly anything at all beyond the passing of his wife. Yeah, the Indian squaw he'd taken in to help raise his sons had shared his bed and, as much out of obligation as anything, there'd been times when they coupled. But toward the last, before she passed, too, any such urges from either of them had long faded. After that, when his boys went to visit the whore cribs in New Town, Moses merely shook his head at the waste of time and money and felt grateful he was past such foolishness.

But now this sultry, dark-skinned Consuela had come along and awakened yearnings in him he thought he would never experience again. Watching the way she moved as she worked over the stove and passed back and forth from there to the table—the sway of her hips, the shimmer of her long, glossy hair, the occasional flash of bare leg through the tear in her skirt—brought back all the things that the nearness of an all-over fine woman could do to a man.

In fact, it had been the nearness of her when she was tied behind him in the saddle, the womanly curves and the heat of her pressed against his back and the smell of her filling his nostrils, that had first gotten Moses's attention. From there, his continuing awareness of her, his savoring of her, had only increased to the point where he could barely take his eyes off her.

Even when he'd sat admiring the prize guns in their custom case, his gaze had lifted from time to time to rest briefly on Consuela. And now, when she passed close to him as she began serving the meal, his hand reached out a time or two, as if by its own volition, to gently brush against her hip.

This attention, the weight of his eyes and certainly the awkward groping of his hand, did not go unnoticed by Consuela. It made her skin crawl. But, at the same time, the desperately determined part of her mind that was fixated on doing whatever it took to make her break from these animals so she could return to Bucky, calculated how finding favor in the old man's eyes might provide an opening to help facilitate her escape.

Nor was Consuela the only one who noticed the way Moses was paying attention to her. While Wiley remained mostly oblivious, both Harley and Cyrus were quick to catch on. This kind of behavior from their father came as a surprise and also a point of sly amusement, causing more than one knowing elbow-nudge to pass between the two older brothers when they caught the old man gazing longingly.

"You were sure right about the señorita being able to cook, Pop," spoke up Harley as he forked a bite of ham into his mouth. "This here's a mighty tasty feed. Gonna be kind of a shame to hit the trail again too fast, without takin' time to let these good eats settle a bit."

"What needs doin', needs doin'," replied Moses fatalistically. "Those town nancies may have given us a lead by not takin' out after us right away, but we can't afford to squander it. There's a practical side to takin' this time to give our bellies a good fillin', but we dasn't tarry too long."

"You still haven't packed your things yet, have you?" asked Cyrus.

"Don't worry about that. It won't take me long," Moses assured him.

"What about feedin' the women?" said Wiley. "Are we gonna let them have something to eat, too?"

Moses seemed to consider a moment, then said, "Reckon it's only fittin'. Especially the señorita, since she did some to earn it. I don't give too much of a hang about the floozy, but we can't hardly leave her starve."

After she'd prepared and served the meal, Consuela's wrists had again been bound and she was left to stand by the end of the hot stove, still neck-looped to its leg. Alora Dane remained where she'd been since they got to the cabin, sitting on the floor over by one of the front windows, bound and neck-looped on a shorter tether to a shutter bar hook.

"When we're done eatin'," Moses continued, "we'll untie their hands and allow each of them a plate of food. No forks or knives—they can make do with their hands."

"Even the señorita?" asked Cyrus.

Moses scowled. "What do you mean?"

"Well, that's kinda shoddy treatment . . . I thought maybe, you know, since she cooked so good for us and all you might want to . . . hell, I don't know. Never mind."

Moses's scowl intensified. "That's right. You *don't* know. Just worry about eatin' what's in front of you and let me do the thinkin' and worryin' about how we treat our hostages."

Having tied their horses at the top of the wooded slope that ran down on the eastern side of the Shaw cabin, Bob and Simon Quirt had then worked their way down to the flat where they now crouched in deep shadows just within the tree line. An open area of trampled grass and dirt, no more than thirty yards across, separated them from the cabin. Before leaving the higher ground, Bob had taken a piece of mirror out of his war bag and held it up to catch a glint of moonlight, sending a signal flash to the slope on the other side of the natural bowl in which the cabin sat. After what seemed like an agonizingly long pause, he got a return flash from the opposing slope, indicating that Vern and the rest of the posse had arrived and were in position.

Speaking in a low whisper, Quirt said, "Lights burning inside and, even with the shutters closed, there are enough chinks in those walls to see movement of somebody in there. If it's the owlhoots we're after, though, wouldn't you think there'd be some horses tied and ready out front?"

"What you got to remember," Bob replied, "is that the one whisker of honest work the Shaws ever did was horse trading. Look at the corral on the other side with a dozen or more horses in it and the four saddles straddling the rails. Since the Shaws know horses and have plenty to choose from, seems reasonable that they'd strip down the ones they rode in on, turn 'em out to the corral, then figure to saddle fresh mounts when they're ready to ride out again."

"I guess that makes sense," Quirt allowed. "So what's our next move?"

"You're right about plenty of lights burning inside. But see that one window on this side? The dark one that *don't* have any light leaking through?" Bob jabbed a forefinger, pointing. Then, without waiting for any acknowledgment from Quirt, he went on. "My guess is that must be a room apart from the rest of the cabin, where all the lights are. I'm thinking we ought to move up on that dark side and have ourselves a closer look."

"Just sashay right up like we owned the place, eh?"

"You're the one who said you work good in the dark."

"I do—long as I don't smile. Or unless I got a paleface tagging along to take away my natural advantage."

"Paleface? That's kinda stealing from the Injuns, ain't it?"

"Trust me, us blacks have our own terms for white folks. But I was trying to be polite."

One corner of Bob's mouth twitched with a wry smile. "No matter. I'm moving up on that cabin regardless."

"Not like I expected you'd change your mind. Lead the way."

In a matter of minutes, they had moved across the

open area and were pressed up against the outside of the house. They froze that way, silent and motionless for several beats, alert for any sign that their advance might have drawn unwanted attention. When there was no such indication, they crouched low and edged around to the front of the cabin. Quirt stayed low and between boards found a sizable chink that he could peer through. Bob straightened up a little higher and chose a seam where the closed window shutter fit poorly and gave him a look at the interior. When they'd each had a good long gander at how things stood inside, they eased back and retreated to a wood-pile just off the back corner of the house.

"Well, it's them, all right," whispered Bob, some-what breathlessly. "Bunched together like fish in a barrel."

"Only trouble is," replied Quirt, "those particular fish are armed to the teeth. And then there's the matter of the women."

"Yeah, I wasn't likely to miss that. Right there close at hand, sure to be at risk in case any lead starts flying."

"Did you see how they've got 'em tied up?" Quirt hissed in a disgusted tone. "Wrists behind their backs and then neck-roped like they were a couple damn dogs or something. Varmints that low deserve noth-ing but—"

"Yeah, I think we're pretty much in agreement on what they deserve," Bob cut in. "But how we deliver it without putting the women in worse danger is the question. The important thing right now is seeing that the gals are still alive and they don't appear to have been beaten or abused too bad other than the way they're bound. If we can get 'em back without 'em having to endure any worse than that, we'll be doing okay."

"You figure they're just stopping here to take on supplies and swap horses, right?"

"That's how I see it, yeah. They might have fooled themselves into thinking that, by taking hostages, they kept a posse from following immediately on their heels. But ol' Moses is clever enough not to rely too heavily on that. I can't see him wasting too much time here."

"The way they're sitting there filling their faces don't look like a pack of wolves in an over-big hurry to me."

"Given what lies ahead for them, providing the old man is planning a long, steady run from here, like I figure he is, stopping to chow down on a big meal before they head out ain't necessarily a reckless thing. But staying *too* long—like to grab some shut-eye or something, if that's what you're thinking—no, I figure Moses is smarter than that."

Quirt shrugged. "In that case, the solution to our problem don't seem so difficult after all."

"Oh?"

"If they're gonna be heading out again before long, we just set ourselves up to be ready for 'em. I hope you're not figuring to try and take them with any of that 'Reach for the sky, you're under arrest' bullcrap, are you?"

Bob's expression hardened. "As long as they've got hostages, anything like that would only result in giving 'em a chance to put guns to the women's heads and we'd be right back to a standoff."

"Exactly. So instead we do it with, say, me and you waiting at each corner of the shack. Hell, there's only four of 'em. Even if they come out dragging the women on the ends of ropes, we could cut 'em down before they ever knew what hit 'em."

"Not a bad idea. Except for a couple hitches."

"Such as?"

Through clenched teeth, Bob said, "What if they decide they've gotten enough use out of having the women as hostages and they're not worth dragging along any farther? If their thinking runs that way and they go ahead and kill the women before leaving, it'll make it easier for us when they do pop their scurvy heads out—but it'd be a little late."

"Shit, man. That'd be a helluva cold-blooded stunt to pull."

"You see anything back in Rattlesnake Wells to make you think they *ain't* cold-blooded?" Bob's tone was bitter. Then he went on: "All I'm saying is that it's a possibility. But is it one we want to gamble on? And if they decide to keep the hostages alive, then that leaves open the possibility for something else. From what we saw, it appears like no ravaging of the women took place yet. But you can damn well bet it's on the mind of some of those animals. Even if he wanted to, the old man won't be able to keep those boys under control for very long. While they're already stopped to take on supplies and grub, who's to say he might not decide to allow a couple quick turns to let 'em get it out of their systems, at least temporarily? You know what that could lead to where Cyrus is concerned—is that another possibility you want to *wait* for?"

In the deep shadow of the woodpile, Quirt's face was mostly obscured but his eyes flashed like hot coals. "Jesus, Marshal! The way your mind works, it's a good thing you're on the right side of the law."

"I have that hope every time I pin on this badge."

Quirt heaved a ragged sigh. "So if waiting for 'em to come out when they're ready on their own don't fit your pistol, you got another idea?"

"Matter of fact, I do," said Bob. "I'm thinking we hurry them along on their decision to leave that cabin."

"And we do that how?"

"We smoke 'em out." Bob pointed upward. "See that smokestack poking up out of the roof there? The one whose smoke first caught our eye?"

"Indeed I do," said Quirt, quickly starting to see where he had a hunch Bob was headed.

"I'm willing to supply the jacket to stuff down that pipe in order to turn the smoke back around on those inside," said Bob, "if you're willing to kick off your boots and supply the cat-footedness to crawl up on the roof without being heard. You're lighter and— don't let it go to your head when I say this—sprier than me for something like that."

Quirt grinned. "I'm also better-looking, not to mention a whole lot of other things. But we'll leave it go at handsomer and sprier for now. All I ask is that, when they come boiling out, you leave at least one of 'em for me to shoot."

"I'll do my best. Now get those boots off."

CHAPTER 43

"Okay then," announced Moses Shaw as he pushed his chair back from the table and his emptied plate. "I believe now is the time for me to go back to my room and pack up the personal items I intend to depart with. First and foremost, a-course, bein' this little baby right here." He reached down to pat the gun case that had been leaning against the side of his chair, then went on. "It won't take long, but it'll give you boys a few minutes to let your eats settle. When I come back out, we'll all head for the corral to pick our mounts and saddle up for our journey."

"However you say, Pop."

Getting a grip on the gun case's handle, Moses stood up. "I think what I'll do," he said, sweeping his gaze over his sons, eyes taking on a curious look that seemed to convey a hint of suspicion or perhaps a challenge, "is take the señorita back with me. With her hands still bound, but in front, she can hold the lantern for me. That'll help me find what I need quicker."

Wiley blinked. "Well heck, Pop, if you want a helpin' hand I could—"

"I said the señorita," Moses snapped, cutting him short. "If you want to be useful, go ahead and untie her from that stove leg and give her a lantern. Then you boys just relax for a spell, like I said. Enjoy takin' it easy while you can." The challenging glint in Moses's eye was stronger than ever.

As Wiley knelt at the stove leg and began untying the rope whose opposite end was looped around Consuela's neck, Alora Dane suddenly thrashed in her own restraints. "You leave that girl alone, you filthy old pig!" she shouted at Moses. "You dried-up, shriveled-up old bastard, you probably don't even have—" Alora worked herself into such a state that she yanked so hard against the loop around her own neck it choked her off and caused her words to end in a sharp gagging sound.

"What about this one? What do you want us to do with her?" asked Harley.

"For starters, teach her to show some respect and mind her foul mouth . . . for her own good," said Moses.

Harley and Cyrus exchanged glances.

"Damn you all!" cried Alora, finding her voice again, though it now came in a harsh rasp. "Take me, if you must! But leave that poor girl . . . Don't—"

Cyrus shut her up with a hard jerk on the throat loop, turning her words once again into a fit of gagging. That done, he turned to face his father. "Anything else for this one?"

"Like what?"

Cyrus licked his lips. "Well, it occurs to me, since we still have some time left, that maybe I got a few more things I might want to pack. If I had somebody to, er, hold a lantern for me so's I could take a closer look, that is. You know, to make sure I didn't miss nothing. This floozy, as you call her, would probably do for that. Might even help keep her quiet if she had something else to concentrate on."

Moses's eyes again passed back and forth between Cyrus and Harley, just as Wiley was handing him the rope attached to Consuela. "Go ahead then, if you think it's worth the effort," he said in a measured tone. "Just see to it you're done when I come out of my room."

Cyrus and Harley smiled thin, smug smiles.

None of them had noticed the single scuff of sound that had come from up on the roof a minute earlier. And, so far, none of them were yet showing any awareness of the smoke haze starting to thicken in the air around the stove and gradually spread outward . . .

Consuela's heart had started thundering inside her, faster and faster, from the instant Moses stated his intent to take her into his room. To hold the lantern for him while he packed his things. She realized, of course, the hidden meaning in those words. The thought of that naturally sent an immediate wave of fright and repulsion through her. But then, strangely, there also was a surge of excitement as she recognized how this might provide her the chance—alone in a room with the vile old man, separated from the others—to attempt an escape.

When Alora Dane suddenly protested on her behalf, it had surprised Consuela and then sent a pang of guilt knifing into her. She never expected anything like that from the entertainer, a woman she barely knew, a woman she had made up her mind she would be willing to abandon if it improved her chances for getting away and making it back to Bucky. And now Alora was not only speaking up for her but was actually offering to sacrifice herself as an alternative.

When Cyrus so roughly jerked Alora's neck loop, Consuela had started to voice her own protest. But she held her tongue. She knew it would do no good and, if she put up too much of a fuss, Moses could possibly change his mind about taking her into the room. It might be insane for her to *want* to go in there with him, but she was desperate enough to weigh the potential opportunity against the possible horror. It was the only glimmer of a chance that had come along so far and she couldn't count on anything better showing up if she waited.

The thing that was giving Consuela her hope of turning the tables on Moses, if she had him alone and out of sight of the others, was the weapon she'd managed to covertly slip into her apron pocket. All the while she'd been preparing the meal, especially when she was using a carving knife to slice the ham, she'd been alert for something useful she could secrete away for the appropriate time.

But she wasn't the only one alert for such a thing. Wiley was watching her specifically for that kind of sleight of hand and he made sure that every tool or utensil she touched got returned and accounted for . . . except for one item. The curve-handled, blunt-tipped lid lifter that hung from a bent rack on the side of the stove. It was a small, practical tool for lifting hot lids off pots or the even hotter circular covers off the cooking surface of the stove itself. It was small but had some heft to it and the blunt tip of its working end—designed to slip into notches on the aforementioned lids or covers so the tool could be used, leverlike, to raise them without risk of burning one's hands—had enough of a point so that, with enough force, it could be driven into vulnerable parts of a person.

If Moses gave her the slightest opening, Consuela had no doubt she could muster the physical force to drive that tip repeatedly and fatally into his neck . . .

CHAPTER 44

Outside, as he moved along the darkened outer wall of the cabin, Bob made a surprising discovery. The single window there had its vertical shutter dropped down, as if closed, but it wasn't bolted. In fact, it was cracked open a couple of inches, held that way by a small wedge of wood, apparently to let in some fresh air. Neither Bob nor Quirt had noticed this when they'd edged along the wall earlier on their way to find some chinks they could peer through in the front.

However this new discovery might have altered their plans if they'd known about it then was a moot point now; it was too late to change what was already set in motion. Quirt was already up on the roof and there was no way for Bob to signal him without risking unwanted attention. Still, he squatted under the window in question and pondered if there was any benefit to be gained from finding it this way.

Then, before he had the chance to conclude anything, there was sudden activity in the formerly darkened room. The door opened, light flooded in, and there was the scrape of feet entering. Bob dropped lower and shifted his position, searching to try and find a suitable chink between boards that he could peer through to see what was going on inside. When he found one, a bolt of agony and then rage shot through him.

Through the opening, he saw Moses Shaw leading Consuela into the room, tugging her along by the rope around her neck. Consuela's wrists were bound in front of her and she was holding a lantern. Her expression was a carefully controlled mask—a beautiful one—but Bob knew her well enough to recognize the tremors of anxiety fluttering under her smooth cinnamon skin. He wanted to groan, to scream. His hand formed an empty claw, wanting to close around the grips of his .44 and aim it to blast Moses Shaw to Hell.

But he couldn't. Not right yet. A sudden, reckless move at this juncture would only elevate the danger level for Consuela and practically guarantee her catching a bullet in what followed.

Bob was close enough to the window opening to hear Moses speak.

"Put the lantern on the table, señorita."

"I thought you wanted me to hold it closer for you. So you could better see to choose your things for packing," Consuela replied.

"There is time for that. Just do what I say."

There was an odd, singsongy gentleness to Moses's voice. For the moment. Bob knew that would change suddenly if Consuela resisted too much. And Bob had no doubt—whether she resisted or not—what the evil old patriarch ultimately had in mind. The mere thought made his guts convulse. Being this close, within sight and sound, if the old bastard went too far, Bob knew he wouldn't be able to hold back—no matter what.

Where was that goddamn smoke?

Shouldn't it be filling the cabin by now?

Reluctantly, Bob edged toward the front corner of the cabin in hopes of getting a quick idea of what was going on in the rest of the interior. Hoping it wasn't just his imagination, he thought he could smell stinging trails of smoke starting to waft out of the structure. And then, for certain, he heard coughing from within.

A moment after that he also heard the loud bark of Moses's voice issuing out through the partially open window. "What the hell is going on out there?"

"Pop! Pop!" The voice of one of the sons, only fainted muted by the flimsy old walls, called out in concert with a pounding on the door of the room containing Moses and Consuela. "Something's wrong! The stove is on fire!"

"Well, put the damn thing out!"

"It's real bad. The smoke is gettin' so thick we can't hardly see."

More coughing. From several different sources, by the sound of it.

"Pop, we gotta get the hell out of here," came the voice of a different son. "This ol' tinderbox is gonna go up in flames!"

"Get out then, you blunderin' damn pups," Moses hollered back. "This place ain't nothing to us no more anyway!"

"You'd better hurry up or you won't be able to see your way through all the smoke."

"Just go! You think I ain't lived in this dump long enough to pick my way through a little haze. Git!"

Bob could hear more coughing and then the frantic scramble of feet coming from the main room of the cabin.

The marshal suddenly found himself in a quandary.

The Shaw sons—and Alora Dane, presumably—were going to come boiling out the front door any second. Right according to plan . . . Except that stubborn old Moses and Consuela would be lagging behind. So if Bob, Quirt, and maybe the rest of the posse members coming down from the other slope, opened up on the initial bunch, then that would provide a warning to Moses before he showed his ugly damned face. And, given such a warning, the treacherous old bastard was certain to put his gun to Consuela's pretty head and try to wangle another deal.

Bob was torn. But only for a moment.

He was pressed against the outside of the cabin, halfway between the front corner to one side of him and the partially open window to the other. If he didn't go to the corner and join in the confrontation of the Shaw sons when they came pouring out, he'd be leaving the task completely to Quirt—and *maybe* Vern and the other posse members if they'd worked their way in close enough. But if he joined there, he would surely be abandoning Consuela once again to the mercy of Moses.

No way he was willing to do that.

Pivoting sharply, drawing his .44 as he did so, he

returned to the window. He poised there, gun gripped in one hand, the other partly raised, palm out, ready to shove open the unbolted shutter.

Tendrils of smoke were curling out through the propped-open gap along the bottom of the shutter. Bob's breathing had quickened, making it unavoidable to inhale some of the acrid smoke. But he willed himself not to cough.

At the first crack of gunfire from out front of the building, Bob lunged into motion. He thrust the shutter back and up with his left hand while at the same time leaning in through the opening and extending his right arm with the .44 gripped in the fist at its end.

The room was small, no more than eight feet across. Moses and Consuela were in the doorway that led out to the main area, their shapes blurred by the increasingly heavy smoke. Consuela still held the lantern. Moses was pushing her ahead of him, gripping the rope around her neck in one hand, the case containing the prize guns in the other.

"Shaw!" Bob hollered.

The old man spun around, shifting his body so that it was no longer aligned with Consuela. Exactly what Bob wanted. He didn't hesitate to trigger his .44, the bullet it spat smashing square into the center of Moses's forehead. Moses was slammed back against the doorframe, immediately going limp. He started to slide down, as he did so letting go of both the rope and the case. Before he crumpled completely to the floor, Bob pumped two more rounds into him, his shots cracking in concert with the barrage of gunfire he could hear coming from the front of the cabin.

In the doorway, Consuela turned slowly, as if in a

dream. The expression on her lovely face, no longer tightly controlled, was stunned, confused. Not even when her eyes found Bob through the smoke haze did it change. Not until he'd made it through the window, struggling somewhat awkwardly to keep the shutter shoved up even as he pulled himself in.

And then he was moving toward her in long, urgent strides. "It's okay, 'Suela," he said huskily. "I'm here now."

CHAPTER 45

"I don't understand . . . I thought you were dead," Consuela kept repeating, even after Bob had her in his arms and, together, they were exiting the smoke-filled building.

"I'm a long way from dead. And so are you," he assured her. "No matter what else, that's the main thing."

Outside, they found things pretty much as Bob was confident they would be. Even without him, Quirt had been more than a match for the Shaw sons—especially with some assistance from the other posse members, who'd accurately read the situation as it was unfolding and had moved in close enough to throw some lead to help ensure the outcome. The three bodies were sprawled lifeless only a few steps outside the door.

Alora Dane, wrapped in a jacket provided by Big George O'Farrow to cover what Cyrus and Harley had wasted no time exposing as soon as they got their hands on her, was standing several paces away, still being protectively steadied by Big George. Murmuring something that Bob didn't quite catch, Consuela pulled away from his arms and rushed over to Alora. The two women embraced and then stood that way, holding each other, for some time. Big George respectfully backed off a few steps.

Quirt came over and stood beside Bob. "You're a real generous fella, I got to give you that," he said. "I asked you to leave me at least one of those Shaw rats to shoot—you gave me three."

Bob grinned. "I always try to be accommodating. I knew you could handle it."

"Not that I *couldn't* have," Quirt came back. "But, just to make sure, I also found me some reinforcements who showed up to lend a hand."

Bob nodded. "I see that. Truth is, for my part I ran into some complications back around on the side that sort of delayed me."

"From the way it looks," said Quirt, gesturing toward Consuela, "I'd say it was worth it. And, judging from the shots I heard coming from inside, I'm guessing Daddy Shaw is headed for a warmer climate along with his sons?"

"Be a lot of disappointed people in this old world if it ever turns out that ain't the way it works."

Vern joined them, looking somber. "How do you want to dispose of the bodies, Marshal? You want to take 'em back into town for burial?"

Bob considered a moment, then heaved a sigh before replying, "Seems to me we've already got plenty of trash in the ground back on Boot Hill. How would the boys feel about doing a little digging right here?"

"Probably wouldn't be thrilled about it. But they

ill, if that's what you want." The young deputy made
a face. "Not exactly a picnic either way. Those Shaws
stunk bad enough alive, they sure wouldn't smell no
better starting to ripen belly down over their saddles
on a ride back. The more I think about it, I think
burying 'em and doing it pronto is the best thing all
the way around."

"Then set a gang to digging," Bob told him.

Following the tracks of the larger posse group, the
one led by Vern after splitting away from Bob and
Quirt, Clayton Delaney and his force of men reached
the base of the slope that bordered the Shaw ranch
on the north. Without ascending all the way up, they
rose high enough to be able to look down on the
ranch buildings and the activity taking place mostly
in front of the cabin. Several lanterns were in evidence, along with the illumination from a small
campfire and the silvery wash from the moon and
stars overhead, to provide a good view of the scene.

Aiding the view, for Delaney himself, was a pair of
high-powered binoculars that had been handed to
him by Iron Tom. Lowering these now, Delaney
smiled as he said to the group of horsemen gathered
around him, "Gentlemen, you will be pleased to
know we have succeeded in our undertaking. Which
is to say that the posse we've been following has also
succeeded in theirs, and have led us straight to the
scurvy dogs—or their remains, to be more accurate,
from the way it looks—who took the item I so badly
want back in my possession."

"Meaning," Iron Tom added, the lower half of his

face split by a wide smile of its own, "it's just a matter of time before it soon will be."

"I sincerely hope so," said Delaney. "The only question is, what's the best way for us to make that happen?"

Frowning, Iron Tom said, "Guess I'm missin' where any question comes in. Back in town, after that Eames polecat tried to ventilate you and you got all worked up over it, you swore you was ready to return to the old ways. No more pussyfootin' around something you wanted bad, you said. We'd just haul off and take it."

Delaney cocked a brow somewhat dubiously. "Yeah, I guess I did say that, didn't I?"

"For a fact. So what you want is down there for the takin'. Why, then, is there any question about ridin' hell-for-leather smack over the top of those who got it and claimin' it away from 'em?"

"How about," Delaney responded, "for the sake of not exposing ourselves unnecessarily to the injuries that would surely be suffered by some of us if we went about it that way? We'd have the element of surprise and we'd be catching most of them on foot, true, so there's little doubt we would prevail. But it would still be at a cost. Why pay that toll if we don't have to?"

Iron Tom's frown turned into an uncertain scowl.

"I think I've got a better idea, that's all I'm saying," urged Delaney. "Hear me out. If you think it amounts to too much 'pussyfooting,' then we'll do it your way."

Bob and Consuela had separated themselves somewhat from the others. They were seated on a pair of

awn-off stumps back by the woodpile. They hadn't
brought a lantern with them but there was still plenty
of light for Bob to drink in the finely chiseled features
of Consuela's face. She had never looked lovelier.
And he, damn fool that he was, was finally getting
around to appreciating the full impact of that.

Consuela reached up and pushed back the wide
brim of his hat, exposing the lumpy bandage that
Doc Tibbs had applied seemingly so long ago back in
Rattlesnake Wells. Her fingers gently touched the
sweat-damp gauze. "I still can hardly believe it," she
murmured.

Bob grinned. "What? That a bullet bounced off my
skull? You, of all people, should know how danged
hardheaded I can be."

"This is true." Her lips spread in an alluring smile.
"In the past I haven't always found that a feature to
be appreciated. But now, thank God, what a blessing
it is."

"Be careful. I'm gonna remember you said that."

"Be my guest. There is much about this day, this
night, it will be best to try and forget. But that needn't
be part of it."

Bob let his gaze drift past her for a moment and
swept it across the others scattered in front of the
cabin. The bodies were in the ground now and his
jacket had been pulled down from the roof, leaving
the cabin dark and mostly thinned of smoke. But
nobody had shown any interest in going back in
there. Somebody had built a small campfire while the
two cowhands, Earl Wells and Heck Hembrow, went
to fetch the horses down off the slopes. Their saddlebags provided the makings for strong, hot coffee, a

couple pots of which were bubbling on the edge of the fire now. It hadn't been decided yet whether or not they'd stay the night here and then return to town in the morning, or if they'd go ahead and strike out within the next half hour or so. But, either way, bellies would always welcome some hot coffee.

As he scanned the members of his party, Bob could see enough signs of exhaustion to make him inclined—even though he was as eager to get back as anybody, mainly so Bucky could see that both he and Consuela were all right—toward finishing out the night here, grabbing some rest, and starting out fresh at sunup. The night was going to be plenty cool, but not unbearably so. The men could handle a few hours of cold wrapped in their bedrolls; they'd come more or less prepared for it. And they'd be certain to make sure the women were properly cared for. There was always the interior of the Shaw cabin, but Bob was pretty sure nobody would be interested in that option. Ultimately, he was thinking, he might leave the choice between riding out or waiting the night up to the women.

"Bob," Consuela said, drawing him out of his reverie.

His gaze returned to her. "Yes? What is it, 'Suela?"

"I was wondering if you would like for me to get you a cup of coffee?"

So like her. Even after her own harsh ordeal, here she was still ready to think of his needs. How big a fool was he for having had this lovely creature in his life for so long yet, in his mind, keeping her pushed off to one side?

"I think," he said softly, "that after all you've been ᴛhrough, the last thing you need to be worrying about ɪs waiting on me." Bob reached out and placed one hand gently on each of her shoulders. "In fact, I think it's time for the two of us to start making a lot of changes. It took the horrible thought of possibly losing you for me to finally open my stupid eyes. But now that I have—"

This time it was Bob's words that got cut short.

"Hey, Marshal! Marshal, you'd better come see this," called Vern, an urgent tone in his voice. "Looks like we've got company."

CHAPTER 46

After calling ahead the standard "Hello, the camp!" announcement, Clayton Delaney nudged his pinto forward until he came within the splashes of illumination thrown by the campfire and lanterns. In front of him, he saw those spread out before the cabin draw together as he got closer. He noted once again, as he'd done when looking through the binoculars, that there was no sign of any of the Shaws—other than the women they'd taken as hostages—while at the same time all members of the posse were present and accounted for.

Further evidence that the robbers had been dispatched, in addition to the freed women, came in the form of an accumulation of firearms lying in a pile near the campfire. Since the posse men were all still armed, the only logical conclusion was that the pile of guns had been taken from the Shaws. Nor was it missed by Delaney that accomplishment of all this against the ruthless clan, while suffering no losses of their own, spoke highly of the posse's competence. He hoped that Iron Tom and others of his gang

...o'd initially been in favor of simply charging ...own on these men were also taking this into consid...eration.

But, above all, what Delaney's appraisal did not miss, was the leather case resting on the ground beside the pile of confiscated guns. The case containing the prize guns that were at the heart of all the other pieces.

"Delaney," said Bob, stepping to the head of his group and then fully recognizing the visitor who reined up before him. "What in blazes brings you out here?"

Delaney smiled. "Seems we have a way of running into one another whenever we venture out into the wilderness, eh, Marshal?"

"Maybe," Bob allowed. "But I've got a hunch that you showing up this time amounts to more than just us 'running into one another.' Why don't you light down, then you can fill me in more. There's not something wrong in town, is there?"

"No, not in the way you mean," Delaney said, shaking his head. "Which isn't to say there haven't been some incidents. That's what brings me here, actually, but it's really more a matter of personal concern to me than to you. As far as your offer to light, thanks but no thanks. I'm good right here in the saddle and I expect to be riding off again in very short order."

Bob nodded toward the pillow he was resting on. "I can see you're right comfortable. But it don't make good sense to have ridden all this way and not want to stretch your legs a mite. Plus, we've got some good, strong coffee brewed and ready."

"Again, I must say thanks but no thanks. What I will

accept from you, and what I came here expressly resolve, is the retrieval of my property." Delane pointed. "In other words, that case over there—the one containing the prize guns you all saw me win fair and square at the conclusion of Gafford's shooting contest."

Bob's brows furrowed. "Wait a minute. You rode all the way out here for that? You couldn't wait until we brought them back to town?"

"Something about this seems mighty fishy, Marshal," said Vern, who had moved up on Bob's left. "How did he even know where to find us?"

"You and your deputy have a right to your suspicions. I'll grant you that much, although I would advise strongly against offending me," said Delaney. "I really owe you no explanation for my motives or methods. Those guns are legally mine. Everybody here knows that. All I want is to take possession of what belongs to me and then be left to ride away. You will never see me after that."

Quirt moved up on Bob's right, keeping a respectful distance away from the marshal's gun hand and holstered .44. "What he's saying might be technically right," the gunman said in a low voice. "But I got to go along with your deputy—something about it is damned fishy."

"Careful not to listen to bad advice, Marshal," advised Delaney calmly. "This is really a very simple matter. Don't make it more troublesome than it has to be."

"I'm all for keeping things *un*troublesome," said Bob, the tone in his voice as flat as the gaze from his eyes. "So you can have your precious guns. Like you aid, they're rightfully yours. Hell, you can take that case and keep it hugged tight against yourself if you want . . . while you ride with us on back to town."

Delaney's expression didn't change, but a muscle twitched faintly under his left eye. He gave it a beat before saying, "Sorry, Marshal, but I'm afraid that would be taking me out of my way. I'm headed east, you see. The business opportunity I'm looking to invest in, like I told you about the other day? I've decided on one in particular, but I need to move fast in order to make the best deal on it. Going back to Rattlesnake Wells, I'm afraid, would cost me time I simply can't afford."

"That's a real shame," said Bob. "Because *not* going back to Rattlesnake Wells with us is gonna cost getting those guns handed over to you. At least for now. I'm unwilling to do that until I'm satisfied everything is okay in town."

"Your precious town is fine! I told you it was."

"Then tell me the rest—what brought about the way you're behaving, this wild sense of urgency you're showing? And don't try to feed me some crap about it being a matter of personal concern that I don't need to worry about."

"You stubborn damned fool, you're *making* it something you have to worry about," Delaney said with exasperation. "You want the rest of it? Here it is." He slowly raised his left arm and pointed at the wooded north slope where Vern and the posse had been just over an hour ago. "Up on that slope are a dozen men with rifles trained on you and your group right this minute. They may not be quite the marksmen you or I are, but they're plenty good enough to riddle you and yours to pieces if I give the signal. It will be over before you have any chance to retaliate, and the carnage will regrettably include the women you just went to so much trouble rescuing."

"You're crazy! You're bluffing."

"A demonstration, then, if you insist."

Delaney swung his arm down suddenly. The next instant, by prearrangement, a shot boomed up on the slope and simultaneously one of the coffeepots on the edge of the fire hopped into the air and fell back, clattering and rolling across the ground with a thumb-sized hole punched through it.

"That could have just as easily been somebody's head," Delaney said as the sound of the shot faded in the night. "If I signal again, it will be."

"No matter how many rifles cut loose, you think one of us can't get you before we go down?" said Quirt through clenched teeth.

Delaney kept his eyes on Bob as he answered, "But will it be worth it? Will it especially be worth taking the women down with you?"

"I don't know what his game is, but I think this fancy-hatted bastard is bluffing," said Quirt.

"I agree," added Vern. "He may have one shooter up there. He may even have two or three. But I don't believe he's got no dozen."

It was at that moment that Eugene Boyd, who up until then had shown himself to be nothing but a solid posse member, made the move to reveal his true colors. From where he'd been standing to one side and slightly in back of Consuela, Boyd suddenly stepped over, wrapped a fist in her long hair, and yanked her back against him while at the same time

ressing the muzzle of his revolver against her
emple. "You can worry about the rifles up on that
hill all you want," he said through clenched teeth,
loud enough to draw everybody's attention. "But,
just in case you'd like to know, you got another little
problem right here in the midst of y'all."

Heads snapped around and growls of anger and
frustration escaped from the throats of the other
posse members.

Delaney chuckled. Then he said, "Allow me, Marshal, to provide a formal introduction—a more
thorough one, I expect, than you were previously
given. Mr. Boyd happens to be a longtime associate of
mine. We go back many years. Encouraging him to be
part of your noble posse was a hunch that I thought
might prove beneficial, although I wasn't exactly sure
how. Lo and behold, it is now paying off in a timely
and critical way."

"He harms the girl," Bob grated, "that hunch will
turn out to be your ticket to Hell."

Delaney heaved a dramatic sigh. "Empty words,
Marshal. Empty words. I understand why you feel
compelled to say them, but we both know you aren't
in any position to back them up in the least." He cut
his eyes to Quirt and gave a faint thrust of his chin.
"You, Mr. Dangerous Gunslinger with disparaging
things to say about my hat, go fetch me that gun case.
Step to it, boy!"

With hate burning in his eyes like molten steel,
Quirt turned slowly and walked back to where the case
rested on the ground. Just as slowly and purposefully,
with the hate never leaving his eyes, he brought it

back and held it up to Delaney. After taking the case Delaney motioned Quirt back to where he'd been.

Hefting the case for a moment, Delaney then raised it for all to see. A wide, smug smile spread across his face. "All you pathetic fools . . . So many who've gone through so much . . . Here, back in town, elsewhere . . . Not one of you has an inkling of the true value this contains. Not the mere pittance represented by a splash of gold and a few jewels. No. So much more . . . So much more than your feeble imaginations could ever begin to understand."

He paused, continuing to smile, letting his words—words whose exact meaning brought puzzled yet transfixed looks to the faces of those listening—just hang in the air.

And then that moment of quiet was abruptly ripped apart by an agonized, bloodcurdling scream that made everyone freeze in a stunned, startled way far deeper than anything mere words could cause.

The horrible sound came from Eugene Boyd. It came as the result of action taken by Consuela—action taken out of rage and desperation. Rage at once again being manhandled and victimized, treated like little more than a piece of wild animal bait. Desperation at seeing how the situation seemed to have reached a hopeless point. Unless . . .

Remembering the lid lifter she'd slipped into her apron pocket back inside the cabin, thinking it might serve as a weapon but never having gotten that chance, she decided now was perhaps the time to still try and get some use out of it. It was still there in the pocket, forgotten in the interim until now. Everyone was concentrating on Delaney, her hands hadn't

en retied, and her captor seemed so confident he
ad full control over her that the gun by her head was
no longer even touching her temple . . .

Consuela slowly slipped her right hand into the
apron pocket, tightly gripping the curved handle of
the lid lifter. Then, bracing herself, she pulled the
tool free and swung her arm up and back in a hard,
fast arc. Reaching over her shoulder, she plunged the
blunted tip of the lifter into the soft flesh of Boyd's
throat, under his jawline and just off-center of his
Adam's apple. Feeling it sink deep, she then jerked
and pulled as hard as she could—not to extract it, but
rather to slash and tear, do as much damage as she
could.

Hot blood pumped down over Consuela's hand
and wrist and Boyd's scream of agony filled her ears.
He twisted violently away, releasing his hold on her
hair and dropping his gun so that he could reach
with both hands to try and close the terrible gash in
his throat. Consuela lost her grip on the lid lifter and
stumbled, almost falling. Boyd dropped to his knees.
His screams turned to wretched, bubbling gasps as his
life fluids gushed down over his chest and stomach.

Bob was the first to react to this bloody diversion,
seeing in it a chance to try and break Delaney's hold
on the situation. "Crash the lanterns! Take to cover!"
he hollered. In the same instant, his hand was skinning the .44 from its holster and, before all the words
were out of his mouth, he was fanning a trio of rapid-
fire shots square into Clayton Delaney. The gang
leader took all three slugs to the chest, grouped
tightly over his heart, and was slammed into a backward somersault out of the saddle.

Delaney's body hadn't hit the ground yet whe[n] Bob wheeled and broke into a run back towar[d] Consuela. On all sides of him, the rest of the posse members were also scrambling, diving for cover wherever they could find it.

Bullets began screaming down from the slope, sizzling through the air, kicking up geysers of dust as they whapped into the ground.

Vern ran forward, drilling a pair of shots into the head of Delaney's pinto. When the unfortunate beast sprawled dead, he dropped down behind it. The carcass provided cover and it also yielded Delaney's Winchester '73 from the saddle scabbard—far superior to a handgun for returning fire to the shooters on the slope.

Quirt and Pecos Ryan flung themselves in behind a couple of the tree stumps poking up out of the ground.

Big George immediately wrapped his arms protectively around Alora Dane and pulled her into a shallow depression where he continued to brace his body over hers, shielding her from the incoming rifle fire.

Earl Wells and Heck Hembrow managed to make it inside the cabin, kicking out lanterns as they went and also snatching up a couple long guns from the pile of confiscated weapons they ran past.

Bob reached Consuela in long, running strides. He grabbed her, whirled her, pulled her to the ground, and then rolled, the two of them wrapped together, in behind a gnarled old tree stump. Bullets immediately smashed and chewed into the stump as they ducked low.

CHAPTER 47

For the next handful of minutes, there was an intense exchange of gunfire. The shooters up on the slope poured a hellstorm of lead down on the posse men. The latter, once they'd scattered to cover, poured it right back. The most effective return fire came from Vern and the two deputized ranch hands who'd managed to grab rifles. Although the range was barely within reach for those with only handguns at their disposal, it did little to keep them from joining in regardless.

But it was Vern and his keen marksmanship, targeting on the muzzle flashes of the slope shooters, who played the biggest part in swaying the tide of the brief battle. Twice in very short order his bullets scored fatal hits.

With Delaney and Boyd taken out right at the get-go and now two more of their force cut down, the remaining members of the Delaney gang quickly lost heart for keeping up the fight. Iron Tom tried to

convince them otherwise, but the argument again
him was hard to overcome.

"Without Delaney's contacts for something bigger,"
insisted Largo, speaking for the rest, "those lousy
guns by themselves ain't worth it. A few scrapings of
gold and some jewels to split between us? And killing
lawmen to get even that much? It's too thin, Tom—
even if we *could* come out of this on top. Ain't nothing for it but to cut our losses and ride the hell out
of here!"

With nothing more to be said, that's what they did.
Throwing a few random shots as they retreated to the
top of the slope, to where they'd left their horses tied,
they mounted up and spurred off into what was left
of the night.

Even after the shooting stopped and they'd heard
the sound of hoofbeats fading away, Bob cautioned
everybody to stay down and keep to cover in case of a
trick. Only when enough time had passed for some of
the men to start getting antsy and for him to be satisfied that the shooters had departed for sure, did the
marshal signal an all clear.

Those who could, emerged from their cover and
rose to their feet. But it was quickly clear that the ri-
flemen on the high ground had taken a toll before
they called it quits. Bob, Consuela, Vern, Earl Wells,
and Alora Dane were all okay except for scrapes and
bruises. Big George O'Farrow, shielding Alora, had
given his life to the effort—one of three rounds to his
broad back having penetrated through to his heart,
killing him instantly. Heck Hembrow had taken a hit
to the thigh just before he made it inside the cabin.
Pecos Ryan had suffered a shattering hip wound.

And then there was Quirt.

He was only able to push himself to a sitting position and then fall back again, tipped against the stump he'd managed to scramble behind when the shooting broke out. But he hadn't made it before taking rounds to his side and stomach.

By the time Bob got to him, he didn't have much left. Beads of sweat stood out on his dark face and the trembling hand he was pressing tight to his middle was painted bright crimson.

He looked up as Bob knelt beside him. "Those dirty so-and-sos got me, Marshal . . . Got me good."

"You just try to take it easy," Bob told him. "We're gonna wrap those wounds and get that bleeding stopped. Then we'll get you back to town and Doc Tibbs will be able to fix you right up."

"Don't waste your breath. That's a lie and we both know it . . . Reckon I must've forgot to not smile."

Bob licked his lips, tried to find words.

"But there's something I want to make sure *you* don't forget," said Quirt, his voice weakening.

"What is it?"

"That gal of yours . . . she's really something, ain't she? . . . I want you not to forget what you said about not dragging your feet when it comes to tellin' her how you feel about her . . . P-promise me that, you hear?"

And then he was gone. Before Bob could agree to the promise . . . at least out loud.

Bob remained kneeling there for a minute, his breath suddenly coming double time, as if he were trying to breathe for both of them. He reached to thumb Quirt's eyes closed. Finally, he rose to h.. feet again.

Vern was standing close by. "There's an old wagon in one of those sheds over there," the young deputy said. "Me and Wells figure we should get a team hitched to it for hauling the women and wounded back to town. Consuela's patching up Ryan and Heck as best she can. But they need to get to a doctor as quick as possible. Especially Ryan, his hip is tore up pretty bad."

Bob nodded. "Sounds like good thinking. Go ahead, set it in motion. While you and Ryan are getting the wagon ready, I'll start saddling some horses."

Vern hesitated. Holding out his two hands, palms up, he said, "There's something more. There's this."

In his right palm was one of the prize pistols. In his left there was a small, cuplike item and a tightly folded piece of paper. After studying this display for a moment, Bob saw that the cuplike item was actually an ornate cap that was meant to fit over the end of the pistol's handle. With the cap off, there was a hollow area visible inside the handle. The paper, Bob reasoned, apparently came out of that hollow area.

"When you shot Delaney," Vern explained, "he naturally dropped the gun case. It broke open when it hit the ground and the pistols spilled out. The end cap, as you can see, came loose from this one and that paper was in the cavity."

Bob carefully unfolded the paper as he carried it over closer to the still-burning campfire where he had better light to see by. It was a sheet of top-quality stationery filled with flowery script done in a woman's ıand. Bob read it through, a frown forming on his face as he did so.

"What is it?" Vern wanted to know.

"It's a suicide note," was Bob's short answer. "But, more than that, it's also testimony to a serious crime—a murder and a cover-up. It's signed by a woman named Hester Lorsby, dated almost two years ago. Her husband—Edgar, she calls him—is the one she accuses of being a murderer and driving her to take her own life out of shame. And, if I'm reading it right, she also indicates he's a senator."

"Let me see that," said Vern, reaching to take the paper back. He scanned it quickly, intently. "Yeah. Yeah, I remember this. It happened just across the river, in Illinois, only a little while before my brothers and me left Iowa to settle out here. The suicide of the wife of a big shot senator, yeah, that had a lot of people talking . . . but I never heard nothing about the senator being accused of murder."

"Because it got covered up," Bob said. "Just like she's telling it there. And then, I'm guessing, the reason behind her suicide also got buried."

"So how did Delaney know about it? I mean, that had to be the reason he was so driven to get his hands on the guns—to get to the note. Right?"

"Seems like," Bob allowed. Then he shook his head. "But *how* he knew about the note, I have no idea. Can't even take a stab at a guess. What it would have gained him, though—blackmail leverage over a sitting U.S. senator—makes it easy enough to see why he wanted it so bad."

Vern scowled. "It also fits with that gibberish he was

spouting about the guns having so much more value than the gold and jewels. More value than the rest of us poor fools could ever imagine, he said."

"I ain't sure I got my head wrapped around all of it, even now," Bob said. "But there's time to sort out the rest later . . . What's more important right now is for us to get these wounded men back to town where they can be properly taken care of. C'mon, we'd better get to it."

CHAPTER 48

It was well after daybreak the next morning by the time they made it back to town. When they got within a couple miles, Vern rode ahead to spread word they were coming in.

Upon their arrival, a whole contingent of folks was waiting. Prominent among them were Bob's other two deputies, Fred and Peter, along with Mike Bullock, Angus McTeague, the Tuttles, Doc Tibbs—and Bucky. The boy came running to meet the wagon, driven by Bob, and clambered up onto the rig while it was still moving. He alternated between throwing his arms exuberantly around his father's neck and warmly embracing Consuela.

Bob reined up in front of the doctor's office, where the crowd was gathered. From there, a handful of townsmen assisted in getting the two wounded men inside. That left the canvas-covered bodies of Quirt and George O'Farrow still in the wagon bed. Alora Dane had ridden all the way from the ranch sitting beside the shrouded form of Big George, sobbing softly every foot of the way. Only at the urging of

the other members of her entertainment troupe did
she finally leave it and allow them to help her down
from the wagon.

When Titus O'Malley, the undertaker, stepped forward to take charge of the bodies, Bob said to him
somewhat huskily, "There are two of the finest men
you're likely ever to lay to rest. Treat 'em that way, you
hear?" When O'Malley nodded somberly, Bob added,
"Out at the Shaw ranch, there are four more bodies.
Me personally, I wouldn't care if they got left for buz-
zard feed. But this badge won't let me make that call.
So, later on, take some men out, plant 'em right
there. Absolutely *not* anything special for them. They
can join the Shaws in the same ground they went in
earlier . . . and join 'em in Hell, too."

With the wounded and the dead being taken care
of and the crowd starting to thin a bit, Bob looked
around and realized somebody was missing—
somebody who should have been certain to be on
hand.

"Hey," he said, still looking around. "Where's
August Gafford?"

"Might be best," answered Fred, "if we went on
over to the jail and talked about that."

Some minutes later, a select group was reassem-
bled around Bob's desk in the marshal's office. Present
were Bob, his deputies, Mike Bullock, and Angus Mc-
Teague. Bucky and Consuela had gone with the Tuttles to wait for Bob at the Bluebird Café.

Fred was doing the talking, teetering slightly on his
crutch at one end of the desk. He'd just finished

elating to Bob and Vern how Ben Eames had tried to kill Delaney in his hotel room and ended up blasted to death on the stairway landing instead.

"That was the start of it, you might say. The start of the suspicions Peter and me both began to have about some things that just felt wrong," Fred related. "Eames's attempt to get rid of Delaney so he'd be next in line for those guns seemed to fit in one way, but at the same time it also sounded awful bizarre. And those two 'business associates' of Delaney showing up in time to help gun down Eames—anybody could tell, just by the look of 'em, the only kind of business those two owlhoots were likely to be involved in had to be something on the shady side. And then when Delaney disappeared and was reported to be seen riding out of town with them, that made it smell even fishier."

"So what does any of that have to do with Gafford?" Bob wanted to know.

"I'm getting to it," Fred assured him. "Gafford didn't figure in until some of this stuff started turning up."

The "stuff" Fred indicated was a display of items spread out on the desktop before them. A skeleton key, a fringed war bag not too different from the one Bob carried when he went out on the trail, and some loose pieces of paper.

"I remembered how, on the day he signed up for the shooting match," spoke up McTeague, "Eames told us he didn't like being too close around people so was camping a ways out of town. When Fred and Peter expressed to me their suspicions about what other motive the man might have had for going after

Delaney, I suggested they might go looking for hi
camp and see if they'd find something there to possibly help with some answers."

"And we sure did," confirmed a sling-wrapped
Peter. "We turned up that war bag. And some of the
contents in it opened up our eyes to a lot of things
about Mr. Ben Eames—or leastways the fella calling
himself that."

"Take a look at the papers," said Fred, gesturing.

Bob plucked up the largest of the somewhat crumpled sheets of paper and shook it out to full size. He
found himself looking at an advertising page from
one of the many so-called Wild West shows that
toured to great popularity back East. This particular
extravaganza appeared to have been built primarily
around a renowned marksman and trick-shot artist
billed as Benjamin "Eagle Eye" Emerson. The picture
of Eagle Eye, though duded up with a good deal of
rhinestones and fringe-cuffed gloves, was unmistak-
ably a somewhat younger version of the man who'd
shown up in Rattlesnake Wells calling himself Ben
Eames.

"So he was a ringer," Bob muttered. "A professional
shooter looking to cash in on a bunch of boomtown
suckers."

"A ringer, for sure," agreed Fred. "But not necessarily in it strictly for himself. Take a look at the
telegram laying there."

Bob picked up a second piece of paper, a telegram.
It was dated six weeks earlier and had been sent from
the telegraph office in Cheyenne. It was addressed to
Emerson and signed *Gafford*. The message contained
specific instructions for arriving in Rattlesnake Wells

s one Ben Eames and adhering to the routine Eames had subsequently followed. It emphasized *no contact outside the contest participation* and, near the closing, reminded Emerson/Eames *you know how much is riding on this.*

"That conniving damned skunk!" Bob declared. "Gafford had the contest rigged right from the beginning . . . or thought he did."

"Until Delaney came along and turned his plan on its ear by outshooting the ringer," said Vern after scanning the message for himself. Then, cutting his gaze to his brother and Fred, he said, "So was Gafford also in on the plan to kill Delaney?"

"No doubt he was in on it to some degree. Hell, he may have been the one pushing for it the most," Peter replied. "But we'll never know that part for sure."

"The final straw for Gafford," said Fred, pointing, "was the skeleton key. We found it on Eames's body. It fit all the second-floor locks at the Shirley House. When we took it to Draeger, the manager, he remembered loaning it to Gafford that morning because he claimed to have locked himself out of his room and had left his own key back at the Crystal Diamond. He was supposed to bring it right back. Obviously, he didn't. And then Draeger got busy with other things and it slipped his mind . . . until we showed up asking about it."

"That was supposed to be Eames's insurance for getting to Delaney," Bob said, starting to put all the pieces together. "If he hadn't found Delaney present when he went to the room, he would have let himself in and waited."

"That's how we figured it, too," said Fred. "So

that's when we went to Gafford and confronted him with everything. We were hoping we could get him to break down and confess. If not, we were ready to throw him in the clink anyway, until you got back."

"What we weren't ready for," Peter said, "was for him to break down as bad as he did. To turn into a blubbering, sobbing, wailing mess. Repeating over and over how sorry he was and how his life was ruined and on and on. Right up to when he asked if he could reach into his pocket—for a hankie, he said." Peter paused, his expression turning grim. "He brought out a hankie, all right. But wrapped in it was a big bore derringer that he stuck in his mouth when he raised the hankie to his face. If anybody cared to bother, they'd still be scraping his brains off the wall of his office."

Once Bob and Vern had been brought up to speed on everything that transpired in town while they were gone, it was their turn to share all they'd encountered on their chase after the Shaws. What they revealed about Delaney and his gang showing up certainly raised some eyebrows, but at the same time it provided a measure of satisfaction for Fred and Peter about the suspicions they'd rightfully had over Delaney and his "business associates." The revelation that came next, though, about the suicide note in the gun handle and the repercussions it could have, reaching all the way to the U.S. Congress, was the stunner of the whole discussion.

Luckily, McTeague not only had a good deal of familiarity with the incident, at least as far as the nitized version of Mrs. Lorsby's suicide, but he also had several high-ranking friends back in Illinois. As did, he added, banker Abraham Starbuck. Bob's relief at hearing this was matched only by McTeague's offer to set things in motion for seeing to it that the right people—people who could be trusted and were in significant positions of power—were made privy to this delicate information and would pursue it to the point of Senator Lorsby finally being held to account for his actions.

At that point, Bob called a halt to any further discussion. He knew full well that his involvement with these matters—the in-depth questioning and detailed testimony that lay ahead—was far from over.

But, for the time being, enough was enough.

He felt exhausted and sore and irritable and all he wanted to do in the hours directly ahead was to step away from all the thievery, double-dealing, and death and just spend some quiet time with Bucky and Consuela . . . his family.

He had a promise to keep.

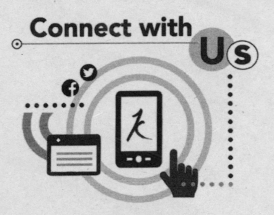